WE ARE
WATCHING
ELIZA BRIGHT

WE ARE WATCHING ELIZA BRIGHT

A. E. OSWORTH

GRAND CENTRAL
PUBLISHING

NEW YORK   BOSTON

Copyright © 2021 by Austen Osworth
Reading group guide copyright © 2021 by Austen Osworth and Hachette Book Group, Inc.

Cover design by Sarah Congdon
Cover copyright © 2021 by Hachette Book Group, Inc.

Hachette Book Group supports the right to free expression and the value of copyright. The purpose of copyright is to encourage writers and artists to produce the creative works that enrich our culture.

The scanning, uploading, and distribution of this book without permission is a theft of the author's intellectual property. If you would like permission to use material from the book (other than for review purposes), please contact permissions@hbgusa.com. Thank you for your support of the author's rights.

Grand Central Publishing
Hachette Book Group
1290 Avenue of the Americas, New York, NY 10104
grandcentralpublishing.com
twitter.com/grandcentralpub

First Edition: April 2021

Grand Central Publishing is a division of Hachette Book Group, Inc. The Grand Central Publishing name and logo is a trademark of Hachette Book Group, Inc.

The publisher is not responsible for websites (or their content) that are not owned by the publisher.

The Hachette Speakers Bureau provides a wide range of authors for speaking events. To find out more, go to www.hachettespeakersbureau.com or call (866) 376-6591.

Library of Congress Cataloging-in-Publication Data

Names: Osworth, A. E., author.
Title: We are watching Eliza Bright / A.E. Osworth.
Description: First edition. | New York : Grand Central Publishing, 2021.
Identifiers: LCCN 2020053570 | ISBN 9781538717639 (hardcover) | ISBN
    9781538717622 (ebook)
Subjects: GSAFD: Suspense fiction.
Classification: LCC PS3615.S93 W43 | DDC 813/.6—dc23
LC record available at https://lccn.loc.gov/2020053570

ISBN: 978-1-5387-1763-9 (hardcover), 978-1-5387-1762-2 (ebook)

Printed in the United States of America

LSC-C

Printing 1, 2021

To and for my community, my people,
my collective voice

WE ARE
WATCHING
ELIZA BRIGHT

CHAPTER ONE

Normally, we wouldn't see her. On any other day, we would see only the city and its more standard occupants. Windy City. Every detail of it. The *buzz-crackling* of electricity in the power lines, the flickering neon signs on bars and lazy lights in shop windows closed for the night, the tooth-splitting bright fluorescents winking in offices sixteen stories above us. Cars speeding along four-lane drives or crawling down one-way streets. Strange public art no one asked for. Our own reflections in the buildings' glass windows; sun bounces off those windows during the day and the streetlights take over at night. A man-made jewel, always glittering. And of course, we would see each other. The city is never empty. So perhaps less like a jewel and more like a galaxy. Constant motion. The bakeries are where we meet; the coffee shops and street corners; the stoops on buildings we know and those we're only dimly familiar with; the walking lanes on bridges, the docks, the old factories, the parks. We are all over every part of it, and we are talking to each other. Or fighting with each other. Or laughing with each other. Or laughing at each other.

Even the most villainous among us would, in the end, choose to protect the city. If you see something, say something, and all that bullshit. Well. We would say something. Because we love it here. It is a novel place. Endless space.

Normally, we wouldn't see her. She would be hidden, visible only to her friends. But then we do. And here is where we start: a shadow stalks Circuit Breaker. A tall silhouette stands out against the reflecting, refracting sea of electric stars echoed in the windows. It looks like a paper doll cut from deep space; the outlined figure is where light goes to die. It is Black Hole, and we know him well. A supervillain. He punches at nothing and she appears, falling to the ground. She is a stereotype. Tall and enboobened, her figure tightly hugged by her ever-present supersuit in burgundy and black, with a shock of blonde ponytail atop her head; her mouth is pert and perfect. She is such a stupid character; we gasp when she appears. It is like sighting a rare bird, even if she is a dumb cunt. "What the shit?" she says from the ground and scrambles to her feet as fast as she can. She puts her hands up, ready to fight. Electricity gathers around them; her superpower. Generic. She is angry. Good.

Two others appear next to her. They are just as exciting to witness, just as rare. The first, a Black man we know as Runner Quick. Where Circuit Breaker's even curvature epitomizes symmetry, Runner foils her with his imbalanced body: his legs are massive, muscular. To understate it, he can run. He can run around the world and not even feel winded. He adjusts his goggles. His scarf blows in the wind; he is in love with the way the orange streetlamp light backlights it, how it glows, the sound it makes as it snaps in the breeze. He knows its red silk looks great against his brown skin. He becomes aware that he is now more visible and puts his hands on his hips like he is posing for a magazine.

The third figure is ugly and she says something shrill: "Now that was fucking uncalled for, what the motherboarding Christ was that about?" It is Chimera the Protector. Chimera, like Circuit Breaker, is another sort of balanced creature, though she looks cobbled together by a chaotic God with no sense of aesthetics or respect for anyone who must lay their eyes upon her. Her hairy ape arms are large enough to be another set of legs. Curled up on her back like two sleeping animals rest a pair of large, black bat wings. All this melds elegantly into a gold-skinned androgynous head, angular in the face with hair as black as clear ice on tar. The result of these disparate parts of people and animals is a hero reasonably good at almost everything: strength, flight, brains and brawn. Skill points in all the right places. When it comes to beauty, she's like a taunt, unconcerned, in our direction. We would rather see Circuit Breaker naked.

Black Hole drops to the ground as another supervillain saunters up next to him. Doctor Moriarty. We know him well too. A perfect gentleman. His blonde hair is neatly parted and swooped as if he is an advertising executive; he wears a grey suit, a pipe peeking from his front jacket pocket. His gun, oversized and expensive, glows a brilliant green and purple. He laughs maniacally. A deep *mua-ha-ha*. Like he's been practicing.

We start to show up in earnest now: people in nondescript suits and glasses, pencil skirts and sensible flats, librarian sweaters. Though we are dressed as our alter egos, we know each of us is a superhero or maniacal villain; every last one.

We hear Chimera say, "Really, Lewis? Really?"

"Suzanne!" says Doctor Moriarty. "You're not supposed to use real names in-game."

It is not as though the illusion is shattered. There's not, if we're honest, truly an illusion. It simply is. *Guilds of the Protectorate* is a skin on top of our reality. A dual truth. Just as real as meatspace. We live in a time where almost everyone has at least two bodies, and the second life is far more thrilling than the first. We are watching Circuit Breaker get the punch to the back of the head she deserves; we are watching Eliza Bright, who is controlling this avatar from her apartment in New York City. Both are true.

Fight!

theyr gonna go

i think they work here

runner quick op

black hole ftw

10/10 would staff brawl again lolllllll

We clamor. We type and shout and hoot and scream and we do it so loud that the shutter click is almost inaudible. Zoom in on one of us, the psionic private eye prone to walking through walls. He wears a trench coat and a close-cropped high-and-tight haircut. In Windy City, he's known as The Inspectre. He doesn't carry a gun; he carries a camera with a cartoonish flashbulb. He deals in secrets, information. We know who to talk to when we need dirt on rival guilds, secret cabals, Avenger-esque bespandexed groups. We wonder how he keeps track of it all—it can't be due entirely to his character stats, he's too fast. He appears any-where the Fancy Dog Games employees appear, at any time of the day or night. He is always replete with facts and rumors about the company, the game itself. So many questions: Does The Inspectre ever sleep? Does he have a brain that catches facts and keeps them like fireflies in a jar? Does he have a wall full of photos with red string between each face? Is he, perhaps, actually an investigator-for-hire in the "real" world? Is he more than one person playing on the same account? We will eventually come to know exactly who he is, but for now, let's maintain the suspense. The telling is half the fun.

Runner Quick says, "Y'all?" and turns outward to face us. The group notices our presence. Not The Inspectre's, per se, but the truth is we don't need him tonight. We are all watching. And it dawns on each of them, even Black Hole and Doctor Moriarty, that our involvement in any fight could go either way. "Maybe cool it?" Runner continues. Circuit Breaker drops the electricity around her fingers.

"Fine," she says, and the group slams the invisibility function back on. Friends only. To the rest of the world, Circuit Breaker and her cronies may as well not exist. We groan and our frustration shakes the glass and the cabs and the very sky above us. We begin to disperse, to wink into our own invisibility or to sign off. But not all of us. Never all of us. We're always here, on the internet, eyes trained on our cast. On Twitter, Reddit, even in Windy City, we can find out a lot. And what we don't know, we can guess; or we can ask; or we can invent.

CHAPTER TWO

et's jump to the next morning: Eliza is the first one of the three-person team to arrive. She gets in the elevator, ascends to the fifth floor, one above where she used to work in the Quality Assurance department. Fancy Dog takes up two floors in a larger office building. Three, if we count the existence of the test floor (which we aren't supposed to know about yet). Preston Waters moved his company in and renovated the shit out of that place. He transformed what was once stodgy cubicles and solid walls with cheap doors into a glass and wood open-plan paradise; now it looks clipped from a brochure for the latest, hottest startup. Perhaps because this is, in fact, the latest, hottest startup. Those few walls that exist are lined with framed art of classic superheroes, villains, and contemporary reimaginings of comics past. We are so jealous from our shitty day jobs, our challenging high-stakes careers, our school desks, and we stalk staff selfies on Twitter, repost to subreddit, swoon; what wouldn't we give to work there.

Eliza is exhausted, having not slept all weekend. Fancy Dog Games has a tradition—when someone new joins a team, he picks something to do, a new feature with a pie-in-the-sky design document or an update or a fix. "To keep everyone on their toes," the CEO says. Eliza is coming off the nonstop weekend of Red Bull and heavy metal coding playlists. She wants to prove herself; it doesn't matter that work is hectic. Given the confluence of Holiday and the huge secret project we shouldn't know about, the one that will be announced shortly, she wasn't required to partake in this particular tradition. But here she is anyhow, having volunteered. An overcompensation for being new or self-taught or shitty at this or the girl. Or all of it. Being a hero in the hope no one will notice ineptitude of any kind.

She rush-completed her part of a brand-new feature, a massive fucking lift, in a mere seventy-two hours and then stayed up late to play the very game she works so hard on. Even we acknowledge it's impressive, if compensatory for other shortcomings. She powers on her computer, a new workstation with different software and a view of the city if she turns and looks over her left shoulder, which she does and grins. She is so proud of herself—she said she'd rise in the ranks and she is well on her way. Her first hours on the three-person development team will be marked with a splash. She is going to kick ass at this. Kick ass and take names. Or perhaps she won't even take names, she won't have the time for it; she'll be one big ball of forward motion, rocketing toward her goal, toward the reveal and release that we aren't supposed to have a clue about. She takes a deep breath, signs herself on to the server and stares at the screen.

//80085. Fleishman will fix.

Below is a section that she is responsible for: code that allows players to bone each other in the game, a feature we've requested since time immemorial, an update we'll all later call the sex patch.

She scrolls down and sees //80085 scattered throughout, on all her code, everything she's done that weekend. There are some other comments as well, in the sections that aren't hers: //JP section, consent (y/y, n/n) and //team two plug in here and //VD point values lol. But only on hers does she see the mysterious code number, always associated with the word "fix."

This is her first assignment—they'd asked her what she wanted to do, and she'd picked this. Already it is borked. She is mortified.

Eliza allows herself a moment to feel the sour cry-feeling behind her face. Imagine: a pout on her rodentish lips. When Eliza was little, about second grade, she was on a class trip to the Museum of Natural History. This kid, she can't remember his name, pointed at one of the prehistoric rat skulls and started calling it Elizasaurus. She stood there, looking at the rat skull with its pushed-forward teeth, and wanted to refute the claim somehow. But when she put her hand on her mouth to check, she found she couldn't think of anything to say. The boy wasn't wrong, after all. Eliza is a six on her very best day.

She breathes deeply, pushes the crying feeling away. She counts to ten, puts her hair up and clicks the file open. Someone's set up the text-editor skin so that all her code writes hot pink on a pastel pink background. She rolls her eyes and changes it to navy and cream—still gaudy, but not pink.

The code in the local copy is flawless. "Oh fuck yes," she says in a relieved hiss to no one at all. She checks Github. People changed it after her—there, there in the logs. That must be what 80085 means, she thinks: accidentally garbled during edits.

We can't believe she doesn't see it, say half of us.

See what? say the other half of us. Those of us who get it make fun of those of us who don't. But for the sake of brevity, let's move forward.

CHAPTER THREE

To: [Lewis Fleishman], [Jean-Pascale Desfrappes]
Subject: Borked Section!

Message: Hey guys! I noticed the comment in my section about the royal borking. It looks like the latest version got accidentally messed up during some other edits, so I reverted to a clean copy. No worries Lewis! Just emailing to make sure you don't stay late or anything to fix the buggy version. Works fine now!

Eliza

PS—what does 80085 mean? Is that the number for accidentally edited? Are there other numbers I should be aware of? Let me know!

CHAPTER FOUR

When Jean-Pascale Desfrappes and Lewis Fleishman receive Eliza's email, they aren't JP and Lewis. They are Black Hole and Dr. Moriarty, and they are getting some supervillain time in before work.

Jean-Pascale created Black Hole, Destroyer of Light. Originally, he dressed him in an all-black bodysuit and a black mask, but after working at Fancy Dog and befriending someone in art, he changed to the now-familiar silhouette with glowing orange eyes. His appearance was so popular after the switch they contemplated adding a silhouette option, standard, for everyone. Jean-Pascale badly wanted to be the only one with this kind of avatar, so he volunteered to, once yearly, turn NPC for a spell and run a server-wide evil campaign. Black Hole became a canon character, though minor and only on one server. His uniqueness was left alone.

Most people refer to Jean-Pascale Desfrappes by his full name, but his girlfriend and co-workers occasionally call him JP for short. He has shoulder-length, curly ringlets, a little bit greasy in texture. Jean-Pascale's height rebels against that of his parents: for some inexplicable reason, he is six feet and four inches, while every other man in his family halts at five feet and nine inches. When Jean-Pascale moved to the States, he converted this popular conversation topic out of the metric system to be better understood. Because he still thinks in the metric system, however, he makes sure to write the new, foreign numbers down in the back of his notebook, and glances at it until he has them memorized. When asked why he constantly carries a composition book, he replies *"pour les idées,"* which is honest, but he doesn't mention the running list of phrases in the back. *Cold shoulder. Wild goose chase. Ice breaker. A perfect storm. Royal borking.*

A note on Dr. Moriarty: We love Lewis Fleishman. He is just like us. He's been playing so long, the sheer amount of resources at his disposal is dizzying. The gentleman can make anything happen with the power of purchase, and he never uses meatspace currency to further his digital fortune. He is an old-school gamer—everything is hard earned by fantastic strategy and finesse. Often he laments the casual iPhone games where levels and items are bought with "real-world" money. As such, their lair is spectacular.

It could probably be said that Lewis's character looks the least like its creator out of everyone we follow in this story, and we are of course counting Chimera and Black Hole. At least Chimera retains Suzanne's wavy hair. At least JP matched Black Hole's height to his own. We suspect Lewis invented Doctor Moriarty (no tagline) by selecting the diametric opposite of everything about his own physical presence. Where Lewis is short, Doctor Moriarty is tall. Where Lewis has frizzy brown hair, Moriarty has a neat blonde style, almost British schoolboy. Lewis is doughy. Moriarty is buff. Lewis dresses in tee shirts and jeans. Moriarty is never without a suit. Lewis does what other people tell him. Moriarty tells other people what to do. Lately he is striving to change this last part, to be a little more like Moriarty in his bossness—having Jean-Pascale around, someone who's so obviously a skilled gamer and who does what he says, helps.

Because Jean-Pascale plays a canon character and is, thus, always visible, we can go into The Lair when they're not there—sure, their stuff is locked down, but we call on them like they are British aristocracy. We gawk at their things, their architectural acumen, their nefarious ideas; living vicariously is fun. Or we avoid it, a few of us. Some of us are good. Some of us play superheroes. Some of us wouldn't be caught dead here.

It is underground, The Lair. Three floors. The topmost, an entrance with a fountain in the middle. It is nondescript, chrome, and a little mall-like; a more expensive imitation of the rest of our houses, apartments and secret places—that is to throw people off. If those who don't know what they're looking for stumble in, they might stumble out just as quickly. But we know better.

The next floor is Doctor Moriarty's, and if he hadn't bunked up with Black Hole, we wouldn't get to see it. We are grateful for his sacrifice in privacy; his aesthetic is ripped from the pages of *A Study in Scarlet*: a perpetually lit fireplace, a springy-but-worn red rug, a stag's head on the wall. Even a violin on the mantelpiece, strategically placed with the hunting trophies.

"That is a little messed up," Black Hole said when the Doctor first put it there.

The Doctor just shrugged. "Sherlock Holmes is kind of a prick and he had it coming."

Off Moriarty's floor is the treasure room—we can't get in there, but we can see it if we maneuver ourselves up against the wall and change the camera view to third person. It is arranged with care to resemble a cross between Smaug's cave and Scrooge McDuck's safe. Performative; they know we are watching. Maybe not at this moment—it's difficult for anyone to imagine, unprompted, a burning spotlight in specific moments—but in general, they're aware.

And then comes Black Hole's floor, which features smooth-sliding doors and a physical (as well as chemical) laboratory. Catty-corner, an old-timey gurney that recalls the days of unfettered institutionalizations in primitive asylums. "Dude, you think my violin is messed up?" the Doctor said when he'd first noticed the gurney's presence. He'd pointed at it. "That's really fucking messed up."

Jean-Pascale had just arrived from France at the time, and Lewis was extremely welcoming so he tried some slang he'd heard around.

He began his sentence with "Nah, brah," and it felt like he'd shoved a bunch of marshmallows into his mouth. But Lewis hadn't even laughed, so he kept going. "It is just part of the décor. The atmosphere. We are playing a game, and we are playing as villains." The gun safe lies just beyond, and it is impressive. They have enough firepower to take over the world. We wonder why they don't.

We are like tourists in a museum, but it is enter-at-our-own-risk: Doctor Moriarty is so rich in-game that he's rigged all the floors with wires that can electrocute a character with one press of a button; he carries that button with him, and uses it whenever they come home. Most of us can do a room, maybe, before we get nervous and flee. Nowhere is safe in The Lair if you aren't one of those two.

Case in point: Lewis says, "Ugh, shit." He presses his button and fries two of us, forcing curses and respawns he will never hear or know about (except of course when he picks up the possessions we unwillingly leave behind). "Check your email," he continues, as he collects the drops and double, triple checks that none of us remain in The Lair.

There is silence, and Black Hole stops moving. Then: "Shit." And it sounds a little like "sheet" with his accent.

"Listen, we know that shit is fucked. I put it in myself," Lewis says. "I bet she's fucking lying to save face. I had no idea she was on the server."

"I thought we had to enter her patch because she wasn't?"

"Don't they give her, like, orientation or something?"

"Apparently no." Jean-Pascale collapses Black Hole into a chair and has him turn on a jazz record. The tinny sounds of false horns signal relaxation time. Their tongues loosen accordingly. "It is frustrating," he says. "We are not running a school."

"It's got to be some quota thing," says Lewis, kicking off his role-playing as his character kicks off his shoes, dons slippers and a smoking jacket. Normally Lewis is hardcore into role play, no job stuff or real names or anything in-game. But it is his lair. He can change the rules whenever he likes.

"There were always two kinds of girls at my university, back in Paris." It is strange to picture Black Hole, Destroyer of Light, going to university in Paris. Or it isn't. "Either they were total bitches to us or they tried to trade us."

"Trade you?"

"They'd have sex with us and then get us to help them with their work."

Lewis snorts.

Jean-Pascale smiles; American humor is a bit different from what he is used to, and even though he's been in the US for a while, he likes when he gets it right. "I don't know what it is about girls who go into games. I guess they have to be a bit different from other girls, since normal girls aren't that interested."

"We should have had a week without her on the server. Not just a weekend."

It is JP's turn to snort. "Or a fucking warning."

"If they were going to let her on that fast, she could've done all that work. We shouldn't have had to do it."

"Fancy Dog School of Coding. We are the training wheels."

The conversation continues as the rest of us, those who avoided the frying by clinging to the ceiling, sign off in fear of discovery.

CHAPTER FIVE

Eliza's face is hot after hitting send on the email. Even the space behind her eyes is hot. It is a ridiculous thing, she thinks, to be embarrassed about, given it was not ultimately her fault. But she is embarrassed all the same. It's a fast fix, putting the clean copy back on the server, but she internally falls down a spiral staircase, wondering if she deserves that promotion.

Or she doesn't find herself mortified at all; she doesn't have any sense she even should be embarrassed for throwing the team off-kilter, for blowing a hole in the SS *Fancy Dog* mere days from a huge announcement. She cares only for the job title on the website, is secure in the fantasy that the borked code was perpetrated entirely by Lewis and JP. She doesn't once think about her promotion the week prior. She simply embodies a false confidence, knowing well they need a woman because nowadays society forces us to hire them, and she can't be fired or demoted unless something truly egregious happens. Fucking with camaraderie or code won't matter. This, the second option, sounds more accurate to us.

Let us break it down: Fancy Dog Games. The name of the company has an "s" at the end, but it is an aspirational plural. They only have one game: *Guilds of the Protectorate*, a massively multiplayer online role-playing game. And honestly? One is enough to support the weight of our fandom, that's how good a game it is.

Guilds, as it is called by its acolytes, obsessives and creators, is similar in gameplay to *World of Warcraft*, but we think it's even better. It's got an equally (or more) devoted following. What is different, though, is the world. MMORPGs are frequently flavored with orcs, wizards and knights—largely not our thing. *Guilds'* world contains superheroes and villains, high-rise buildings and underground secret layers set against the grit of Windy City, a fictionalized mashup of Chicago and New York that borrows liberally from each real-world landscape. Players can choose to be heroes or villains, but it is far more complicated than that. There is more to alignment than Good and Evil: The Lawful Good of a Superman, the Chaotic Good of a Batman; The Chaotic Evil of the Joker, the Lawful Evil of—actually, Eliza can't place a Lawful Evil supervillain; she has trouble wrapping her brain around the paradox that is "lawful" and "evil" describing the same character. She thinks perhaps the best example is Emperor Palpatine, but hadn't he overthrown the actual law, or found a loophole in it? Was he truly deserving of "lawful" if he didn't adhere to the spirit of the law? Or perhaps Eliza can think of a million Lawful Evil characters. Perhaps she disdains them the most—rigid and cruel, and she doesn't like to think of herself that way. Either way, she never chooses to put herself in their shoes. We know she's never made a Lawful Evil villain. Not very self-aware of her.

Though we have the opportunity to play both heroes and villains with unlimited character creations, according to the analytics, most individual players choose to play only one type of character—one moral alignment—no matter how many we make. We are part of the Protectorate in their individual shards or we are trying to shatter the world, laughing maniacally.

The game was a surprise hit—the company started as two dudes dicking around in a university computer lab. "We just wanted to make a game that we wanted to play," says co-founder Preston Waters in his interview on *The Daily Show*, from back in 2014. Eliza gets a kick out of watching it every so often—he looks so shocked, like he wants to reach out and touch Jon Stewart to make sure he isn't made out of pixels. The once-shy coder is wide-eyed. He looks tired and energized, nervous and elated. "We didn't know it would be this popular," Preston continues. "Don't get me wrong, we're glad it is! And we're working full speed ahead! We're hiring more and more people even as I sit here!" He seems confident, this one. Poised. Young. The barest hint of muscle, not showy, like perhaps he's hiding abs under his shirt but isn't, ultimately, defined by them. A man with everything. We've seen him play, when he streams—it is like reading a poem, watching him shoot a gun or swing a sword or—anything, really. We would watch him play anything.

Eliza's been working on *Guilds* for the better part of a year and a half by the time we meet her, by the time our story starts. She is one of those shotgun new-hires Preston talks about on television, brought on as a quality assurance peon. She spends the year and a half we aren't focusing on her struggling through long nights on Codecademy and Treehouse. She teaches herself how to program because what she wants more than anything in the whole damn world is to make Fancy Dog Games into a true plural. The next big hit is going to come from her own head, and to get there she has to ascend somehow. She is determined. She is cocky. That spitfire. That cunt.

She thinks about her promotion, only three days old, imagines it in detail. She is grateful or she is smug or she is spiraling: "If that's your goal, we'd be happy to support your journey in that direction," Preston says, grinning. "Let's fill out this Career Tree together." The company is still small enough that she sees this man, this genius, on the daily. He is, miraculously, somehow right there in front of her, encased in a glass-walled office of his own design. Eliza hauls herself off the sinking couch, jostling the dog that put his head in her lap.

True to its name, Fancy Dog is full of dogs. Big dogs, small dogs, cute dogs, ugly dogs—the office looks like a P. D. Eastman children's book to us. By now, Eliza's accepted the prevalence of canines, pausing only to wonder where all the dog people had worked before the age of startups. What she still doesn't believe (and what most of us can't believe either) is that the dogs have uniforms, issued to them by the company on the day their human checked the "I will be bringing my dog to work" box—small tee shirts in royal blue that say things like "Marketing Dog," "Backend Dog" and "Customer Service Dog." These spawn spoof shirts, courtesy of overinvested employees with too much money: "Yo Dog," "(Let Me Sniff Your) Backend Dog," and "Dog, Stop Sending Me Email." The dog she disturbs is wearing a shirt emblazoned with the phrase "I Am Dog," because that is, in fact, his name. Preston's dog is just called Dog, and Dog is the original Fancy Dog. He is big and white with a curly mop of fur that covers his eyes—he is also a minor internet celebrity, at least with us; we follow Preston's Instagram, and photos of Dog garner the most likes.

Eliza pats Dog on the head and sits down at the computer.

She sympathizes with Preston's *Daily Show* appearance more than ever—she, too, feels like perhaps this is a highly realistic hologram, a simulation, some pixels of her own invention. For a second she wants to grab his hair in her hands and is immediately revolted by that impulse.

He is her boss! People do not touch their boss's hair, no matter how touchable that hair might be. Instead, she clicks harder and faster, filling in radio buttons with wild abandon as she maps her goals at Fancy Dog. Or she is overcome with lust, breathes heavily, tries to focus on work and fails because women can't keep their minds on the job. Or she sees her opportunity, begins to concoct the plan—how can she make herself the most attractive to him? How can she use her body to become indispensable?

Eliza does have a body to use, even if she doesn't think so. Aside from her rat mouth, we'd perhaps increase her score from a six to a seven on a day we are feeling generous or horny. Her meatspace appearance is very different from Circuit Breaker's: Eliza is five feet four inches and skinnier than a praying mantis on a diet, though not for lack of trying. She can hoover an entire eggplant parmesan sandwich, wash it down with a milkshake, top it all off with some French fries and still she looks breakable. We think that's dumb as fuck. What kind of girl complains about being skinny?

She wears glasses. Big, honking glasses as thick as tar with tar-black frames. She doesn't mind them now—she once did, and she tried all sorts of different ones. But the younger Eliza found that, due to the crazy thickness of her lenses, none of the other frames looked quite right. So back she came to the big black frames until, all at once, her unavoidable glasses became a signifier of Williamsburgitude; of the ability to purchase daily Starbucks with a simultaneous disdain for those who didn't seek out better coffee; of cool, or coastal elitism. She is grateful and embraces the requisite uniform of lumberjack-like flannel and skinny jeans accordingly. She is whiter than an Easter lily, and she wishes she looked a bit healthier but can live with her complexion. What we're saying is, it would be possible. Her body's an asset, an unfair advantage. Undo a few buttons on the flannel, put contacts in, wear something besides ChapStick. It's possible.

It is an ambitious climb up her Career Tree, she and Preston both agree. "You'll need to have a wide perspective on the business, I think. I was impressed with your coding test—you're teaching yourself?" he asks as he prints her a copy.

Eliza nods.

"Brilliant!" Preston continues. "A stint in development, so you know what's possible. Starting next week, I think. You already have the QA—brilliant, brilliant job debugging the Medusa Lovely arc, by the way! Details!" He whips into his next thought, so smart, able to turn on a dime. Every word from his mouth sounds like a staged monologue. No ums or uhs. Full-throated and fully thought out. "Details are so important. In the meantime, try your hand at designing a tabletop game. Really, in the end, it's all about gameplay, and nothing gets that across better than not having pretty graphics to fall back on."

"You want me to design a tabletop game here?" Eliza asks.

"Ha." Preston's laugh is a bark, a sound made only by someone unafraid to take up space. "No, no, not for here, I don't think we'll be expanding to tabletop just yet," he chuckles. "I mean on your own time. To get the experience of it, the feel for it."

"Right, of course," Eliza says, feeling the tiniest touch of red spread across her face and up her nose. Or she blinks, doe-eyed, coquettishly LARPing a damsel in distress.

"Listen, I'm going to give you some real earnest advice. It's why I talk to everyone personally, mentor them. Give it some real thought—do you want this? Because if you really want to be a decision maker, a game changer, in this company and in games, you have to eat, sleep, breathe and live *Guilds of the Protectorate*. You have to understand how everything works from all corners. You have to totally immerse yourself. And that's not even counting the semi-magic creative factor in all this. Even if you ascend in the ranks, it doesn't guarantee the muse will visit you. It has to be something you have to do." Preston ends his speech seated calmly at his desk, hands folded, with the kindest eyes. The buttery sunlight makes his very-windowed office feel corporate, happy and chic. He looks like the startup superhero, exactly the kind of person who should be featured on the cover of *Wired* with the headline "Hacking the Gaming Industry."

"Do you want it?" he asks. "Do you want it badly enough to do all that, to not have a life outside of this for years, and then to potentially fail at it because the muse didn't catch the right train?"

Eliza is breathless, her heart beating quickly. She licks her lips. "I want it, yes. And I will not let you down." Then, wait—"Mr. Waters?" She'd never called him by any name before, never addressed him directly.

"Call me Preston. We're not a 'Mr. Waters' kind of company, Eliza, get a grip."

"Right, yes. Preston? Did you just promote me?"

"Yes, I did. You've earned it."

Eliza rocks back in her chair. Did she? Did she, though? "I, uh. Wow. Thank you."

"Oh," says Preston as he reaches beneath his desk. "And one

more thing." He slides a brand-new nondisclosure agreement across the glass.

"But I already work here? I mean, I've signed this already."

"We're asking all devs, every team, to sign it again. Your colleagues already have. Just a precautionary measure. A reminder."

"Oh—okay?" Eliza says, but she signs it nonetheless. A quick dash off with a blue Bic and Preston taps his nose. "Come with me," he says. He retrieves a box from his desk and stands. Eliza is bewildered.

He leads her to the elevator and, taking his badge from his pocket, he waves it in front of the small black square affixed under the buttons. Eliza's eyebrows snap together. "But we don't have any keyed floors," she says.

"That," says Preston, enjoying the delivery, the suspense, "has changed."

They shudder down to floor three, which we are not supposed to know about. But of course we do. Fancy Dog, like every other organization of human beings, has the structural integrity of a sieve. Rumors fly. The doors open; a plain, concrete room stands before them, solid and entirely nondescript. There are no windows. At the corners where the walls meet the ceiling are what look like security cameras. Green lights wink down at us as we look around, follow Eliza's gaze, imagine the floor into existence based solely on descriptions and disparate nuggets of experience with expensive technology.

At the edge, a high table; it's one long standing desk, unused charging cords neatly protruding from organized square holes. A large monitor attached to a short tower are the only items currently sitting on the surface.

Preston leans against the table and slides the closed box—about the size and shape of a boot box—across the table at Eliza. "Okay. Now you can open it."

She does and: "Preston. Oh my God. Are we—?"

Preston nods. "Yup. This is now your equipment. That's what your colleagues have been working on for months and months. We're going to announce beta testing publicly—very soon, actually. Right now, only developers and a few key departments, a few necessary people, know what's going on. Not even all the narrative designers are in the loop. We have a very lean set of devs acting as high-level QA. A difficult decision, to be sure, a risky one—it's made our lives much harder, but we don't want any leaks. We'll take it to the rest of the company in the next week or so, so you won't have to keep the secret for very long. It's been killing your friend Devonte."

Eliza lifts the lid on the box and slams it shut again. "That's— that's— oh my God that's so cool." She paces around in a tight circle. "Oh man, Preston—can I play with this? I mean, is it already possible to play *Guilds* with this?"

Preston pushes off the table and walks into the center of the room, empty for such a clear reason now. "That's why I brought you down here. It's an entirely new software, rebuilt from the ground up, so we're still working out the kinks. Play for now, but not too long! Be ready on Monday for full speed ahead. You're really going to have to hit the ground running! Now normally I'd have new people pick a project to bring to their team—it's kind of a team building exercise— but considering the amount of work you're going to have to do for this announcement—"

"No wait, Preston. With this—I have a brilliant idea. Something people have been requesting forever. I know there's some half-baked plans for it already, but with this it's even—"

"You're not going to have time." Because of course she won't have time. She can barely code as it is, and her co-workers are going to have to teach her everything.

Eliza glances down at her phone to look at the time and pushes her glasses up on her nose, ignoring her own incompetence. "If we email them this morning, I have all afternoon. All evening. All weekend. I can basically do the bulk of it. Just hear me out."

"Okay. But I can't get you on the server until Monday morning."

CHAPTER SIX

At this point, we should talk about Preston Waters, co-founder and CEO of Fancy Dog Games. Preston is a golden boy with a very symmetrical face and thick, brown hair that waves over his right eye in a natural 1940s swish. A quick glance back even further and we can see him grow up with his mother insisting, loudly and publicly, that his face is so perfect it should be on a coin. His father takes that to mean he should expect the boy to be president. Preston is the kind of guy who, no matter how much time he spends at the computer and no matter how many cookies he eats, still retains a healthy layer of muscle. He is never effortful nor effortless, hardworking without being a try-hard. Never too serious nor too frivolous, always the right amount of lulz. His jawline is as sharp as his intellect. He commands respect without asking for it.

We watch for his character in *Guilds* constantly. The original, the proto-character: Human Man. So clever, to name him something so close to Everyman. Anyman. Preston Waters is all of us. Any single one of us could become him if we follow his pattern closely. And his superhero persona is an extension of everything classic about *Guilds*. It isn't hard to emulate Human Man; *Guilds'* default settings match Preston's character, such that anyone who is eager to get playing makes an exact copy of Human Man. Middle skin tone, middle brown hair, the standard red unitard and cape. He is, therefore, invisible by default. His neutrality grants him anonymity.

He is asked about it on his *Daily Show* segment, from way back when—"Of course, those are the default options, those are my favorites!" he says as we hit the play button again and again. "I almost named my character Superman but—" He stares at the camera, eyes wide. An expression jolts across his face. Excitement. He is in the process of revealing his genius on national television. We would get a boner too, if it were us.

He comes back to himself. "It didn't sit right with me, ripping off Jerry Siegel like that."

"Jerry Siegel?" asks Jon Stewart.

"He was one of the great men who created Superman. But I wanted to pay homage to an icon."

"So, you went with—Human Man?"

"Human Man! I sure did."

We memorize his answers. He only sleeps four hours a night, so we try this. He carves out bandwidth for his ideas by replacing most of his meals with protein shakes, anytime he doesn't get takeout. This is appealing. Who wants to think about food ever? It takes up too much time, the maintenance of a body. We buy Vitamix blenders. He devotes an hour every morning to brainstorming the next big thing before he hits the Starbucks for his morning coffee; we do too, and we buy apps for mindmapping and transfer our thoughts to slide decks. We understand Preston Waters with the precision of a collective of naturalists or devout monks. We are ready for our own success. We are ready to join his ranks.

"We didn't know it would be this popular," Preston continues. "Don't get me wrong, we're glad it is! And we're working full speed ahead! We're hiring more and more people even as I sit here!" The only thing we do not understand is what he sees in Eliza Bright. Why he promotes her when the world is full of us, those that wouldn't need to ask him a single question because we can telegraph his every thought.

CHAPTER SEVEN

JPDes: hey, Eliza, just curious—what games do you play?

JPDes: like outside of this one?

EBrig: Oh it varies! Comes and goes, whatever I'm interested in. Mostly I play this one, but I've been really into that Stardew Valley thing that came out in February

JPDes: the farming game?

EBrig: yup!

JPDes: you don't think that's a little boring?

EBrig: oh not at all—especially for someone who lives in a city.

EBrig: plus that guy is super cool—he made it entirely by himself! that's exactly the kind of thing I want to be able to do. in the context of a company I want to be a lead designer, but I want to be *able* to make the whole thing myself start to finish.

JPDes: good for you.

EBrig: thanks 😊

CHAPTER EIGHT

JPDes: fucking STARDEW VALLEY

LFleis: figures

JPDes: she couldn't name any others

LFleis: figures.

JPDes: lolololol

LFleis: she probably plays the sims or some shit. fucking girl games. and her code is all fucked up too wtf is she fucking doing here

LFleis: why do u think they promoted her?

JPDes: numbers

LFleis: ?

JPDes: to have women n stuff

JPDes: so we dont look liek sexist assholes

LFleis: fucking takeover

JPDes: ya

LFleis: wait

JPDes: ?

LFleis: u think she fucked somone?

JPDes: ?

LFleis: like fucked somone to get the job?

LFleis: liike the women who traded at yr school?

JPDes: that would make me really angry. i thought i was done with that bullshit when i graduated

JPDes: i cant sleep with someone to get promoted

LFleis: lol unless preston is gay or somthing

JPDes: lolololol

CHAPTER NINE

Someday, Preston often says, he'd like to have a campus with a café on it, like Apple has. Preston is obsessed with the café on the Apple Campus. But until then, Fancy Dog has catered lunch three times a week. It is the first time Eliza isn't the pickiest eater, and she revels in the consistently present vegetarian options, not pescatarian, which is cheating (and she is allergic to fish, this we know for sure).

Let's watch them eat, that afternoon after she logs into the server with her shiny new credentials for the first time. She sits down with her lunch next to her own personal *Guild*, the employees The Inspectre calls "the Diversity Squad." Devonte (Runner Quick) is a gameplay developer but has been temporarily reskinned as high-level quality assurance, and Suzanne (Chimera the Protector) is one of only a handful of customer service employees and nominally in charge of them all. These three, while they have never all sat together at one desk or been on the same team in the office, are near-constant G-chat companions. Inseparable in the digital world, seriously lacking in physical hangout time outside of work. They cling to each other, labeling the rest of us outsiders. If we were back in middle school, they probably wouldn't let us sit with them. Who the fuck do they think they are, to ostracize us?

Devonte is already sitting; he tilts his head toward the empty seats around him. Eliza slides in, but Suzanne remains standing and yawns.

She drinks her chocolate milk while balancing it on her dull cardboard takeaway container, a harbinger of a desk lunch.

"Up late playing?" Eliza asks.

Suzanne shakes her head, her mouth still sucking the straw rising from her chocolate milk, her full lips pouty or smirking. "Nope," she says when she finishes. "I dealt with a particularly nasty fucker yesterday on the phone, complaining about normal-ass regular shit that happens in a game." She snorts. "Play late. Just because *you* have to 'eat, sleep and breathe' the game doesn't mean *we* have to. Some of us would rather just eat, sleep and breathe."

We've never seen Suzanne Choy without eye makeup that looks professional, as though hours of watching YouTube makeup tutorials have transformed her technique. Some of us wonder why she doesn't record a few of them herself; it would let us watch her more. Something to rip to our computers. We'd have to take her swimming on the first date, to check. To make sure. Make sure she looks like she says she does. Her skin is luminescent, golden and always blemish free or covered in those dishonest cosmetics. She wears glasses most of the time, because touching her own eyeball freaks her out. She does not like her glasses. She does not like her cheeks—she thinks they look stuffed, like those of the viral video hamsters eating tiny burritos in the cutest corners of the internet. She does like her hair, which seems to rebel against her mother's and her mother's mother's hair: it falls in soft waves instead of pin straight. She always lets it air-dry. No curling iron, no hairspray. In short, she is beautiful and we imagine Eliza is jealous.

"We'll get you at dinner then?" Eliza asks.

Suzanne raises a well-defined eyebrow. "If I finish my Helpfulness Target. And my second-in-command's Helpfulness Target." She rolls her eyes. Suzanne is not a team player. It isn't his fault that CS dude number two has to leave for a dentist appointment. And she should be grateful to work at Fancy Dog. What a demanding witch.

Eliza looks to Devonte, who takes a giant bite of his sandwich. Devonte Aleba is tall and gangly, with just the barest hint of muscle suggesting perhaps he doesn't spend all of his time at the computer, just most of it. He does not have the ability to grow more than a skinny mustache. When he tries, Suzanne likes to attack him with a tissue and try to rub it off. "Not cool," he says, and he bats her away. He has an impressive collection of snapbacks and sneakers, his peacock plumage. The collections each grew more impressive when he graduated from Stanford with a degree in computer science and went straight for Google. He'd been snatched away from Silicon Valley by a very shiny relocation package from Fancy Dog when they needed to scale up fast— they had the resources to make it worthwhile, it was closer to home and he'd always wanted to work in games; who wouldn't want to?

"So how is it?" Devonte says around a mouthful of sandwich.

"Good. I think."

Devonte raises his eyebrows. "You think?" He takes a bite out of his banana.

"I mean, yeah, I think." Eliza pauses. "I dunno, Jean-Pascale and Lewis seem weird."

He snorts. "It's a game studio. Everyone's weird."

Eliza smiles. "Yeah. I dunno. They seem like they've got their own little bubble and I'm not allowed in."

"Well you're new," Devonte says. "It'll happen."

"Like, they have their own language. It's like feral twins. They have this thing they mark code with? Do you guys use the number 80085 for anything?"

Devonte, still eating his banana, slows his chew down. His eyes unfocus. "Did you ask them about it?" Devonte says, careful, like he is picking his words out of a case filled with bone china or camera lenses.

"I emailed but they haven't responded. I'm supposed to know stuff. They'll think I'm an idiot if I ask again. I'll figure it out."

"Yeah," Devonte says without smiling.

CHAPTER TEN

Here's a brief history of Lewis in games:

When Lewis's mother brings her first boyfriend home, she buys Lewis *Kid Pix*, which all of us certainly know about, but those of us who are currently in high school aren't familiar with in an end-user way. It's a painting program directed at children, made for the friendly-looking Macintosh living on a dusty table in their basement. Perhaps we can't entirely call it a game, but she parks her son in front of it while she partakes in adult activity for the first time in years. It is 1992 and he is four. He draws a portrait of her. Red lipstick, curly brown hair, big smile with all the teeth showing. He is mesmerized by the things he can do. When it comes time to show her the picture, he can't find her anywhere in their lightly run-down Brooklyn home. Some doors are locked, so he can't be sure. But he is not afraid, being the man of the house and all. He grows bored and uses the mixing tool to swirl the colors in her face, her lips, her hair, all together as if he is finger painting. He doesn't have the words to say it yet, but he thinks the essence of her is still present in this whirling new likeness.

Math Blaster: In Search of Spot, 1994. In first grade they have a computer in the classroom, perched on a desk set atop the corner of the blue storytime rug, and everyone can sign up to use it during free enrichment. Lewis signs up the most out of everyone so he can play *Math Blaster*. As a result, he aces quizzes left and right. He is promoted to Gifted and

Talented Math come second grade and, as a reward, his mother buys him *Math Blaster* and one other game—*Are You Afraid of the Dark? The Tale of Orpheo's Curse*. A spooky point-and-click mystery that occupies hours of bright Sunday afternoons. He has to know the end of the story, he just has to. He is so angry with himself every time he dies. He doesn't notice he is playing as a girl; or he doesn't care. The drowned magician in the tank, a victim of his own hubris with his inability to escape his self-imposed confines, gives him nightmares. But even when he wakes in the middle of the night, covered in so much sweat he is convinced he's been submerged in choking water, he doesn't cry out.

When his mother brings her third boyfriend over, that's when he gets the console. A Super Nintendo, with *The Legend of Zelda: A Link to the Past*, *Super Mario World*, *Super Mario Kart* and *Star Fox*. He's never seen such a treasure trove, and the last is his favorite. It moves so fast and Lewis is fascinated by his ability to operate in three dimensions on a two-dimensional screen. It's magic, he thinks, and: this is what I want to do.

He subscribes, then, to *Nintendo Power*. He wants to learn everything he can (and we should step outside our timeline once again to mention that he remains a subscriber until the last issue, December 11, 2012. A regret: that he was not subscribed at birth so he could have owned the first and the last, slipped reverently into plastic sleeves).

When the Nintendo 64 comes out, that's when we calculate that Lewis manipulates his mother for the first time. He throws a fit about the boyfriend. (It isn't a difficult fit to throw. Lewis doesn't like him anyway; the strange adult yells, looks right at him and accuses Lewis of things he's never done.) The tantruming child receives the newest console as consolation. When *Star Fox* is released, he does it again. He has to experience the Rumble Pak with its vibrational feedback—it is gaming history. He must continue James McCloud's lineage with the new character, Fox McCloud, and the flying; oh, the flying! He bonds with boys over barrel rolls. They draw the characters for the games they promise each other they will make one day. "You'll be the first one to play it, pinky swear." If they are not doing that, they sit under the overhang by the cafeteria, Game Boys in hand, trading Pokémon and helping each other through *Wario*.

Let's skip a few, because we have made our point. Lewis loved video games. He loved the same ones we loved.

World of Warcraft, 2004. Argent Dawn server. He and his lost boys lose entire weekends to role-playing and drinking soda out of liter bottles. They are a player-versus-player guild; as long as it serves the story, there are no rules. This—this is a feeling deeper than love. It is an obsession. A second life. A way to attempt feats they would never have the strength or courage to do in physical space. There was a sweetness to their face-splitting cruelty; it was imaginary, consequence-less. A product of boyhood. Fuck anyone who calls it toxic.

CHAPTER ELEVEN

DAleb: Okay so its like

EBrig: ...

EBrig: what?

DAleb: dude, trying to figure out how to say it

EBrig: Devonte, don't make me guess.

DAleb: okay, okay, this is not a big deal. they're just being stupid

DAleb: I just hate to be the one to tell you

DAleb: have you looked at it carefully?

EBrig: what?

DAleb: the number? the code they're tagging with?

EBrig: what code?

DAleb: 80085?

EBrig: what do you mean carefully? ive seen the number

DAleb: look at it

EBrig: Devonte, what am i not seeing?

DAleb: write it down

EBrig: oh god.

DAleb: do you see it?

EBrig: it says boobs

DAleb: yeah. it says boobs.

EBrig: all my code was marked with this. i went back and looked. and then this afternoon it wasn't anymore

DAleb: yeah.

EBrig: devonte. are you telling me Lewis and JP marked all of my code with the word boobs?

EBrig: that is what you're telling me

EBrig: they marked all my code with boobs. 80085. boobs.

EBrig: this is because I'm a girl

DAleb: I think so. They don't do it to any of the guys who have boobs.

EBrig: Devonte.

DAleb: and it's a company full of nerds, there are plenty of guys who have boobs

DAleb: you're making the sex patch. is it possible they're referring to actual boobs?

EBrig: i don't think so

EBrig: they commented on those bits with the actual word boobs

EBrig: this feels different than that, now that i know

DAleb: listen, they're just being idiots, okay? i dont think theyr used to working with women

CHAPTER TWELVE

EBrig: IT MEANS BOOBS, SUZANNE

SChoy: what now?

EBrig: Boobs. 80085. Boobs.

SChoy: of course it does

SChoy: didnt you ever have a calculator? what did you do during math class, actual math?

EBrig: jp and lewis marked all my code with it

SChoy: o shit

SChoy: on the work server?

EBrig: yep

SChoy: thats dumb as shit, someone could see it.

EBrig: theyre never going to take anything i do seriously

SChoy: did you honestly expect them to?

EBrig: suzanne, i'm like three steps away from crying rn

SChoy: dont cry

SChoy: youre in their line of sight, right?

EBrig: yeah

SChoy: you cant cry. if anyone sees you, theyll think you cant handle your shit rn.

EBrig: what do i do about this?

EBrig: suzanne. are you still there

SChoy: nothing

EBrig: what?

SChoy: you don't do anything

EBrig: what do you mean? i hafta do something. shouldn't i, like, tell HR?

SChoy: all theyre gonna do is slap them on the wrist, maybe make them do, like, sensitivity training or something

EBrig: well good! they need the training

SChoy: but like, what are the odds its gonna make a difference?

SChoy: and then they know it was you, that you reported. who else would've looked at the code?

SChoy: and you still hafta work with them after

EBrig: well shit

EBrig: i didnt think of that

SChoy: reporting someone is why i left my last job

EBrig: no shit, rly?

SChoy: yeah. made it real weird.

SChoy: would have been better if i hadnt said anything

CHAPTER THIRTEEN

Eliza needs to go to the bathroom. She needs to go to the private bathroom, so she can cry alone. In her hands, she clutches two things—her phone and a printout of the Career Tree she filled out with Preston just last Friday. We aren't sure why she grabs it. She intends to rethink it? Or she wants to stare at it for a while. Perhaps she wants to rip it up and flush it down the toilet; we hope for the third option. She repeats to herself that this might not be a big deal, that she is making something out of nothing, that this only feels so shitty because it's never happened before, that a heap of tears and a splash of cold water can make everything fine again, that all new jobs are hard for a while. We think she's being a little bitch. It's not a big deal! She's making a mountain out of a molehill, and at the first sign of actual gaming culture, she's running away and crying. If she can't do the job, she doesn't belong here. But whatever, cry alone. Go for it.

Using that bathroom means passing the glass wall that does a bad job of hiding Preston's office. When asked why he designed it that way, Preston's answer is always, "Transparency!" She sees him in there, gesturing to no one, practicing some presentation or another—probably for the big announcement. Beyond is New York, darkening quickly with office buildings reflecting what remains of the harsh winter sun. For a breath or two, she thinks she is in Windy City. She'd rather be. If she were, she'd be tall, tan and blonde instead of short, skinny and rat-faced; she feels certain that she'd know what to do if she were a superhero. She wouldn't be running to the bathroom to sob if she were Circuit Breaker, hardwired to ignore rules in favor of chaos, all to further what is good. What is right. What is fair.

We should interrupt here to clarify: we don't know exactly why she does what she does next, especially since all of us agree, even those of us who have a molecule of sympathy for her, that of the million ways to handle this, what she chooses is the worst one. Eliza herself will say the same after it all happens. But we do know one thing for sure: nerds like us, like who she's trying to be or pretending to be, love a Chaotic Good protagonist. A hero who can say "fuck the rules!" Someone whose moral compass is greater than the law, than a bureaucratic government or social propriety. Chaotic Good is romance. It's standing up for the little guy. It's robbing the rich to give to the poor. It's bold. It's big. Our mythos is built on the individuality, the genius loner nobility of Chaotic Good. The Robin Hoods, the Wolverines, the Kvothes. Perhaps it is a moment of weakness or insanity, but most of us think this stumble-step moment is a simple—if ill-advised—realignment, a wish that life was a little more like the world she helps to build, where her own personal idea of justice is served and consequences are pixels. It is the only explanation we can offer for how she changes her mind, midstep. Or perhaps she's just an idiot. That could work too.

So, let's continue.

Eliza examines the last few minutes—she's taken a swing into Lawful Neutral and has been coasting, stuck. Or perhaps, she thinks, she's transformed from a superhero into someone who needs rescuing. When had she gotten complacent? she wonders. When had her alignment shifted without her noticing? When did she start taking the safe option instead of the brave one?

Instead of bursting into Preston's office like the Chaotic Good badass she wishes she is, she retains the good sense to knock. She longs for a proper wooden door—it would make a good smacking sound and she could use a hearty *thwap*; she could imagine an in-game bubble stating her sonic results, like a comic book, one made of candy-colored polka dots and bold, satisfying outline. *Knock! Bam! Thwap!* But the glass makes a hollow *clink* against her knuckles. "Preston?" she asks, fighting the prickly pins behind her eyes threatening to push tears out.

"Yes?"

"I'd like to have a Conversation with you. Is now a good time?"

Preston's smile falters. Fancy Dog corporate culture says that Conversations (capital "C") are a gift. But no one ever has Conversations for positive stuff (even though it is encouraged). Good things are reserved for regular conversations without the capital letter, and what is left over is critical feedback. So Eliza knows that Preston knows that what's coming isn't anything super. And you are supposed to give the recipient control over when they hear it, except everyone knows that's bullshit: no one can ever say "not fucking now" even if it isn't the right time, because Conversations are gifts and one should always be willing to receive a gift.

"Yes, of course! Did you want to talk some more about your Career Tree?" Preston asks.

"No." Eliza hesitates. Suzanne's words rattle in her brain. But—and we truly do not understand why—she keeps going. "It's about— I think I'm experiencing some sexism? On my team?"

Preston's eyes widen. He is shocked. "Come in, come in. Close the door." He remembers that his office is glass. He wonders if either of the two deaf people on staff can read Eliza's lips. Would they tell anyone? Should they both face away, toward the windows? Or could sound travel through glass? He thinks about the collaboration rooms, but they're glass too. And accusations like this—they spread things. Things he doesn't fucking need.

"No, wait." Preston pushes Eliza back out the door and closes it behind them. "Let's go to dinner. I mean, I'm taking you to dinner. My treat, obviously. Well, the company's treat. A business meeting. Let's talk this out." He walks two steps forward and remembers it is cold out. He backs up and grabs his coat from the spiny coatrack.

"I don't have my coat," Eliza says because there is nothing else to say.

"We can stop by your desk, not a problem."

Eliza considers saying she isn't much hungry, or that she has a ton of work to do; she considers saying she just found out about all this, and she needs a minute; she considers backing down entirely, but she doesn't. Preston accompanies her to her desk. She puts on her coat and they leave in the elevator together.

CHAPTER FOURTEEN

LFleis: did u see that

JPDes: yes

LFleis: we were right

JPDes: are you sure?

LFleis: she just left with him!

JPDes: i know

LFleis: i bet theyre not coming back

JPDes: we dont know, tho

LFleis: of course we do

LFleis: she totally fucked her way to the middle

JPDes: i guess your right

JPDes: sad

JPDes: i thought more of preston than that

LFleis: me too

LFleis: well at least we know

JPDes: i feel like i felt when i found out père noel wasnt real

LFleis: ?

JPDes: pere noel.

JPDes: father christmas

JPDes: santa claus, you asshole

LFleis: 😜

CHAPTER FIFTEEN

And now A Brief History of Eliza In Games narrated by only those of Us who Love her and want her to succeed which means a collective of queers and folks without genders that at this point has very little to do with the story but who will become Very Important later on—We have Temporarily Expelled the others

Her first one: *Star Fox* on the Nintendo 64 though We suppose if We're being technical it was *Stunt Copter* on her mother's old Macintosh computer—she doesn't think of it as a game in the same category as *Star Fox* when she gets the Nintendo 64 for her birthday because to our Plucky But Realistic Heroine a game is only such with a Dedicated Piece of Machinery on which it is played—she rips open the package and slots the cartridge in while leaving the Rumble Pak by the wayside and noticing it later after she's gone half through it— the controller feels like a Hug between her fingers and the relationship between joystick and flight is seamless and Elating—Eliza has never felt so free

When her next-door neighbor who is of course a boy (for now) comes over to see the system he sneers and says "that's a boy's game— let me show you how to really play it"—and the very first mission— which is one that she's only completed but not won—turns into a success when he shows her how to rescue Falco and make it to the Cornerian waterfalls—she still plays occasionally after that but only casually and

We are in Mourning with her—the fervor evaporates—the Joy gone from joystick until she feels stuck

Pokémon in 1998—first, she sees the show and the monsters are cute but she fears it might be another "boy thing" (Our Heart, it Breaks!) and then she sees Misty—Misty with a side ponytail and a shirt that Shows Her Midriff and a Sisterhood of feminine girls in bathing suits by her side—she begs and begs her mother to get her a Game Boy for the video game's impending US release—"But you barely play the Nintendo as it is" her mother says while driving the red minivan to ballet

"This'll be different" a small Eliza replies and she doesn't follow it up with "Girls play this even if it's called a Game Boy" because her mother's response won't be helpful—her mother would say "Girls can do anything that boys can do" and her eyebrows would knit together to make one long eyebrow—and We Agree!—but Eliza knows better—perhaps that is true in her mother's world, but everything is gendered in the language of ten-year-olds—girlhood matters (We Feel Compelled to leave a footnote here that not everything Eliza thinks as a ten-year-old Reflects Our Opinions but in the interest of Honesty which is a Core Value of Ours We must tell it like it is even though We wish We could go back into this History and Reparent her a little bit)

In the end it is her father who caves and she wakes one morning and discovers both items—the Game Boy and *Pokémon Red*—on the little white desk where she does her homework—she isn't the only girl who plays—but she is the only one in the Early Kids program—her high-powered advertising executive parents drop her off in the gymnasium each day on their way to work a full forty minutes before school actually starts and that forty minutes is spent on hard blue bleachers playing Pokémon with ten-year-old boys (for now) in backwards ball caps and white-soled, gym-teacher-approved shoes and she's right there along-side them in a Laura Ashley floral dress with a side ponytail like Misty's and no one cares—the memory of boy games and girl games begins to fade (Huzzah!)

Neopets in the year 2000—it was the next logical step from *Pokémon*

and she picks a Kau with its friendly farm-animal face but it is a short-lived obsession because she tries to be one of those people who have a ton of money and can partake in all the quests—it seems no matter how hard she tries she is at the bottom of the barrel—she wonders how much time people spend on here and she tries not to think about her Kau suffering without her to take care of it as she goes days then weeks without playing—understanding now that games can be played on her computer she asks for two for her birthday

Secret Paths in the Forest and *Secret Paths to the Sea* also the year 2000—they are a little older and a little outdated but she has it on good authority from *American Girl* magazine that she'll be able to see herself mirrored here—story! she thinks: This is how I want to see stories—not from tedious books and This is how I want to tell stories—not in essays no one but my teachers will ever read—but when she sits down to write a game it feels pointless without the skills to make little fantasy people move around dream worlds on a screen—instead she draws with abandon because it is the closest she thinks she could get without being good at math and without having already started to tame the computer—She Is Twelve! and decided already on the impossibility

There are more games of course but We will skip to 2004—*Ultima Online* and an awkward flat-chested sixteen-year-old girl who has stopped growing far earlier than her teenaged compatriots and who eats lunch in the guidance office and offers periodically to organize files in return for a safe and unawkward space to Peacefully Contemplate her cucumber-and-cream-cheese sandwich and her iced tea—she works summers at her parents' advertising agency and takes art classes where other students both shy and navel-gazing leave her in a corner to paint on her own and when one of the art kids whispers with his eyes on the floor that he plays *Ultima* and hopes to see her there sometime—that it is Stupid Fun—she buys the game and signs up for the subscription using her leftover summer job money and she doesn't tell her parents because they think games are a waste of time for a young lady beginning to look at colleges

Her character tames horses—she can tame anything to ride and she sells steeds to those whose skills lie elsewhere and she finds the Shy Art Kid and he introduces her to the other Shy Art Kids and they form a Shy Art Kid Guild and Eliza finds she can actually talk to them in the game with the keyboard standing sentry between her and the scrutinizing eyes of others—the fantasy aspect isn't necessarily for her—she has never been a girl who is into princesses and dragons—but the Bravery and the Camaraderie and the Automatic Conversation Topics when she sees the others at school—she'll take that any day—they build their castle and design their own crest: a paintbrush crossed with a sword and they take on dungeons and Eliza tames them each and every one an ostard or a warhorse or whatever they want—for Herself she tames a unicorn—it is a mount only women can ride

CHAPTER SIXTEEN

W e catch up with her an hour after Preston takes her to dinner, when Circuit Breaker pops into existence. She flees to the outskirts of Windy City, ignoring us all, and starts cracking down suburban trees with lightning. She thinks blowing up some stuff might make her feel better. It doesn't. She collects the wood to build things for her fortress. Any other day it is tedious but necessary work. She undertakes it now because she hopes the exploding little plants will grant her satisfaction. They don't.

Circuit Breaker hears the unmistakable *thunk thunk* of Chimera's knuckles on the ground. She sees the sound bubbles long before her fellow hero arrives. Chimera says nothing for a while. She grabs trees by their skinny necks and pulls them from the ground like weeds, dwarfed in her mighty fists. She breaks them in two—it requires no effort at all—and adds hand-split wood to the pile. "What are you planning on building?" she asks.

Eliza shrugs even though Suzanne can't see her (even though we can't see her). "I dunno," says Circuit Breaker.

"Okay."

They blast things. They uproot things.

"So you told Preston?"

"Chimera," says Circuit Breaker with a warning in her voice. "I don't want the real world in here. As much as possible. Right now."

"Ugh, fine. You told Human Man?"

"Yeah."

"And?"

"I dunno. He shook his head. Said he was really disappointed. Said those guys had been with him from the first hiring round, some of his best. He took me to dinner and then sent me home for the rest of the evening, so I came here." She cracks another tree, this time with a good deal more electricity. Instead of usable wood, the two heroes gaze upon the pixel-perfect equivalent of a spent match. It is at least a little satisfying. "He did that thing where he seems to want to squeeze his own head until it's a tiny square."

"The thing with his palms on his temples?"

"Yeah."

"He's gonna start breaking out. Zits for days."

They keep blasting trees.

"Why are you here, anyway?" Circuit Breaker asks. "Shouldn't you be working?"

"You bet I should." Chimera pauses. "This felt more important. I'm taking a break. I'm on the couches. I have a laptop with me, I'm surprised you can't see the lag."

"He said he'd talk to HR," Circuit Breaker says after a while more.

"How do you feel about it?"

"I really have no idea how I feel about it. It was such a spur-of-the-moment decision. And I think, maybe, it wasn't the best—" They hear a camera click and we shudder with anticipation. Yes. Yes. More information.

The telling dust trail and Runner Quick, Winged Feet of America and the World, stands at her side. Devonte knows it is a long, ridiculous tagline; that is part of the fun.

"Y'all don't have private turned on," Runner says immediately, and we all curse.

"Fuck," says Circuit Breaker, for a different reason. Or rather, the same reason from an opposing viewpoint. We could hear them. We want to continue to hear them. They wink from existence, but we know they're still there. Ghosts.

But it's fine, it's fine, we know what happens. We know we know what happens. We can keep narrating. "Preston called HR into his office as soon as he got back," he continues, once he is sure their voices aren't being broadcast.

"And?" Eliza and Suzanne say, both forgetting the role-play rule this time.

"Jinx," Suzanne says.

"Come on, dude," says Eliza, rolling her eyes.

"I dunno. They talked for a while in the glass office. Joe told me."

"Joe with the hearing aids?" Suzanne checks.

"Joe with the mad lipreading skills. He says it's not exact. But he seemed pretty sure of himself, regardless."

"Well then," Eliza says. "You have to know what happened."

"I dunno. I mean, I do know, but do you really wanna know?"

"Uh-oh," Suzanne says.

"Yeah," Devonte replies. "Joe said it looked like mandatory sensitivity training." No one is playing now. Their characters are the opposite of disembodied, standing there. What is it called when one only has a body, we wonder? Reverse ghosts?

"And?" Eliza asks.

"Have you, like, not been listening?" Suzanne says into her mic. "That's all that's going to happen." She pauses. "Right Devonte?"

"Joe didn't say anything else. Just that."

CHAPTER SEVENTEEN

JPDes: i feel bad

LFleis: why?

JPDes: preston seemed upset

LFleis: he just has to be

JPDes: ??

LFleis: he has to call HR in

LFleis: and pretend to be upset

LFleis: so he can say he took care of it

JPDes: i dunno

LFleis: look, he did teh minimum okay?

LFleis: thats how u know

LFleis: if he were really pissed abut it, hed do more

JPDes: i still feel bad

LFleis: your choice dude

JPDes: i guess we know shes not sleeping with him

LFleis: we dont kno that

JPDes: ???

JPDes: she went out with him to rat on us

LFleis: they culd have done that in his office

LFleis: but he took her out insted

LFleis: do u take women to lunch or somthing if your not gonna fuck sometime?

JPDes: i take my sister to dinner when she visits from paris

LFleis: dont be an asshole

LFleis: you kno what i mean

JPDes: i guess

LFleis: theyr definitely up to somethign

LFleis: you think shell be mad at him that he didnt take her side?

JPDes: dunno

LFleis: i bet hes not getting any for a LONG time

LFleis: lol

LFleis: JP?

JPDes: lol.

CHAPTER EIGHTEEN

Most of us identify strongest with Jean-Pascale, unaware and unassuming, a brilliant technical mind, so he is deserving of our eyes and ears and focus for a moment or two. He hangs his keys on the board as requested by Delphine. She is wearing an apron and making some kind of asparagus over some kind of quinoa. He winces: asparagus isn't in season and he hates quinoa. He wants something with meat in it, and in a bigger portion. But Delphine, an actor-dancer, is very particular about what she can eat, so he usually picks at what she puts in front of him and goes out for burgers late at night.

Delphine is so very cool or so very fake, depending on which of us you talk to; we either want to fist-bump Jean-Pascale in celebration, or sit him down and ask him what he is thinking. She has a French name but not a drop of French blood in her. Samantha Delphine Stewart, middle name selected by a Francophile mother. It came in handy when Jean-Pascale chatted her up in a bar. "My middle name's Delphine!" she'd said when they talked about his move from Paris to New York.

"Delphine's a very French name," he'd said as he sipped his beer and pretended to like it. He's called her Delphine ever since. Her mother is thrilled about it. He wishes for bar snacks in lieu of whateverthefuck she is cooking. The best part of America is the junk food.

She turns around with a baking sheet in hand and sees his face. "What's wrong?" she asks. She is so in tune with him. She can spot his upsetness. We wish we had girlfriends that paid attention to us like that.

"Hello to you too," he says, his shoulders slumping. He doesn't really want to talk about it anymore—he feels like he's been talking about it for hours, with HR and Lewis and inside his own head, feeling shitty about it all.

"Tell me everything," Delphine orders as she scoops some vile dinner onto his plate. So he does.

"80085," she giggles and covers her mouth so Jean-Pascale can see only her tiny nose and mischievous eyes, squinting at the corners. She is like a Disney princess—animated, perky and perfect. "JP, that's so mean." She pauses. "But so funny. It's clever, using the numbers like that. Certainly this side of offensive."

Jean-Pascale smiles. "You think it's funny?"

"Yes. Comedic genius."

His smile breaks into a grin. Or grimace. "That's what Lewis said. I'm not sure anymore."

"Ugh. Lewis. Your boyfriend." She emphasizes the *oy* in "boy" as if she's been transported back in time to the playground. Delphine chews her bite of quinoa. Jean-Pascale rubs his eyes. "Aww, honey"—she puts down her fork—"you really feel weird about this?"

"Yeah."

"Okay. Well here's what I'm going to do. I'm going to go take a bath—I've been sore all day anyway, that new choreo is a killer. And I'm going to use some bubbles and some candles and stuff."

"Uh. Okay?"

Delphine smiles. "That's so when you order in the burger I know you get at least once a week at the diner, I won't smell it. And you won't have to leave."

"You know about that?"

"Of course I do. You smell like meat when you get home. Meat and fried things. And popcorn? I don't know why popcorn. They don't serve popcorn. But you smell like popcorn and that diner smells like popcorn. And anyway, you can eat your burger and play your game and hang out in cyberspace with your boyfriend—"

"—he's not my—"

"—and you won't have to worry about anything at all. Good?"

Jean-Pascale doesn't know how he's gotten so lucky. "Sure. Yes, good."

"Okay then." Delphine gets up to clear the plates.

"Delphine?"

She turns around. "Yeah?"

"You don't think something worse should have happened?"

"Jean-Pascale, you are a wonderful person. If we can't joke around anymore at work, then maybe we should all hide in basements somewhere and never speak to each other again."

"So you don't think it was that bad?"

"JP. Let me tell you. This isn't sexist. Yesterday I left an audition because it became abundantly clear that I wasn't getting the spot unless I slept with the choreographer who was twice my age. When it comes to shit that happens because of sexism, we have way bigger things to worry about."

CHAPTER NINETEEN

Lewis isn't doing anything particularly interesting tonight, but we should check in on him anyway because this is the last evening of calm before the maelstrom, and we feel like we should see him in his normal state, before it all goes to hell, before his inertia is disrupted. He logs on to *Guilds of the Protectorate* so he can be Doctor Moriarty (no tagline) for a bit. He doesn't think one thought about HR or Preston or Eliza. Sometimes he thinks about how much of a pussy JP had been, and during these moments he shakes his head. But then he gets sucked into the game again.

He lives in midtown with his mother—or more accurately, his mother lives with him. His apartment has a fabulous view of the city where he can see Manhattan in layers, as if it's shedding petals and exposing a center only the luckiest pollinators would ever see. If Lewis were to look out over the city, maybe he'd think about how lucky he is. How he has this place in the middle of things that lets him really know New York in such an intimate way, a bee dipping into a concrete flower. The New Yorker building with its red letters. Yellow cabs look like skittering cats on the street below, that's how small they are. Maybe if he were to survey it all with a bourbon in hand, he'd have some other thoughts too. And maybe those thoughts would drift to Eliza. Or to his mother, snoring softly in another room. Perhaps, with such a quiet moment of reflection, he'd be better able to handle what's coming. But we disagree on this—some of us see Lewis as the tragic hero in the classical sense. Predestined, the sort of person tragedy hunts down and finds with little provocation. His flaws are coded into him. What else is he to do?

But some of us think he could choose to turn back. We'll point out when we think the moment is, where—should he listen to his chorus—he could throw his hands up and walk away. But that's the thing with tragic heroes—we'll never know, because they never listen to their narrators.

Anyhow. Instead of doing any of that, he sits in his dark apartment missing the clouds brewing, rolling in against a sky inkier than Black Hole, Destroyer of Light. The blue shine from his computer blasts his face. It lights up the window with a cold, lifeless LCD hue while every one of his neighbors' windows shines a buttery yellow.

CHAPTER TWENTY

The next morning, we watch Eliza brazenly change the subject after Preston calls her in to tell her the situation has been taken care of. Entitled to his time and the direction of the conversation, like she belongs. Completely without the deference required for the CEO of Fancy Dog. "I don't understand," she says after listening, her lips growing tighter and tighter over her ugly-ass rat mouth. "I don't understand why they just got a slap on the wrist. Don't you believe me?"

Preston sighs and rubs his temples, squeezes his head. His eyes dart to his giant glass wall and to the prying eyes beyond. "Of course I believe you, Eliza." He pauses. "But it's a complicated thing."

"Can I ask you to explain—?" She clears her throat. Her mouth is dry. "Explain it to me?"

"You could, but I wouldn't have to." Preston is getting annoyed. "How management decides to deal with its employees is really only the concern of management. Above your pay grade, as they say."

"But"—Eliza points to the glass wall—"what about transparency?"

Preston sighs again. "Okay, fine. Come on, sit down."

After Devonte signed off the night before, Suzanne and Eliza talked. "Okay," Suzanne had said. "If you're insistent upon it, if there really is no turning back, you need to be really clear and cool-headed about it. You can't go in there and cry. You can't go in there and say 'systemic issue,' because men don't want to hear that they're part of the problem too. You have to go in there with solidly reasoned points as to why this actually matters, because Preston isn't going to instinctively know why. He's not. He's never going to have experienced something like this, and he never will." They'd gone over everything she could possibly bring up. Gone over it twice.

"Can you just tell me what happened?" Eliza starts, because she isn't exactly sure how to begin, despite the preparation. She is nervous. She hopes he will throw her an anchor, a place from which to begin. Or perhaps she hopes he will trap himself.

Preston sighs once more and glances at his watch. "I pulled them into the office with a Human Resources representative. I let them know you had seen a tag on all of your code and had come to me about it, that you were concerned about sexism and I wanted to get their side of the story."

"And?"

"And they said they were just keeping an eye on your code because you're new—to the position and to programming—and they thought this was a funny way to do it, being you're the only one who has—well." Preston blushes. "They didn't mean anything by it and were sorry if it hurt your feelings. Lewis expressed a sadness that you didn't come to them about this first, as they would have apologized and corrected their behavior without me getting involved."

Eliza is about to defend herself, but stops short—perhaps she should have gone to the two of them, no fuss? Some of us think so—it's the same dilemma we have with Lewis. How much can her actions change things? If she is someone's tragic hero (certainly not ours), or if they both are, then she's hurtling through destiny toward the inevitable. But if not—what if she'd called Lewis and JP jerks to their faces and left it at that? Then we'd have no story. Nothing to watch. Do we prefer it this way? Or do we stick to our ideological guns and say shame, shame on her?

"They're undergoing mandatory sensitivity training so that they will

better understand what kind of humor is office-appropriate in future."
Preston pauses. "I've also let them know your promotion was earned
and that you're a spectacular coder, you know a lot for having started
fairly recently and you've come along so far so quickly. Off the record,
I told them they were great big morons for not trusting your code."
Preston smiles shyly. He feels like this is winning, paying her this
compliment.

Eliza glances out the office window. She could decide this is
enough. She almost does. Except it isn't. To her, it isn't, and Eliza can't
pretend. She is so close to swerving around her tragic flaw: the need
for vengeance. The part of her that is Circuit Breaker won't stand for
it because it's not fair. She shouldn't have to deal with this, she thinks.
We think she's just a whore. A slut who wants to get Lewis and
Jean-Pascale fired for a stupid joke. Not the tragic hero at all, but a
villain. So: "May I have a Conversation about the work environment
this places me in?"

The last thing Preston wants to do is give her permission. But: "Of
course, Eliza. Conversations are always gifts. I'm all ears."

"First, I want you to know that I feel it is unlikely that Jean-Pascale
and Lewis will ever take me seriously, given that before my first week
on their team was even over—before it had even begun—they reduced
me to a body part that is associated mostly with women."

"Now Eliza, we can't—"

"May I—" Eliza clears her throat again, turns redder. "May I finish
having a Conversation with you first, Preston?"

Preston closes his mouth, embarrassed. It is a policy of his own
invention, after all. "Certainly. I apologize."

"Okay, so I find it unlikely that they will take my work seriously
because they reduced me to a body part. And I also think that giving
them mandatory sensitivity training might not address the environment
that's been created now that they know I've spoken to you about sexism.
Their sexism."

"I'm not sure I understand."

Eliza sighs. "They know I told on them so—"

"Oh, right, of cour—"

"They might take that out on me, you know? Professionally? And then lastly, I think that giving two people mandatory sensitivity training fails to address, um, the systemic—the, uh, larger issue of sexism in the gaming industry—in the world at large, right now—that will inevitably color some of our, um, the women's experiences here, even in a place like Fancy Dog which is largely—or, um, entirely—almost entirely— progressive."

Preston pauses. "Are you finished?"

"Yes. I think."

"Well, I want to say that I hear your concerns. But to have a Conversation about your Conversation, when you said that there's a systemic problem here, frankly that made me feel hurt." Preston takes a good deal of pride in the "action-feeling" speak. Concrete action, personal feeling. He is better at this than anyone else. He will win this Conversation, he is sure. "Because I try very hard to be one of the good guys. I promoted you with next to no professional development background because I believe that you really can do great things. You've shown immense drive, which is why I'm so surprised that your co-workers playing what is, in the end, a silly and stupid little joke has thrown you so much. Or at least, I perceive it has really taken your mind off work and off the goals that we set together. Moving forward, I would suggest working on forgiving and forgetting—don't let adolescent pranks stand in the way for you. Let me handle them and you just keep your nose to the grindstone. Do good work, be a good person, that's all anyone cares about around here."

Eliza almost blurts out that no, they also seem to care that she has boobs. Instead: "Does it weird you out?"—she tiptoes around her words carefully, like they might bite or escape out a sliding French door before she can close it; or, she calculates—what tone of voice will make this seem natural, like she is not a conniving bitch?—"that they chose to label my code with an area—a part of a woman's body that's normally extremely sexualized? That doesn't, I don't know, create a tension that doesn't belong in a workplace?"

Preston is in the middle of sipping from a glass of water when she reaches the word "sexualized." He stops, puts the glass down and blinks at her once, twice. "Are you saying that Jean-Pascale and Lewis sexually harassed you?"

"I mean, maybe! I don't know! I've never been sexually harassed at work before, is that what this is? I've always thought of harassment as, like, wolf whistles when walking by construction sites. But even Fancy Dog orientation says it's harassment when someone feels uncomfortable, and I feel extremely uncomfortable."

Preston neatly folds his hands on his glass desktop and looks out through his glass wall. He sees Joe turn his head back to his computer. He can't even speak to the man about eavesdropping—he isn't sure where the ADA stands on that.

Preston turns back to Eliza. "I want you to think long and hard before we fill out paperwork stating that. I want you to think very, very carefully before you accuse anyone of anything. Look, candidly, just between you and me: all it was was stupid. You didn't get hurt, your job is safe, I don't think less of you, no one thinks less of you. No harm was done, they were just idiots. And they're not even normally idiots! They're good guys. They write great code. They do nice things. They just fu—slipped up. Once. If you say sexual harassment, I have to pull HR down here and put them on documented training with notes all over their records or terminate their employment with no references. But I want to stress to you, remind you, that no harm was done to anyone. It was just a joke and I really don't want to ruin anyone's life over this. Now. Knowing that I am strongly suggesting you let this go, don't let it bother you and we'll just keep moving you toward your goals here, what would you like to do?"

"Preston, please, I don't want to ruin anyone's life here either. But I do think they're getting off pretty lightly for what could be a really big deal."

"Let's not keep score, Eliza."

"And I do think harm was done—I have to work with these guys now."

"Well what do you propose I do?" Preston snaps, losing his cool. He will regret this later, but now he looks at Eliza and feels only rage because she is wasting his time, his brain space. What if this is the very moment he is supposed to be coming up with his next big idea, and instead he is dealing with this? "Demote them? Fire them?"

"How about informal probation, no notes on their records?" Eliza asks, tentative. "That way, if they do something else to me, or to anyone, something more serious could be—"

But Preston is shaking his head back and forth, and some of us are doing so too; we know the policies. "No. We don't offer probationary periods at Fancy Dog for any reason. It makes people feel like they're not part of the team." The only sound for a few seconds is the blowing heating vent as the hot air clunk-clunks through the system. It is extremely uncomfortable.

"Move me!" The idea sneaks up on her suddenly and pounces. "Move me to a different team. It's still in line with my goals. I would love working with Devonte."

Preston rubs his temples with his fingers. "There are no lateral positions on any other team right now. I'd have to promote you or demote you. And frankly, I'm not prepared to do either. You shouldn't get demoted for something you didn't do. And you shouldn't get a promotion until you've earned it. And no one in this company is moving at all until we—" He stops short, remembering the wall and Joe. Joe is not part of the team that knows about the launch. Leaky Joe would give us more on 4chan if he were. Joe can't keep a secret.

"Then I don't know what to do," Eliza says. "But it just feels like— something. Something should be done. It should be addressed some-how. It feels like—it just feels like a big deal to me. It feels like an injustice."

"I have dealt with it. I have addressed it." And we agree with him, yes. It should be over. "Now, you go and do your thing, working for Fancy Dog. And I'll keep doing mine: running it. And making decisions like this."

Eliza stands but doesn't move toward the door.

"Unless of course," Preston continues, "you'd like to say they harassed you. Sexually. Then we're not finished here at all." We are all on edge right now. We don't want her to ruin their lives over this.

She stumbles from the glass office. Preston leaves by himself under the pretense of grabbing coffee, needing to get out for a few minutes, to breathe air, to be unwatched. He Instagrams the butchered name the barista writes on his coffee cup: Pearson.

CHAPTER TWENTY-ONE

LFleis: here she fucking comes

LFleis: joe says she asked for promotion

JPDes: no shit, rly?

LFieis: yeah. she didnt want to work with us anymore

LFleis: and she almost accused us of sexual harassment

LFleis: cunt

JPDes: i mean, okay

JPDes: we definitely didnt do that

JPDes: how are we supposed to handle this?

LFleis: dunno. just a joke

LFleis: if she were cool at all, shed just laugh

JPDes: i guess

LFleis: delphine laughed, right?

JPDes: yeah

LFleis: see? delphine is cool

JPDes: but she didnt say sexual harassment?

JPDes: in the end?

LFleis: joe says definitely no

LFleis: p talked her out of it

LFleis: then they talked about a promotion

JPDes: if she gets a promotion

JPDes: im gonna be pissed

JPDes: even if we were mean

JPDes: thats not fair

LFleis: if she gets the promotion

LFleis: shes definitely sleeping wit him

LFleis: joe said he didnt do that tho

JPDes: see shes not sleeping with him

LFleis: it dosnt mean shes not

LFleis: i just said if she got the promotion, then she definitely is

LFleis: if she doesnt, that doesnt mean shes not

CHAPTER TWENTY-TWO

Eliza walks up to her workstation. It would be too kind of us to call it a desk; it is a sparse, long table she shares with one of the other developers, someone on Devonte's team. Across from her at their own long table sit Lewis and, next to him, Jean-Pascale. Their view of her is unimpeded by cork walls or any other cubicle accoutrement. It is, at the moment, an open-office purgatory. As she sits, unsmiling, she notices Lewis's raccoon-like eyes pop up above his monitor for a second, and then flick back down to his screen. He begins to type such that the clacking from the keys on his keyboard isn't separate: instead, one long, slightly varied click, modulating according to the difference in applied pressures between a pinky and a middle finger.

Jean-Pascale types back. Slower, but banging heavy with each keystroke. It isn't normal for him; he generally has an incredible amount of finesse. Silence. Then Lewis again.

Eliza needs to finish her part of the project, so she begins working. But she isn't above the keyboard Morse code as emotional display—she hacks away furiously, like the semicolons offend her, hoping they'll interpret it as her own discussions with allies on the other side of the screen. It isn't a difficult charade to pull off—she is angry. And uncomfortable. In actual fact, neither of her allies are particularly responsive: Suzanne is fielding questions about rumors that there's a big launch coming, though what it is no journalist can say. As we pepper her with questions, she can rightfully reply she knows nothing about it. Devonte debugs at breakneck speed, or what passes for it in the glacial environment of programming. Runner Quick is an apt alter ego for him; relative to the rest of the world, he is fucking fast. The way he interacts with his computer is practiced, elegant, efficient. Like watching an ice skater glide or a cowboy ride a horse.

No one speaks out loud to each other for as long as is sustainable. Jean-Pascale and Lewis keep volleying their clicking noises back and forth; Eliza figures they are lobbing balls of pure hatred over the net at each other. In her effort to broadcast her feelings, she ham-fingers everything. Eventually she looks down at the two lines she's added and can't even figure out what she was trying to do. It feels like she's dipped her hands in the tension and it's hardened, gluing her fingers or possibly her brain and making her clumsy.

"Hey," says the programmer next to her. "Are you okay? You're turning a bit green in the face." He has discarded his headphones and looks concerned; he's been watching her struggle for a while. In his lap sits a dog, a pug with bulging eyes wearing a tiny tee shirt that says "UpDog." The dog's tongue sticks out in perpetuity. We have barely seen this dog on Instagram. He pets it absently.

"I'm fine. Fine," Eliza says. She forces a smile. "Thank you." Except she doesn't sound grateful; she sounds tight-lipped. Peevish. She grimaces.

"I can't concentrate with all this noise," Lewis says to the air around him. "We may as well skip right to our pre-announcement meeting, if we're going to talk instead of working." He unplugs his laptop from his monitor, flourishing his fingers and savoring each cord pulled; "pointed" is the word, we think. He is pointedly undocking. He stands, computer under his arm. Once he is halfway to the stairs, he turns around. "Jean-Pascale? Are you coming?"

Jean-Pascale looks up, startled. He's fallen into his work and has forgotten all about everything. "Uh. Yes. I—I suppose I can't concentrate so well up here either. Plus we can, er, talk openly there. About the announcement." He unplugs quickly. Lewis opens the door to the stairs and disappears. Before JP follows, he turns. "Eliza?" he says, and he clears his throat. "There's uh. Does that work for you?"

Eliza forces a smile, one that makes her look like a wolf with a facial tic or a violent offender. She half salutes at JP—what a weird gesture—and it looks so much like she's raising her hand to hit her deskmate in the face that he flinches in his chair. "Sure," she says. "Yes, coming. Just give me a minute to wrap up." She can't make herself say thank you. He turns his back to her and Eliza's shoulders slump forward. She becomes bean shaped as she pushes her glasses up her nose. Dog moseys up to her and whines; puts his paw on her knee. She scratches his white mop of a head and pushes the fur out of his very sincere eyes.

Eliza leans down and whispers in Dog's ear. "Even all the dogs are male."

"Hey." Her deskmate is back in her field of vision. "I have this ginger gum if you're nauseous. It works wonders."

"Thank you, I'm actually not—I'm just going to go. To the meeting. I'll be fine. I'm fine." She undocks her laptop as well and sets off toward the collaboration room, almost catching up to her two teammates.

"Hey!" she hears from behind her, and she rolls her eyes as she turns around. The programmer jogs up behind her, his dog now sitting at the computer as though it were in charge of the *Guilds of the Protectorate* landing page and not the human.

"What?" Eliza says, fixing her face as best she can. For someone with an unfixable face.

"When you feel better, I'd love to ask you out for a drink or something. Maybe tonight, even. To celebrate the announcement." We imagine what she thinks of him—that he is asking her out on a date when she's visibly distressed and at work is bad enough, but then he waggles his eyebrows up and down. See, this is why we hate her. She thinks he's a nerd, and so she shoots him down.

"I'm sorry, I have a boyfriend," Eliza says. Perhaps at another time, she'd have been flattered, some of us think. Almost all of us think she should give the nice guy a chance. He isn't bad looking, and he works for Fancy Dog, so he is clearly smart, competent. Maybe the eyebrows are a joke; maybe he is funny. A few of us, though, we get it: everything is sour. She just wants to work, and now this.

Out of the corner of her eye, she sees Lewis and JP turn to face each other, but she can't see what their faces do in that moment of connection. We can see it, however, and it is a knowing smirk, Lewis's lips curling up in disgust.

They settle into one of the collaboration rooms. That's what Fancy Dog calls the very tiny conference rooms created for the teams to meet together. Big screens hang on the walls for employees to dock their computers so everyone can see their work. They are honeycomb shaped and fit together in a cluster of six on Preston's floor, their floor-to-ceiling windows facing his glass wall. It wasn't consciously intentional, we don't think, but he probably put them there so he could get off on seeing these people he brought together succeed together. Because he does; he figuratively gets off on that a bit, who wouldn't? Who doesn't look every so often at the moving parts of something they've created and think, fuck, I am good?

The meeting should be short: they are close to finished with their part, with only the documentation left to write. Tricky problems have been solved. The code is so neat it looks like poetry. There should be a hefty amount of congratulations, even in the face of the all-nighters the entire company is going to pull. It should be the kind of meeting where employees can be excused for popping open a bottle of cheapish champagne, doled out in recycled-paper cone cups from the water cooler. Instead there is silence, a quick divvying up of the remaining work by Lewis, the unofficial captain, and more silence.

The tension is too much for her shitty sense of self. Or she is sure that she'll be immune to consequences if she confronts them. Or she takes another swing into chaotic again; what she psychotically believes is Chaotic Good. Eliza clears her throat. "I know what 80085 means."

"We know you know," Lewis says. A beat passes. Jean-Pascale looks down at the wood floor. "We know," Lewis continues, "that you asked for a promotion."

"I didn't," Eliza says. She can't figure out where to set her gaze, so she looks out toward Preston's office. He sits at his desk staring at his computer, and Dog sits on the couch, his watery eyes on her.

Lewis clears his throat again, heat rising in his face. He is awkward even at the least awkward of times, and this is not the least awkward of times. "We know you accused us of sexually harassing you."

"I didn't, I actually don't think—"

"Do you know what that does to a guy? To have that accusation on his record? What, are you just trying to slash and burn us to claw your way to the top? And fuck all with the established team, the people who have been here all along? You think you're too good for us—"

"No, I—"

"Yes, you do," Lewis snaps. He is emboldened now that he understands what we have always understood: there is protection in the brotherhood of gaming; the company understands that sometimes men need to yell at work. Someone might have a Conversation with Lewis about it later, but then he will apologize and his point will still have been made, incontrovertibly burned into Eliza's memory, and that's what he needs. The Conversation mechanism is there to protect him, a leader, as he does what needs doing for his team. Or he loses his cool, forgets that Eliza and Preston are almost certainly sleeping together and that whatever he says might cause the CEO to retaliate. Or he knows it and will deny saying anything later. It'll make her look even more crazy, like a lying bitch.

"You can't take a damn joke. We all got poked fun of and hazed or whatever when we first started—we're used to it, from high school. And what, you think you should just get to be here? Some popular hack who jumps into games the instant it's cool, the instant it won't get your ass kicked." Lewis stands; his hands curl into fists. "That you don't have to do what we both did." He gestures to Jean-Pascale, who looks up, wide-eyed and surprised to be included. "No, there's a process. A set of dues. You don't just waltz into the gaming world and take a great job from someone who's studied for years, played games for years, put up with bullshit for *years* to get here. And you don't do it in a way that none of us can. Marching all over the place, accusing us of sexual harassment. Fucking your way to the middle. We know about you and Preston." Lewis's eyes bug out, like a dollar store toy being squeezed and squeezed. "We can't sleep with Preston to get a job or to ask for a promotion, and you shouldn't get to either."

"We are absolutely not—!" Eliza shouts back, alarmed. She wants to finish the sentence with the word "fucking" but it is work and she isn't sure if she can or should say it. Or she's taken so much by surprise that she can't respond, outshouted or outwitted by Lewis. Or they are fucking, and she finds it difficult to lie. Once again, Eliza looks around, this time for witnesses to this outburst she can barely believe is happening. JP is jittery like he's taken a caffeine pill, scratching his arms and looking anywhere but at Lewis. Her eyes light on Preston's glass office once more and, of course, he is working too hard to have noticed the commotion. Dog, though, has risen from the couch and sits at the glass wall, staring, mouth open in a silent whine.

"Oh, sure, sure, you didn't, you're not, whatever. And then you tell Andy you have a boyfriend. Well, you didn't before and now you do, now that you have a promotion. Did he pay you with that promotion, huh? Is that how you see it? Preston's too good to see it that way and you're going to suck all the fucking life out of him and then eviscerate him when you get what you want." Lewis is more controlled now, more like Doctor Moriarty. A small spark of glee lodges somewhere behind his diaphragm: he's embodying all those opposite parts, those choices he would make to be a different person, if he could. To be more powerful. To take the power that is rightfully his. He draws himself up and looks down at Eliza. He is short, but so is she, and it looks intimidating. "We were doing fine before you got here."

"I don't doubt that, but—"

"We'd have made this patch without you."

"Okay, but listen—"

"And we'd have launched Vive support without you. We did all of that anyway."

"I understand, I only knew for a couple days—"

"Your stuff doesn't deserve special attention, it just doesn't."

Eliza stamps her foot on the ground and shouts, "Did you even look at the part of the patch I wrote? Really look at it? Or did you just copy it in all chopped up without paying attention and decide it was filled with errors?"

Lewis turns his back on her. "I don't need to look at anything created by a feminazi whore who asks for promotions over her seniors. Because I know. I just fucking know." He turns back around, eyes narrowed, teeth bared. Yes, yes. We feel this face. Deeply. We feel it so often. Lewis Fleishman is our hero. "Go run to your boyfriend."

Lewis steps back, fast, because Eliza gets what we'll call dead shark eyes. Something turns off in her. Any sort of human compassion for another person flees her gaze and all that is left is darkness. Here is the villain we know she is, in her eyes at this moment. A few of us disagree, think we understand: she is tired. She is finished. Still more of us think she is on the rag: do eyes go dead when that happens, when you're that emotional? She stands up and walks out of the collaboration room.

When she arrives at the bathroom, she can't even cry. She would have thought that's what she'd do—she's never been called a feminazi whore before. She's never been accused of sleeping with her boss before. If she'd told past-Eliza about this moment, past-Eliza would have predicted tears.

Or, when she arrives in the bathroom, she splashes water on her face and sets her mouth in a thin line, ready to take revenge.

Or, when she arrives in the bathroom, there's a twenty-minute gap between this piece of the puzzle and the next, because she does cry. She takes care to do it silently; if anyone hears her, she will be judged too sensitive, too feminine. Because she can't get a good wail on, it takes longer than normal.

We don't really know what she does in the bathroom.

CHAPTER TWENTY-THREE

The entirety of Fancy Dog files into a movie theater Preston rented. The theater employees are under strict orders to stay out of the screening room; it is at the very end of the hall, up the stairs. The walls are soundproof. No one will be able to overhear the announcement outside.

Eliza is buzzing on coffee and excitement while also weighed down with the knowledge of 80085, being accused of having an affair with Preston, and the proof positive that it still means something to be a man in this world, that there are still people here who would put her in her rightful place. It is a strange cocktail of emotions that results in a floating feeling, like breathing helium from a balloon. She can't quite feel her face.

"Welp," Devonte says as he turns to Suzanne. "We have to go up front."

"What?" Suzanne asks around a mouthful of popcorn.

"Eliza and I have to sit up front. We're part of the announcement. We have cues to hit and everything."

"You mean you both know what this is?"

Eliza and Devonte nod.

"Son of a fucking bitch," Suzanne says, shaking her head. Eliza worries that Suzanne is angry until she sees the little smile. "I can't believe y'all didn't tell me."

"They made us sign a thing," Eliza says. She wishes she'd said it with her own mouth full of movie snacks, but when she'd gotten up to the counter, she found she was too nauseous to want anything. Almost as if her body latched on to her deskmate's suggestion.

"It was killing me," Devonte says, a Twizzler protruding from the corner of his lips like a celebratory cigar.

"How long?" Suzanne asks.

"Fuck, more than a year. Close to two."

"I only had to do a few days," Eliza interrupts. "I can't imagine keeping it for longer."

"This is where we leave you." Devonte salutes Suzanne, who discreetly flashes a middle finger below seat level. Devonte snort-chuckles and turns toward the front.

"Dev," Eliza says. "Make sure you're sitting between me and that guy?" She points at the back of her tablemate's head.

"Who, Andy? What's wrong with Andy? He's a nice guy."

"He hit on me right before this. Which is, like, whatever. I just don't wanna deal."

He snort-chuckles again. "A little too nice, maybe." When they get to the front row, Devonte puts his body between Andy and Eliza.

"Do you have yours?" Devonte says.

"Yep. It's in my bag." She holds up a cloth sling purse, weighed down by what a careful observer might guess to be very large binoculars; perhaps a scuba diving mask.

In response, he holds up a strangely shaped Whole Foods shopping bag, which he stuffs down under his seat. "Weirdest-shaped avocados ever," he says, and Eliza laughs. She is starting to have fun; being with Devonte is always easy. He's calm, calming. The smile slides from her face, however, as Jean-Pascale and Lewis enter from the back. They are both carrying conspicuous neon-yellow backpacks and wear smug smiles. Their heads are raised like they are being led by the chin and they gaze, king-like, upon the uninitiated, their own personal unwashed masses. They are reasonably proud, given what they've accomplished in such a short amount of time. Eliza's body shoots through with anger and her stomach flips upside down.

She nudges Devonte with her elbow. "Do the teams have to sit together?"

He nods and gestures down the row at the rest of his five-person crew. Andy lifts his hand to wave and Eliza turns quickly away. We sigh with relief: everyone in the front row—all the engineers (junior and senior), all the user interface designers, everyone who knows about the launch—all of them are men. Except Eliza. And except Devonte, all of them are white. No matter what they try, we aren't obsolete yet. We're still here, in the upper echelons, where we belong. But they're encroaching—Devonte and Eliza are proof of that. So even though we know well that the "perks" of diversity are fake, we have to be vigilant. We don't want us, or our representatives, taking up any fewer seats in rows like this.

Eliza turns in her seat and looks back. The entirety of HR is comprised of women. It's the acceptable place for diversity efforts, one that doesn't require any hard skills. Customer service is equally split— Suzanne sits next to her co-worker, what's his name, that fucking fruit. She nudges Devonte again. "How did they get away without telling the animators and the character designers?"

Devonte holds a finger up while he swallows the last of his Twizzler. "They design and animate in 3-D already. We just got really specific about sizes, specs, that shit."

Lewis and Jean-Pascale sit down next to her. She stops talking. They sit in silence. Not a comfortable silence; imagine the silence after a beer is spilled on a laptop. That's the kind of silence we're talking about. Fortunately for everyone, Preston and his co-founder, Brandon, step onto the stage. The lights dim as everyone begins to clap and cheer.

They never see much of Brandon in the office, though he is a co-founder and certainly the COO, maybe even the CFO. In fact, Eliza thinks this is the first time she's ever seen him in person; but we see him a lot, especially those of us who have purchased stock in Fancy Dog

Games—this is the man who addresses stakeholders, did all the pitches when they were gunning for VC funding, writes articles on Business Insider, Quartz and in the *Wall Street Journal*. He looks like he is Preston's age, but his hair is already mostly grey. He attempts a smile— and why not, it is a very exciting day—but his face looks unused to flexing those muscles. In all his photos, his suits are bespoke expressions of sartorial grace, and the kind of skinny velvet modern that can go out of style any second. Today is no exception—a dark maroon with a coordinated (but not matching) tie and pocket square. His tie clip is a Space Invader. He looks like a J.Crew take on a classic nerd. His glasses are small and wiry, circular and very hip. Eliza touches her own black frames and hopes they aren't returning to the style corner from whence they came.

She blinks—she feels like something is missing from the stage. Aren't there senior software engineers, vice presidents of such and such, to join them? At the very least, a business strategy team? Until this point, she's assumed they have a small army running the company. Could it really mostly be the two of them, even after they'd gone public? She reels from imagining all that responsibility until she remembers the board.

"Settle down, settle down," says Brandon.

"You'll have enough cause for noise in a bit, we promise," Preston adds. Eliza's eyes shift to him and—

"Oh no." She leans her head over to Devonte. "He's not—"

"What?" Devonte says.

"The clothes? Preston's clothes?"

Preston wears a black turtleneck and blue jeans, an impersonation of the Steve Jobs announcement uniform. To Eliza, it reeks of striving, of intentionality. "You don't think that's a little—I dunno, embarrassing?" Eliza whispers.

"Why would it be?" Devonte whispers back.

"Do you really think it's a fair comparison?" Eliza says, and Devonte thinks for only a second before nodding an affirmative.

"Shhht," Lewis hisses. "Always so distracted. Distracting." Eliza rolls her eyes while also feeling thoroughly chastised. Her stomach grumbles. Her face is burning red with embarrassment and anger.

"Before we get started," Brandon continues, "HR is coming around with another nondisclosure agreement and some pens for those who need them." Papers rustle and a blonde woman appears in the aisle, smiling as she passes out forms. Smiling big, even though she has no idea what is about to be announced and she knows she is looking at a group of insiders.

"We know, we know!" Preston says. It sounds rehearsed, like he expects there to be groans in the audience even though there aren't any; Eliza thinks the shine on Preston might be tarnished for her, and it makes her sad. "You've all already signed agreements, but the following announcement is, well, it's major. And it falls under the category of business secret. Consider this new NDA a reminder." He winks. At what, Eliza isn't sure, but she hears someone sigh behind her. The reedy tones of idol worship. It reminds her of wanting to dig her hands into Preston's hair, of wanting to climb onto his shoulders. She tries to resummon that feeling with little success. Trying to be in the moment, to get swept up with JP and Lewis right next to her, is like trying to meditate in the presence of a heat lamp. It is hard to let go, be present, with the words "feminazi whore" blazing next to her. The triumphant look on Lewis's face.

Brandon and Preston wait until everyone's signed and all eyes are back on them. "I'm going to keep this short and sweet," Preston says, and everyone hushes. "This is an idea Brandon and I have been playing around with since 2012, when we attended a demonstration by a software company that will change not only our own lives but the future of gaming and storytelling alike. Because truly, that is what games are all about. Since the beginning of human existence, we've been creating our own mythologies. And with those mythologies eventually come exclusivity. We have come up with all sorts of gates and gatekeepers to make sure only certain people get to tell their stories. Massively multiplayer online role-playing games are doing a lot to democratize that—to put the power of myth, fable and story back into the hands of the people where it rightfully belongs.

"We think that what we—what you all—are doing is so important, so life-changing, that we wouldn't settle for hardware less stellar than that," Brandon continues, seamless. "We want to leap forward into a new world of user experience so vivid, so real, that our heroes don't only get to create their mythologies through play: they get to live them."

It is Preston's turn again: "The technology just wasn't there in 2012, however, when *Guilds of the Protectorate* made its public debut and Fancy Dog Games officially launched. At the time, they didn't have their hardware together. We kept our promise. We didn't settle. But we foresaw great things. We had a plan for integrating this new product, this new paradigm, from the outset." There are murmurs once again— Eliza picks out that same sigh. "He's so smart," the voice says, and it is everything Eliza can do to keep her face steady, to not react.

"When the company contacted us and officially let us know a new, updated developer kit would soon be available, we went ahead with the plan. We called together our team of developers and they began the process of building an entirely new Windy City." Brandon tries a tight smile. He is simply not as charismatic as Preston, we think. But in the end, that doesn't matter. He is still alpha. He is still important. It gives us hope. "Earlier this year, when the consumer version hit our hands, we knew we'd made the right decision."

Someone behind Eliza gasps. "The Vive," the voice whispers to a neighbor. "It has to be the HTC Vive." Her voice rises at the end; excitement.

"Virtual reality support?" the neighbor whispers back. "No shit." Eliza smiles a little. Despite her anger, her disappointment, a part of her is still excited to be here. To be a part of this. She glances over at Devonte—his smile is huge. Seeing his unfettered happiness makes Eliza's stomach drop further; she can't be entirely ecstatic. They've wrecked it for her. In this moment, she is more than a witness to history: she is making history. But she can't feel purely electrified. And then with a pang, she realizes how unfair her feeling is. Devonte didn't ruin it for her. And he's been at it for so long. He deserves all that happiness. She feels like the monster we know she is. She tries to focus her attention back on Preston.

He says something Eliza doesn't catch in her distraction, then winks again. A few people chuckle. "Ladies and gentlemen," that's the cue. Eliza, Devonte, Lewis and Jean-Pascale plunge their hands into their bags and strap the gear to their faces, keeping their heads bowed as if everyone hasn't already guessed. Preston keeps going: "I give you." He pauses to let the front row turn around.

"*Guilds of the Protectorate*. On. Vive."

The crowd goes full Bacchanalia; it should be exhilarating to face everyone going bananas like that, even if she can't see them through the eye-gear. Eliza can hear someone shouting, "I knew it! I knew it!"

From the back, she hears Suzanne crow, "We beat *EverQuest*! We're doing it first! First VR MMO!"

Someone else: "Is it gonna work with other shit? Is it gonna work with Oculus?"

"Settle down, settle down," Preston says into his microphone. We can hear the smile in his voice; he doesn't want anyone to settle down. He is loving every second of the rave and revelry. "We have to go over what the next couple of weeks are going to look like. We're all going to have to hit the ground running!"

Devonte throws one of his hands in the air and starts jumping around. He tips into Eliza once, then pops his headset up onto his forehead for better balance. Lewis jumps up and down too, and keeps bashing into her; she is sure she'll have bruises up her right arm. When she turns to look at him, his Vive is already up on his forehead. Some of us think he steals sidelong glances every few jumps; he knows he is hurting her and doesn't care. But most of us think it's just the excitement; he has no idea. Eliza stands there, her thin smile evaporating. She feels like a wet spaghetti noodle among the party streamers.

CHAPTER TWENTY-FOUR

It is already dark by the time they file out of the movie theater. It is shocking how small Fancy Dog actually is, given what they produce, given how many of us there are. Only filled one theater. Eliza is wondering what to do, how to proceed. Does this thing with Lewis and JP still fall into the realm of not so big a deal? Had they crossed some sort of imaginary boundary? Could she make it something she could ignore? We think she both should and could. This is the way the world works. This is how jobs are. Not only gaming jobs. All jobs. She has to learn to handle the real world. Move the fuck on. Keep making the game, that's what we pay them to do. We pay for play. Make play for us.

She is contemplating her failures as a programmer and a woman when she sees Preston leaning against the movie theater wall. He isn't with the rest of the company, not even with Brandon. He isn't wearing a coat, even though it's cold. His face is upturned, smiling, in the never-dark of Manhattan. Caressed by a streetlight. He isn't smoking, but we wish he were. It would be the perfect, classic image. The James Dean of nerds.

She walks up to him and ruins it. "Preston?"

"Eliza, hi."

She hesitates here, afraid to spoil his reverie, his celebration. It was a very successful internal announcement. He knows it will be leaked. He plans for it now. He's never had a colander for a company before, but he's getting used to it. Using it to his advantage. They only ever leak stuff like this; nothing that would truly hurt him or Fancy Dog.

Or she continues boldly without any hesitation at all, gleeful at wrecking serenity. We're all for disruption but for fuck's sake, think about what you're disrupting! "Sorry, I actually don't know how to say this."

Preston thinks she is about to confess her attraction to him, tries to find a way to prevent this from happening. His face goes on a journey. "Eliza, if this is a Conversation, I think it should wait unti—"

"Even if I wanted to have a Conversation with you right now, we sure don't want to have it in the office in front of Lewis and JP."

"What's goi—"

"Lewis just called me a feminazi whore during our meeting. And he accused us of. Well." She reddens a little and is grateful for the dim light. Perhaps her embarrassment is hidden in it. "Accused us of being together? Like, together together."

Preston's eyebrows nearly touch in the middle. It isn't exactly what he was expecting, but it's just as bad. If not worse. "Like, boyfriend girlfriend together?"

"I think the insinuation was a little more vulgar than that."

Preston looks around. The company is almost entirely out the doors now, and most of them haven't noticed his hiding place on the side of the building. It is safer to go from here, he thinks. She's right. It's better to do it outside the office.

Or perhaps it continues to be her idea. "Why don't you take me to dinner?" she says. "It's been kind of a rough day." She stands coyly, her shoulders collapsing toward her chest, one of her feet popped up on one single toe, knee turned in. Her eyes are big with seduction, with ambition, with entitled greed.

CHAPTER TWENTY-FIVE

LFleis: i told you

JPDes: it is wierd.

LFleis: i told you

JPDes: but not conclusive

LFleis: told you told you told you told you told you told you told you

JPDes: she's probably telling on you.

LFleis: nope

JPDes: what do you mean nope? it was a lot.

LFleis: well maybe also that

LFleis: but you saw them leave together FROM THE BACK OF A MOVIE THEATRE

LFleis: i mean come the fuck on

LFleis: not even subtle

LFleis: if i get fired for this i swear

JPDes: no one said anything about getting fired

LFleis: if i get fired for this, you have to promise to stick up for me, okay?

LFleis: like, do something

JPDes: and what would that be?

LFleis: i dunno

JPDes: dude no one is getting fired

JPDes: just stop being a dick

CHAPTER TWENTY-SIX

The Inspectre follows one set of IP addresses in particular. He keeps an encrypted document full of all the numbers currently and previously associated with this 4chan ID, those couple of Reddit usernames. He attributes all these numerals, names and posts to one man. One employee at Fancy Dog, the one we all call Leaky Joe. Some of us think the Leaky Joe among us is a myth. Some think he is multiple employees, because how could one person spill everything he does and not get fired? In this way, Leaky Joe is our Shakespeare. But The Inspectre has his finger on the IP pulse, nonetheless, and whether or not it comes from one guy or many, he deems these communiqués genuine.

So when Leaky Joe complains on KotakuInAction, that most illustrious subreddit, that this bitch of a co-worker just threatened sexual harassment allegations against two gameplay-feel programmers to try to get a promotion and lol, it failed, looks like the world isn't as fucked as we thought—well. With the help of The Inspectre, we know to which company Leaky Joe is referring. A company with a few small development teams. One of which is made up of two fine gentlemen and one conniving cunt. How dare she. A modern witch. A blemish on the face of the world.

Click save. Add bookmark. Remember this post, for it is one more of the shattered puzzle pieces we assemble and reassemble. We love

The Inspectre. We love how he caresses each piece of information, how he gleefully hands it to us bit by bit. We love his rage, especially. The towering inferno of it, barely masked; it matches the heat under our own skin. We love to see it burst through to the surface.

The Inspectre is intrigued as he sits in his lair. It is a large square room at the bottom of a hole deep enough to kill those who don't know the precise jumping pattern from ledge to ledge on the way down. There is no door to this windowless basement cell he calls home; one must be able to walk through walls to enter. He looks at his latest screenshots, hung aesthetically and appropriately by a length of clothesline—photos of Black Hole, of Doctor Moriarty. But Circuit Breaker is missing from most of his shots. He does have a few of the squabble, when the Diversity Squad was (abnormally) thrown into the public eye. Invisible to all but friends, those three. The room is baked in the red glow of developing film, and he feels his face flush with that same sort of heat. How dare she be so inaccessible to him. He has access to everything. Everyone. Invisible, involuntary. She is infuriating.

He wants to watch them closely. Closer, even, than he is already. He has managed to add a few Fancy Dog employees to his friends list, so it isn't that much of a stretch, he thinks. There will be friends in common. It would not be out of the realm of possibility for them to click accept.

He requests to add Circuit Breaker first. Then Doctor Moriarty and Black Hole. He waits for a couple days, but doesn't hear from any of them. He understands entirely why Lewis and JP don't respond to his friend request. They're busy. And they're a guild of two, exclusive, and everyone knows it. His best bet is to gain their goodwill by doing work for them—he'll have to figure out how to approach the duo. But Eliza? Her bias is showing. Her bias against the Inspectres of the world, the straight men, the white men. His rage begins to simmer under his tongue; yes, yes, we love when the anger bubbles up, floods the landscape like lava. Explosive at times, slow and crawling at others. But as transformative. As destructive. He plots. He is about to get his big breakthrough and he doesn't know it yet, but we do.

CHAPTER TWENTY-SEVEN

They duck into the first place that looks private: Castle and Cognac. The walls are cream and the light is dim. A cocktail menu lazes on the table, and both parties ignore it. Some of us can see them; some of us are close enough, in meatspace, to actually touch them. It is unusual, to run into them anywhere that isn't digital.

Preston looks bewildered, eyes wide and metaphorical feathers ruffled from stuffing himself in his coat too quickly. "So what happened?" he asks, a little less professionally than he likes. "What did he say? Tell me everything."

Eliza recounts the conversation in the collaboration room. She sounds meaner than we expected. Strident. Like she's licking her lips with a predatory relish. Or maybe recounting the incident actually hurts. But there is a calmness to her. That, at least, we all agree on. A confidence we don't usually imagine into her mouth. Not the person we imagined coquettishly standing with her foot popped onto her toe and her knee turned in. How does she pull off all of it, this version and that one? How does she manipulate him into liking her when she's not only a six on her best day, but a six with a shrill voice like a goddamn fire alarm?

"Fuck," Preston says when she finishes her story. He covers his mouth. "Sorry. Pardon me. I didn't mean to—" He interrupts himself because he's thought of something. Something that will surely take her down. We lick our lips. "Am I to understand you didn't have a Conversation with Lewis before coming to me outside the theater?"

Eliza blinks. "What?"

"Did you have a Conversation? With Lewis?" Preston repeats.

"Uh. No."

"So what I'm hearing is that you came right to me without having a Conversation with them, rather than modifying your behavior based on our last Conversation and talking to them first?"

"Welcome to Castle and Cognac!" A waiter materializes next to their table, as if out of the miasma of sheer enthusiasm. "Something to drink for you both?"

"We need a few minutes, thank you." Preston has not forgotten his manners; he's handling himself perfectly. The waiter dematerializes.

"I came right to you," Eliza continues. "I had no idea what to say to him. It was blatant sexism. And he thinks you and I—" She pauses, her body not letting her talk and turn red at the same time.

"Yes, that—that is a little embarrassing." Preston looks down at the tablecloth. "But once you've cooled off a bit, you have to start first by telling him about his specific, observable actions and how they made you feel."

"Excuse me?"

"And give him a chance to rectify his behavior." Preston takes a breath and his face becomes the man we see in photos. It's debonair, but—safe somehow. We feel safe when we see him like this, in control of everything around him. Eliza recognizes his company-meeting expression. "Policy is in place for a reason," he begins. "The Conversation policy is there to create a corporate culture of openness and mutual respect. It allows us all to correct each other's behavior without putting any emphasis whatsoever on management—your Conversations aren't less important than mine, for example." Except they are. Eliza knows her Conversations are inherently less valuable than those of the cofounder, original game designer and CEO. We know it too. She is nobody and yet here she is, somehow. "I see you jumping straight to me to have a Conversation about someone else's behavior and asking me to deal with it. That undermines the culture we work so hard to create in a number of ways." Preston holds up his hand and ticks his fingers with his thumb. "First, it teaches everyone to respect my Conversations more. We should be respecting everyone's Conversations. Second, it makes me the referee for all sorts of—"

"Can I get you guys anything?" the waiter asks, pen touching paper in anticipation.

"No, no, we haven't looked at the menus yet," Preston says, smooth, as if that's what he intended the rest of his sentence to be.

"No problem!"

"Anyway." Preston keeps his eye on the waiter to make sure he is out of earshot before continuing. "It makes me a referee for all sorts of interpersonal disputes when I should be running a company. And thirdly, skipping Conversations and going right for me takes the opportunity away from Lewis to correct his behavior. Lewis is a good guy. I'm sure he would have corrected his behavior if you had given him the chance to."

"How can he correct something that's already happened?" Eliza asks. Christ, what a fucking idiot.

"Well he could have apologized to you. Taken it back. Promised to do better in the future. And—" Then Preston smiles. His face softens into something different, but just as safe. Just as welcoming, understanding. What a stand-up guy. We take notes. His posture seems to say, I'm here for your existence, here for your feelings. What a fucking good play. "You might have told him that we weren't seeing each other. In any capacity." He blushes and it looks like he's been dipped in a bucket of bright red bicycle paint. "He could have retracted that statement. Said he believed that we weren't together."

"That's what you're concerned about?" Eliza asks, incredulous.

"Well, that and other things," Preston says quickly. "Of course, other things as well."

"Like the fact that all those statements he made, those things he said, point to a dislike of women that will interfere with any woman he works with and impact Fancy Dog culture and maybe, if he ever gets to design games, affect the kinds of games he produces?" We're surprised; given how flustered we have imagined her up to this point, she is pretty eloquent. We feel ourselves start to nod our heads. Then, wait—we don't believe in this kind of bullshit. It's just games. Games don't affect how you are in the real world at all. Hysteria.

"See, I don't think his little outburst points to that. I think it points to—I dunno—insecurity, stupidity, a lack of social skills." Preston pauses and mutters, "or a lack of a hold on reality." It doesn't occur to him that he might offend Eliza, that he is hitting the we-are-definitely-not-fucking note a little too hard. It does occur to Eliza, we can see it on her face (inside, we scream with laughter), and Preston attributes her horrified look to recent events. "But they don't point to a hatred of women, I don't think."

"And if I disagree?"

"Then you should tell him that his observable actions," Preston stresses that last part, "make you feel disliked as a woman. Because you're a woman. And you should assume his positive intent, so you'll probably want to add something like, 'and I don't think that's what you intended for me to feel.' Or maybe something like, 'and I recognize you were just trying to make sure that all was right with the world.' See, there's a million ways to talk to him about this without accusing him of something that's going to wreck his life. We don't want to wreck anyone's life here."

"What about mine? My life?"

Preston squeezes his lips together and furrows his eyebrows until they join at the center and make him look like a Muppet. "I'd hardly call your life wrecked. You're on a well-paid team that's launching a premium product this week."

They sit in silence for a second. Until: "Hello again, guys! Have you had a chance to look at—"

"NO!" Eliza and Preston both yell in unison. The waiter scampers backward.

"Look, we have to order something soon or leave," Preston says. He squeezes his temples with his palms, eyes closed, tense. "Eliza, why couldn't you have just had a Conversation with him. You're good at Conversations. I've seen you do it—you keep having Conversations with me, for Christ's sake; that's not an easy thing to do. You can't say you were scared of him. Frankly, he's a lot less scary than I am and you seem to have absolutely no issue speaking your mind to me."

Eliza chooses her words very carefully, afraid, we think, that they don't feel like they are in the right order or the right words. "I just felt like this was too big for a Conversation."

"Well it's not. Eliza. You seem to have the idea that this is a bigger deal than it is. If everyone came to me every time they were personally offended by one of my employees, I'd never get anything done."

Eliza pushes her chair back and stands. "Wait!" Preston says. "Where are you going? I'll treat you to dinner, obviously. Consider this the hazard pay for the day." Let's pause here to wonder at something— why is he trying to get her to stay? She's terribly annoying and he won. Is her strange enchantment bleeding into his personal feelings for her? We trust JP and Lewis, and even though we haven't truly imagined it until now, it could be that Preston hasn't won at all. Perhaps he's already lost. Aw fuck, they're totally boning. She's got him entirely under her control.

Eliza looks past Preston's shoulder, and the light in her eyes switches off for the second time that day. Dead shark eyes. Preston visibly recoils; so do we. It is scary, in person, and much scarier for Preston who is seeing the veil ripped off his girlfriend for the first time and realizing there is something grotesque underneath. "I'm going back to work. You said it yourself—I'm part of a well-paid group of people who are launching a premium product this week. Tonight was always going to be an all-nighter. I suppose I should be grateful that I won't be able to sleep anyway."

"Actually," Preston corrects, "I said 'team.' Part of a well-paid team."

"I know what you said." She walks out of the restaurant, passing their very confused waiter, passing us. Her head is buzzing. Electric. She leaves her coat hanging on the back of her chair.

"Wait," we hear Preston say. "Your coat! Your coat!" But she continues anyhow. She doesn't want her coat. She needs the cool night air on her skin or she might spark and catch fire.

CHAPTER TWENTY-EIGHT

To: [Cara Smith]
Subject: Sexism at Fancy Dog
Message:

Ms. Smith,

Due to your recent tweets regarding digital harassment perpetrated by alt-right men's rights activists and Trump supporters,
I thought you might be interested in a situation that's progress-
ing at Fancy Dog right now (I am employed there). I am
reaching out to you because you are a journalist at re/Code.
Please shoot me an email if you're interested in chatting. I am
fine with being quoted.

Eliza Bright
Developer at Fancy Dog Games

CHAPTER TWENTY-NINE

He begins his day the usual way, loosely knotting Dog's leash to the bike rack outside Starbucks. He buys his venti soy latte, steamed to one hundred thirty degrees exactly. They mangle his name on the side of the cup: Princeton. He smirks and takes a photo, uploads it to Instagram. We see the hashtags: #whydobaristasmisspell? #justtofuckwithus. We tap the photo twice; we like the photo.

He reclaims Dog and ascends the glass tower. His glass tower. It is sunny and crisp. The hard outlines on benches, sidewalk seams and garbage cans prove what his mother calls "winter sparkle." He smiles, remembering her theory—in winter it's drier; less moisture makes everything pop. He's never looked it up; he doesn't want to ruin the magic of winter sparkle. His employees are working away in the tower when the elevator doors part to let him in—he sees excitement and determination on every face. He'd gone home and slept for four solid hours; he isn't nervous in the slightest about the public announcement later this afternoon. In short, it is a good day.

Preston just about spits out his coffee when he sees it. The headline. "It's Everywhere: Sexist Culture at Fancy Dog," posted one minute ago. And the copy. It doesn't help that this one is so puntastic. "Fancy Dog proves they're not so fancy—they're just dogs." Lewis is attributed: "feminazi whore." How dare she. How fucking dare she. It's Preston's big day and here she is, forcing the spotlight to turn. His good mood replaced with alarm bells. And all to send the fucking elite media people after us? His phone rings so continuously that, due to its vibrate function, it threatens to waddle right off his glass desk. He is as mad as we are. Let it shatter, he thinks. Let the whole thing shatter.

CHAPTER THIRTY

LFleis: HOLY SHIT THAT CUNT PUBLISHED OUR NAMES

JPDes: ??????

LFleis: LOOK ON RECODE

JPDes: what?

JPDes: where?

LFleis: ITS ON THE GODDAMN FRONT PAGE ASSHOLE LOOK AT IT

JPDes: oh my god

JPDes: OH MY GOD

JPDes: we are never showing our faces again

LFleis: no, wait, look

LFleis: read the comments.

LFleis: at least some people see this for what it is

LFleis: a manhating femoid just trying to get her fifteen minutes

LFleis: or a promotion

LFleis: or to get back at her boyfriend

LFleis: see? like a lot of people are sticking up for us

LFleis: JP??

JPDes: sorry. delphine called

LFleis: y?

JPDes: ask if i was okay

LFleis: delphine doesnt read recode

JPDes: someone told her about it

JPDes: they red it on jezebel

LFleis: JEZEBEL HAS IT????

JPDes: kotaku has it

LFleis: of course they do

JPDes: and then jezebel put it in a roundup

JPDes: lewis, what are we going to do?

LFleis: look, most people are with us

LFleis: scroll down, look at the comments

LFleis: like a lot of people think its funny

LFleis: it was funny

JPDes: what about this one

JPDes: As an engineer with SpaceX, I need to speak to all of you saying no harm no foul. Harm was done here. It's done every day when these attitudes are allowed to continue. These attitudes are what breeds the ridiculous attrition rate for women in STEM fields. It's what leads women to be passed up for promotions. It's what makes us quit. It's what Dr. Ben Barres experienced after he transitioned. He used to be called Barbara. Did you know someone remembered his research from when he identified as a woman and commented that his was much better and clearer than his sister's? Well guess what, Dr. Barres doesn't have a sister. That was his own research from a few years back and it hadn't changed. The only thing that changed was the perceived gender of the person presenting the information. That's it. That's what made the research better and clearer. So yeah, harm was done here even if she didn't get fired or demoted or anything. It's absolutely going to affect her career. It's going to affect mine too. Everyone's.

LFleis: that person doesnt even work in games, how the fuck does she kno

JPDes: dude. that woman is an ENGINEER for SpaceX.

LFleis: dude.

LFleis: its an internet comment. hands down that fuck does not work for nasa.

JPDes: dude we fucked up so bad

JPDes: we never shouldve written nething down

JPDes: we said stuff in public we shouldve just said between ourselves

LFleis: no. we didnt. we were just being people at work joking around and having a good time

LFleis: if thats fucking up, then they r gonna ban all jokes at work

LFleis: she fucked up

LFleis: she drew all this attention

LFleis: look, if were copying and pasting comments now, what about this one

LFleis: listen, i'm pretty sure those guys were being idiots, sure. But do we really need a whole article on one of the most respected tech websites for something that's virtually a non-issue? Literally nothing happened. This whole article is about nothing. Nothing happened.

JPDes: that other one is a spacex engineer

LFleis: who the fuck cares

LFleis: look at the numbers

LFleis: half of these just say lol, id tkae these guys out for a beer

LFleis: my phne is ringing now too

LFleis: blocked number

JPDes: dont answer it

JPDes: lets go to preston

JPDes: there has to be some kind of protocol here

CHAPTER THIRTY-ONE

A sample of what we find in Eliza's G-chats:

DAleb: you shouldn't have done that. they're going to come down on you hard.

SChoy: are you fucking out of your damn mind this is going to suck so bad you should never have done that

LFleis: you shouldnt have done that

Eliza hasn't slept. She hasn't even left—stayed in the office after talking to Preston. She pounds another coffee and checks her code, waits to be summoned.

CHAPTER THIRTY-TWO

Let's pivot to Windy City, down, down, down through the hole in the ground to look at The Inspectre, who has skinned Kotaku with a rare newspaper artifact so he can read it, kicked back in the red light of his lair, without switching to meatspace. He prefers to exist here, to read the gaming headlines from inside a game itself.

And there she is, that cunt, that fascist, spilling names and destroying men. But even in his anger, his lips curl into a smile. We know why; we know the policies. And all of us, including him, know what's coming next. We relish the suspense and we will eat the outcome happily and messily, with ketchup dripping down our chins like blood. She will be fired, we are certain. And they will use some technicality, but we know. We know. They have our back, these men, these soldiers in the war against social "justice." Justice for whom, we wonder? Certainly not us! Our world is being invaded, colonized, and our safety threatened. So we take up arms. Windy City is ours. It's for us.

The Inspectre pops a bag of popcorn and turns on his in-game computer, engages with this *mise en abyme*, this recursive technology, to watch Reddit as we all read, comment, post, discuss. It is a beautiful discourse, free of censorship, a marketplace of ideas, a meritocracy. And we whip ourselves into wind, into a sandstorm, into an inferno: fire her. Fire her. FIRE HER.

The Inspectre cackles.

CHAPTER THIRTY-THREE

Eliza is called into Preston's office almost immediately. Her mind is filled with a sound like a million buzzing bees or clacking keyboards or humming electricity. No one notices the stress radiating from her is different from anyone else's. Almost the entire company has been awake all night. Fancy Dog, on its face, prides itself on work-life balance. Crunching hasn't been required of anyone. But it is common and unspoken knowledge that, no matter what is said, each employee has to stay up all night working if they want to compete with everyone else. Eliza knew she would need a lot of goodwill this morning, so she spent the night plodding through each line of code, distracted by the internal sound of anxiety perhaps. She expects to be talked to. To have a Conversation. We rub our hands together. It will be so, so much worse. How can she not know?

Preston isn't sitting at his desk when Eliza walks in. He stands, arms folded. The biggest thing on his plate today is supposed to be the public announcement. Everything is interrupted. Everything must be recalibrated. The situation has to be dealt with as quickly as possible. We will inflate the internet with the hot air of our constant conversation until it all floats away; it is our favorite kind of ride. And Eliza is so sleep-deprived and nervous she doesn't remember all the details as they occur. She experiences this encounter in vignettes; dark at the edges, flashes isolated from life's normal linear cause-and-effect pattern.

It isn't just Preston. It is Preston, the skinny blonde HR representative, and the other co-founder, Brandon. This is the crowd that appears when people do something majorly wrong. Now she knows. Imagining that shock, the lips parting to form a delicate "oh," the finest her rat mouth has ever looked—oh, such a delicious moment.

Preston grabs the bridge of his nose with his fingers. "I really, really don't want to do this."

Eliza wants to say, "Then don't." And if it were only Preston in the room, she might have. Instead she replaces that "oh" with a grim line, lips pressing together. She inclines her head, lifts her chin like she has something to be proud of.

Preston's lips are tight and his words are short, small enough to escape through the tension as he continues. "But you signed an NDA. Nondisclosure Agreement. You can't disclose anything. And now you have. And if you read the NDA—and you better have read it, you signed it—you know the price of disclosing is immediate termination of your work agreement."

"But I didn't disclose the Vive support! I didn't even talk about the software update!"

Brandon steps into her line of sight. "It's a Conversation with an employee on our private property. That is a business secret."

"What happened to Conversations? What happened to giving me the opportunity to correct my behavior?" Eliza's voice rings small and watery. She hates the way it sounds, almost as much as how her rat mouth must look in this moment, blubbering in front of Preston, in front of everyone, like this. But what she hates most is her inability to do anything about her reaction.

Preston places his palms together as if in prayer, but uses them to point, like aiming a Nerf gun. "This is too big for Conversations." Preston wants to bite his own tongue when he hears the words he uses. He stops. Freezes. His eyes unfocus. We want to reach through the narrative, shake him up, tell him he didn't lose. There is such a thing as too big for Conversations. She crossed the line when she ruined the launch.

Brandon continues. "Why did you do this? You know we're one of the good guys here."

She's not sure how to answer exactly, so she goes with: "What would you have done, if you were me?" She pauses so long Preston thinks she will offer no more explanation. He takes a breath to speak, but she gathers herself and interrupts before he begins. "They think I'm not good at this because I'm a woman. They did something that proved that. Nothing happened. Then they refused to work with me in our meeting, and I came to you about that too. And nothing happened. What was I supposed to do? Can an employee really use the words 'feminazi whore' at work without consequences?"

She doesn't hear his answer—it falls outside the faded outlines of her vignetted experience. Preston knows he doesn't give one. At least, not a real one. Because at this moment, Preston starts to wonder what exactly she should have done and can't think of anything to say. This is his tragic flaw. If we think of him as the hero, which we can sometimes, it is his lack of conviction, here, that leads him to his downfall. That he sits here and thinks about what she should have done instead.

There are more words. Brandon speaks. The HR representative might be speaking too, we don't really know. It's not important.

Eliza looks through the glass wall and sees Lewis and Jean-Pascale. They look like they've come up quickly—Lewis still has his coat on, has a coffee in his hand. He stares at her through the glass like she is a snake in a tank. His wolverine eyes in his sunken sockets fix on her as he shakes his head, lips in a thin line. The realization that his face looks rehearsed, as though he practiced it in front of a mirror, whips across Eliza's face in the form of a twitch. Under other circumstances, it might make her laugh.

Jean-Pascale doesn't look rehearsed at all. His Frankenstein's Monster height isn't matched by any balance in his gawky limbs, appendages that seem to shoot out in all directions. Now, with his hands clasped behind his back and his nervous tick of turning his toes in toward each other, then slowly turning them away as he stares floorward, he looks like a shamed schoolboy.

The HR representative speaks. Small, blonde and pretty; the kind of person whose photo is surely on the Careers at Fancy Dog page. We imagine up a bimbo, attach these words to a face. "We know you'll understand we can't permit you to return to your desk. We will send your personal effects along with Ms. Choy this evening."

And then Eliza is walking, the small HR bunny behind her, out the glass doors and toward the elevators. Everyone is staring. Then she is in the elevator. The doors close. She is gone.

Lewis claps Jean-Pascale on the shoulder. JP's face gets stuck like a frustrated Jack-in-the-box, tension about to spring—a Jean-Pascale-in-a-box. He is livid with her and himself in equal measure, strong feelings in two opposite directions. We are getting used to such contradictions in him, in everyone. Lewis says, "Well, that's taken care of. We can go back to normal." He follows up with a second clap on JP's shoulder before turning and walking into Preston's office. He holds his head high. He feels no fear.

CHAPTER THIRTY-FOUR

Before we move on, let's zoom in on something here: the folder in HR Barbie's hand. All files are computerized, sure, but when dealing with someone individually, files are printed. That's what happens when a company is full of employees who have, at least, the chance of possessing a modicum of hacking capability: HR makes a hard copy before someone can mess with the file. Their file is printed in its entirety: hiring paperwork; any agreements they might have signed—in this case, Eliza's three nondisclosure agreements, her undoing; background check; attendance record; if they've needed any sensitivity training (Jean-Pascale's and Lewis's files both say that, along with the words "pending schedule." Their files aren't printed at this point, however); anything and everything with their name on it—a copy of Eliza's Career Tree (which is by now dead and dropping its leaves); *Guilds of the Protectorate* account name—employees receive presents in-game for every holiday and badges next to their names so they are easily identifiable as working for Fancy Dog. It is all necessary information. Perfectly standard.

During the whole termination, the folder is in HR Barbie's hands. She's bored, mostly—sad someone is getting fired, but bored all the same. She doesn't know Eliza except by sight and has an appointment at the spa with her two best friends for the evening, so she is constantly checking her phone, watching the minutes tick by. This is the kind of woman we imagine here. So simple and so nice to look at.

So watch what she does before she escorts Eliza to the elevator and, subsequently, out of the building. She sets the folder down, not on Preston's desk but on the table by the window, next to which are a few squishy armchairs for more pleasant, relaxed meetings than this. On her way back up, after depositing Eliza squarely outside, she feels her phone vibrate in her pocket. When she looks, the little green speech bubble flashes "adress of spa again?" After that, "*address. sorry. also name?" And she texts her friend about the details on the way back up to her desk. She never returns to Preston's office.

Even if she were to, Jean-Pascale and Lewis are already there, and, though the meeting is far more pleasant than the one she just witnessed, it still looks to us like they aren't to be disturbed. She probably would continue on to her desk anyway. Likely, she would still forget all about the folder, because Eliza is already fired. Out of sight, out of mind. Or in this case, out of building, out of mind. Out of job, out of mind.

Some of us think this is the problem, the heart of it: a nameless blonde woman distracted by a spa. We will argue about its importance—the shields-up cucks among us will tweet in all caps that we are being UNFAIR, that the problem started with 80085 or even with how Lewis holds Eliza accountable for her actions. Some of us will argue that the fault lies entirely with The Inspectre. But the majority of us lay blame here, with a woman we are not sure exists but who has been conjured up as inept. Someone left the folder out.

CHAPTER THIRTY-FIVE

Jean-Pascale and Lewis's meeting with Preston is barely important. There are only a few things we need to know. They use the comfortable chairs. Any questions they get from journalists, they are to immediately refer to press@fancydoggames.com. "We have a whole team with media training and strategies; Legal works at the next desk. Let them take care of all this." Their sensitivity training will start the next day—they are bringing in an outside firm to do it, something off a Feminist Foundation list in hopes that they will tweet about the sensitivity training as a good solution. "Our PR people really are brilliant," Preston says, though he doesn't smile when he says it.

Along with sensitivity training, Lewis and Jean-Pascale will undergo media training. "Just in case," says Preston. "In case this goes further." Because they are now one person short on their development team, their various trainings will take place outside the workday. They will be paid overtime for it. "Work-life balance is still important," Preston says. It's enough to know all that and not hear them speak.

What is important: what happens at Jean-Pascale's desk, after. Remember his composition notebook—he always has it with him, and he brings it to the meeting. He puts it down on the table by the window and picks it up again when he leaves. When he returns to his desk, he sets it next to his keyboard and tries desperately to continue working. They are pushing the sex patch the following day, not to mention beta testers with Vive will be in soon, and he needs to put together some documentation still. He tries, but he fails. He texts Delphine. He goes to get a compostable cone of water from the water cooler. Finally, he grabs his notebook to doodle down some ideas for a game of his own. That's when he sees it: Eliza's entire file, sitting right there on his desk to the left of his keyboard—he realizes he'd grabbed it, stuck to the bottom of his notebook. The color drains from his already-pale face.

He G-chats Lewis only the words "come to desk plz."

"Holy shit," he says when he gets there.

"I have to give this back to Preston right now," and Jean-Pascale makes to get out of his chair.

"No," Lewis says as he catches Jean-Pascale's shoulder and eases him back down. "Look, he's watching us like a hawk right now, he's going to think you did this on purpose. Besides, we could use it."

"Use it how?"

"A little—protection. In case she does something else."

"No, we are not using it for that. Or at all. For anything. I should just shred it." A small aside: we want this folder. We want it so badly, we salivate. We want to post it on Reddit, to comb through it, to caress every detail with our eyes, to do something that feels like defending our territory. We want to build our wall; we want to place digital heads on pikes around it, a demonstration of our power, our seriousness. Too long have we been squashed under the boots of women, of social justice warriors, and we are just starting to take our land back. Give us the folder. We ache for the folder.

"No, you can't shred it," Lewis says, and we sigh with relief. He is our mind reader, our advocate, our representative in the room, just the person to petition Jean-Pascale on our behalf, to convince him not to be such a fucking pussy.

"And why not?"

"Because if they come looking for it, they have to be able to find it."

"No they don't, that's stupid. Preston could have just as easily shred it by accident. Or maybe that's what he was going to do with it anyway."

Jean-Pascale coughs—it sounds wet in his throat, like he is holding something down. "Excuse me," he says, and he runs to the bathroom at top speed.

Out of those of us who think Lewis can back away from his downfall, step away from the precipice off which he will throw himself, only a fraction of us think this is the deciding moment. But it's worth noting, nonetheless. Perhaps he could choose not to do this. But we want him to. We want him to so, so badly. Give us the folder. We need the folder. We need to run our typing fingers over every inch of Eliza's life.

Lewis waits until the door swings closed behind his friend, then he snaps a photo of each and every document, every scrap of paper. He thinks Jean-Pascale is crazy not to want a little information, a little padding. Everyone in this industry knows, after all, how powerful a little information can be. A little information can build an entire world, for Christ's sake.

Lewis is startled when he comes to Eliza's Career Tree—it looks so very similar to his own. Slightly different order, and he is further along. But not by much. His anger flares, and he feels once again the powerful man that stood in the collaboration room. The only way she could've done that was if she was fucking her way to the middle. He is already so resolved; this doesn't change anything, we think. Or if he feels any sympathy, any guilt, any feeling that prevents him from fighting for his place in the world, battling in this war against men, this burns it away.

He walks over to the bathroom and pushes the door open. A retching sound echoes against the tiled walls; it's coming from the handicap stall. He walks down the row and knocks. "You okay, buddy?"

"Not really."

"Wanna go home?"

"I can't. Neither one of us can. Release tomorrow."

CHAPTER THIRTY-SIX

*E*t maintenant une histoire de Jean-Pascale en les jeux.

 C'était un faux ami ça, le mot "donjon." Mais il ne le savait pas. Il a supposé que ça signifie une fortification. Un château. En anglais, "a keep." Eh? Mais oui, nous parlons le français, nous sommes internationaux. But probably we can't all understand that. *D'accord.*

It was a tricky word, the word "dungeon." It didn't mean the same thing in French. But he didn't know that. He thought it signified a fortification, a castle. A keep. He was interested in building things. He spent long days drawing structures, fascinated with two-point perspective. He spent long hours drawing maps. He mapped everything. The aisles in the grocery, the number of steps from bakery to bakery, how he imagined the phones connected to each other, his own thoughts. It was a natural leap, then, to start playing Dungeons & Dragons.

His friends sure did like battle. But he hinted, pushed them to build a stronghold when they were strong enough, rich enough. He drew it. Painstakingly. So that each player had rooms, territory of their own. They never seemed grateful enough; they wanted to keep killing things with swords.

We should mention all his friends were boys. Not one girl in the group. Frustrated by the lack of care, the way they did not seem to appreciate the verisimilitude of his made-up world, he let that group fall to ruin like they let their keep rot.

He went in search of gamers who appreciated the world-building. He found them. Forums with rules and mechanics where one would post and wait, then another would swoop in and do the same, all text-based role-playing. Problem: they were mostly in English. And his English was only okay. So he learned. And he flubbed. But it was fine, because the native speakers weren't that good at English either. He played in the world of *Dune* by Frank Herbert. House Atreides. He never knew the real-world personas of the people he played with. Their realities didn't matter much. It was all about the story.

Ironically, he didn't play a lot of video games until his adulthood—he is a much bigger straight-up computer nerd than the rest of them. Linux, networks, open source software. Hacking. A technical puzzler brain with social graces when he was trying. But he grew into a graceful man, and he found his dexterity suited the simultaneous buttons pressed in arcane rhythms. By then, there was very little difference between the countries—globalization and all. The internet was a vast and wonderful place, now he got games as soon as the United States did. But he still longed for the days when it was smaller. More exclusive. More local. Even as he flew across an ocean to make stories into games, as he had always done. The irony; the hypocrisy. But what choice does one have in this epoch?

CHAPTER THIRTY-SEVEN

Suzanne shows up at Eliza's apartment with a box of stuff and her coat. At any other time, Eliza would be embarrassed at the state of her living space, which can only be described as "piles." Piles of clothes sit both inside and outside the bedroom door. A big pile of greasy dishes sits in the sink, still visible because the kitchen is in the same room as the main space. Everything smells like burnt popcorn because Eliza keeps forgetting the bags in the microwave. The term "forgetting" doesn't even make sense—Eliza keeps losing track while she's standing right next to the whirring machine. Keeps staring into nothing. So inedible brown-black popcorn sits in a pile that fills a salad serving bowl; Eliza can't bear to throw it out and thinks of punishing herself with the charcoal taste.

"You know," Suzanne says, "that's not the way they're supposed to do it. They're supposed to walk you to your desk and watch you clean it out. Sure, that's still awful," Suzanne amends when she sees the stricken look on Eliza's face. "But they're supposed to let you take your stuff home. I can say something to HR if you like."

"Up to you," Eliza says. "Wanna drink?"

Suzanne accepts a whiskey, served in a fine-edged tumbler. "Classy," she says. "Want me to stay here a little while?"

Eliza is about to say "sure" when someone else raps on her front door. "Who's it?" Eliza shouts.

"Devonte." So they let him in and offer him a whiskey.

"I brought fries," he says, and he holds out a grease-spotted paper bag.

"I don't deserve fries," Eliza replies, and for once we all agree. She's been doing the Strong Female Protagonist thing, which means reskinning herself from villain to hero in her own head. In this moment, she finally tires of it. The mental gymnastics of it all—she's just a lonely, stupid girl with no job because she can't take a joke. Since getting embarrassingly canned, she's been drinking and staring at her wall, occasionally crying or chewing on her nails. Hard to think herself the hero then, isn't it?

They all sit on the couch for some time, not saying one damn thing.

"Ya know," Eliza says, and she sighs, "the shit part is all I want to do is play *Guilds* right now. They just fired me and all I want to do is play that stupid game with you guys. And I still feel like I'm going to work tomorrow. I still feel like I should be brainstorming ideas for a tabletop game. Or pacing around worrying about the patch release. About the announcement."

Devonte groans. "They're not still releasing that, are they? After today?" Suzanne is shaking her head too.

"Why wouldn't they?" Eliza says. "I picked it. That's what I wanted to work on. The sex part is mostly mine. And they can't really extricate it now and still release the VR game on time—it's mixed in with all sorts of other software stuff that the beta testers are gonna need."

"Did you wind up emailing that other journalist?" Suzanne asks.

"Yeah. And she connected me with someone else and—" She takes a deep breath. "Suzanne, I think I'm going on *Last Week Tonight*?" Is it glee she feels? The pleasure of striking a match and looking at the flame before tossing it on the curling line of gasoline? Or is it dread, knowing she's about to show her whole ass on television? Is it the longing to still be part of the group, and the need to destroy that which does not want her? All of it, we think. All of it.

Suzanne laughs, shakes her head. "Then they're gonna look bad. They're gonna look so, so bad."

Devonte's eyebrows don't come unfurrowed. "You emailed another journalist? You're going on a talk show? You're going on, like, a famous talk show?"

"Yes."

"Dude. I dunno about that."

Suzanne hauls herself off the couch and puts her hands on her hips. "What don't you know about it?" Her voice climbs a tiny bit in register, her hips jut out to one side. She purses her lips. Strident, so strident, so difficult to listen to.

Devonte recoils, seems to sink further into the couch. "I mean, is that a good idea? Don't you just want to let this whole thing go away?"

"She broke an NDA, Devonte," Suzanne says. And she says it in a way that it sounds like it's all one word and like Devonte is an idiot. "She has to go on the offensive or she's not going to get work again."

"Okay, okay, Christ." Devonte holds his hands up. "I just wouldn't want all the attention if it were me."

Eliza's eyes start to leak tears down her cheeks. She tries to suck them back in, but tears do not work like lower stomachs. "You think I want this?"

"Fuck, no, Christ, I'm the good guy here. I'm on your side, I didn't mean—"

But he is interrupted by another knock at the door. All three jump at the unexpected sound. "Who's it?" Eliza calls again, taking another sip of whiskey.

"Preston?" the door asks, as if the person on the other side isn't sure if that's his name. Or as though he's bewildered about the series of choices that have led him to this place.

Suzanne's lip curls and her eyebrow raises. She throws her hands up in the air and we think she looks like a cartoon. "Do not tell him about this," she mouths. And then she mouths, "What the fuck?" Devonte cocks his head to one side and squints with his left eye. Eliza just sits there, blinking. It is an awkwardly long time before Suzanne gets the door.

Preston stands in the doorway, his hands jammed in his coat pockets and his shoulders up to his ears. He seems a little startled to see the other two. "Hi," he says. No one answers right away.

Let's pause. We know he's there! He has his location services turned on. We know he's talking to her. But if we were Preston, we wouldn't do this. There's so much else to be doing right now. We wouldn't care about her, because she's gone now. But Preston, and this is another one of his fatal flaws, is the kind of guy that cares what people think of him. Even the meaningless people. Or they're already fucking and she's tricked him into actually caring about her, he just didn't expect her friends to be there, to get truly caught. Or they're already fucking and he expected to bone, which even we know is totally misguided.

"Listen," he continues. "I just wanted you to know that I'm really sorry it had to go down that way. I really didn't want to."

"Well you did," Eliza says. She is furious. The buzzing's come back, due to anger or alcohol. "You know my address?"

"You're on my way home," he says. "I wanted you to know that I'm going to do my best to write you a great recommendation for wherever you end up, seriously, anything within my power to contextualize the—"

"It's creepy that you know my address."

"It's part of your paperwork, it's—"

"Listen. Thanks and all. But I really don't want to see you right now." What a cunt. How dare she. He came to check on her.

A Preston more representative of us might say, "Look, I'm trying to help," and then maybe stalk off. We wish he were like that; her response is entirely uncalled for.

Instead, he says, "Okay. Then. Bye." And Preston turns and walks down the hall to the elevator. Suzanne closes the door.

"Well that was fucking weird," she says.

"Yeah," Eliza says back.

"So. He's gone. Just us. What do you want to do?" Devonte asks.

"Be alone and get drunk?" Eliza suggests, but Suzanne is already shaking her head.

"Out of the question. At least, the alone part. The drunk part, we can manage."

Eliza smiles. "Pick a movie." She turns the television on and flips the input to the computer hooked into the back of it, the massive hard drive full of media. She smirks, proud even in her sadness, and we admire her setup that her undeserved job paid for, jealous. Everything is a computer. The only piles she doesn't have are DVDs.

"You pick." Suzanne gestures to the TV. "Just don't make us eat that shitty popcorn."

"I can't pick. I can't care." Eliza adds, "Pick anything but a super-hero movie."

CHAPTER THIRTY-EIGHT

We see three headlines the next day: one in the morning, two in the afternoon. The first reads "Gamer Girl Fired For Speaking Out." It is on Kotaku first, and The Inspectre reads it with a hearty laugh. But that's not where we get it first. Recode actually breaks it with something different; their headlines, however, are always more serious and less alliterative. The Kotaku headline, that's the real good one. We know that one best. It's shared widely.

The second headline comes in the afternoon. It reads "Sexist Game Company Releases Sex-Patch. Oh Yeah, and Virtual Reality Support." It is also on Kotaku. It becomes a consistent part of the feeds, gets shared and reshared on our subreddit and 4chan, upvote upvote upvote. It is ubiquitous, every site seems to have their own version. What is different is the commentary. We are a little more civilized on Reddit—we question the idea of the "sex-patch" being inherently sexist. It's not, we don't think. Nothing is inherently sexist about sex. What Fancy Dog suffers from, we think, is bad timing. Yes, bad timing—they shouldn't have released this today. Optics. Optics for the normies.

On 4chan, we laugh at the timing. The timing is *for* us. We pledge allegiance to Fancy Dog. Subscriptions skyrocket in support of the company. We say the girl who got fired got what she deserved—it's right there in the paperwork. Nondisclosure means you can't disclose. We tweet to each other. We tweet at Eliza.

Not all of us see the third headline. Mostly it is for women, and there are few in this collective who haven't been driven away.

The third article is entitled "#NotAllMen At Fancy Dog Are Jerks." Its tagline is "And Some Of Them Are Eye Candy." It is super problematic, but we, the very few women, are good at compartmentalizing—it is necessary when your hobby hates you. The article is posted on PopSugar and it cites Delphine Stewart as its source. It is populated with photos from Jean-Pascale's Facebook. It starts with "Finally, a Not All Men statement we can get behind—" (vapid fluff) and continues on about Jean-Pascale's innocence as told by Delphine. And Jean-Pascale isn't the only one featured—so many men! So many to pick from! Developer Andy, who is funny and has no problem shooting his shot. Or maybe this one—is this one Leaky Joe? Or are they all Leaky Joe? Devonte Aleba is featured too, making Eliza choke on her breakfast-cereal-for-lunch and cackle. "Eye candy!" she shouts aloud, in her apartment, to no one. It features a photo where Devonte isn't smiling. He looks rugged. Brooding. Desirable.

We think this article is the reason Lewis takes the action he takes, because it identifies both Jean-Pascale and Lewis by name: "'This was all sparked by something his buddy Lewis typed out. JP's been iffy about it from the start. Not all the guys at Fancy Dog are jerks. It's like anywhere else, you know? Any other group of people, you're going to get some jerks and the grand majority of people are going to be perfectly fine. And not all the jerks are going to be men.' Sure, not all men at Fancy Dog are jerks. But #YesAllWomen have experienced sexism at work…" and it continues on and on, quotes from the other articles, unfocused and rambling in a way that can't make up its mind (we could've written it so much better), and drops a mention at the very end: "Programmer Eliza Bright is slated to appear on *Last Week Tonight* this Sunday. We reached out to Fancy Dog for a comment and they have not contacted us at the time of this publication." So perhaps that's why. Perhaps that's why he does it.

CHAPTER THIRTY-NINE

SDSte: before you say anything, they left stuff out

JPDes: no one is supposed to talk to the media right now

SDSte: they left out a whole part about it being a joke

JPDes: i've been called into a meeting with preston

SDSte: they took it out of context.

SDSte: i had no idea they were going to use facebook photos, my god

JPDes: i told you we weren't supposed to talk to anyone

SDSte: you said ~you~ weren't supposed to talk to anyone

SDSte: you didn't say anything about me

JPDes: i thought it was implied.

SDSte: how was that implied??

JPDes: it just was

SDSte: look, if they weren't going to let you say anything

SDSte: SOMEONE had to come in and clear your name

JPDes: you confirmed our identities

JPDes: up until you confirmed our names, it was only her word that we had anything to do with it

JPDes: you fueled the flames

JPDes: without another one, this was going to die

JPDes: now i have to wait more time for this to fucking stop

JPDes: i had to make my instagram private

JPDes: people messaging me, women asking me for dates, was that your intention?

JPDes: people telling me i'm horrible for not stopping lewis.

JPDes: lewis had to make his twitter private too

JPDes: christ, i forgot about my twitter

JPDes: i have like 600 notifications

JPDes: Delphine?

JPDes: delphine, i swaer to god.

SDSte: sorry, I just got a phone call

JPDes: DO NOT ANSWER ANY MORE MEDIA THINGS

SDSte: no, no, it was for me. i got an audition?

SDSte: babe, it wasn't going to die. she's going to be on john oliver's thing for christs sake

SDSte: you think shes not gonna talk about you two?

SDSte: anyway, tell lewis that they took a bunch of that out of context

SDSte: i really wasn't as mean to him as they made it sound

JPDes: lewis isnt even talking to me right now

JPDes: he hasnt said one word since like four people sent him that article

JPDes: you know i came up with the joke, right? i said it first. lewis typed it out, but it was my joke.

SDSte: look, i'm sorry

JPDes: its time for my meeting with preston. we'll talk about this later.

CHAPTER FORTY

DAleb: dude. i had no idea, the press and legal people didn't tell me NOTHING

EBrig: hahahahahahahahaha

DAleb: what, you think it's funny??

EBrig: hahahahahahahahahaaaaaaaa

DAleb: apparently they got contacted and decided the best thing to do was just not acknowledge it

EBrig: lolololol

EBrig: you're eye candy

EBrig: EYE CANDY

DAleb: dude, not funny. i got mad twitter notifications. and they got from that girl that i'm friends with you

DAleb: what, that like guarantees im not a jerk?

EBrig: dont like the attention?

DAleb: no, like, if it was for something different

DAleb: like, if id done something cool. made something cool or something

DAleb: but this eye candy business

EBrig: my twitter notifications are no picnic either

DAleb: ???

EBrig: im actually not sure what to do about this?

EBrig: like, you being eyecandy was the funniest thing i heard all day

EBrig: the rest is like

EBrig: here, i'll copy and paste

EBrig: @BrightEliza u cunt imma rape you

EBrig: or here

EBrig: @BrightEliza fu u tryna ruin shit #gamergate

EBrig: @Bright Eliza u should kill yrslf

DAleb: what? h/o

DAleb: that first one's a threat

DAleb: have you told someone about this?

EBrig: yeah, you. Suzanne.

EBrig: all Suzanne's said so far is "fuckin neckbeards" though

DAleb: customer service is pretty busy today

EBrig: do i wanna know?

DAleb: no. lots of questions

DAleb: we expected it. preston went public with vive last night and some of the calls and chats and emails are about that

DAleb: but it's also lots of weird people emailing just to say they love us no matter what

DAleb: its weird

DAleb: but i mean like police, have you told the police?

DAleb: youre a white woman, the police were, like, made for you

EBrig: lol, and say what exactly?

EBrig: some anonymous guy named GamezMcGee threatened me

DAleb: that's his twitter handle?

EBrig: yup.

DAleb: 😔

EBrig: exactly

EBrig: besides. its not like they know where i live

EBrig: New York is a big place

DAleb: i guess. just watch yourself?

EBrig: i will

DAleb: maybe get out of the house?

DAleb: stop reading the notifications?

EBrig: some are good

EBrig: here

EBrig: .@BrightEliza we stand with you! *raises shield*

EBrig: or here

EBrig: .@BrightEliza just cancelled my Guilds subscrp. until they rehire #raisetheshield

EBrig: there's actually lots of calls to rehire me

DAleb: i guess that's okay

DAleb: but still

DAleb: come out for drinks or something? get out of the house?

CHAPTER FORTY-ONE

SChoy: ive been reading your twitter notifications

SChoy: i have a tab set up and im keeping track

SChoy: looking at them while on all the cs bullshit phone calls

EBrig: well good afternoon to you too

SChoy: are you okay?

EBrig: mostly i think?

EBrig: most of them are actually fine

EBrig: either theyre normal internet rage

EBrig: or theyre in support of me

EBrig: but some of them are just so creepy

SChoy: yeah, i see

SChoy: on the bright side though

SChoy: theyre just internet people

SChoy: def not the worst thing that could happen

EBrig: i dunno, it's definitely the creepiest thing that ever happened to me

SChoy: this is the creepiest thing that's ever happened to you?

SChoy: what about, like, getting followed into the subway by men shouting about your pussy

EBrig: that happens to you often?

SChoy: literally everywhere

SChoy: like once a week

SChoy: that doesn't happen to you?

EBrig: clearly not on the scale that you experience it

SChoy: what about when you were little?

SChoy: no bad birthday clowns?

SChoy: you know there's now a clown you can hire to follow your kid around and it's on purpose scary as hell? that's a thing now

SChoy: childhood is creepy

SChoy: my mother used to scare me with a story about an aunt who got stoned to death for losing her virginity before marriage, though

SChoy: so maybe my childhood was creepier than most

EBrig: the creepiest thing about my childhood was one of my mother's 60's hits tapes

SChoy: what?

EBrig: you know that song? they're coming to take me away? how the voice gets higher like it's on helium or something?

EBrig: once my mother was playing it in the kitchen while i was trying to go to bed and i legit didn't sleep right for a week

SChoy: that's it?

SChoy: that's the creepiest thing besides the twitter molesters?

EBrig: it just creeps me out, okay? look you asked, that's the creepiest memory from my childhood.

SChoy: you had a fucking perfect childhood didnt you?

EBrig: not perfect. other kids were really mean, but not scary scary. but pretty much, i guess. at least as far as horrors are concerned. i accidentally watched a freddy kreuger movie once and that gave me nightmares, i guess, but not like the goddamn funny farm thing.

SChoy: i can only imagine how you would have faired with my mother

SChoy: im still watching the notifications, okay? if it gets bad we'll

SChoy: well i don't know what we'll do but we'll figure it out

CHAPTER FORTY-TWO

We think it also might be this that drives Lewis to do it:

"There are calls to rehire her," Preston says to Brandon in his office. "And frankly, I'm not sure we shouldn't. It's not like she was bad at her job, and the optics—"

"She broke her NDA," Brandon points out. "Protocol dictates—"

"Pardon my French, Brandon, but fuck protocol."

"Preston, there's no need to—"

"There's no anger behind that, Brandon, there isn't. It's just my game. That has to count for something. Overriding protocol has to be something that we can do if we feel like it."

"You didn't ask the rest of us if we wanted to consider hiring her back, which by the way I don't, and I was in that computer lab with you too, so it's just as much my game as it is yours. We'll never be sure if we can trust her again. I mean Christ, Preston, *Last Week Tonight*. She's trying to make the talk show circuit now, she's getting her fifteen minutes—"

"Trust me when I tell you that she doesn't want her fifteen minutes like this. It's going to be as much of a pain in the ass for her as it is for us."

"Even if we hired her back, she certainly doesn't love the game anymore, and we really need our employees to love it here, love what we make, otherwise why do it? You'd have to be crazy to do this without the love. We lost the worker that she was, the second she blabbed to that crazy Smith woman."

"Brandon. Did you just call one of the best, most trusted technology reporters in the industry 'that crazy Smith woman'?"

"Yes, I did! She's out to destroy us, the media is the opposition party here, both of them are—"

"Look, I don't think anyone is out to destroy us. She was hurt, her team insulted her—"

"My team insults me all the time!"

"Brandon!" Preston comes the closest to yelling that he's come throughout this entire conversation, maybe the closest he's come to raising his voice the entire year. "You keep talking over me. If you're going to obsess about protocol, then follow the guidelines we set up so we wouldn't become one of those violently competitive work environments we hate and shut the hell up." Silence.

"Okay," Preston continues. "So here's how I think we should proceed. We put the guys in training right away, we keep advertising that fact like crazy. And we call Eliza in for a meeting as fast as we can—tonight or tomorrow morning. We see if we can rehire her before she makes any television appearances. We promise to change the protocol, set up something about teaching girls to code, I dunno. I can talk to her and see what she wants."

Brandon makes a move to talk here, but Preston plows forward: "Shut the hell up, Brandon. Yes, I know that's giving her an awful lot of power but we look like idiots right now. This will stop us from looking like idiots. Then we capitalize on her *Last Week Tonight* appearance, and whatever else she may have booked since that insane post came out—" Preston shakes his head here, embarrassed. He'd been featured as well, called "eye candy," and Brandon hadn't. We wonder if perhaps that's why Brandon is so ornery. Some of us believe that Brandon did the firing, not Preston at all. But when it's Preston who does it, it makes for a better story. Better drama. "—and her and I go on together. We talk about our commitment to combating gender inequality in the tech industry, and we actually mean it. We actually take all those initiatives we say we're going to take, earnestly and with all of our effort, because people will be able to tell if we don't mean it. If we do it right, if we mean it, if we commit hard enough, we get her, as a worker, back tenfold because we'll put her in charge of those initiatives, whatever we decide they are. And that's how I want to handle this from here on out."

Brandon sighs, his shoulders slump forward. "That's a huge money sink."

"I know," Preston sighs back. Mirroring body language, that's a thing that works, right? We sometimes forget that Preston is twenty-eight, the same age as Eliza, and he doesn't have a business degree or any real experience in running a company. But in these moments, where he takes tips out of CEO memoirs and Business Insider interviews, we remember. What a talented man it takes to disrupt the system like that. A wunderkind. "But look at it this way—it's a problem that needs to be addressed—you've seen all this Gamergate stuff, how some people say that was the harbinger of this political mess—and we'll be at the helm, we'll be at the center of the conversation in a positive way, and that's good marketing. We'll get a woman's photo on the leadership page, which will make articles like this"—he gestures to the "Sexist Game Company" article up on his computer, the one that had taken a screenshot of their leadership web page and used it as ammunition—"impossible to write. Plus it'll stop the steady leak of users we've seen since yesterday. Have you seen this hashtag-raise-the-shield thing? The Vive was supposed to be a huge selling point, and the feminists are poking holes in it."

"I've seen it. But look how many people are signing up in solidarity with us!"

"I'm not really comfortable with misogynists signing up out of spite as our business strategy. You saw the study. More than half of gamers these days are female. This is a long-term solution, I'm telling you."

"You know, they could be signing up because of Vive. How do we know our announcement didn't have something to do with it?" As soon as the words are out of Brandon's mouth, Preston raises a single eyebrow. He does not even have to gesture to the several tabs open, the Twitter responses. Brandon knows he is being stupid. He knows why we are loyal. "Okay, okay. Let's run it by the numbers guys and see what they say."

"Now, do it now."

Brandon sneers. Both men leave the glass office. Preston runs straight into Devonte outside the door. "You wanted to see me?" Devonte asks. "About the eye candy thing?"

Preston looks at his watch. "Oh yes, sorry, I have so many time slots dedicated to the eye candy thing, I'm sorry. I'm not keeping track very well." Preston registers who he's talking to. "Hey, Devonte," he says, his voice sinking into a whisper. "Hypothetically, if I called first, do you think Eliza would be okay with seeing me again, sometime this evening? If I had good news for her?"

Devonte's eyes deaden a bit and he shrugs. "I dunno, man. You heard her last night. You saw her last night. You might wanna try email."

"It's really important, though," Preston says. "If I emailed her, I'd need to be absolutely sure she read it."

Let's zoom in here, slow down, shift focus—Lewis is returning from the bathroom. He passes them, and they are standing outside the office. Outside the glass. Lewis assumes it's about the goddamn eye candy article—he's been trying not to think about it; he can't even look at Jean-Pascale. But when he closes in on them, he hears it: "Hypothetically, if I called first, do you think Eliza would be okay with seeing me again, sometime this evening?" And he passes; the rest of the words land as a mashed string of sounds in his left ear. He can't control his facial expression—his lips twist up and his dark-circled eyes squint.

This is the moment, the one most of us agree on. The moment where, if he could turn back and walk away, he'd have to do it now. Some of us don't think he can. But there's no point in arguing agency versus destiny, because he doesn't. He doesn't turn back, and so we'll never know.

But we know for sure what happens is this: Lewis goes straight to the nearest desk he has access to. It is Jean-Pascale's, who's been visiting the bathroom quite a bit in the last twenty-four hours. His seat is only one step closer than Lewis's own. It's unclear if he uses Jean-Pascale's computer on purpose, but many of us think so. Some say no, they're friends. He wouldn't have done him dirty like that. But some of us know better: Lewis is a computer nerd. A programmer. He has to know what the consequences will be for JP. The photos are on his phone, after all; he could upload them directly from there and yet he chooses his best friend's workstation. Perhaps he doesn't have enough bars to upload that much data from his phone—does Fancy Dog allow employees to sign on to the office Wi-Fi? Or perhaps he is one of those people who finds it tedious to post on forums from a mobile device. Piss-poor excuse—far more likely, we think, that this is revenge. Revenge for what, we're not exactly sure. But revenge for something. For clearly feeling two ways about their joke. For getting Delphine to pin it all on Lewis. For being tall and a man who women think is eye candy.

It doesn't matter: the photos of Eliza's paperwork wind up on Jean-Pascale's computer, and then they wind up on 4chan. Lewis drags them into the trash on the computer once he is through, but he does not even empty it. That has to be a choice too.

CHAPTER FORTY-THREE

DAleb: he wants you to come into the office

EBrig: who?

DAleb: preston

EBrig: huh . . .

DAleb: i think you should consider it

EBrig: i am considering it

EBrig: i mean, is it for what i think it is

DAleb: rehiring you?

DAleb: tbh idk

DAleb: it sounded like it, though

EBrig: the number of people who are using that raise the shield hashtag's grown. i'm surprised.

EBrig: i can't believe people have the bandwidth to fight for me

EBrig: i mean, the other stuff's grown too

DAleb: tell me you aren't reading that still

EBrig: its hard not to

EBrig: ive had more calls from talk shows too

DAleb: trevor noah, right?

DAleb: thats the rumor

EBrig: yeah.

CHAPTER FORTY-FOUR

Eliza walks back into Fancy Dog that night, after many (but not all) employees have gone home. Suzanne is still here, answering phone calls and emails from both sides. When Eliza asks her to stay, she texts "lolololol, im here anyway! bring power bar. coffee. dinner. anything."

She asks Devonte to stay too. He texts back, "of course." She tries her very best to look presentable—she's been holed up in her apartment, in her pajamas. She hasn't showered since she was fired, but she drags her ass to the bathroom and cleans up before arriving.

Jean-Pascale and Lewis are both here too, undergoing their sensitivity training. Jean-Pascale looks worse—dark circles equal to Lewis's, shoulders hunched, curly hair a little more greasy than usual. Lewis looks—fine? As fine as Lewis normally looks. He is speaking to Jean-Pascale again, but his words are stilted and he's smiling like his teeth are made of broken Legos.

We know exactly what time we start, so we know that, as she crosses the threshold, she feels the phone in her pocket begin to buzz. But Preston and Brandon are in the lobby to meet her, and she doesn't pick it up. It is definitely a phone call—the long buzzes instead of the short double Morse code that signifies a text or tweet. She decides to let it go to voicemail. That's what voicemail boxes are for, after all.

The office seems colder than normal. "Take a seat," Preston says. He gestures to the leather chairs, the comfy ones. She sits, pets Dog curled on the floor, and her phone begins to buzz again, loud enough to fill the room with sound. Everyone ignores it. "We have some excellent news, Eliza, truly excellent!" He looks like he really believes it. Preston is so earnest, or so good at pretending to be earnest. "We'd love to talk about rehiring you. Or more aptly, pretending we never terminated your employment in the first place—we're the first to admit when we've made a terrible mistake, and, in your case—" But Preston's eyebrow raises and Brandon's gaze turns to the glass wall.

Eliza spins around in her cushy seat to see Devonte and Suzanne running so fast they practically tear up the carpet. Devonte gets there first and pauses to compose himself, but Suzanne grabs his hand and propels him forward. Of course she does. Entitled. We know she thinks it's a big deal, but can't she see the grown-ups are talking? They burst through the door. Suzanne's luxurious hair, once well kept and the healthy kind of puffy, is thrown into a side ponytail and looks wild, frazzled. Devonte's sneaker is untied and his hat is askew, as though he's been grabbing the left side of his head with his hand.

"You have to see this," Devonte pants at the same time Suzanne says, "I'm so sorry." Eliza's phone begins to buzz anew.

Devonte opens his laptop, logs into his own *Guild* account and presses the Party button to find Circuit Breaker instantly. He turns the computer around so they can all see what we're doing.

CHAPTER FORTY-FIVE

We stand in a ring around Circuit Breaker. Where she once wore a supersuit, she now wears nothing. Her skin is smooth and her breasts stay high of their own accord. Gravity has nothing on girls in Windy City. A man walks up behind her. He wears a black mask and a wide-brimmed hat. He carries two cutlasses, one in each hand. He slides one into a sheath and grabs Circuit Breaker's blonde ponytail. Using the remaining cutlass, he slices into her hair slow as sipping Scotch. This is the beta server, so we are wearing the Vive; it's so realistic. It even looks like it has tension, the way the hair is pulled taut, the way individual strands give way and snap. He holds up the blonde handful and we cheer. The women among us, they leave sneering. And we are blessedly alone again, with no one looking through the clubhouse windows, free! The masked man pushes Circuit Breaker in the shoulders and she falls to her knees. He fades into the crowd, into us. He keeps the trophy.

Another one of us steps out, differentiating himself, in front of Circuit Breaker this time. We holler out, "She wants another one. Give her another one."

Just like that, his camouflage pants vanish and leave bare skin in their wake. One of us calls out, "It looks stupid with your shirt and your jetpack on, take it off!" He obliges and we roar with laughter.

rotflmao

rotflmao

ROTFLMAO

We do not know if he is wearing his headset. He must be. It's a better story if he is.

"Do you want me to fuck you in the mouth," he asks. But it is not a question.

"Yes," Circuit Breaker says, not in her normal voice; it is altered. Impossible to tell who's at the helm. And they begin. Nothing is blurred or pixelated out—it isn't the fucking *Sims*, for fuck's sake. It isn't a game for children. We see his dick enter Circuit Breaker's mouth. We watch Circuit Breaker's head bob up and down.

We yell things. Some are typed:

"giv that bitch wat she deserves"

"best game ever"

"u no she wants it"

Some are verbal:

"You guys, stop, this is gross."

"Is that really her? Fuck, she must be bored."

The naked man says, "You know you want it." It is broadcast. Everyone can hear it, hear it right in our headsets. We marvel at how big everything looks—they are the size of real people. The sky is miles above us, a blue bowl just like the real outside. And these two full-sized human beings are having sex right in front of us, even though we are in our own living rooms, our own basements. What must it be like, to be the people fucking right now? Many of us vow to try it immediately. Others of us shudder at the thought.

"I know. I want it. Yes," Circuit Breaker says. Her voice is computerized, scrambled. Probably not even a woman. Gay, gay, gay, we think, but we don't say it. We don't stop to wonder how she can speak when her mouth is otherwise occupied; we don't ask too many questions.

When each of us fucks Circuit Breaker in the mouth, it has some interesting side effects. It skews our alignment toward "good." We take note of this. We plan our lays to be advantageous to our gameplay. Some of us become disgusted with us, with people, with the internet. Some of us are cucks.

Those of us who are left are delighted to see that we can still perform a critical hit, something usually reserved for extremely successful combat, violence. When the naked man is blessed with such a moment, we all pound our feet on the ground and clap our hands as the red banner flies over his head. CRITICAL +6. We laugh when we see what it looks like: a fountain spray of white all over Circuit Breaker's face. It looks like the naked man pied her. It drips down in thick clumps while Circuit Breaker looks up with wide, surprised eyes. It is meant to be funny. They made it that way.

We are hysterical. We cheer.

CHAPTER FORTY-SIX

Eliza's vision spots a little bit. She grows very queasy. The circle around Circuit Breaker is getting bigger. "Make it stop," she says. "Someone make this stop." Then she remembers: she knows how to shut her own account down. She is a developer and this is basic. "I'll make it stop, give me the computer."

But Brandon puts his arm out to stop her and she runs right into it as she tries to lift herself from the chair. "No, we don't have paperwork from you yet, we can't let you back into the server." She sits back, hard. She feels like the chair is swallowing her; she's never before noticed how small she is in comparison to furniture.

"I don't understand," Preston says quietly. "You have to say yes. You have to click yes, anyone can click no. Was there a bug—?"

"There's no bug." Eliza is talking loudly now, not quite shouting. "I wrote it, I checked it, there's no bug, it won't let you do it until you select yes. We tried it." Eliza blushes red. "Not wearing the headsets. Not with our characters. With plain grey people, they didn't even have faces." Or perhaps things got hot when they were trying it out, and now, feeling awkward around her team, she manufactures all this "harassment" for herself.

"Someone hacked you," Devonte states. He seems to remember that we're still taking turns on Circuit Breaker, plain as day on the screen. He moves to sign out.

Brandon stops him: "We need to see their usernames, every-one around her, screenshot them." Devonte starts screenshotting. The camera sound fills the silent room with computerized shutter clicks, so awkward and unnecessary. Eliza looks more and more green in the face, so he turns the monitor toward the wall and keeps going.

"Don't bother," says Eliza. "Turning it around, I mean. I still know it's happening," she says as she pulls out her phone. She closes her eyes, takes a deep breath. Getting her account hacked is not that bad, she thinks. It is not the worst thing that could happen to her. But then she looks down. She sees the missed call badge—it is at thirty-seven. An-other call comes in. She declines it. She taps on the email icon. "An error occurred, please authenticate again," says the prompt, and when she types her password in, she returns, in red letters, "incorrect password." She taps on the Bank of America app—and receives the same error.

"I think." She clears her throat and tries again. "I think." Eliza leans over very quickly, grabs the trash can next to Preston's desk and throws up (it's what we would do if this happened to us). It tastes like sour milk and is, unfortunately, mostly undigested Lucky Charms. Hearts, stars and horseshoes, she can't help thinking to herself as she tries to hide the rainbow hues and breathe normally again.

"It wouldn't have been hard," Suzanne says to the room. "Everyone knows our usernames."

Devonte shakes his head. "We sign in with our emails, our personal ones."

Preston rounds on Eliza. "Did you ever put your personal email on-line?" he asks. "Maybe like a blog or something, a personal website, do you freelance?"

"No, never, not the one I use for log-ins. It's just a string of numbers at Gmail, it's not even semantic."

Preston's fingers hover over the computer, but he realizes he can't remember how to shut the account. Or that it's changed so much, the system, that he no longer knows how to do it. "We need the sys admins," he shouts out the door.

Leaky Joe is the one who responds; he's been watching very closely. "Brian is work-from-home with the flu, do you want someone to call him or—?"

"Fuck. Okay. Someone pull Lewis and JP out of training!" He remembers and shoots a look at Eliza. "Sorry," he says. "I'm really sorry." Devonte tries to raise his hand; he could shut off access too. He is ignored.

Eliza stares through the glass wall. "Do you think they're actually wearing the Vive?" she asks no one in particular. "Do you think the people doing that are using virtual reality?"

Suzanne kneels down in front of Eliza and grabs her face. The lights from the city sneak in through the big glass window and look like electricity running through Suzanne's wild hair. "Maybe. But you're not. They can't make you wear it. It's not really happening. Don't think about it, just for a few more minutes. Think about anything else."

Eliza tries to follow the directions. "I brought you a Luna Bar," she says, but she is starting to hyperventilate. "Suzanne, I can't log into my bank accounts. I can't get to my email. I think they got everything." Brandon finally looks at Devonte; they exchange a look. Brandon sits at Preston's desk and begins to type.

Lewis doesn't run into the office, but Jean-Pascale does. He flies into the chair so fast it rolls and he has to pull himself back into place. "Lock it!" Preston yells. "The same way as if the player doesn't pay us." It takes Jean-Pascale only a few seconds, thirty at most. And then the room grows quiet.

"Just delete the account," Eliza finally says.

Preston shakes his head. "I'm sorry, Eliza—we need to look at logs, we need to figure out what happened, if there's a larger security breach—"

"Then keep it. Just don't ever give it back to me."

"I know what happened," Brandon says from behind the desk. Everyone turns to look. He rotates the monitor toward the room. The website is instantly familiar—the horrid orange brown, the layout so bad that it renders the page almost invisible.

"4chan?" Suzanne asks.

"It's everywhere," he says. "Reddit. 4chan. Personally hosted websites. All I had to do was Google her name." Everyone leans in to look at what is unmistakably a scan of Eliza's Fancy Dog file—username, password, even her allergies to penicillin and fish. Every email address she's ever had, she'd had to write down on the application and check off if she still uses it or not; a precaution to prevent leaks. Most people lie— who would know? What an idiot, not lying on that form, not keeping something to herself. Doesn't she care about digital security at all? We don't need an ounce of hacking knowledge to get her. It is all out there. Her address. Her phone number. Numb and puked out, Eliza looks back down at her phone. She has voicemails.

She shades her eyes so the rest of the room won't see her face and presses the little recording icon. The first two are fine—offers from talk shows. The third one is intriguing—an offer from *Diverse Games Now!*, for media training, free. The fourth, she puts on speakerphone.

It is a recording of "They're Coming to Take Me Away, Ha-Haaa!" The part where the voice gets higher and higher. "This song," she says, her voice small like the sound of it is trying to fold in on itself, "used to give me nightmares when I was little. That was, gosh, how many years ago? How would they know that? How could they know that?"

Eliza looks up from her phone, still playing—"to the funny farm." Everyone is looking at her. Except Jean-Pascale. He is looking at the computer screen with her file all over it, turning paler and paler like someone is sucking all the red from his face. He pitches forward in his chair and hits the floor with his beak-like nose. Everyone scrambles to him, someone shouts, "Jean-Pascale!" Eliza stands too, but she is lightheaded from vomiting. She sways, and notices Lewis still standing beyond the glass, never having set foot in the office. His eyes meet hers. Nothing goes on in his face; his own version of shark eyes. Jean-Pascale is stirring, his nose bloody and already starting to turn colors.

Eliza, still quiet, still small of voice, wishes for superpowers. Instead of reaching her hands out to electrocute the entire structure of the city, the world, until no computer is left functioning, until everything catches fire and burns to the ground while she watches, she says, soft, squeaky: "I don't want to play anymore."

CHAPTER FORTY-SEVEN

The Inspectre is not the person who takes Lewis's post and spreads it like oil in an ocean, or rather, he's not the only one. One person can't do that by themselves anyhow—we all do it together. He isn't even the person who comes up with the virtual gang rape idea. Or should we call it rape? Some among us say it's not the same thing because it's fiction, fake, digital; the consequences are imaginary. Others point out that, to everyone who sees it, to people who don't know she's hacked, Circuit Breaker consents. Whatever we call it, The Inspectre is simply an involved witness at this point: elated at the crowd gathering, giggling at the things the hacker is making her say. He, of course, wears the Vive. A developer's edition, actually. He has one of the first beta invites (based on the number of hours he spends playing *Guilds*). Surrounded by all these people watching this gorgeous act of violence, retribution for her earlier lack of response, he is turned on. He is in line to take a crack at it; he is hard.

When they pull the plug on Circuit Breaker's account, he gets angry. Some of the other men are grumbling, sure. But he feels such fury—they took his toy away when he hadn't yet had his turn. He is outraged the hacker hadn't seen it coming and prevented it. The Inspectre is the better hacker; he will figure out some way to play on. He pulls up her information—it's easy to find by now—and he digs deeper.

He'd been the first person on her emails, the one to change the password. Sure, the smarter thing would've been to go for the bank account before someone else got it (and someone else did get it), but The Inspectre isn't worried about money. He's worried about information. And emails, G-chats—that's like living in someone's head. He settles in to read the conversations, things Eliza always assumed would be private; he's sure he'll find something there. The ones with the men don't interest him. The only ones with a woman, though, a Suzanne Choy—he starts there, with the most recent.

It takes him seconds; he is so fast. Find. Download. Straight to voicemail, that's what he wants, to leave a message. He wants her to stumble upon it, like tripping into a hole in the ground or stepping on unexpected four-sided dice with bare feet. He cracks his knuckles, imagining her fear and wondering if, like so many others (he supposes), her orgasm face is the same as her terror face. He devours every conversation between Eliza Bright and Suzanne Choy as if they are novels put on shelves for people to access.

CHAPTER FORTY-EIGHT

Brandon rises from Preston's chair, marches over to HR, the keepers of the file now leaked in its entirety, and fires the whole department on the spot.

And that's all. End of chapter.

CHAPTER FORTY-NINE

Suzanne pulls Devonte aside. "It's me," she tells Devonte, and then she realizes that makes no sense. "She told that to me, like, two fucking hours ago. I was talking her through the tweets—we were making fun of them, like thinking of way worse things that could be happening, thinking of creepier stuff. I just wanted her to not be so freaked anymore. I wanted to be not so freaked anymore."

Devonte pulls Suzanne over to the window; it looks like they are contemplating the city. He arranges his posture to look reflective, sad. It doesn't take much pretending. "Talk out this way," he says. "Lewis is right out there. We don't know who else might be watching. Now. Do you think you're hacked?"

"No, I don't. I haven't seen any weird tweets or anything like that, I haven't gotten phone calls."

"Where did you tell her this?"

"G-chat."

"Okay, do you have your credit card associated with your Google account at all? PayPal, anything else? Your bank? I'm talking even log-ins?"

"Yes."

"Don't say which. What we are going to do is calmly go back to your floor, and you are going to take your iPad out of your bag, turn the Wi-Fi off, TunnelBear on, and switch every log-in that uses the

Gmail account to something different—if you don't have another email floating around, make one up. Don't report it to Fancy Dog."

Suzanne nods. She breathes deep. "It's someone in here. That's her internal file. And Christ, Devonte, it could have been anyone—so many people could have grabbed that, copied it and sent it."

"I know. But three guesses who. You go first. I'll follow you down." Suzanne starts to turn, but Devonte says, "Oh—and think of anyone you know who can help us figure out who the funny-farm guy is."

"Someone—anonymous?"

Devonte nods.

CHAPTER FIFTY

@theinspectre: @yrface You sound sexy, Suzanne. Don't be jealous just because your friend

@theinspectre: Eliza is getting all the attention right now. @yrface

@theinspectre: Don't worry, @yrface.

@theinspectre: @yrface I see you.

@theinspectre: Your turn will come. @yrface

CHAPTER FIFTY-ONE

Immediately after Eliza whines that she doesn't want to play anymore, she runs from the office. Flees into the night like the coward she is, can't take a fucking joke. Preston makes it all the way to the street, panting, and finds she has disappeared. He looks both ways, scans the shop windows and heads bobbing along the street—nothing. He even walks up and down, going inside establishments and craning his head between aisles and around corners, checking coffee lines. He knocks on the Starbucks bathroom door and is surprised by a surly, deep voice. Gone, he thinks. So he continues on to her apartment; he knows where it is, after all. The thought stops him in the middle of the street: now, so does everyone else. We know too. His skin tickles as if it's crawling with tiny people, tiny hands and fingers, prying open the fruit of his skin. The entire internet knows where Eliza Bright is on her way to, right now. It makes his face flush. He is hot and cold all at once. He has to breathe intentionally, steadily, with the weight of the internet and our eyes pressing down on his chest. He continues on.

He finds himself almost instantly knocking on her door. He jumps a little, startled to realize he remembers almost none of the cab ride. His hands grow clammy at the thought of his mental faculties deteriorating. Wasted brain space. Wasted on the thoughts of his fuck buddy, this person who has weaseled her way into his affections, conned her way into his consciousness.

When Eliza opens the door, wider this time than before, he notices: that she is a hot mess; that she is wearing next to nothing. Her hair is twisted up in a messy bun, bra and panties—plain white ones—and her glasses jammed slightly askew on her nose as though someone played pin the tail on the donkey and got them mostly where they should be. It isn't unfamiliar, this sight. He knows her body so well by now. The birthmark under her belly button, the scar on the ball of her ankle, the way her lips part when she sees him outside of work.

Eliza opens the door when she hears the knock. We think that is unwise, given her situation, but she is ready to fall into the arms of someone comforting, someone familiar. Or she looks through the peephole and sees her prey. Or she is drunk. Very drunk. She has a bottle of WhistlePig rye whiskey in her hand. Her eyes are red and puffy, her cheeks almost as red as her eyes; her face hurts. "Oh thank goodness," she says, instead of "hello" or "why are you here?" And that confirms it, for us. They've been going at it all along. She falls into his arms at the door and lets herself be taken up, carried back over the threshold. Preston, this is such a bad choice! How could you let yourself be swindled like this! You have a higher purpose, more important things to do, and this actual succubus is going to drag you into hell. Normally we would abandon such a person as a lost cause, but we can't abandon someone who has never abandoned us. Who gives us cause to exist. We'll never abandon Preston Waters.

Preston has no issue hoisting her, but when he sets her gingerly on the couch, she collapses, limbs splaying out in all directions, her insides so obviously pickled in liquor. There is something sexy about her in this state, even though she is a six. Gorgeous in her brokenness. We are hard for her vulnerability. The idea that now anyone could have her, just like we all had Circuit Breaker. More gingerly, Preston sits down beside her, coat still on. We wonder: why doesn't he take his coat off? Does he really have no idea what's coming?

"Whiskey?" Eliza asks. It is almost a purr.

"Fuck yes," Preston says as he takes the bottle, takes a swig. It is rakish, piratic, comfortable.

In spite of herself and everything else, Eliza grins the grin of the satisfied, the demon who has won. The alcohol mutes the echo of the rat skull joke that she always carries with her, that usually prevents her from smiling with her whole mouth.

"Shit," he says. It isn't impassioned, it isn't loud or even really a curse word. It is just a fact, stated plainly. "Shit."

"Yep," she says. He passes the bottle back. Pull; burning in her mouth; pull; burning in her throat, then her empty stomach. At least the whiskey washes the taste of vomit out, replaces it with the memory of taking Preston out, drinking with him until he gave her what she wanted.

"We weren't joking, you know," he says. "About rehiring you. It'll give you institutional support to deal with this. And besides, no one needs to know about us."

"It's over. Everyone already knows about us. And at this point, it's about what we would rather. Do we want to keep doing this, or do we want to work together?"

Preston thinks about all his reasons to rehire her; that they wouldn't look like idiots if they got her back. And then he thinks about throwing her into bed, picking her up and slamming her down. He is too far gone to think about not sleeping with her. A puppet. He wants both things, and damn it, Preston, it gives her so much power. He opens his mouth to argue that they can have all of it, every single morsel or drop or whatever, but changes his mind. There will be time, he thinks. He can convince her, when she needs the lawyers or when it all blows over or— sometime. Sometime in the future, the nebulous foggy future, he is sure he can convince her to come back. Instead: he kisses her. Sweetly, then passionately. She bites his lip and draws a little blood. All she can think of is grabbing Preston's hair, pulling it. That same exact electrifying feeling from the office, back when she had a career. Back when she could imagine herself behind Preston's desk one day, or at the very least launching a game of her own. An image arrives, unbidden: unzipping his skin and climbing inside. She bites harder and he yelps. It is the closest she can get. She inhales the small squeal, pleasure and pain, but mostly she drinks in the power. The power she has over his body in the moment; the power she has over his mind more generally. When she pulls away, she does her best to look into his eyes as the whiskey rocks her back and forth. She has just enough presence of mind to set the whiskey bottle on the table before he reaches under her shirt, something he's done a thousand times before.

CHAPTER FIFTY-TWO

O r it could've gone this way:
Preston makes it all the way to the street, panting, and finds Eliza has disappeared. He looks both ways, scans the shop windows and heads bobbing along the street—nothing. Gone, he thinks. So he continues on to her apartment; he knows where it is, after all.

He finds himself almost instantly knocking on her door. He jumps a little, startled to realize he remembers almost none of the cab ride. His hands grow clammy at the thought of his mental faculties deteriorating. But no, he is just worried. Concerned for Eliza, concerned for the future of Fancy Dog. Nothing about this afternoon went to plan.

When Eliza opens the door, wider this time than before, he notices: that she is a hot mess; that she has furniture—nice furniture; the computer and the hard drive poking out from behind the television; the white walls are mostly bare and her bookshelves are lean—he can relate to that, the minimalism.

Eliza opens the door when she hears the knock. We think that is unwise, given her situation, but she hasn't thought of it because she's a dumb cunt. She has a bottle of WhistlePig rye whiskey in her hand. Her eyes are red and puffy, her cheeks almost as red as her eyes; her face hurts. "Why bother with a glass?" she says, instead of "hello" or "why are you here?" And then, to answer a question she thinks she can see in Preston's face: "It's from my pre-no-income days. I guess I'll buy cheaper next time."

"I didn't say—didn't even think—"

But Eliza laughs, mean. "Sure you did."

"Eliza, I swear, no judgment. About anything. No judgment at all." Both stand still, looking at each other across the threshold. Eliza tries to remember how to exist in her numb body. How do limbs move?

She takes another pull from the bottle. "Welp. I suppose you should come in." And she turns around and leaves the door open for Preston to walk himself through and shut. She collapses on the couch, limbs splaying out in all directions. More gingerly, Preston sits down beside her, coat still on. We wonder: Why doesn't he take his coat off? Does he really have no idea what's coming?

"Whiskey?" Eliza asks.

"Fuck yes," Preston says as he takes the bottle, takes a swig.

"I would've got you a glass," Eliza says.

"You said it yourself: why bother."

In spite of herself and everything else, Eliza grins because she didn't know he was like this. She sees only his professional self, and then only the self that fired her. The alcohol mutes the echo of the rat skull joke that she carries with her always, that usually prevents her from smiling with her whole mouth.

"Shit," he says. It isn't impassioned, it isn't loud or even really a curse word. It is just a fact, stated plainly.

"Yep," she says. He passes the bottle back. Pull; burning in her mouth; pull; burning in her throat, then her empty stomach. At least the whiskey washes the taste of vomit out, replaces it with the barest hint of impending questionable decisions. She wriggles in her seat, suddenly very aware of how close he is to her. He radiates heat next to her and she can't concentrate on anything else she wants to say.

Something comes over her; it is the whiskey and the accusation and the realization that he isn't her boss anymore. She kisses him. Hard. It is the closest she can get. Or she is simply fucking her way to the top, exactly like Jean-Pascale said she would. Or sex would feel good after the shit day she's had. Or she's drunk, it's that simple. And Preston is the beneficiary of good timing. We like Preston. We wish we were Preston too. Sex is always good, even with a six. A sad six, especially. She will be feisty; she will do things to annihilate her body, to make herself forget.

Eliza bites his lip and tastes the breath from his yelp and the copper from his blood. When she pulls away, she does her best to look into his eyes as the whiskey rocks her back and forth.

He looks surprised, but not shocked. She has just enough presence of mind to set the whiskey bottle on the table before he kisses her back.

CHAPTER FIFTY-THREE

O r how about this way:

He finds himself almost instantly knocking on her door. He jumps a little, startled to realize he remembers almost none of the cab ride. He was so distracted by the idea of us, the threat of us. We wish we could tell him we mean him no harm, none whatsoever.

When Eliza opens the door, wider this time than before, he notices: that she is a hot mess; that she has furniture—nice furniture; the computer and the hard drive poking out from behind the television; the white walls are mostly bare and her bookshelves are lean—he can relate to that, the indecisiveness about what to put on them, in them. He hadn't really looked when he'd shown up earlier. He was mostly focused on how stupid he'd felt. Now, though he's frightened, he doesn't feel quite as stupid. There's no audience.

Eliza opens the door when she hears the knock. We think that is unwise, given her situation, but she hasn't thought of it because she's a dumb bitch. Or she looks through the peephole and sees her prey. Or she is drunk. Very drunk. She has a bottle of WhistlePig rye whiskey in her hand. Her eyes are red and puffy, her cheeks almost as red as her eyes; her face hurts. "Oh. You," she says, instead of "hello" or "why are you here?" And then, to answer a question she thinks she can see in Preston's face: "It's from my pre-no-income days. I guess I'll buy cheaper next time."

"I didn't say—didn't even think—"

But Eliza laughs, mean. "Sure you did."

"Eliza, I swear, no judgment. About anything. No judgment at all." Both stand still, looking at each other across the threshold. Eliza tries to remember how to exist in her numb body. How do limbs move?

She takes another pull from the bottle. "I suppose you should come in. You're here, after all. Again." And she turns around and leaves the door open for Preston to walk himself through and shut. She collapses on the couch, limbs splaying out in all directions. More gingerly, Preston sits down beside her, coat still on.

"Whiskey?" Eliza asks.

"Fuck yes," Preston says as he takes the bottle, takes a swig.

"I would've got you a glass," Eliza says.

"In situations like this, why bother with a glass?" He pauses. "Shit," he says. It isn't impassioned, it isn't loud or even really a curse word. It is just a fact, stated plainly.

"Yep," she says. He passes the bottle back. Pull; burning in her mouth; pull; burning in her throat, then her empty stomach. At least the whiskey washes the taste of vomit out, replaces it with the feeling of tears, which she promptly shoves down into her chest.

"So I came to take you to the police station. I figured we can report the funny-farm thing. That's harassment." He pauses, wishing for the whiskey to teleport back into his hand. Eliza reads his thoughts or his face—she supplies his right hand with the bottle. His pull is long. He shakes his head after, looks at the label. "This stuff is good. And then we can talk for real about rehiring you, that way our lawyers—" But Eliza is already shaking her head.

"Preston. When I said I didn't want to play anymore, I meant it. All of it. Someone leaked that file—someone I know. Someone who works at Fancy Dog. I never want to look at *Guilds of the Protectorate* again for as long as I walk this earth."

Preston opens his mouth to argue, but changes his mind. There will be time, he thinks. He can convince her, when she needs the lawyers or when it all blows over or—sometime. Sometime in the future, the nebulous foggy future, he is sure he can convince her to come back. Instead: "Well, let's get to the police station anyway." He stands and turns toward the door. "That funny-farm business is no fucking jo—"

"Don't you dare." Eliza stands too, and grabs the front of his coat before he has a chance to get out the door, or to convince her. Preston stumbles. The end result is face-to-face, chest-to-chest. "Don't you fucking dare. You fired me, and now I can say whatever I want, and you don't get to—"

She wants to explain to him that she has everything under control. Before getting wasted, she'd called the bank, the credit cards. Someone in the litany of humans she spoke to said "how did this even happen?" in the crackly, accusatory way one person can talk to another when neither party can see the other's face on the phone: anonymity at its worst. She thought about calling her mother; thought better of it. By the time she grabbed the bottle of whiskey she's now drinking, exhaustion had already set in. The kind that makes it impossible to believe doing anything, let alone explaining her situation to stone-faced New York City police officers, is worth it.

When she opens her mouth to say all this—to say that people are by and large lazy and she doesn't think anyone will waste their time coming to look for her apartment, or that weird internet boys won't expend more effort than it takes to tweet at her or leave a creepy message on her phone, or that she isn't that damn important—all she can think of is grabbing Preston's hair, pulling it. Back when she could imagine herself behind Preston's desk one day, or at the very least launching a game of her own. An image arrives, unbidden: unzipping his skin and climbing inside.

She bursts into tears.

"Whoa, whoa, whoa, hey," he says, short-circuiting a little. This is not how he thought this would go. Or it is, just not quite so ugly or so close.

"Please leave. I'm begging you, I really just want to be alone right now and this"—she sniffs hard and Preston can hear the snot gurgle in her face, her throat—"this is very embarrassing."

"It's not very safe to be here alone, Eliza."

"It's not very safe to be anywhere with anyone," she retorts. Then she giggles and it is a horrifying sound, a horrifying face. "The call is coming from inside the house. I don't know who to trust. It could've been you! You could've leaked it!"

"Listen, like—at least let me stay here? I'll stay here! Strength in numbers, in case people show up." He pauses. "And it wasn't me. I wouldn't ever do that."

"If you stay here," she says, "I don't want to talk to you. I don't want to look at you. I will go in there and you will stay out here and you can, I dunno, watch my door. As penance. Or whatever."

Dumb fucking cunt.

CHAPTER FIFTY-FOUR

Devonte's apartment is in the financial district. He's thought about cooler places with fewer meat-headed finance bros, but he likes the big picture window through which he can see the river. He both loves and hates the way people looked at him back when he moved in. They wondered openly, with the unhidable contours of their rubber faces, if he should be there, with his fancy sneakers and his snapbacks and his brown skin. Walking through his building, he set his mouth somewhere between a grim line and a smirk as people's eyes flicked over him, trying to hide surprise. Eventually they got to know him and it stopped. Mostly.

Today there is no smirk. He turns his key and collapses in his chair. His most prized possession: a record player accompanied by an ever-growing collection of vinyl he hunts down in dusty shops when he isn't staring at a computer. He pours bourbon into a Glencairn glass and sets the needle carefully down, paying attention not to the music but to the welling up of sound in his body, in his bones. His apartment fills with rich reverberations that only emanate from physical media—digital never comes close. He sips the bourbon, torn by his haves—on the one hand, is it really fair that he has and his cousins have not? On the other hand, they told him he never would—"The nerds shall not inherit the earth," or maybe "Stop being such a fucking pussy," they'd say as they left him behind or, on the truly bad days, worse. Much worse—

blackened eyes and toilet-water hairstyles worse. That makes it all the sweeter that he has and they have not. He smiles. It's complicated.

When his body soaks up enough good resonance and liquor, he powers up his hand-built computer. He emails his Anonymous friend. "Not here," he replies. "IRC." Internet Relay Chat. It's where the hackers live.

CHAPTER FIFTY-FIVE

Eliza and Preston aren't even finished when someone knocks at the door. They want to ignore it, but the knock comes again, loud and frustrated. Eliza pulls on her pants so fast that she puts both legs in one, mermaid style, and has to begin again.

Or she comes out of the bedroom with her whiskey bottle as Preston gets up from the couch, coat still on, unsure of what he should be doing now that he is sitting vigil in her apartment.

She looks through the peephole and frowns; leaves the chain on and opens the door, talks to the pizza delivery man through the crack.

"I didn't order a pizza."

"Eliza Bright?" the delivery man asks, and she nods. "I have an order for Eliza Bright at this address. Three large pizzas with pineapple, anchovies and hot sauce, no cheese, plus two liter bottles of root beer. Man, that is some weird party you're having in there." The delivery man shakes his head.

Preston is up and behind her. "You guys actually made that?" He draws himself up tall and looks down the bridge of his nose. Eliza thinks he is fairly terrifying—that way he has about him of being smarter than anyone else in the room, directing it at people in these concentrated moments like a pinpointed laser. "That's inedible. Anyone with two brain cells to rub together can see that's inedible. You guys didn't think this was a prank?"

The delivery man turns a little red—Preston is in his boxers, bare-chested. Eliza blushes too, and wonders why he couldn't have put on some clothes. She's managed. Or he is fully dressed, overdressed even, and the collar on his coat is popped up; he looks like Sherlock Holmes. Rich. Intimidating.

"I—I—it's pay on delivery," the pizza guy stammers.

"We are not paying for inedible pizza we did not order," Eliza says. Embarrassed though she is for the pizza (and the boxers and the boy, if our theories are correct), she is absolutely not shelling out any cash. She closes the door.

"That was weird," Preston says.

Without replying, Eliza pulls her laptop toward her and checks her Twitter. She sifts through the notifications: "80085, you like pizza? Lol, this is a important question, you like pizza?" she reads aloud. She Googles her name. Then the number, 80085. She finds our subreddit. "I hope the bitch really is allergic to fish," she reads aloud and turns to Preston. "I am, by the way. Allergic to fish. Ah, yes, here"—she squints at the screen—"from the allergies listed on my intake forms. Yup, they know." Eliza is calm—calmer than she should be, we think. Calmer than we were hoping she'd be, those of us who sent the pizza. How quickly does one get used to this? Or is this what she wanted, this attention from us? Our eyes are all on her, waiting for the tweet, for the sign that she got our little joke.

Preston wants to say "This is fucking sick." Or he is impressed with our ingenuity. Or he feels like Doctor Frankenstein, wondering how something he brought to life could have become such a monster. His mouth hangs open, but no words come out. Someone knocks at the door again. Eliza rises to answer, but Preston shakes his head and looks out the peephole himself. "You've gotta be shitting me," he says as he opens the door to a bicycle-helmeted delivery guy carrying white bags with giant red characters on them.

"I have an order of salmon teriyaki," he begins, reading off a receipt.

Preston interrupts him before he can get going, "I'm sorry, there's been a terrible misunderstanding. Any orders your establishment gets for us tonight aren't for us, okay? Someone's—playing a joke, okay?" The delivery guy blinks a few times, slowly, like he has to compute each word, as Preston shuts the door. He turns back. "Please, Eliza, we have to call the police now."

Eliza snorts. "And say what? We'd like to report a pizza?"

"Well we wouldn't have to put it like that, that'd just get us laughed at, that's not—"

"Preston. Do you know what I've had to do today? After I left? Not even today, just this evening. All my bank accounts, my credit cards are frozen right now. I literally don't know how I'm going to pay rent come January first, let alone buy Christmas gifts, because of course I haven't done that already. I changed every password I can think of for every account I can still get my hands on; my Gmail has been hacked so bad that the password's been changed, probably a million times by now, and I'm waiting for Google's customer service to get back to me on that. They've left Twitter and Facebook pretty much alone—I can only guess they want me to see all the messages they're sending me, because they didn't seem to have any restraint at all with my Tumblr. That's covered in porn. And not just any porn. Violent porn that they have photoshopped my face into."

She takes a breath, hoping Preston will ignore the slurred, mushy quality of her diction. "Preston, this took them two hours to do." She looks at her phone to check the time; she is nothing if not precise. "Three, I guess it took them three hours to do. My phone is filled with this fucking horrible song. They're all calling me 80085 now. So no, no I don't want to call the police. I don't want to do anything right now. I want to die, basically. Or just to stop existing. I don't even want to expend the effort required to die." She looks anywhere but at Preston so he can't see how close she is, yet again, to crying. It's what she feels like doing; it's what would get her sympathy; it doesn't matter anymore, that professionalism, because they've fucked. Halfway fucked. Or: It doesn't matter, that professionalism, because she has all the power and she doesn't work there anymore. Or: It doesn't matter anymore, that professionalism, because nothing matters when the world is a strange mirror and the day, twisted and refracted, ends so very differently than how anyone could've expected.

Someone knocks at the door. Eliza pushes Preston out of the way, saying "For the love of—" as she careens, unsteady on her feet, toward the peephole. But she changes direction, ends instead with "Oh thank God." She pulls the door open for Suzanne and grabs her by the wrist, pulls her inside.

"Whoa," Suzanne says as Eliza flings her arms around her friend's neck. Suzanne takes the sloshing bottle of whiskey from Eliza's hand and sets it on the coffee table next to the key dish. "You're hammered, that didn't take you very—" Her eyes land on Preston, who is still half naked. Her eyes widen.

Or, her eyes land on Preston, who is still wearing his coat and looking small and confused because he isn't quite sure what his role is, here. And he is so used to being sure. To knowing what should or could be done. To being in charge, ordering folks about, and he hasn't been listened to once this evening.

"Okay," she says. "We're gonna talk about that later." She pushes Eliza away so she can look her in the face; Eliza sways on her feet. "We're gonna make you some coffee, sweetheart, and then we're gonna talk about—"

"They're sending me fish, Suzanne."

"Hm?"

"The internet is sending me death fish."

After Suzanne sits Eliza on the couch and coaxes information out of her, pieces together the fragments and says "oh hell no," or "nope" many times, she takes down the phone number that, even now, is providing a steady drip of eerie '60s music to Eliza's voicemail without ever ringing her phone. Then she texts Devonte because it is the only thing she can think to do.

CHAPTER FIFTY-SIX

Suzanne: Devonte?

Suzanne: Devonte?

Devonte: hold ther fuck on, I'm tracking down this anonymous person i used to know

Suzanne: can you track a phone? like if i gave you a phone number rn?

Devonte: hell no

Suzanne: but you know this code shit

Devonte: it's not the same thing and besides i've got a pretty strong aversion to breaking the law. things don't go well for black dudes who do that and telecomms are straight up evil

Suzanne: i thought everyone learned this stuff by hacking

Devonte: well i went to stanford instead, so

Devonte: but save the number my friend might be able to do something with it

Suzanne: i just googled it, it's a bufffalo ny number

Devonte: congrats, you know more about it than i do, i nominate you the law breaker for this group

Suzanne: tho i suppose it doesn't necessarily mean he's from buffalo, if its one of those prepaid burner things, and like, i would make sure it was a prepaid burner thing

Suzanne: dev do you think he'd be more likely to put a buffalo number if he lives in buffalo? does this mean this little shit is, like, fairly far away from here?

Suzanne: Dev?

Suzanne: Dev?

Devonte: hold the fucking fuck on, i got him

Suzanne: the phone guy??

Devonte: no the hacker

CHAPTER FIFTY-SEVEN

Eliza reaches out and grabs Suzanne's arm, eyes wide. "Wait. How did you get up here?"

"The doorman waved me through," Suzanne says with a shrug.

Preston's eyebrows furrow. "Without calling up first?"

"Well, based on my delivery history for the evening, he probably thought I was having a party," Eliza says. She looks at the whiskey on the table and wishes it was still in her hand. "Never mind that I've never had a party here in my life."

"I'm on it," Preston says. He puts his pants on, then a shirt. Eliza is thankful. Or, he simply walks from the door, having never once taken his coat off.

The instant the door clicks behind him, Suzanne wheels around to Eliza with her eyebrows raised as high as eyebrows can possibly go while remaining attached to a human face. "What the fuck?"

"Should I have told him to be careful? When he left?" Eliza slurs. "Was it weird that I didn't?"

"That's what you're worried about right now? Details, before he gets back. What the fresh hell is going on?"

Eliza shrugs. Her movements feel like a bourbon slushy, all soft and watered and drunk. "I dunno. It just happened. He was just—right there in my face, I dunno."

"Well, like, do you like him?"

"Yes? I mean, he's a good guy. Smart guy."

"Who also just fired you."

"Yes."

"And then tried to rehire you."

"Yes."

"To make himself not look as bad."

"Yes."

"Well okay then, as long we all have our eyes open here."

Or: The instant the door clicks behind him, Suzanne wheels around to Eliza with her eyebrows raised as high as eyebrows can possibly go while remaining attached to a human face. "What the fuck?"

"Listen, he just showed up here! And like, I was already drinking, I am very tired. I didn't have the energy to send him away." She pauses. "Can you do it?" She hiccups.

"He's still my boss! You do it!"

"But you're—you, I dunno, you can always say anything you want and people thank you for it. How do you cultivate that superpower?"

"Why did he say he was here?"

"I think he thinks he's protecting me? I think he feels bad."

"Yeah, no shit, he has manufactured literally every situation you've found yourself hip deep in, at least all the ones in the last seventy-two hours."

"Listen, if I keep him on the hook, I can get something out of this. If he keeps feeling like he made this bad, he'll feel like he owes me."

They both stop talking abruptly when Preston walks back in the door.

Or: The instant the door clicks behind him, Suzanne wheels around to Eliza with her eyebrows raised as high as eyebrows can possibly go while remaining attached to a human face. "What the fuck?"

"I don't know, it's kinda sweet."

"Sweet? He keeps showing up at your house unannounced!"

"Well you showed up at my apartment unannounced."

"I didn't fire you, did I?"

"Listen, I don't super want to be alone when everyone knows my address. It's like I can feel them watching me. It's horrible."

"No doubt, but like, he fired you. He's my boss. Wait." Suzanne puts her hands on her hips again. "You don't like the guy, do you? Like, like like him?"

But before Eliza can answer, the door is creaking open. Instead of using words, she swats Suzanne on the arm.

"He knows," Preston says. "He won't send anyone up, not even a delivery guy." He walks into the kind of silence that only exists after stumbling into a conversation about one's own self. His eyes dart to each one of their faces and he holds his hands at his sides like they are rubber ducks taped onto wrist stumps: awkward, unmovable, weird. What does one do with rubber-duck hands? His feet want to shuffle, but they are as embarrassed as the rest of him. His eyes, having gone to all the reasonable places and found them embarrassing, settle on the ceiling.

"Anything interesting up there, buddy?" Suzanne asks, smirking smugly. Or she ribs, jokingly. She is mean, Suzanne. Or: She is sharp, Suzanne. Or: She is funny, Suzanne.

She's a lot.

"I—er. I— Does anyone want a snack? I can make a snack!" He shoots into the kitchen, and glances, woeful, at the half wall that won't hide him from the women in the living room.

"Well. I don't like talking to pigs, but I don't know what else to do. I'm calling the police," Suzanne says.

"I didn't want to," Eliza protests. "It's been—so much. Plus it's only pizza. Japanese food."

"From the looks of it, also Thai," Preston says, looking out the window, frying pan in hand.

Suzanne's smirk morphs into an openmouthed sneer. "You don't have to call. I will. This shit is creepy."

CHAPTER FIFTY-EIGHT

@theinspectre: do you want a pizza too, @yrface?

@theinspectre: @yrface i bet i can find you

@theinspectre: i havent yet, @yrface, but i will

CHAPTER FIFTY-NINE

\<**d3vgenius:** yo>

\<**d3vgenius:** its devonte>

\<**evrlrnr:** i know>

\<**d3vgenius:** why do i have to chat with you here?>

\<**d3vgenius:** pain in the ass>

\<**d3vgenius:** you have gchat like everyone else>

\<**evrlrnr:** you said you wanted to talk about hacking>

\<**evrlrnr:** i dont do that on gchat>

\<**evrlrnr:** google will just give shit right over to them>

\<**evrlrnr:** did you even read that julian assange thing>

<d3vgenius: they never asked me for anything when i worked there>

<evrlrnr: well they wouldn't have to>

<evrlrnr: they have implicit permission>

<evrlrnr: probably several back doors>

<evrlrnr: googles dirty top to bottom>

<d3vgenius: then why are you still talking to me?>

<evrlrnr: youre the exception>

<evrlrnr: not the rule>

<evrlrnr: now what can i do for you>

<d3vgenius: i have a friend who needs help>

<d3vgenius: she got doxxed today>

<d3vgenius: you mighta heard about it>

<evrlrnr: from your job?>

<d3vgenius: yes>

<evrlrnr: you bet i heard about it>

<evrlrnr: sent over a salmon burger to offer my condolences>

<**d3vgenius:** what?>

<**evrlrnr:** you haven't seen that thread yet?>

<**evrlrnr:** people are sending her fish>

<**d3vgenius:** why?>

<**evrlrnr:** because she's allergic>

<**evrlrnr:** get it?>

<**evrlrnr:** it's funny>

<**d3vgenius:** man, wtf is wrong with you>

<**d3vgenius:** you used to not be this much of an asshole>

<**evrlrnr:** please. this is comedy>

<**d3vgenius:** what happened to you? You're disgusting, man.>

<**evrlrnr:** ah yes, and I suppose you're rolling in pussy?>

<**d3vgenius:** wtf is that supposed to mean?>

<**d3vgenius:** like that's not even related>

<**evrlrnr:** listen, when the dust settles, she'll be drooling at the mouth to please everyone who gave her a hard time>

<**evrlrnr:** that's how women work>

<**evrlrnr:** i'm out here doing it for the culture. shell be easier to handle after this, trust me>

<**d3vgenius:** ho, fuck off>

<**d3vgenius:** i'm out. don't talk to me again.>

<**evrlrnr:** you came and found me, pal>

<**d3vgenius:** YOU ARE NOT HARD TO FIND. YOU LIVE IN THE WORLD. YOU WORK A REAL JOB.>

<**evrlrnr:** before you go>

<**evrlrnr:** tell your buddy preston to be more careful with his location services>

<**d3vgenius:** he's my boss, not my buddy>

<**d3vgenius:** wait, why?>

<**evrlrnr:** because I can tell he's at that chick's apartment rn>

<**evrlrnr:** I won't blow up his spot>

<**evrlrnr:** she's not, like, bad looking, better than a five, so I get it>

<**evrlrnr:** id put it in her>

<**evrlrnr:** but his phone is obvious. the only reason everyone doesn't know by now is because no one is looking at him>

<**d3vgenius:** then why are you?>

<**evrlrnr:** because im a better hacker than everyone else>

<**d3vgenius:** cool. fuck off and never talk to me again>

<d3vgenius is Leaving . . . >

<d3vgenius disconnected from server>

CHAPTER SIXTY

Suzanne: its like the police have never been on the internet

Suzanne: felt like they were two steps from asking me what a twitter was

Suzanne: the only reason they didn't was, like, cnn puts our new presidents tweets on the news

Suzanne: never forget, the police are white nationalists. theres been studies

Suzanne: devonte?

Suzanne: you cant be asleep already its early

Suzanne: they wont take a report over the phone

Suzanne: they need her to come down to the precinct to do it

Devonte: sorry, feeling weird. like scattered.

Devonte: preaching to the choir re: white nationalists

Devonte: dont go tonight

Suzanne: well no shit

Suzanne: people showing up here in the dark

Suzanne: imma stay here, even

Devonte: ill meet you tomorrow we'll do it tomorrow just, like, let me chill tonight

Suzanne: k

CHAPTER SIXTY-ONE

Have we mentioned it is almost Christmas? Usually, Eliza loves Christmas, especially Christmas in New York City. Any other year, if she'd had a day free like this, she'd go for a walk in Central Park and pretend carriage horses weren't being treated cruelly as she watched them clop by. She'd wear her fancy coat and a faux fur muff and she'd stroll about by herself, pretending to be in a different era. She'd maybe Instagram one photo for us and resist posting a million more of her beautiful day, her beautiful life.

She'd come out by the shops—look in the windows at Bergdorf Goodman, Saks. She'd go into Tiffany's and lament that she didn't have a reason to buy herself a necklace or a bracelet or something pretty. But she'd go in just the same because everything about the inside of Tiffany's felt like Christmas, gilded with red-and-gold ribbon and smelling of pine. She'd pop into the glass cube Apple store and play on computers, installing things at the command line and futzing around, even before she'd taught herself to code in earnest. Coding is the closest thing to having magic. You know the right words and you can make things happen. (That's what she used to think; so naive.) Perhaps she'd buy Christmas gifts. Perhaps she'd buy one for herself.

Today, though, we find her filing a police report instead of doing any of that. Preston leaves in the early hours to go home, shower and get dressed for work. Eliza is surprised he doesn't want to come to the police station, given how insistent he was the night before. But she realizes with a jolt that he can't be seen missing work to file a police report with her, and certainly not this early in the morning. It dawns on her, slow, like the coffee is kicking in sluggish: no one can know he spent the night. No one who doesn't already, at least.

Devonte shows up with bags under his eyes, something ill or haunted in his face.

Suzanne hasn't looked at him but two seconds before she asks, "Are you okay?"

"I'm fine," he says.

"Shouldn't you be at work?" Eliza says. "Shouldn't you both be at work?" She hasn't eaten breakfast, barely slept for a second. Preston had been there, hot as a space heater or a napping dog. Eliza stared into the darkness, wondering what Suzanne was thinking on her couch. She'd spent the long hours wishing desperately for a baseball bat.

"I called in sick," he says, and he puts air quotes around it. It's not as though they won't know where he actually is. It's not as though we don't know where he actually is.

While Eliza talks to the receptionist, or whatever one calls the officer who sits at the front desk of a police station, Suzanne pulls Devonte aside. Eliza is aware of it, but dimly. Background noise in comparison.

"Your person?" she asks. "Your hacker?" She drops her volume so the word "hacker" is mouthed.

Devonte sets his mouth in a line so severe his lips all but disappear. He shakes his head. "Won't help."

Suzanne tilts her head to the side but doesn't press, not here. They turn their attention to the thick, bald police officer with a tattoo of New York State on his neck. "But do we know where they are? Do we have physical locations for these people?"

"No, they're sending me messages on Twitter." Eliza hands over printed screenshots. "This one says he wants to behead me." She points to the paper as his eyebrows furrow. "This one says he wants to post an ad on Craigslist asking someone to come rape me."

"Do we know who these people are?" the police officer asks, his face puckering up like he's bitten a lemon. "These look like fake names. Who is actually harassing you?"

"I don't know what their names are in real life, Officer"—she squints at his name, the tag printed clean and rigid on his left breast pocket—"Hunt. These are screennames."

"We would need names, at the very least, to file a report."

"What about a phone number?" Devonte pipes up from behind Eliza. "She has a phone number too."

"These people have called you?" Officer Hunt is interested, leans forward. "What did they say?"

"They left me a recording of 'They're Coming to Take Me Away.'"

"Is that another internet thing?" Officer Hunt asks, his eyes unfocusing and staring at the wall behind Eliza.

"No. It's a song. Do you want to hear it? I haven't deleted any of them."

Eliza pulls out her phone and plays a few bars, listening to the voice rise in pitch like it's filled with helium. Goosebumps erupt on her skin. The word for that, we know, is "horripilate." The erection of hairs on the skin due to cold, fear or excitement. Which is it, Eliza? We want to know. She taps the pause button on her phone.

Officer Hunt shakes his head. "We don't know what that means. It's creepy as fuck—pardon my French, ladies—but technically not a threat."

"But it is!" Suzanne can't keep silent anymore. "She told me on G-chat that the song freaks her out. It's a threat."

"What's G-chat?"

Suzanne purses her lips, tries to lock a sigh inside her lest it escape and ruin the chances for a police report. "It's an online chatting service. You type to each other and have a conversation. It's not public, not like Twitter. He hacked into her account and got the conversation—"

But the officer shakes his head again. "It doesn't directly threaten her. Listen," he says. "You can file a police report right now, this stuff is harassment regardless. But with an unknown perpetrator we'll have to close the report right away."

So she does. Eliza fills out every piece of paperwork they give her. Devonte runs to the bathroom to splash water on his face—he hasn't slept well, and he is tired. Suzanne types on her phone, her fingers moving frenetically, bumping letters and numbers she doesn't intend. "How to track phone." Or, "how to track phone number only." Or, "how to hack." Or, "how to exorcise spectres."

CHAPTER SIXTY-TWO

Preston goes to work on Sunday as if he isn't familiar with Eliza's plight or her body or her apartment mess. He knows calling in sick isn't an option, and that if everyone is working overtime, he must do the same. Christmas is coming, and the already-established marketing plan for the holiday season needs to be changed in response to the situation. And there's Brandon's personal investigation of who leaked the records. And, of course, the Vive. We suspect that, with all else going on, virtual reality is an afterthought for Preston, but certainly not for Fancy Dog. It is finally settling down—more and more of us are posting play-throughs, videos, reviews of *Guilds of the Protectorate* on Vive as the beta list grows and grows—Eliza is no longer the only press Fancy Dog is getting. It only took a few days to catch up. The verdict is in: we love it. It's amazing. All the locomotion problems somehow smoothly solved. Those who can fly feel like they're flying; those who run at superspeed watch the world blur by; those who shape-shift change size and height and perspective. It is, in short, creation. A whole new world, a whole new plane of existence.

What's insane, truly, and all of us agree on this, is that life—human existence—is completely different after the Vive announcement; everything. And that's not an exaggeration. Perhaps people in the larger world, the "real" world, don't think so because it's a game. But we are literally seeing another planet created. It's like Aslan making Narnia over here. We cannot stress enough how important this is. And how strange it is to be watching anything else. But it is the human way to stare at strife, to speculate and construct and talk until we could take off with the buoyancy of our own hot air. But we digress. And see how strange it is to consider what is perhaps the biggest game changer of the decade, of the century, a digression. The small versus the big; human drama versus history made.

Preston Instagrams the erroneous name on his Starbucks coffee cup—Peter—with the comment, "I come here literally every day. Sometimes twice or three times. #theyrefuckingwithusonpurpose." He thinks he is pretty funny and is smiling when he walks into his glass office. When he finds Brandon sitting in a chair by the window, his smile evaporates. We should come up with a different word. "Evaporates" sounds like something gradual. This is instantaneous—a smile, then not-a-smile. Binary.

"The investigation's finished. You aren't going to like it," Brandon says.

"I know I'm not going to like it. It doesn't matter who it is, it's internal, it's one of my—" He stops his sentence short, eyeing his glass wall. He frowns. "Perhaps we should go somewhere else to talk about this."

Brandon's mouth jumps to one side. He is so twitchy. It's no wonder his hair is grey. "Why?"

"People tend to—know things. After I talk about them in here."

"So? Let them know. Transparency." Brandon pauses and clears his throat. "Besides, they'll know soon enough anyway."

"Just let me get coffee in my mouth, okay? Don't fuck over my day yet, it's too early." Preston does his best to slow down and sip coffee, to breathe, to let the tension out of his face. But Brandon doesn't look out the window or leave the office, as would be the polite response to Preston's request. He focuses his eyes directly on his co-founder and drums the windowsill with his fingers, one at a time. It makes Preston jumpy. Jumpier.

Brandon didn't use to be like this. He used to be fun. Shy, quiet, sure, but still a person who could drink a PBR in a seven-person-college-house garage, fantasizing about what his future would be and arguing the finer points of digital narrative, game design. He used to be the kind of friend Preston could rustle up with a minute's notice, knock on his door at any time and propose anything, from lunch at the university student center to starting an entire, world-changing company. And Brandon, a person who gets things done, would smile and put a paperback book in his back jeans pocket, and say, "I'm down. Let's go." Calm. Collected. Optimistic. An easy smile and forward momentum at a steady pace. Now he's a butt.

Preston finally turns toward Brandon, unable to finish his coffee. It is close enough. "Okay. Who is it?"

"One of your developers. One of your favorites. We found the files on his computer. Didn't even delete them." Brandon smirks. "Didn't even make it hard for me. I thought I was going to be here all night. Hell, all week. I thought, we have a company full of computer people here, but I suppose they're just as dumb as us business boys."

He slides a folder across Preston's desk. Preston looks down at the manila tab. The name on the folder, as we have guessed, is Jean-Pascale Desfrappes.

CHAPTER SIXTY-THREE

It's Sunday, the day of Eliza's appearance on *Last Week Tonight*. And she is nervous. She hasn't slept at all—is being destroyed by an internet mob really as newsworthy as making a game or writing a book? she wonders. She's just been shat on pretty hard by the internet; she knows it might be interesting, but it feels strange to her. Upsetting on top of upsetting. John Oliver, or his producers, know about our obsession with this drama, want to feed it. Our appetite, a hunger, to lay eyes on her, to hear her words, to laud her or rip her apart in response; we will shred her. The buzz is out: Gamergate, the harbinger of American "fascism." Lol. We are now a sought-after demographic, and in turn, so is she, this antagonist. It almost doesn't matter what she says; it almost doesn't matter what we think of her. What we want is to put our eyes on her, to possess her, to be involved. We want to know everything. And everyone wants to know everything about us.

More than a few times she wonders if John Oliver is going to make fun of her—he is a comedian, after all. His entire show is satire. Is her situation funny? She still can't access her bank account. No one can email her. The Tumblr with photoshopped pornography continues to multiply like worms, reblog after reblog, while Tumblr takes its time to decide if it violates anything. So far, the company hasn't taken it down. Is this funny ha-ha? Is this funny in the sense we (humans, not us specifically) make better zoo subjects than animals, with our messy contradictions and our mistakes? Eliza doesn't know. But she is pretty certain that if she doesn't do something about all this, she'll crumple into a ball and do nothing forever. So *Last Week Tonight* it is.

CHAPTER SIXTY-FOUR

This is what Jean-Pascale looks like after getting fired from his dream job: his nose is swollen, his eyes still bruised from falling face-first to the floor earlier in the week. He comes home and lies down in bed, a deflated version of his former self. He doesn't bother to turn on the lights; he doesn't have the oomph to get up and pull the shades down. He doesn't take his clothes off. He doesn't get under the covers. Instead, he lies there on his back as the light changes in the room hour by hour. Different shadows grow to monstrous sizes and shrink, their reign of terror over. Squares of light from the windows morph shapes on the walls as his watch clicks softly from his wrist, a metronome for his mourning. He wonders why he still has a watch—he just looks at his phone anyway, he can't remember the last time he'd shaken his sleeve off his wrist to look at the time. It occurs to him that everyone does that—an entire generation has reverted to pocket watches.

Delphine comes home with Trader Joe's paper bags full of vegetables she can't get from the Greenmarket in the winter. By now, it is dark and Jean-Pascale hasn't told her what happened. He wonders if his firing is being reported on the internet yet. Perhaps, he thinks, he's already been made into a snappy headline and Delphine has read it. Or not, it is a Sunday, after all. If she doesn't read the headline, if neither of them do, does the headline exist? We see it when it happens, weekend or not. It exists for us.

He doesn't sit up or shout for her to come in so he can tell her the bad news. He lets the dark darken while she cooks dinner; the smell of lemon and olive oil fills the apartment. He can hear her mouth snap on carrots while she clunks a wooden spoon against several pots. He hears the soft "hm" when she, he presumes, looks at her phone and realizes what time it is. Realizes he isn't home yet, when he might normally be. Realizes dinner will soon be done.

He is suddenly overwhelmed with the simultaneous desires to see and not see Eliza appear on *Last Week Tonight*. It feels like half of his body tries to tear away, to get up, while the other half becomes more stubborn, more leaden. He fights himself like that for a while.

He hears Delphine make a noise in the back of her throat—her exasperation call. Despite himself, Jean-Pascale grins. Perhaps this is what it's like to be finely attuned to a child's cries, something he has never experienced before.

His phone begins to ring, but not where Delphine expects it to be. It is in his pocket. "What the—?" Delphine says, as she comes into the bedroom with her phone pressed to her ear. Her forehead shows wrinkles—Jean-Pascale knows her confusion must be acute, for she normally tries not to move her face too much when she isn't acting. She flicks on the light.

"Honey, what's wrong? Are you sick?" She sits down on the bed. Jean-Pascale gets angry, which he knows is ridiculous. But he can't believe she assumed he was awake. What if he'd been sleeping? She would have woken him up.

He manages to punch through the anger. Probably because what he says next makes him so sad—like throwing water on his internal fire and watching it sizzle out. "I'm not sick," he says. "I'm fired." He curls up and faces the wall with the windows. He doesn't hear the things Delphine is saying over the buzz in his own head, over the white paint he fixes his eyes on. He is aware that she is rubbing his back, but it isn't really at the forefront of his consciousness.

"…that bitch…" she says at one point. "What are we…" he hears, a fragment cracking against the silence; "…don't worry, I'm sure…" He isn't even trying to hold on to her sentences. He doesn't find them meaningful just now. And frankly we can't be assed to make up the rest of them. If he isn't interested, neither are we.

He eventually sits up. "Can I eat?" he asks. She nods, aware that he hasn't responded to anything she's said. Jean-Pascale drags himself to the kitchen to serve himself carrot salad and homemade veggie burgers. He eats while having a staring contest with the remote. The remote wins.

When he is finished, he checks his email. There are six messages from Lewis Fleishman. Jean-Pascale swipes all of them, one by one, into the trash while thinking how good it would feel to put them into a real garbage can instead of a digital one. The last new message is—

"I got offered a job," he says. His eyes are wide. He grabs his own curls with both hands like he used to do when he was little and loud noises startled him.

"What?" Delphine starts laughing, smiling big. "That's amazing. You haven't even been on the market a whole day."

"'I understand how things can get blown out of proportion,'" he reads aloud from his computer screen. "'I don't want your life to be ruined by some stupid prank and some overblown publicity stunt. Your work must be good—Fancy Dog wouldn't have hired you otherwise. Consider yourself head hunted, my man. I'd be honored to have you down to the New York City branch of Phasix Studio as early as tomorrow morning so we can give each other a try.'" By the end of the sentence, Jean-Pascale's lip is curled up of its own volition. He hasn't processed the emotion entirely, and he doesn't know where it's coming from, but he can name it: disgust. Or he thinks perhaps the world he knows, loves, just isn't built for him anymore and wonders if he should pick another career.

Delphine interprets his thinking, his weighing, and says, "Okay, so it's not quite a job offer. But hey, that's a really solid interview or trial period or something! That's a really solid something. Nothing to feel bad about there."

Instead of responding to either Delphine or the email, Jean-Pascale pushes himself away from the table, goes back to the bedroom and lies down again. He does not speak once before falling into restless sleep.

CHAPTER SIXTY-FIVE

Preston can't decide about watching *Last Week Tonight*. He'd never been on this show, but he liked the experience of going on *The Daily Show* as much as he could have at the time. He thinks perhaps he forgot to truly enjoy himself, to savor it. But he pushes that away. The idea that he is missing something he can't get back scares him.

In the end, he clicks on the interview just in time to hear John Oliver say, "...you know. It's my job to make fun of the news, I'm a comedian. But—" He pauses in that signature John Oliver way, where we can sense him taking a big breath because he is about to race-shout through several sentences at once. His hands pushed against the top of his desk, his entire body pointing toward the camera. John Oliver lets out his string of words, like machine-gun fire or the speedy banter from old movies: "I can't really make any of these threats into something funny—"

He turns the television off before he knows what he's doing, before John Oliver inevitably gets to the punch line, his awe and anger made somehow funnier by the posh British accent. Preston tries to will himself to push the little red button, to hear what Oliver will say next, how Eliza will respond. He can't do it. He thinks he could've been on there with her; she could've been rehired, there could have been a redemption story here. Or: She was always going to use this to get her fifteen minutes, that worthless slut. Or: He is pining, he's fucked, he's cucked, he's lost. Instead of watching, he walks in circles around his almost-empty living room. He thinks perhaps he'll play *Guilds*, but then he is struck by the realization that he hasn't played—really played, not just tested something—in months. That isn't the most surprising part of his epiphany, though. For Preston, the strangest thing about it is the realization that he doesn't want to.

CHAPTER SIXTY-SIX

They have a woman named Aisha on here too, this feminist game critic," Mrs. Fleishman says as she shovels Cap'n Crunch into her mouth, sitting on the couch in front of the television. "God, he just keeps calling all these women out. They're sitting on risers, there's so many— Lewis, you can't tell me this has happened to all of these people?"

"Ma. I don't want to talk about it." Lewis stands in his living room. When he realizes his mother is home, he tries to change course to his bedroom, to email Jean-Pascale again, when he freezes, staring at the program his mother's watching on his big screen.

"I can't really make any of these threats into something funny. I'm not talking about everyday internet abuse, of which I'm more than aware. I'm talking about the kind of direct threats that make people fear for their safety. And if you think that doesn't sound like that big of an issue, congratulations on your white penis." The audience roars as he continues his spiel, as tweets, Facebook posts and Reddit threads all begin to rapidly flash in that false floating box over his right shoulder. All the women in the audience scream with laughter; it's so shrill. What a disappointment. "Because if you have one of those, you probably have a very different experience on the internet than our guests today." The audience applauds. "Please welcome—"

But we're not paying attention to John Oliver. Instead, we imagine

Lewis's face, his mouth open like a Nutcracker. He doesn't want to hear the rest of the broadcast but he can't seem to make himself walk to his bedroom, shut the door. "Ma," he says, wanting her to look away from the television. "I think you should turn it off, you don't really like the technology stuff anyway."

Mrs. Fleishman's hair is in rollers—she is a young mom, only at the tail end of her forties. She has an array of red lipsticks on the coffee table in front of her, to be decided on and applied when she's finished her cereal. She wears a dress—a bright navy blue with repeating white anchors. It is too bright for winter and certainly too bright for New York City, but when Lewis pointed this out to her upon its purchase, she'd snorted and said, "Like I give a fuck." Lewis always hates the classic New York–ness of the way she says "like." It sounds like "loike." He's battled that pronunciation his entire life.

Mrs. Fleishman's red high heels are resting, upright and waiting, next to the couch. Lewis turns a little crimson—his mother is going on a date. Judging from the cereal, she isn't quite certain about the restaurant choice. "Thai food," she's said sometime in the past, "I could take it or leave it." Lewis blushes deeper at remembering that, in his mother's pronunciation lexicon, "Thai" and "like" almost rhyme. He gets angry and swallows, scratching at his neck. As an adult, Lewis has tried to talk his mother out of dating on several occasions, each of which has been unsuccessful.

Mrs. Fleishman lifts a well-tweezed eyebrow. "They've said your name on this show. You better believe I'm watching it." The space above where Lewis thinks his stomach is starts burning. "Your friend Jean-Pascale," she continues. "He was fired today." She points at the screen with her dripping spoon. "I can't say I don't think he deserved it."

Lewis runs through several responses in his head: of course she thinks he deserved it—the mainstream media always makes white men the villains. Or, Jean-Pascale absolutely did not deserve to be fired and you know absolutely nothing about it, don't fucking talk about shit you don't know. Or, yes, he did deserve to be fired, but not for the reasons they're saying here. He chooses instead to say nothing. He makes a mental note, as he does every day, to kick his mother out of his apartment, and he finally wrenches himself away from the television, from his mother, and closes the door to his bedroom. Puts headphones on.

We should focus on Mrs. Fleishman for the thirty seconds after her son leaves the living room. She puts her bowl and spoon down because her hands begin shaking and she thinks perhaps she'll drop them. She touches her own face, her own forehead, and she wonders what to do about her son; she's wondered that many times in her life, some of us think. And she did not expect to have to wonder it in his adulthood. She wonders what she's done wrong. Others of us, we think she's cruel; she hasn't thought about her son much at all. If she'd only done something before this, something for him, perhaps he wouldn't do what he does. Lewis Fleishman, what becomes of him, is her fault.

CHAPTER SIXTY-SEVEN

Preston finds himself standing outside Eliza's building after the *Last Week Tonight* broadcast he didn't watch, mere hours after firing Jean-Pascale. He is about to simply go up, tell the doorman, but within steps of the entrance he realizes how insane he's being, not asking first yet again, and he ducks into a café, texts her.

"Mind if I drop by?" he types out as he juggles between apps so he can pay with Apple Pay. Swipe, check, done. Receipt email. He now has coffee and a scone, slightly stale from the day. He checks his cup—no name to Instagram.

"Sure," pops up in a white bubble. "But I'm not home yet." The messages are careful. They are spelled properly, punctuated. We can't tell what that means. Trying to impress? Angry? Wary? Aware she's being observed? Doesn't actually want to see him? It grows later, darker. The city begins to shimmer with cold rain as only December can provide. The café doesn't close. His coffee grows cold, but he doesn't feel like making another purchase, so he nurses it nonetheless.

He watches as she gets out of a black car—did they call her a car service?—and enters the building. She stumbles a bit. Of course, he would have gone out for dinner and drinks with the rest of them too, if he were in her place. It was probably a good interview. It probably required celebration. She probably didn't want to watch the broadcast, and why would she? She's living it.

"How about now?" he types, after a safe amount of time.

"Sure—I'll be showered by the time you get here."

She expects him to be at work or at home, like a normal person. He sips his coffee. He doesn't feel the need to tell her he's across the street, that he saw her only moments ago, just as we saw her moments ago. He plays a game on his phone. He shuts the game. He flips his phone over. He wonders how long it usually takes him to get here. It feels like he's been coming here forever, like the past few days have each contained within them an entire revolution around the sun. How long should he sit and pretend he is en route? His scone is aggressively mediocre; he chews it anyway, counting to one hundred and counting to one hundred again.

Why is he here? We're not sure he knows, exactly. Booty? To rehire her, try again? Jealousy at her television appearance? A need to be in proximity to her as she blazes, white hot, with the heat of our attention? The base need to try and save her from the many-headed monster that is us? That last is too mean for Preston; we are his people.

Finally, he approaches the doorman, who buzzes him up. He is about to knock on the door when it opens. He almost knocks Eliza right in the face, right in the mouth. "I got a job," she says, unfazed by the fist so close to the end of her nose. "Or at least"—she turns away and leads him in, toward her computer—"an interview? I have something."

She sits on her couch. Preston stands, not moving into her apartment any farther than he has to. He shuts the door behind him and he almost forgets to lock it (stupid!). Her smallness reminds him and he turns to click the deadbolt.

"Here's part of it," she continues, not noticing he hasn't stepped past the entrance, past the little square mat immediately beyond the threshold: "'We saw you on Last Week Tonight and believe what happened to you at Fancy Dog was morally reprehensible. We're impressed with the VR drop and know you were critical to that patch going through. We'd be honored to fly you out to sunny Santa Cruz to interview you' blah blah blah self-contained project blah." Her eyes skim down the page as she holds a wine glass up to her lips. "You know that project's going to take more than ninety days," she mutters. "Oh hey, 'A little bit about us,'" she keeps reading to Preston. "'Fifty percent of our four vice presidents are women, as is one of the co-founders, so nonsense like—'"

"Okay, stop," Preston says. How dare she! How brazen, how hurtful! He hops a tiny bit forward, like he wants to rush in and cover her mouth with his hand, but he doesn't shout.

"What, Preston, I'm only reading you what these people at"—Eliza squints—"See No Monkey Studios sent m—"

"Oh great, 'See No Monkey.' What a stupid name."

"God, Preston, I—" But Eliza stops. She isn't sure how she feels, or how she means to finish the sentence. We try a couple endings out for her:—was seeing if you believed I didn't know See No Monkey is one of your biggest competitors?—was genuinely excited?—wanted to try to get you to leave and stop coming here? She isn't sure which is the true sentence ending; we aren't sure they all aren't true at the same time. It is getting harder and harder to separate, to use ||, the "or" operator that we love so much. Perhaps that is the lesson we are supposed to be learning: people, even those we deem titans or villains or tragic heroes, are soup.

Preston, however, knows much more about his feelings in this moment. "Did it occur to you that I wouldn't want to hear this?" He lets the tension out of his face and sits next to her on the couch. "Look, my offer still stands. I still want to rehire you."

"Even after—?" Eliza's question dies midthought.

"Yes, even after—" Preston feels silly saying it and he feels silly not saying it. Or it's not about sex at all (but it's definitely about sex). "Look, we could figure that out." His face is very close to hers again.

Eliza is drunk, like last time. Her phone is still buzzing. She switches it off. "Could we though? Could we really?" She doesn't move her face back.

"I'm sure we could." He kisses her. He is angry and he is kissing her. "We built a whole world, after all," he says when he comes up for air.

They do finish, this time. They down a bottle of wine while waiting the requisite amount of time, and finish again. He falls asleep, neither one talking about the job even though it is on the tip of Eliza's tongue. Once again, she lies sleepless. Everything is cold and scary here; "Sunny Santa Cruz" doesn't sound like a bad option. She wants to talk it all out with him, the thoughts that are bouncing around in her head like so many rubber balls. They give her a headache but still she doesn't say anything; she doesn't want to see his face tense up again. Or she wants to play her cards right, get the most money, the most advantageous position possible. Or Preston is on the couch, and none of this happened. Or she falls asleep. We can still use the || operator, after all.

CHAPTER SIXTY-EIGHT

I t is around six in the morning and she thinks she's dreaming. A hollow *pok pok pok* echoes in the hallway. It sounds distant and she doesn't want to wake up. It might not even be real, and she's only sunk into sleep two hours prior. Eliza curls herself into Preston's side; he takes up so much space in the bed, and her semi-sleeping brain can't decide if she should shrink to fit or grow in protest. Or she spreads all her limbs out like a starfish, hogging the whole bed from no one because no one will ever fuck her. She falls back into unconsciousness.

When she wakes, she smells breakfast. She has the sudden urge to wrap herself in her bedsheets instead of getting dressed. Just like they always do in the movies. Like they're modest. Like they're wearing togas. She does this, because why not? Why not perform a little when everyone is looking at you? She glances at herself in her mirror and frowns. She is far from looking like a movie star and she blushes deeply, her shoulders and collarbones turning red along with her face; starlets never look like they're drowning in their own bedding. Starlets have perfect teeth, gums that don't look like bones covered in a thin sheet of skin. She turns away and heads into her living room. Preston is fully dressed, ready to leave. "Watcha makin'?" she asks.

"Bacon," he rhymes, and they both smile.

"It's fake bacon, you know," she says, listening to the limp sizzle that heralds tempeh.

"Oh, it's impossible not to know. I am deeply aware that this isn't real bacon." They are silent for a little while. Eliza is served eggs, toast and facon. It's nice. She never would have made the tempeh for herself. It would have sat in her freezer for a long time before she admitted it was never going to get eaten, or until she moved. To Sunny Santa Cruz, maybe.

"Did you watch it?" she asks. It's on HBO Go, after all. She would have canceled her account, except canceling things is just as difficult as getting credit card information back.

Preston shakes his head. Eliza is disappointed. We think it is excusable that he hasn't watched. We wouldn't either. It is impossible to watch people think you're wrong and say so publicly to the tune of applause. We're keeping tabs for him, so he doesn't need to.

"I'm going to do the interview with See No Monkey."

Preston's grip tightens on his fork, but he tries his best. "How much are they offering you?"

"Offering me? It's just an interview, people don't offer money when you're at this stage—well, maybe they do for you. But honestly, it's not about the number, whatever it winds up being. It's about the chance to just—not be here anymore."

Preston frowns as if he is imitating a frown. It seems too deep to be honest. "Okay, look. Just promise me you won't take an offer until I've had a chance to try, okay?"

Eliza wants to ask, "Try what? Try to hire me? Date me?" And we would like to know as well. Instead: "You're going to get ketchup on your shirt"—she points at the fork. It is dangling eggs dipped in red. She shivers. Ketchup on eggs looks barbaric. Let's pause here—we can't quite imagine her inflection. Is it sweet, the way Delphine would talk to Jean-Pascale? Simpering, fake, the sonic equivalent of an exaggerated pout? Is it thin, hard, sarcastic? A way to point out a flaw, however small, in this great man who volunteers to protect her, even if the threat is imaginary?

Preston checks his phone. "I have to go. To work," he clarifies. "Christmas marketing waits for no man." He does not mention the PR nightmare; he wants to pretend it will not be a substantial part of his day.

Preston shoves the last two bites of his eggs into his mouth, leaves all his tempeh save for one attempt at a bite and plods to the door, opens it. Eliza isn't facing him when he opens the door, pauses briefly and then slams it. She jumps at the sound. "Nope," he states, his voice wavering even as he tries to cram it down, repress this sign of weakness. He opens the door just enough to poke his head out and looks both ways down the hall. "Nope. Nope." He slams the door again.

Or. Or it all could've gone this way: Eliza is still sleeping as Preston is trying to sneak away. She is still tangled in bedsheets, now more ensconced since he got up. Or he rises from the couch and brushes his teeth with his finger, not having planned to stay over because they aren't fucking, but still trying to be a knight in shining armor. A superhero. Still convinced his presence is a shield. Perhaps no breakfast is had by anyone. Perhaps no sex is had by anyone. Perhaps they both want to have sex and don't. Perhaps they fuck until the wee hours and now they're exhausted, energy sapped, unprepared for the rest of their days, their lives, spending their life force on something so fucking trivial. Get back to making our game, you absolute losers!

One thing is for certain. In the moment Preston opens the door, he's alone with it. He has to make a decision. He hesitates, unsure of what to do. He shakes his hands as if they're wet or made of spiders. Too slow, too slow, his body throbs even though the danger isn't real! We wouldn't actually hurt them. Come on now; Eliza is out of her fucking mind if she thinks we would cross that line, even with her, as much as she's the fucking worst. Preston is probably catching all his fear from her. Finally: he runs to the bedroom and heaves her from bed, dead weight, and he is strong in a way he doesn't expect but is running on adrenaline and so remarks at this with some distant part of himself. Or he runs across the apartment and grabs her body off the kitchen stool, sheet and all. She is yanked to her feet. Wherever she is scooped from, we can hear exactly the way she reacts in our heads. "Preston, what the fuck?" Eliza says.

"Nope. We're leaving. Nope." His voice is getting higher, louder, shoutier. She sits back, resists being pulled further. "What's going on?" From her perspective, Preston looks insane. But we know what's going on inside Preston's head, even though she doesn't. Picture his thoughts like a circuit board; his mind is usually very organized. But an electrified pulse of terror surges when he sets his eyes on it, and now his circuits can only communicate a wordless, thoughtless flight response. Where he has worked so hard to be rational, now everything is flooded. No longer capable of sensical communication, he slings her over his shoulder and carries her toward the door. "Preston, what are you doing? Stop, I don't have clothes on!"

Eliza starts to feel burning fear drop into her stomach, the same feeling induced by the helium-affected voice in the song. Eliza's fear feels so different, less like it will flood her sense of self or the way she thinks, and more like something terrible she's eaten. Indigestion. Bodily. Perhaps because she hasn't seen it yet. Or because women aren't intellectual in the same way.

It is very apparent that Preston isn't slinging her over his shoulder to be romantic, to take her to the bedroom. He grips her tight and his entire body is one white-knuckled fist, and he is clenching on to her out of terror. "Preston, what's wrong, what's—what are you doing? Put me down!" She doesn't expect him to be able to lift her like this, but in a strange, logical part of her head responding to all this insanity, she supposes he can. He's much bigger than she is.

"You're not staying here" is all he manages to blurt out. He is breathless, from carrying her or from fear. Or both.

"Preston, put me down, put me down," she says again and again as she feels his body open the door once more. She slaps his shoulder a few times with a flat palm, not wanting to hurt him but hoping to startle him into coherence. "Preston, I am an adult person, I can walk or run out of here on my own after I put some damn clothes on, just fucking tell me what—" And then she is in the hall, looking back at her own door and coughing as his shoulder digs into her stomach.

At first, she thinks it is a Barbie. Just a Barbie, naked and nailed to her door. *Pok, pok, pok,* she remembers. Her eyes trace its feet, pointed but flexed at the toes in a perpetual approximation of high-heeled contortion. Up to its waist, so tiny as to look permanently and unrealistically corseted. Nipple-less breasts, as neutered as the smooth plastic between her legs. Barbie's shape when she is wearing clothes is ideal, most definitely. Seeing a naked Barbie, however, is disturbing. With pride, she thinks that Circuit Breaker surely has nipples and a vagina, until she remembers that she definitely knows Circuit Breaker does. She's witnessed the violation.

Up to the swanlike neck, and that's where she thinks the doll ends. Headless. But no, not quite, for there is still brown hair. Eliza wonders where one can get a brown-haired Barbie doll—is it still called Barbie when it isn't blonde, or does it have some other name? A red carnation is—what?—nailed over its face? That's what holds it to the door, the same thing that obstructs—no, no. The face is cut away almost lovingly, the edges are so smooth, carefully curved, carved like waves, and the flower is stuffed into the now-obvious void.

We want her to scream, but she doesn't because Preston's shoulder is still digging into her diaphragm. Or she doesn't because the fear is too much. It is choking her, this thing that she is swallowing, that's stuffing itself down her throat. She forgets she has a mouth; forgets she has a face. She is only trying to stomach it. Only a helpless girl slung over a shoulder. Or she is not scared at all. A lizard person, feelingless. Scream, you bitch. We want you to scream. It's how this kind of story goes.

The doorman looks at the odd couple, his brow furrowed. He puts his hands up to perhaps push the sheet back onto Eliza—it is slipping; we know from the security cameras. From the photo we are sharing over and over, replicating like a virus. Eliza scrambles to cover her almost-exposed chest, but each of Preston's too-quick steps smashes and jostles her. As he runs through the door, the sheet bursts out behind them and billows, like a superhero cape, in the cold December wind. The sunlight springs through it and she is an Athena. Or an Artemis. Or a Venus. Or a girl, rat-faced and terrified, drowning in a sheet.

A shutter click. The sound a phone makes when a photo is snapped. Gorgeous, gorgeous. A swooning, skinny woman. Bare-breasted, looking up at the building. A terrified CEO pushing her, and her body bending like a tree in a storm, about to break but still—supple enough. Here is their first intersection with The Inspectre in meatspace, where three bodies pass each other, almost colliding. But no one sees him. No one sees him, yet we all know he's there. He uploads the image, the art, to 4chan. To Reddit. Tweets it. He walks away.

CHAPTER SIXTY-NINE

Here is a partial list of things that happen right after Eliza and Preston find the faceless doll:

From the cab, Preston calls the police. They agree to search the apartment, the building, to make sure no one is still there.

He also calls the super, who questions the doorman. He provides a list of who he's let in that morning: a locked-out resident for whom he can vouch; a Fresh Direct delivery to apartment 2F; a Con Edison meter reader. We know Con Edison sent no such person. They do not. No one checks.

Preston stashes Eliza in his minimalist apartment, lends her clothes. He tweets something about oversleeping his alarm. He goes to work and tells her not to leave. He walks out of his apartment, leaving her to steep in her bewilderment. There is almost nothing here. A couch. A television, large and mounted to the wall. A bed. The computer. How does anyone live like this? she thinks. We know it's about a clean mind, a slate for ideas, a font for his own creativity. There's no art. There's barely a surface to sit on. But the windows—he's on the top floor and the slanted roof is made entirely of glass. She stands in borrowed sweats and surveys the Flatiron District. Preston's building is high but not too high. She watches people moving below, on the street. She wants to walk around, resents Preston for giving her orders. She doesn't work for him anymore. He can't boss her around.

She settles onto the couch, snuggles up with Dog. Dog always looks some mixture of sad and confused, even as his tail betrays his happiness. She finds it amazing how small a ball he can curl into. He snuffles his nose into her lap; such a good boy. While Eliza isn't a stranger, she is not a fixture in this apartment, and yet Dog welcomes her with open paws. Eliza almost emails See No Monkey to schedule a flight out. She almost logs on to Todoist to add "purchase new dumb phone" to her daily tasks, but she changes her mind. She is paranoid, but not without reason. We could probably see the task if she'd just enter it; we own her accounts now. But she has learned, and so quickly too. She grabs instead a piece of paper and a pen, both difficult to find in the non-clutter that is Preston's apartment. This is the point at which she screams. Not the kind we want. It's angry, like a raging barbarian. It is not being able to find a simple pen and paper that unlocks this primal yell. If she could be in her own space, she would be able to find it. But instead she's in a strange, soulless apartment, with none of her things around her, not one ounce of comfort. It's like trying to live in someone else's brain. Good. Good that she feels she can't go back. This is the kind of thing we want her to feel.

She receives a series of direct messages on Twitter:

> **@franglais:** hey, so i know you don't want to hear from me right now.
>
> **@franglais:** i wouldnt either if i were you
>
> **@franglais:** but do you want to grab coffee?
>
> **@franglais:** i have some apologizing to do

For most of the day, Eliza isn't going to respond to these messages, which is a little harsh, we think. Even if we put ourselves in her shoes, JP is offering an olive branch and the least she could fucking do is hear him out. If she doesn't let him talk to her, it's as good as censorship.

Preventing him from saying his piece. But the messages itch at her like bugs on her skin or in her head. Eventually she relents and gives him a set of streets at whose intersection he can find a Starbucks. She makes sure to pick one close, but not the closest. She also doesn't call it a Starbucks. She calls it a coffee place and trusts that he will figure it out. See? Learning. Except here, she is actually paranoid. We left her Twitter alone, so we could shame her in public and she could watch. She changed the password right away. We couldn't get into her direct messages; someone would have to socially engineer her password out of her, and Eliza is on her guard. And make no mistake, we're all dying for information. If someone made it available to us, even the most Lawful Good would likely click on it eventually. But we digress.

> **@BrightEliza:** 3:30pm. Today. Let's get this over with.

> **@franglais:** fair enough.

Eliza refuses to listen to Preston. She takes cash from her wallet—some of the women on the show had given it to her the night before, after learning what was happening at the bank. They'd bought her drinks too, and dinner. They'd said so many things, so many horror stories and so nonchalantly. Or perhaps Preston gives her the cash; maybe he feels guilty. Either way, she puts on some ugly sports sunglasses she finds in a small, neat pile next to his bed, where a bedside table might be in a more maximalist apartment, borrows a big puffy coat and a knit cap from a mostly empty closet and walks until she finds a Best Buy. She purchases a phone that she is assured doesn't connect to the internet at all. She prepays for her minutes, her texts, in cash. She turns off her smartphone and wonders if it's too dramatic to throw it into the Hudson. Instead, she slides it into the street and watches a taxi run it over.

She's put only a few numbers in the phone. She thinks perhaps she should text Suzanne her new number, but she is afraid to do so—do they have access to Suzanne's phone? Her texts? The funny-farm thing came from their chat, so it's possible. She calls See No Monkey and tries to schedule a flight out.

"Okay, well—I guess let us know when you can get back into your apartment? We can't really—schedule—a flight under these conditions. Or an interview. I guess let us know." The recruiter seems so disinterested. Eliza's entire body tenses. She spends the rest of the afternoon watching *Doctor Who* on Preston's giant screen and crying. She interrupts herself before her appointment with Jean-Pascale only once, to take Dog out for a stroll—would they notice that Dog wasn't with him today? Who would guess? She hasn't seen the photo we have, she doesn't know that no guesswork is necessary. When three o'clock comes, she puts the sunglasses, the coat and hat back on. She sets off, planning to wait at the Starbucks. Jean-Pascale, however, is already there.

CHAPTER SEVENTY

@theinspectre: your friend didn't like her flower, @yrface

@theinspectre: see, @yrface? she doesnt look happy at all [expand to see photo]

@theinspectre: you are proving much more difficult to find, @yrface

@theinspectre: congratulations, @yrface

@theinspectre: @yrface and thank you. I do love a good puzzle.

CHAPTER SEVENTY-ONE

Suzanne: Eliza, are you seeing these tweets?

Suzanne: that means hes here

Suzanne: he sent a photo of you, fuck

Suzanne: and what the fuck, he left you a flower? at your literal, actual apartment?

Suzanne: fucking talk to me, Eliza, are you okay?

Suzanne: shit was it him? this photo is everywhere? i'm seeing it everywhere

Suzanne: fuck. how many people do you think know here?

Suzanne: at fancy dog?

Suzanne: probably everyone

Suzanne: everyone with a reddit account at least

Suzanne: which is everyone

Suzanne: listen, im not a programmer, but you are. can you find out where it came from?

Suzanne: shit, fuck, Eliza, text back. I'm calling rn

Suzanne: okay, pick the fuck up, your phone is going straight to vm

Suzanne: devonte has the photo. he says its going around

Suzanne: i dont like this

CHAPTER SEVENTY-TWO

Suzanne: im gonna go over there

Devonte: you absolutely cannot go over there

Suzanne: like fucking hell i'm not going over there, she's not picking up, she could be fucking dead

Devonte: wait, really, dont go

Suzanne: i have to check on her

Devonte: no i mean dont go to her apartment, she isnt there

Suzanne: ???

Devonte: in the photo

Devonte: shes getting into a cab

Devonte: prestons with her

Devonte: preston tweeted this morning that he overslept

Devonte: hes lying

Devonte: shes at his apartment

Suzanne: do we know where he lives?

Devonte: no?

Suzanne: can we find out?

Devonte: . . . not ethically?

Suzanne: screw ethics

Devonte: I don't screw ethics.

Suzanne: well is it ethical to let her get hurt?

Suzanne: dev?

Devonte: okay fine

Devonte: wow, i found that fast

Devonte: people are already talking about it. like other people did the work, i didnt have to

Devonte: maybe you dont want to go over there?

Devonte: anyone can find this rn

CHAPTER SEVENTY-THREE

When Lewis sees the photo, it is a cocktail of emotions. Livid; vindicated. A heady mixture, intoxicating. Proven right and also deeply wronged. The mixture is more than that, even, though those are the two main flavors. There are also notes of longing, of wishing to be closer to Preston. Jealousy. And on the nose, we have the smell of Eliza having ruined his chances at this closeness, a mentor-mentee relationship that was budding and is now dead. On the finish, we have something extremely familiar. The specific rage of victimhood. The one caused by forced impotence, of external forces colluding against him, making sure he can't get ahead, and all because he had the great misfortune to be born a straight, white man. No one wants to take responsibility for their own misfortune anymore. And so they have crowned a boogeyman. And we are that monster. Lewis is that monster.

If they'd step back for just one second, they would see it for what it is: another form of egregious discrimination. Instead of their precious fucking equality, they're turning around and standing on our necks instead. And that isn't the way forward! But everyone's letting them do it because they're fags or females or illegals or whatever. Whatever fucking sob story of the minute they're peddling in their latest race to the bottom, to be the most denigrated and most degenerate, their Oppression Olympics. Everyone's letting them do it, and what are we supposed to do in response? They're taking away our successes, our opportunities. There's a reason we're the greatest country on earth. And it's because of us. We're rich and powerful and no one fucks with us, and why? It's not because of them. They'll come crawling back when their beloved experimental society fails. They already are.

It isn't hard to find out where Preston lives. And if Lewis doesn't do it, someone would. Leaky Joe, The Inspectre, Evrlrnr. It's just not terribly difficult to do. But no one has done it yet, when Lewis sees the photo. It used to be much easier; Instagram pinpointed every user on a map. But they got wise, killed the feature, and now we have to do a little more work. But not with Preston. Preston's building has several businesses in it: a comics shop, a dry cleaner and, yes, even a Starbucks. And with his location services turned on, it predicts and automatically tags those three every time. It doesn't require a rocket scientist, and Lewis is smarter than most.

CHAPTER SEVENTY-FOUR

Here is another point at which we very accurately know what's going on, and in real time. Some of us are right here, in meatspace, in the Starbucks. If straining ears made sounds, Eliza would hear the whine and creak of them as she walks in. We say nothing, not to her. She doesn't need to know, doesn't deserve to know. We know, though. We know, and so 4chan knows. Reddit knows. When we know something, we know something. We all know it.

Eliza decides not to hurry. Her hair is tucked up under Preston's hat and she leaves his sunglasses on her face. Jean-Pascale doesn't show any sign he recognizes her. She steps up to the counter to order a coffee, black; she feels so tired. When she takes her cup and sits down across from him, he starts and looks up from his phone as she removes her silly disguise, lets her hair fall from the hat. Our suspicions are confirmed. We pull out our phones. We begin to type the conversation, the parts we can hear. He settles back in his chair, but he is not settled. He is leaning forward, magnetized. He is uncomfortable.

"Hi," he says.

"Well," she says.

He lets out a puff of air he's been holding in his chest. "Thank you. For meeting me. You didn't have to."

"You're right. I didn't." Eliza taps her fingers on the table. It feels strange when she's mean. We're not used to her being mean. Not openly, at least. We are much more used to the candy-coated, rat-mouthed girl, even if the caramel is hiding a rotten apple.

"Listen. It's weird, what I wanted to say. I wanted to, well, apologize." Jean-Pascale pauses, grimaces. "And I wanted to say that I think it's all wrong, what happened. Is happening. It's just all so—wrong. And that moment, when you got fired." He winces, takes another deep breath. "I wanted to let you know I've been fired."

"I know," Eliza interrupts.

"And that I didn't do what they say I did. But I'm not fighting the termination."

Eliza's been looking out the window, making her disinterest plain. Now she turns her head. "Wait," she says. "It wasn't you who posted my file?"

Jean-Pascale shakes his head so hard he looks like a little boy. "No. But I took the folder. It was an accident, but I didn't give it back. I was afraid—what it would look like—Lewis said they'd think I stole it—I tried to hide it."

"So who put it online?"

Jean-Pascale's eyes flick around. We imagine he doesn't want to answer the question—we could be listening, after all—but Eliza's stare wins. "I think it could have only been Lewis. He's the only one who knew I had it."

"That fucker," Eliza says, with emphasis on what sounds like every letter. A mother glares at her from one table over and gestures to her toddler girl. "Sorry," Eliza mutters. "Why aren't you fighting the termination, if it wasn't you?"

Jean-Pascale winces again. "I let it happen. I thought the code—80085—was funny. I made it up, actually. I didn't put it on the server, but I thought of it. I didn't turn the folder back in." He pushes his coffee cup around the table with his pointer finger, not looking her in the eyes. "And I think the worst thing is I looked at your part of the patch again. You were right. We introduced errors. You're a good developer and I know it. All this, and we lost someone good."

"That's what I told you. That I was careful, I knew shit, I'd given games my pound of flesh. You didn't believe me before."

"I know. I am sorry. About that too."

Eliza pauses long here, and we tap away on our phones. "There's someone on the internet who's trying to get to me in real life. Someone was at my apartment this morning."

"What?"

"You don't think—it couldn't be Lewis, could it?"

JP is about to say no, absolutely not, Lewis would never do such a thing. But he pauses, too long and hard. "I don't know" is what he finally settles on. "I don't actually know."

"He seems so—involved. If he released the folder, if he made sure you took the fall for it."

We pause here. Could The Inspectre be Lewis Fleishman? We ponder this; we know how it shakes out, of course, and with the timeline, well—it would be impossible. But we only know what the newspapers tell us about the whens of things and about who gets accused of what; it would make sense. It could make sense for Lewis to have a backup character, make sense that The Inspectre always seems to be around—being on the game at work is, after all, his job. He's close enough to Eliza in proximity to take action. What if we rewound all the way to the calm before the storm, when we watched Lewis Fleishman play video games in his apartment, his window glowing electric blue. What if he was playing as The Inspectre, and not Doctor Moriarty? And we didn't check in on him last night— what if, in his bag, he had a box with a Barbie doll in it, a bouquet of bodega flowers? What if he spent the broadcast cutting the face from a doll, and if his apartment is searched, we will find the discarded countenance flattened on his desk, pressed like a blossom with the weight and heat from a coffee cup? What if, after his mother went on the date, after she didn't come home, he left his apartment in the wee hours of the morning and nailed his art project to Eliza's door? Hung around to take the photo? The Inspectre is one of us, but he must revel in the speculation. Because unlike the rest of us, he isn't very forthcoming.

A third person sits down at their table; Eliza jumps. "Suzanne," she sighs, relieved she knows the intruder. We fight not to turn our heads, to openly stare. Things are getting good. "What are you doing here?"

"Surprise," Suzanne answers, her voice flat. "We need to go." She narrows her eyes at Jean-Pascale while reaching for Eliza's elbow, ready to haul her up by the arm. We notice she's hyperaware, her eyes darting at all of us. They land in all the wrong places. They land on stereotypes, the people she thinks we are. But they don't linger where they ought to. Stupid. It's also stupid she doesn't grab Eliza and march her directly out the door. Her fingers on her friend's arm are soft. They lack conviction. "What are you even doing here?" This isn't a question for Eliza, but rather JP, who nervously stares down his cup of coffee.

"I'm apologizing," he says, without looking up.

"Too little too late, friendo."

"He didn't do my file," Eliza interjects.

Suzanne snorts. "Sure. Convenient. Let's leave. Leave time now."

"No, I swear I didn't!" JP says, alarmed. He doesn't like being accused of lying, not at all.

Suzanne smells blood, metaphorically speaking, and she forgets us. Her focus is laser-like on JP. "Oh. You swear?" Her eyebrow cocks up like she's preparing to shoot a gun.

Eliza tunes out the sparring, but they continue. Eventually JP stops defending and takes it, each small verbal cut, looking intently into his cup with basset hound eyes. She's more uncomfortable than she'd have previously expected, watching Suzanne excoriate Jean-Pascale like this. She hadn't been about to forgive him, not in the slightest. She was going to give him the requisite hard time. Or she was going to sue him and eat his soul. They all do. But we can see her face soften as he withers under Suzanne's biting tongue. Eliza knows being in her friend's cross hairs is harrowing. "Shouldn't you be at work?" she interrupts and checks her watch—Preston's, actually. Another thing she borrowed.

"Yeah. I'm letting everything go to voicemail like we're closed. And if anyone argues with me, well—" She runs her eyes up and down JP, who still hasn't looked back up at her. "They've frankly got bigger issues right now."

"Why are you here, though?" Eliza asks.

"You ignored your texts, your phone calls."

"Oh," Eliza says. She holds up her new phone.

Suzanne curses and the air turns blue around her. Babies cry; dogs howl; stay-at-home wine-moms get very angry. "You could've told a bitch," is where she ends up, followed quickly by, "but this is not our biggest problem right now—"

Eliza grabs Suzanne's arm right back. "Wait, Suzanne. How did you get here?"

"It's part of what I came to tell you—it's easy to find Preston. And there's a photo. Of you and him. Everyone knows. Everyone knows you're at his apartment, everyone knows his address. And everyone knows where you're sitting right now, too. I have Google alerts on everything to do with you, and I was on my way to his place when another one hit, so I changed course. People are in here. People are in here with you and they're telling the internet about it. Look, it's all over Twitter and I don't want to haul you around like you're a child or a suitcase but we have to leave." She offers up her phone as evidence. Eliza takes it, looks at the screen. The Inspectre's Twitter profile is pulled up—the default egg on a green background, the bar at the top of the app that tells the user there are more tweets to be loaded, recent ones. Suzanne intends for her to see the photo of her and Preston, but Eliza taps the bar. Refreshes the page.

She gasps. Drops the phone in the middle of the table and whirls toward the window, eyes wide, lips parted like a sex doll. Suzanne and JP lean in, over the phone, stare down at it.

We have, of course, seen it by now. Even those of us watching the interaction in person. Especially us. Sure, it is tweeted publicly, and so we can all enjoy it. But there are only a select few of us who can see her face. Priceless like a Mastercard commercial. Eliza has just seen a photo of herself, Jean-Pascale and Suzanne sitting in the Starbucks, framed by a window.

"**@theinspectre:** well hello, @yrface. It's nice to see you."

Jean-Pascale leaps up and runs out the door, paces in front of the building and squints at passersby, trying to see if anyone is loitering, if anyone is holding up a phone.

Let's pause here for a second: no matter how we feel about Eliza, about Suzanne, about The Inspectre, every single one of us loves Jean-Pascale more in this moment. The outburst of collective love, entirely unspoiled by dissent, is difficult to justify. Why the fuck do we feel like this? And why so sudden, so strong? Because this is our story and because we can pause and digress as much as we want to interrogate it. Because it isn't logical, the feeling, and it requires examination.

Neither is it logical that Jean-Pascale gets up and hunts down an errant photographer when everything we know about The Inspectre suggests he'll be gone and hidden before he hits the send button. He's in a building or around the corner or even in a taxi, speeding away. Things change in a second; everything is instant. And even if The Inspectre makes a mistake, even if he sticks around—what's Jean-Pascale going to do, exactly? He finds The Inspectre and then what? Holds him down while someone calls the police? For tweeting a photo in a public place? Will he take a swing at him? Jean-Pascale isn't a violent person outside Windy City—he is not big on the consequences of fighting. And none of us know at this point what The Inspectre is capable of. The Inspectre could shoot him, stab him, tase him. JP doesn't think about that.

It is in this logical failure that we find the catalyst of our love. His action is reactionary, chaotic. But not only is it that—it is paternal, it is protective. It is good. Our gasp of feeling correlates to the precise moment that JP's alignment changes; where we all align ourselves with him. We're all Jean-Pascale.

But back to it: He tries to find the angle where the photo was taken, but when he realizes it could have been zoomed in, flipped on its axis— The Inspectre could have been across the street in either direction—he comes back inside. But Eliza and Suzanne, they're already reading the other tweets. There are so many more.

CHAPTER SEVENTY-FIVE

@theinspectre: i'm so sorry, @HumanMan

@theinspectre: but you crossed a line today, @HumanMan

@theinspectre: @HumanMan you hid a cunt from me

@theinspectre: @HumanMan there's a code, you know

@theinspectre: the more crass among us would call it 'bros before hos' @HumanMan

@theinspectre: @HumanMan I prefer to think 'misters before sisters'

@theinspectre: but it's clear, @HumanMan, that she's not your sister

@theinspectre: @HumanMan i can respect that

@theinspectre: many men do stupid things in the name of pussy, @HumanMan

@theinspectre: you got in my way, @HumanMan, and you broke the code

@theinspectre: so I broke my code too, @HumanMan

@theinspectre: i promise i won't do it again, @HumanMan

@theinspectre: @HumanMan as long as you promise not to break yours again

@theinspectre: and don't worry, @HumanMan, he didn't pay the ultimate price

@theinspectre: @HumanMan just a small fine

CHAPTER SEVENTY-SIX

W hat the fuck does this mean," Suzanne states more than asks. Jean-Pascale looks green again, and Suzanne reaches over to pinch his arm. "Buck up, wuss, this isn't about you."

For a second, Eliza doesn't know what this could mean either. It sounds like nonsense. The ramblings of an internet crazy. But all at once she drops the phone as though the battery has heated up, the second time in what feels like seconds. "Dog," she says. "Dog is in the apartment. He didn't take Dog to work today because I was there." She tears out the front door, Suzanne and JP close behind.

"Wait!" Suzanne is shouting. "I'm dialing the police, you can't just go in there, he could still be there! He could still be in there." We lose sight of them as they rocket down the street; we are now glued to our phones, reading everything twice, three times. We want to suck every inference, every hidden nuance in each 140-character bite. Eliza, fueled by adrenaline or perhaps simply small and fast, outstrips her compatriots. The doorman stares at her as she runs in, but recognizes her and lets her pass. She pushes the elevator button and, mercifully, one is already on the ground floor. She wishes fervently for the Wonkavator—to move diagonally and let her directly in without running down the hall. She wishes for teleportation.

When Eliza arrives at the front door, she wishes she hadn't gotten there as quickly. No one is behind her; she has no backup. But the door is ajar. The whole doorknob has been removed and now there is a yawning hole. She can hear Dog whining.

We can pause here too, because here is where another gasp of feeling escapes, one that surprises us even more. Because this time, we love Eliza. We love her like we do Jean-Pascale. It is so confusing. We love that damn fool as she flies toward an open door, to where her stalker may very well be waiting, all for the love of Dog. Whatever we feel about her before or after, here is the moment that changes us forever. In this brief moment, we repudiate The Inspectre. We cast him out. He is not us. We didn't make him. He acts alone.

She pushes through. The door bangs against the wall, leaving a divot and announcing her presence. There is blood on the floor, but not as much as either she or we were expecting. "Dog?" Eliza calls out— she isn't thinking clearly, or she wouldn't make a sound. She hears another whimper and runs toward the bathroom just as Suzanne and Jean-Pascale squeeze, two at once, through the doorway. Eliza opens the shower curtain to a scared, shaking Dog. He is whining and bloody, and minus a tail, but otherwise appears to be fine. It has been excised with precision, the knife-line sharp and accurate. It is the same loving cut as the doll, we think, and we are not sure how we know that. But we do. Tiny Eliza lifts Dog bodily—he is not a small dog—and starts heading back toward the door. Jean-Pascale is looking suspiciously green, the same as when we last saw him faint. "Fucking pull it together, JP, and Yelp a vet's office," Eliza says from underneath Dog. She grunts.

"I'm waiting for the police! In the lobby, with the doorman!" Suzanne calls after them. Eliza laughs, bitter. And we wonder, we wonder— Where is the tail?

CHAPTER SEVENTY-SEVEN

The vet's office had been nice enough to give them their own room once Preston had arrived to take over with Dog. The large windows in the waiting room had been making her jumpy. His mood was strange—distant, perhaps adjacent to angry. Eliza can't help but think of the person at the bank who asked how she could've let this happen. In his eyes, she'd seen panic. And he'd said—something. It was fuzzy. First, "Is he okay?" Second, "Are you okay?" There was a lot of "oh thank God" and "Jesus H. Christ" and there was, at one point, a wooden hug, stiff in its awkwardness. And somewhere in all that, Eliza thought she felt *how could you let this happen.* But perhaps, she thinks, she is making that up. A coping mechanism. A way to deal with feeling that way herself.

Or Preston said it. Flat out said, "How could you let this happen?"

And Eliza spat back, "How could *you* let this happen? You're fucking famous, your location services are on, and everyone knows where you live. That one's not on me, pal."

Or there was no overlap. They'd been sidelined while Dog was taken to the back, and then Preston came in and took over. A vet told them they'd been given another room, and that they could leave whenever they wanted. That if the police had questions, they'd be in touch. And that left Eliza to stew, to wonder—how did Preston feel about this?

How did she feel about this? Things happen so quickly. She hasn't had a lot of time to feel things.

Now the two of them sit in the unused exam room, eyes as wide as dinner plates or full moons, trying to see a path forward, unable to picture anything but the bleeding animal. They stare into treat jars and syringes, stacks of baby food and an exam table scale.

"You can't go back there either," JP says to a blood-coated Eliza. "He knows where Preston lives."

She only snorts in response. "I just got his dog's tail chopped off. I don't think I'll be invited to return."

Eliza jumps as Suzanne bursts into the room, shouting, "Mother ass bitch, all cops are bastards, that's for fucking sure."

"Suzanne, you just made my stomach drop out of my butt, can you maybe knock before you appear places?"

"Sorry. It's just. They took my phone."

"What?" JP jumps in.

"They bagged my phone as evidence."

"But—why?"

"Because they didn't know how else they were going to be able to see tweets again."

No one speaks for a second. Because that is really, really fucking stupid.

"So you're just—down a phone now?" Eliza asks.

"I guess. Did you know they have a whole unit for animal cruelty? There's, like, special cops for it. It's a thing I just learned. And this isn't the first time they've seen a tail chopped off. They say it's usually worse. Usually it's with scissors. This one was more precise than that."

A moment of silence for the temporarily fallen Dog. JP chimes in again, uncomfortable in the silence. "I can't believe that just happened."

It is Suzanne's turn to snort derisively. "I can."

"Oh come on. You can't tell me you would've predicted this."

"Let's call the feeling Shocked-But-Not-Surprised, then."

Eliza dips her head into her hands, defeated. "Where do I even go? Who hasn't he touched yet? Who hasn't he proven he can get to?"

JP wants to volunteer. But his thoughts snap immediately to Delphine and he thinks better of it. It would be one thing if he lived alone. But Delphine—he couldn't put her in danger. Besides, she doesn't usually get along with other women.

"Well it sure can't be Devonte. I think he's about to crack."

Eliza raises her eyebrow.

Suzanne continues: "Before the police bagged my literal entire phone—gosh, I can't fucking get over that—I texted him. He said as soon as Preston got the call, Fancy Dog descended into chaos. You'd have thought The Inspectre assassinated Elon Musk. Everyone's on the weirdest warpath about it."

"Weird how? We all love Dog," JP interjects.

Eliza sighs. "Because no one gives a shit about him harassing me, JP."

"Ah. Yes."

"They've got Devonte answering phones in my place. I'm excused, of course. He keeps texting 'I have not been trained for this' over and over. Besides. He's got the world's smallest one-bedroom anyhow, no one else can fit in there. It may as well be a studio."

Eliza squishes her face between her hands; she can see how Preston finds it comforting. "It's New York City, Suzanne. Everyone has the world's smallest one-bedroom, if they're lucky." And we think she has a point. It's not like Windy City; space cannot expand at the request of the User Experience team.

"Let me—make a call," Suzanne replies, simply and mysteriously. She takes Eliza's burner phone and steps from the room, leaving JP and Eliza sitting across from a picture of a cat sniffing a daisy.

"I really am sorry, you know."

"I know."

"Can you—do you—accept my apology?"

"I'll get there."

Suzanne bursts back in the room, startling Eliza a second time. "It's settled, then. You're coming to stay with me."

"Where do you—" JP begins to ask, but Suzanne is having none of that.

"Absolutely not, you wimpy traitor. Please leave now."

After he departs, Eliza turns to Suzanne. "What the fuck was that about?"

"I didn't want him to know this place exists. All we know for sure is he took your folder and then it ended up online via his computer. I'm not giving him shit to work with here."

And that is how Eliza winds up invited to stay at the Sixsterhood of Healing, Arts and Literature.

CHAPTER SEVENTY-EIGHT

We have kicked the reddit people out—though We are a small group, We are mighty and the others have no concept of this place—they Cannot Imagine It—modeled after the warehouse art collectives in the Bay—it's the best grab We can make for what We imagine New York City used to be—Communal, Creative, and not only for rich people—something akin to the Sweet, Glorious Freaks who lived in the Chelsea Hotel, paying in art and Doing It for the culture and trying not to die So Desperately Young

but where in the city are there warehouses that We can still rent this way—where zoning law isn't enforced and profit hasn't led to forcible eviction? Queens! Brilliant Friends! Queens! is where, and in particular one warehouse in Queens where certainly no one sleeps no one stays overnight it is simply studio space and studio space only We swear, officer

New York City is one of those places you can be Very Close Friends with someone and not know where they live—two people can witness the Birth of each other's children and not once darken each other's doorsteps, go through life without ever seeing the spot in the entryway where magazines pile up—it is just the way of things and it is not surprising to us that Our Splendid New Friend Eliza—even as she is a Giving and Perceptive Friend—has not one single clue that Our Suzanne—that

Luminous Star of a Person—accidentally lives in the perfect solution, a place to get lost

Eliza the Brave stands outside Our unassuming building—it is tagged with spray paint and accessible only by key fob—which our Gorgeous Suzanne hands her immediately—she walks up, not to the loading doors but to the regular, person-sized door, and says "Welcome to the Sixsterhood," as she pushes it open—Eliza is expecting a grander entrance considering Our Loyal Suzanne has up until this point protected it—protected Us—but it isn't so very grand at first glance—just a stairwell—"Let me give you the tour"

Suzanne—Our Perfect Thoughtful Unicorn—opens the door to the left and a massive cavernous space—bathed in sunlight and covered in what looks like bright streamers with big blue mats on the floor—spreads itself before Eliza the Resilient—"So here's the aerial silks—it looks like Bunny finally rigged up the lyra—that hula-hoop-looking thing—but it's more like a trapeze really and back there is the recording equipment—we've soundproofed it pretty good but sorry where you're staying you'll definitely be able to hear it—" Suzanne closes the door and when she opens the door on the right the scent of wood shavings wafts through and Eliza breathes deeply filling all the corners of her Lithe and Beautiful body with the sweetness of it appreciating the Home Depot smell—"Welding, carpentry, general building this way—unless you have a secret talent for metalwork, probably you won't spend much time in there"—she closes the door and continues up the stairs—"up we go"

Eliza has had a long day—her legs weigh so heavy when hung with all that stress, understandably so—and she asks "Isn't there an elevator?"

"Not exactly"

They hoist themselves up step-by-step until they turn on a landing and Eliza gasps: A huge welded sculpture of a lion head looks out over the stairwell with rivets that shimmer like oil slicks and jagged teeth juxtaposed with friendly eyebrows and a majestic mane—a banner is painted above: "Resilience—Vulnerability—Strength"

A good banner—a good mascot—We came up with it, all together—home! home! home!—everything here seems more real-brighter-bigger—the scale of it is as though We're in Windy City and it's Our superhero lair—and Our Intelligent Protector Suzanne has never told anyone about it

Through the door on the left: a large, almost industrial kitchen with pots and pans hanging from the ceiling over a giant steel island—Our Gorgeous Friend Eliza is overwhelmed by the sheer amount of kitchen gadgetry: mixers, pasta makers, instant pots—it looks like a food blog in here except Decidedly Grungier—like a food blog where no one gives a Fuck about aesthetics just about food, some of which We lift from the restaurant dumpsters and some of which We collectively purchase from the organic grocery store—except We have a huge dining room table made of a barn door from the Hudson Valley placed lovingly in front of massive windows so We are not wholly unconcerned with Aesthetics—and sitting there We can look out over a view of dingy semi-ungentrified Queens—from the second floor of course so the view isn't spectacular—but the sun shines in all the same as it sets early

Eliza—We are watching her closely, experiencing her Taking-In—feels a pang of—is it nervousness? Yes and it's too strong to be only nervousness—We can see it spasm through the tiny muscles in her face watch it settle in her limbs as it arrives on her body—it's fear—a strong desire to get away from the windows through which someone might see her and she registers surprise at how reasonable it feels: both the action and the emotion behind it—the obsession and compulsion "Back there are bedrooms—Jack, Bunny, Lil and Lyle, Dee, they all live on this floor"

"How many are you here?"

"Eleven—Twelve soon—And I guess you so thirteen?"

Our Gentle, Brilliant Sun Goddess Suzanne takes Eliza's hand and leads her back through the stairwell to the door on the right and pushes it open: "I expect you'll be a particular fan of—" and We can tell she is about to finish the sentence with "this room" but Eliza gasps once again—such Good Taste she has, in spaces, in Communities—and steps in running her hands over two shining Alienware towers, two drobos and—

"A Vive, even? This place is—wow, this is the full ideal setup"—She looks around, absorbs the large room, again with the windows (pang in her stomach, We can see it)—most of the center is empty which is Perfect for wandering weird worlds with the headset on and the back of the room is occupied by long standing desks and power strips—a sectional runs into the corner and two of Us are cuddled there staring at a laptop and crunching on popcorn—We are Perfect Peacocks of People with piercings on our faces and tattoos on our necks, fingers and wrists—Eliza isn't sure of our Genders, and We don't tell her—aren't always sure Ourselves and of the things to know about Us it is the Least Relevant and also the Most and in the absence of a meaningful space to share Our Deepest Selves, We ignore it like neutral weather—a fact of existence

"Lil, Lyle, this is Eliza—" Our Suzanne introduces Us—or rather a facet of Us—Our representatives in this moment

We stand, smiling—*Hi, hello, welcome*

"Are you—is this all yours?" Eliza gestures to the Vive and the computer towers

We shrug: *It's the Community's though We're the ones who are trying to use it the most—We want to make sure queerdos aren't left behind in the VR revolution—neither one of Us studied shit like this though so We're making it up as We go*

"How's it coming so far?" Eliza asks

We—pretty much just know how to play that archery game—

—But We're taking a lot of notes!—

—On what makes a successful UX, what a compelling story is in this space, what sorts of Possibilities We see—

Eliza smiles and her face hurts—she tries to quickly count how many hours she's been awake and how many times she's cried (crying is Courageous!) and fails—it seems like the day has extended the length of a few rotations at least—stretched beyond the horizon that way

Our Exquisite Attentive Suzanne picks up on her friend's exhaustion and ferries her out of the room before We can ask to show her Our Radical Feminist Unity Project—which We of course wouldn't do—We can see she's tired and sad—We can provide distraction later and a place to sleep now—later! later! We will Embrace her later!

"Upstairs is all individual studios and bedrooms—I'll show you mine" They huff up one more floor and Eliza's quads are burning as she tops the rise and sees the rooms, which are less rooms and more stalls, partitioned with cubicle cork and flimsy doors; "Here, this one's me" Suzanne opens one and—

Eliza lets out a gasp for the third time—not because of computer equipment but because what's beyond is so unexpected—and We agree because Our Composed Blossoming Sunflower Suzanne passes—for straight, and for wealthy and for someone logical and people don't think of her as an Artist outside the Community—her tiny allotment of personal space is mostly made up of those huge glass windows and one bed with a crazy amount of blankets all piled in the center and an easel on which sits what looks like a Renoir if Renoir had ever lived in a warehouse in Queens and knew what a trans person was—It is a painting of the view outside her window which is garbage and a chain-link fence and all, but in her Hands and Eyes and Talent it is somehow brighter and lighter as if despite all its Desperate Grunge and its pigeons and its poop this corner of Queens is Suzanne's happy place—is as treasured as a fancy boat ride or a Sunday in the park—she is today's impressionist and We're impressed—We always are—she is Us after all—Our Sweet and Exceptional Muse

"Suzanne!" Eliza almost shrieks "You—I thought you were normal!"

"Uh—thanks?"

"How have you—fuck, this is beautiful—how have you not mentioned this?"

Suzanne shrugs—"I like my private life private"

"But—we're friends! At least how did I not know you painted? Christ, why are you working in customer relations? You could be in NPC character design easily—never have to talk to another customer again—if you wanted to, I don't know, render hundreds of heads—"

But Suzanne—Insightful and Self-Aware and Well-Boundaried—is shaking her head as she says "I like my job and my art very very separate"

Eliza whirls around and says "This place is—it's magic"—her face falls—"Do they all know? Are they all okay with me being under this roof?"

"Surrounding you in off-the-grid people—people We're sure We trust—seemed like the best idea to Everyone—besides"—Our Cunning and Beautiful Dormouse Suzanne smiles—"my name's not on the lease—everything here down to the security cameras and the key fobs connect only to Our own servers—I have never had location services turned on—I'm nearly fucking impossible to find which means now you are too—" Eliza's mind flickers to the windows and "what if" echoes in her ears and in her mouth and in the back of her throat: what if he followed and what if he can see in here? she crams it down as Our Suzanne says "you're in the guest room—I'm afraid it's not quite as nice"

She leads Eliza to the very back of the warehouse past other cubicles and a bathroom where one of Us is showering and filling the air with Blessed Comforting steam—she turns into what Eliza thinks is a dead end except it's not: there is an elevator—an open one—with a red lever stuck in the "locked" position just outside the door and inside there's a bunk bed made up with thin sheets and a ratty pillow and fairy lights twist around the posts because We have done Our best to combat the dark which is to say We lean into it and make it feel like the fort We

251

all wish We had as children—Hygge and Cozy—a Mother-Bear-Ready
dark den

"Suzanne?"

"Yes?"

"Am I sleeping in the elevator?"

"Yes"

CHAPTER SEVENTY-NINE

Outside of Our door We see a man and he looks Very Confused—he carries a suitcase and he is tapping at the key fob and We do not know this man

He hears an electronic whizzing—the articulated arm on one of Our Beautiful Creations—and he looks up and sees the camera wake and point its lone eye at him

Then We speak—*WHO ARE YOU?*—and it's loud and grainy and sounds like it was lifted out of a Dilapidated Burger King Drive-Thru because that is where We got the speaker from—We stole it! Be gay do crime!—as he looks closer at Our camera he realizes that too is Old—Repurposed and Re-Engineered—We love a good Reduce Reuse Recycle

"Devonte"—he says to the machines—"Devonte Aleba"

WE DON'T KNOW ANY DEVONTE ALEBA

"I'm with Suzanne!" Devonte yells to the air and the door because he can't see where We might have hidden the microphone—"I have Eliza's stuff"

WE DO NOT KNOW ANY ELIZA OR ANY SUZANNE—YOU MUST BE MISTAKEN

"No," This New Stranger Devonte replies "I know they're here—she's my friend—they're my friends—I work at Fancy Dog"

YOU MUST BE MISTAKEN—NO PEOPLE WHO HAVE CHOSEN THOSE NAMES EXIST HERE

A. E. OSWORTH

"I brought this suitcase for them"

OF ALL THE PEOPLE HERE WHO USE THEY-THEM PRO-NOUNS NONE ARE EXPECTING A SUITCASE—PLEASE EXIT THE STAGE LEFT OR WE WILL RELEASE THE BEAR

"No no—I mean for both—look, can I just come in and drop the suitcase off?"

SORRY—THIS IS A CLOSED STUDIO—NO VISITORS—IF YOU DO NOT LEAVE WE WILL BE FORCED TO CONTACT OUR COMMUNITY ALTERNATIVE TO LAW ENFORCEMENT

This Persistent Fellow Devonte smirks and says "Better chance of them showing up then"

PARDON US—WE DID NOT HEAR THAT LAST BIT

Devonte hears a familiar tone—a muffled voice he would recognize anywhere—and of course he does because he interacts with his two closest friends via microphone so often that even the "what? Someone here?" from the Janky speakers fuzzing out onto the stoop is an instant Antenna-Raiser and he cries out "Suzanne! Eliza! I have your things and I have things to tell you!" and then he hears Us talking in the Wah-Wah of assenting Peanuts incomprehensible adults

OH—YOU CAN COME IN THEN!

The door clicks open and Our New Friend Devonte mutters "Jesus Christ"

CHAPTER EIGHTY

Our Three Wonderful Protagonists gather in the elevator and draw the curtain across—a gesture toward privacy as the doors are halted in the open position—We can still hear them even as We try not to and Collaborator-In-Safety Devonte crosses his legs on the creaking bed—"This place is wild" he says and Yes! it is and We can tell he is Unused to living with Community or he might speak a little bit quieter and We Swear We are trying not to Eavesdrop but it is Impossible and now they are Part Of The Thrum and Hum of our Heart-Place and We Absorb their sounds

"How did we not know about this?" Eliza asks

"I didn't tell you" Our Suzanne replies

"Why the hell not?"

"Because I didn't want anyone gawking at me—I seem like I'm not private but I am and I've only known you two a couple years—give me a fucking break"

Eliza (who is So Lovely and Wonderful) turns to Devonte (who is also So Lovely and Wonderful) and says "You said you had things to share?"

"Yeah—I went to your apartment and I expected it to have—I dunno—crime scene tape or look like it was investigated somehow but when I got there I didn't even need to use the key you gave me because it was still unlocked"

Our Suzanne (who in this moment stands in perfectly for Our Reaction) raises her eyebrows—"'Still'? what do you mean 'still'?"

"I mean it looked like no one had been in there since Eliza and Preston—like the food was still out—I know what you were eating— So I went down to the doormen and asked if any police officers had been by or if they'd requested it be left exactly as it was and Eliza—no one ever came"

There is a pause and it's a long one—Our Three Courageous Souls breathe and they smell the must and dust of a Very Old Elevator

"Devonte" Eliza begins (too calmly in Our Humble Opinion) "are you telling me"—she takes a breath—"that the NYPD showed up"— she takes another breath—"for an animal welfare complaint"—a third gulp of air and We can hear the cracks this time in this Manufactured Zen and We can even hear the Tears beginning to brew at the corner of her left eye and then her right—not a cry of sadness but one of rage— "And did not show up for the doll? for harassment?"

Our Strong and Sensitive Devonte knows that his answer will bring those teetering tears tumbling down Eliza's cheeks and he doesn't want to speak his single word out because he doesn't want to make his friend cry or yell and he'd rather avoid this whole thing but he does it anyway because it's the Truth and because silence is the same answer so he says "Yes"

"What the absolute fuck!" Eliza wails and her two friends move out of the way as she whales her knuckles against the pillow and then when it's not satisfying enough We hear the crash-bang of a hand hitting a wall and We grow Concerned for the Safety Of Our Community because she doesn't know yet that the way We deal with Powerful Anger is to call a Powerful Anger Circle in the silks studio and participate in a Group Primal Scream and We will have to find a way to tell her that hitting a wall creates a Hostile Environment but We are not Unreasonable and We know that Straight People by and large haven't been taught to deal with their emotions healthily

"Whoa whoa" says Devonte because he'd expected yelling but not punching

"Stop hitting my house!" Suzanne bellows and the elevator shaft is a Sound Artery so We all turn toward it and We wish We could remind her to tell Our Overwhelmed Eliza about the Possibility of a Powerful Anger Circle but instead she says "Come on you're hurting yourself—stop!"

Eliza gasps for breath and her knuckles are bloody and This is why We have Powerful Anger Circles! "I am so fucking fucked!" she says and "what do the police even do?"

Our Incisive and Intelligent Suzanne replies with "kill Black people and turn New York City into a Capitalist Hellscape we can't even afford to park in while providing white families headed by cis men with the illusion of a safety that doesn't exist"

Devonte elbows her and stifles a laugh he doesn't think is appropriate and he wonders how he hadn't guessed at Suzanne's living situation given the things that come out of her mouth—then again how could anyone guess at this exact housing? We have made whatever it is that We wanted and most people aren't Us—They don't have the Capacity to set about wanting what We have

"You need a Band-Aid—We have those" Suzanne continues "And we need a plan"

"We?" Eliza asks "Neither of you have to— I mean you didn't even have to put me up—It's my problem"

"We are not going to sit by and watch you suffer—Right Devonte?"

"Right" he says and We can hear the reluctance—it's a split-second hesitation and a sound like a throat clear but subtler—Our Suzanne is one of Us and used to operating in Community so she picks up on it as well and she flags it for her attention later

"So we need a plan" Our Suzanne continues "and I still think that plan involves hacking"

"So lawbreaking?" Devonte asks

"Necessarily yes—the police aren't doing anything to help Eliza so the law isn't exactly working out—I think it's time to come at this vigilante-style"

"There's just one problem" Our Astute Eliza says "I'm not a hacker"

"You code and you can build shit—I'm sure you can get your way into—" but Eliza is shaking her head before Our Suzanne finishes—Devonte is too—and Suzanne halts her sentence and cocks an eyebrow—it is a look We know well—Stubborn Taurus Energy combined with a Mercury in Scorpio and a Mars in Aries

"Hacking isn't about the computer" says Devonte "Not really"

Our Suzanne looks like she's about to say "what the ever-loving hot fuck do you mean?" as she crosses her arms with her eyebrow still raised but instead she says "go on"

"It's—if you've got a hacker that's all about what he can make the computer do that's called a script kiddie—there are hordes of them and they're just copying things—they don't really understand—you don't hack a computer—you hack people—computers might be the gateway but you're really interacting with the people who use them—how do they think? what do they need their data for? what does safety mean to them? who do they trust? what does that person look and sound like? it's—it's much more social than television would have you believe—some of the most socially aware people on the planet are hackers—they aren't basement boys lacking the ability to read faces—they just—use their powers questionably is all"

Eliza and Suzanne are quiet—"It seems like you really know what you're talking about" Suzanne says after a moment

"I did once" admits Our Smart and Currently Very Lawful Devonte

Eliza chimes in "I know enough to know I'm not a hacker regardless of what I can make the computer do And The Inspectre—he seems good—experienced—I don't know that I could touch him"

Our Suzanne turns back to Devonte "So it's down to you then"

Devonte stares at his friends incredulous and says "Look I just made it sound really romantic and all but it's not—people go to real jail for this and I—I cannot go to jail"

"Plenty of people never get caught ever" Our Suzanne points out

Devonte purses his lips "Yeah but the way I see it, your best bet is to do the phone company—try to get his location through his phone number—and the phone company is hella litigious—the stakes of doing that—astronomical—probably no one will catch you but if they do that's very very illegal and whatever phone company you fuck over will make sure you hurt forever"

CHAPTER EIGHTY-ONE

@theinspectre: tsk tsk tsk. you didn't stay with @HumanMan long enough, @BrightEliza

@theinspectre: he's so sad at the vet's office right now

@theinspectre: @yrface @BrightEliza but you're heartless. you didn't stay long enough for me to catch up

@theinspectre: I'll find you eventually, @yrface @BrightEliza

CHAPTER EIGHTY-TWO

Suzanne: Dev, do you see it?

Devonte: Yes

Suzanne: What do we do?

Devonte: I defer to Eliza, honestly

Suzanne: Dev, she's not on this group chat anymore, she doesn't have her phone

Devonte: Oh right

Devonte: I mean, if we were to do something

Devonte: IF

Devonte: having him contact you more and not less is what you want

Devonte: so maybe poke him in the eye a bit?

Devonte: just, like

Devonte: make sure your location is really really hidden

Devonte: use a computer with a VPN. incognito mode. the works

CHAPTER EIGHTY-THREE

@yrface: To @theinspectre (and yes, I'm going to Storify this all, immortalize this shit)

@yrface: That was a dick move, attacking @HumanMan's dog like that @theinspectre

@yrface: We thought you had a code, @theinspectre

@yrface: @theinspectre Turns out, you're just a psycho-punk chopping tails off animals

@yrface: @theinspectre and then, what, taking them?

@yrface: Don't fuck around with @HumanMan, @theinspectre

@yrface: you're hurting animals because you're too afraid to come after us, @theinspectre

@yrface: @theinspectre or maybe it's because you're not smart enough to find us

@yrface: either way, @theinspectre, we win.

@yrface: yes, to all who are asking—Dog is okay. #LongLiveDog

("Here, use this computer for it. I set it up already, they can't trace us."

"What do I even say?"

"Devonte says to make him keep talking to us, maybe something will slip. Make him reckless. I think the best thing is to make it seem like he's losing. It'll make him try harder."

"It sure seems like he's winning to me. I'm sleeping in an elevator."

"Come on. This is cool. We worked really hard on it. It's a really well-appointed elevator.")

> **@BrightEliza:** To everyone who believes in #GamerGate and to any cowards who attack helpless animals for your "cause."

> **@BrightEliza:** #GamerGate is a bunch of crap. It's not about ethics. It's about scaring women. I am not quitting—I never will.

> **@BrightEliza:** I am not scared, I never will be.

("You sound really fucking brave. Is all that true?"

"I don't know—I'm definitely scared, so that part's not true. About the quitting, though, I did get a maybe-something from See No Monkey—"

"Holy shit, that's wonderful. Fucking congrats."

"They seemed to back off, though. After the doll thing this morning. Gosh, was that this morning? It feels like years ago."

"Ugh. I'm sorry. That's balls and they're cowards."

"Even if they do offer, though, I don't know if I'd take it."

"Why the hell not?"

"That's the thing. About the not quitting. I don't know if that's true.

I don't know if I want to do this anymore. Look, I know I did this all wrong, but I don't think I deserve this? I like games but—like, all this is over a *game*. This whole thing is over games. That's kinda fucked. I don't know if I can really do this, sacrifice myself like, this, for a fucking game."

"Fair enough. But like—games. They're never *just* games. Just like they're never *just* memes or *just* a joke. It's all the culture, you know? Like all this, it's the fabric of our lives. It's all a reflection of everything we do, everything we believe. It's how we communicate what we value to other people. It's the way we socialize, the things we talk about. You know it's not just games."

"But it also is! It also is just games! The stakes are supposed to be lower about games, that's the whole fucking point of them! And there are one million other ways for me to participate in culture. I could disappear into the sunset and make an anonymous meme account. I could, I don't know, draw comics. I wanted to do that once."

"That world is no better. Same world. It's all the same world."

"Also, since when are *you* so romantic about games?"

"I play this thing just as much as you do, don't erase me from it. Who do you think turned Us on to the VR shit? It certainly wasn't Lil and Lyle by themselves."

"I would miss it, though, I think. If I quit. The good parts. For sure. And I don't want to, like, let them win. I just don't know. I'm so scared.")

CHAPTER EIGHTY-FOUR

We are back now, us, the real us, not those candy-ass bitches. This is our story. Ours. Devonte stops tweeting. Runner Quick stops showing up in Windy City. They both step out of our story for a bit. And we know why:

Devonte, restless and worried about what they are asking of him, walks twenty blocks away and hails a cab back to Manhattan, dreaming of his peaceful home, sans demands. Even Suzanne, who should know a little bit more about what she is asking, doesn't seem to. They don't seem to understand that lawbreaking means something different for him, in his body, than it does for them. It's just like women, to ask the big strong man to assume all the risk. Devonte is exhausted; the work-horse of the group, meant to run errands and stay strong in the face of all the destruction and dysfunction, still expected to show up to work in the morning when Suzanne has been excused, able to work from home if she does it carefully. Preston gave him no such recompense. And we figure that figures—the men go underappreciated here, when the man is the one able to solve most of the problems the girls face. The only one with experience in social engineering and computer engineering, both. See, this is why they'll come running back to us when their ideal world crashes and burns. He has earned another bourbon or time to listen to his records or maybe even the opportunity to play *Guilds* with the Vive alone, blessedly alone. The important part, we think, is "alone."

The opportunity to relax by himself, no expectation, no guilt. It is late. It is dark.

When he arrives, however, his hallway is packed with four other humans, three of them tall and square and looking like they don't fit in the space. Because it is narrow and they are not; because it is posh and they are not. One is much shorter, braids reaching down her back, a look on her face like she's sucked on a lemon.

"Aunt Ida, what—"

But Devonte cannot finish because he is interrupted by a smack on the back of his head. "What the hell did you do?" Ida hisses. She is keeping her voice down because sound bounces in this building, but her anger is apparent, nonetheless.

"What do you mean?" Devonte asks, and he barely gets the question out.

"Let us inside. We've been out here for hours. It's a damn miracle your neighbors haven't called the cops."

Ever the obedient nephew, Devonte unlocks the door and ushers Aunt Ida and his cousins, Jacob, Isaiah and David, all into his apartment. He notices the duffle bags, Jacob carrying two of them, and he begins to panic. A deep, time-traveling panic that now rockets forward, something that sat deep in his youngest self, a sensation we know so well. The boys shoot him dirty looks and, if he were a different person, Devonte might feel nostalgia for the split lips, the nut flicks, the running and hiding of his youth. But he doesn't, because he hated his cousins and no amount of childhood magic could make them into jolly giants. In short, they were mean, idolized, cool, and probably still are; children that meat-headed don't often change. We know. They were our oppressors, these football brick houses, these popular boys.

Ida had been different, though, when Devonte was growing up. She took pity on her soft nerd-boy nephew, smaller than her children by a head and shoulders at minimum. She always got him books for Christmas; she let him bake cookies in the kitchen instead of playing basketball, a sport at which (like all team sports) he was abysmal; she did nothing more than raise a single eyebrow and say "change it back" when he'd mess with and break her family's computer. He would sweat until he'd figure out how to put it right, but he always did. She never rushed him or hassled him or yelled at him, and in return she never had to go to the principal's office on his behalf. He never let her down.

All that kindness is gone from her face as she interposes herself and her family between Devonte and his record player. "What kind of sick practical joke are your friends playing on you?" she asks, voice only marginally louder. It is after midnight and walls are thin.

"I don't understand."

"Earlier this evening, me and my boys are sitting down to dinner. Jacob starts to say grace when I hear someone knock once at the door. Except it isn't a knock, it's a crash. They broke down the door, Devonte! They broke down the door while we were eating dinner."

"Who?"

"The SWAT team," says Isaiah.

Devonte goes cold, like someone is breaking a water balloon over his head.

"They broke the door right off its hinges. They shouted 'get down' and 'active shooter.' We all hit the floor, right out of our seats." Devonte can see, now that he is looking for them, the elbow scrapes that come with diving out of a chair onto coarse carpet, the bruises on cheeks that come with cracking one's face against the ground. "They said they were looking for you. Devonte Aleba. Someone reported you had gone crazy, were taking hostages. They had our address and everything."

Without responding, Devonte pushes past his family and sits at his desk. He is self-conscious about the roll top; he pushes it up as quietly as he can, as if his cousins won't notice. But they are watching him. David, closest to him in age, smirks, his meanness unaltered by the events of his evening. Devonte powers up his computer and pulls up Reddit and there he needs only type his own name, hit search.

"That fucking bastard," Devonte says. Evrlrnr—Evan, that smug shit who thinks his handle is so cool, or that crazy kid with the conspiracy theories, or that man who knows what taking matters into his own hands truly looks like, because now he's cut off the one real, useful resource the ladies have at their disposal. He's released Devonte's old address, from back when Evan knew him well. When they went to school together, Devonte's permanent address had been—

"Aunt Ida, I'm sorry. I've been going through something, and this guy, he's fucking nuts."

Aunt Ida draws herself up and she seems to grow until she is mythic, terrifying. "Nothing illegal." It is supposed to be a question, but the force that is Ida transforms it into a statement.

"No, of course not."

"Well then." And her face does get a little kinder. "Whatever it is, whatever got you here. Don't do it again. Now." She looks around, sizing up the place. "It's a bit small but—"

Devonte's stomach drops. Of course they are staying. He learns that Isaiah nailed the front door shut to keep their stuff from being stolen. He blows up an air mattress. On the way to the bathroom, David punches him in the side something savage. Aunt Ida takes Devonte's bed only at his insistence, and he is left in the living room with his personal childhood wolves. Does she know they will torture him the whole night? That he will wake up with hairy penises Sharpied on his arms and face? And this, this is where we feel for Devonte, regardless of how we felt about him before. We know what this is like. Most of us were teased and tormented too. When it comes to family—when it comes to bullies—nothing changes.

CHAPTER EIGHTY-FIVE

<**d3vgenius:** you bastard>

<**evrlrnr:** what?>

<**d3vgenius:** whyd you dox my cousins?>

<**evrlrnr:** your cousins?>

<**evrlrnr:** meant to dox you>

<**evrlrnr:** youre hiding that female>

<**evrlrnr:** after she got that dev fired>

<**d3vgenius:** you fucking bet i'm hiding her>

<**d3vgenius:** from the crazy fuckwads like you in the world>

<**d3vgenius:** you fucking know what happens to Black people in this country, evan?>

<**d3vgenius:** do you understand what you could have done?>

<**evrlrnr:** dont use my real name>

<**evrlrnr:** i couldve changed it, you don't know>

<**d3vgenius:** fucking give it up, evan>

<**d3vgenius:** no one is after you>

<**d3vgenius:** you are not that interesting or important>

<**evrlrnr:** cuck. slaving at the feet of females. i was right to do it. im going to find her. we all are>

<d3vgenius is Leaving . . . >

<d3vgenius disconnected from server>

CHAPTER EIGHTY-SIX

Because we can't find Eliza, let's look in on Delphine. A proper lady. Someone doing this whole womanhood thing right. Gorgeous. Devoted to JP. Someone who wouldn't have complained about a joke, gone to the media. Right now, she is at an audition. *Taming of the Shrew*. Shakespeare, that cultural bastion, relevant (instructive) even four hundred twenty-six years on. She recites, clear-eyed, doe-eyed, a misty expression.

"I am asham'd that women are so simple
To offer war where they should kneel for peace;
Or seek for rule, supremacy, and sway,
When they are bound to serve, love, and obey.
Why are our bodies soft and weak and smooth,
Unapt to toil and trouble in the world,
But that our soft conditions and our hearts
Should well agree with our external parts?"

The casting director isn't even looking at her. Not even at the headshot, the most simpering one in her rotation right now, used for ingenues, nor the résumé stapled to the back. He is looking at his phone. Internally, she rolls her eyes, even as she continues. It is typical. Probably Seamlessing food or scrolling through Twitter. He turns to the woman next to him, probably an assistant, and his phone tilts a little bit. Delphine sees Eliza's face on it, a face she has never met in person but has come to know very well over the past two weeks. The bane of her existence. Jean-Pascale had been the breadwinner in their house, and New York City is expensive. Between her mother and her boyfriend, she'd managed to maintain her status: the only one of her group of friends to not sleep two to a room in bunk beds. The only one not working a food service job of some kind. She'd gotten domestic partnered, and therefore had health insurance. And those animals, Eliza and Lewis, took it all away with petty squabbling. It's just a stupid joke; a stupid game.

We, of course, don't agree with her line of thinking. But at least she's not out here pretending to be interested. Not trying to convince us she's some fake geek. Not trying to co-opt games for cool points. Neither does she bother JP for his attention while he is playing. She is content with whatever he gives her. Loves him. Will cook for him and put out for him. We cannot think of a better woman; one who leaves us alone and who pays us so much attention at the same time, who constructs her body, clothes, behavior for the way we watch. It is the ideal.

She falters on "but now I see our lances are but straws" when she sees that rat mouth and she thinks, Great, another way that cunt has cost me money. Naturally this happens when the casting director looks up. She stumbles further, and she mentally kicks herself. A true professional wouldn't have let that throw her, wouldn't have hung up on "but now— but now," as though she'd forgotten the line. But of course the casting director loves to see a woman in distress, and Delphine's face changes from serene to troubled. Normally she would have plowed through— that's what actresses are taught to do. Entirely out of character, she hunches her shoulders and crosses her arms. "I'm sorry," she says, and she gestures at the phone as though she is still performing. And perhaps she is. "My partner is one of the programmers wrapped up in that mess."

The casting director, who had been about to tell her that the role of Kate was certainly going to go to someone famous and not to someone untried, leans forward. "You have firsthand knowledge of this whole thing?" She nods and starts walking toward the door, anticipating the dismissal. "Wait, sorry," the casting director continues, and she halts. "This version of *Shrew* is—updated. The director has this vision to do it, if my understanding is correct, sort of Tinder-inspired, very reliant on this internet stuff. This is—kind of perfect, actually. Do you happen to have 'no shame but mine' prepared?" The assistant has begun scribbling some notes.

Of course Delphine has the other monologues prepared. She is perfect at what she does. She sets in on it, jumps into it.

"Angrier!" the casting director yells, and she takes the note, twanging against the new energy in the room, pulling the string she can now feel between herself and the table, and for a second it is time travel. A bending of space. This lightless box with its grey floor becomes, somehow, both Renaissance Padua and the stage on which she will perform as Kate, a leading role. The room electrifies and everyone can see the future. "Use what those men did to your girlfriend! Fuel it! Light it on fire!"

Delphine realizes the mistake, but launches directly into the next line, taking the note anyway. Both the casting director and she see the narrative spinning out before them, more valuable than any acting talent she might possess. What gets a girl hired here is the ability to chum the media waters. To link her name in a direct line to the Fancy Dog scandal, to us. It is the first time she considers that feminism might be a tool. What a depraved vulture. She will correct them, eventually, but only halfway. She will let them think she has always had a complicated relationship with Jean-Pascale's actions. She will profit, profit by throwing him under the bus.

Every woman is a cunt. This proves how ridiculous the female gender is. As soon as even the tiniest whiff of success, of fulfilled ambition, scents the air, drips into the water, they'll always, *always* turn on men. All the money and the health insurance in the world wouldn't fix them. Jean-Pascale deserves her attention! He's the reason she's got an advantage, the reason she can be at this audition at all! We are livid on his behalf. She should be grateful and instead she looks down on him, looks down on all of us. We are seething.

She will go on to star in the 2019 Broadway revival of *Gaslight*. That craven bitch.

CHAPTER EIGHTY-SEVEN

On the night they strategize—after Devonte leaves and after they tweet at The Inspectre—Our Heroine Eliza goes back to the elevator and lies down—she can hear everything We do in the warehouse—Our sounds paint themselves into the dark and tiny room and echo up the elevator shaft: One of Us plays acoustic guitar well into the night and then there is The Sex—We are Always Having Sex—a bed-shaking rutting that feels closer than it could possibly be, amplified by the Sheer Number of us Fucking in Various Combinations—but even without all of the Beautiful Noises of Human Love and Connection Eliza's brain is grinding in on itself—every echoing footstep becomes a break-in until the toilet flushes, and every undulating shadow becomes a stalker in the night as Eliza jolts awake more alert each time until she is fraying at the edges

She is still awake when the sun inches under the curtain in the morning and her eyes are round as dinner dishes—when Our Suzanne knocks on the wall Eliza says "I'm sorry—I never slept—I think I'm—I must be sick"

"Want me to bring you breakfast?"

"No thank you" and she would pull the curtain shut if she had ever opened it but she didn't—she doesn't want to lay her eyes on Our faces because it would be too overwhelming and We understand and We do not understand—All Feelings Are Valid and also hasn't she heard about the Healing Powers of Community and Especially the Powerful Anger Circles?

She does not eat that day and We grow So Concerned—she waits for the floor to clear and for all our morning Rituals to finish crashing into each other—when Our noises move to more distant locales (and she can hear Us all and she begins to draw a sonic map in her head) she crosses to the bathroom and drinks out of the sink with her hands—if she would venture out there would be a glass for her in the kitchen but she knows We are there and ready to Embrace Her—even with those of Us who leave to work there are enough that We're always around—too much Chatting and Noise and Embracing and besides—the windows—she should stay away from the windows—it is a Reasonable Response and also We fundamentally Do Not Understand It because We are comfort when We're together and We want her to have a water glass and to experience Our Stability and We wish she would eat and she should take all the time she needs

She pokes her head out to make sure the floor is truly devoid of Us and she heads for some dusty bookshelves lined with Our second-hand reading—We are who We are so mostly it's heavy with Judith Butler and Maggie Nelson but We like that good sweet book candy as well! We are not humorless! We love A Whimsy! it's possible to find Our very favorite fluffy stuff—Our literary teddy bears—some high fantasy titles in the bottom corner and some young adult titles in the bathroom—ladies dressing as boys to become knights and queer teenagers finding romance in the rural Midwest—exactly what she is looking for—she sits on the bed still in her pajamas and feels the gloss on the cover and the raised yellow letters and she can't remember the last time she's touched a physical book—We are So Happy to share

Eliza shoots through two books from the comfort of her elevator and then it is midnight and she is finally tired so she sleeps but she dreams of being Haunted—the big red lever is pulled by a wayward spectre and the elevator drops and she jolts and sits up gasping—safe—

nothing actually happened in the waking world and she sighs through her mouth—she is drenched in sweat

She steps up to the curtain and opens it and stares down at the space between the elevator floor and the floor floor—between the potential for Movement and the Promise of Stasis—and she thinks she might be hungry and she tries to lift her foot and place it outside into the hall— her leg simply does not follow the instruction—she's lost all get-up-and-go and she thinks what is another day of reading fairy tales? of taking some Radical Self-Care Time away from capitalism and declaring one-self A Being in need of Rest in a world that wants to monetize every second of Our time?—eventually Our Suzanne knocks on the wall

"How ya feeling?" she says through the curtain

"Still not good" Eliza lies and tells the truth—Fear is an illness and it isn't

"Good enough for food? want me to bring breakfast up?"

Eliza hesitates because it is such a burden and she doesn't want to be a burden but she is so hungry and she cannot imagine the long journey to the communal kitchen so she finally decides to answer "Yes" but immediately she feels bad and she feels that Yawning Chasm of Fear and the need to cocoon oneself after trauma and so she doesn't stop her friend even though she feels terrible about it

Our Suzanne returns and knocks again and says "I've got tea and eggs and toast"

"Just leave it out there" Eliza replies "I don't want to get you sick" and on some level she knows Our Suzanne can't catch what's keeping her in bed—though fear *is* a contagion, We have spent all our lives dealing with fear and it's now static in the background—We have become accustomed to everyone wanting Us dead and gone and We all remember the moment—different for each of Us but fundamentally the same—when We realized that Safety was a lie and that We had to make it ourselves if We wanted any of it

"Okay" says Our Suzanne through the still-closed curtain but she doesn't sound convinced and neither are We—when Eliza hears

Suzanne's footsteps grow distant and go down the stairs she reaches under the curtain and pulls the tray in and winces at the scraping sound and the slight slosh of hot tea—she eats and wonders what to do with the plate and cup so she tiptoes across to the bathroom with panic rising in her throat each second she is out and rinses them as best she can in the bathroom sink by scraping the stuck egg off with her fingernails and she wonders if she should leave them outside the curtain and she decides no that's too weird—like she thinks Our Suzanne is a maid—she's sure she'll be able to go down to the kitchen soon—sure she'll be able to walk a greater distance than across the hall—she decides she'll wait until then—she keeps reading

Our Suzanne shows up again midday and says "I brought you lunch—No-meat sandwich and chocolate milk for a little bit of Understandable Regression—can I come in?"

"Just leave it out there" Eliza says through the curtain and Our Suzanne raises an eyebrow because Eliza sounds muffled like her head is buried in the pillow "I don't want to get you sick"

"I promise I won't get sick—the Rage burns all the germs out" Our Sweet Jokester Suzanne is cajoling because she thinks it will get her the best response and she doesn't want to push her friend but it is frustrating for Our Suzanne at the same time—as much as she loves Us Suzanne is a person who leaves for work during the day and she is unused to spending all her time here—We know We are A Lot and Eliza is her connection to outside—when no reply comes she continues to speak, more insistent this time—"Eliza, I need to get your breakfast dishes"

Our Suzanne hears footsteps and when Eliza peels back the curtain her hair is crazy and her bed is unmade and despite having slept her eyes are surrounded by dark circles and the room smells stale—Our Suzanne twitches and wonders how a room without a door can smell so Strongly of anything let alone the ephemeral subtle stench of depression

We want Our Suzanne to be a little more understanding because it has only been a day though it has felt like years and years and We all know that recovering from trauma requires care and time and even though We think she needs Community Care that Eliza needs to feel the Beating Heart of Her Own Agency and that Mercury is in retrograde anyway and all communication will go very poorly but that doesn't matter to Suzanne's underlying lizard brain and her instinct says run away from this—that this is a black hole that will suck her in and that it already has

Our Suzanne breathes deep three times because she is a Pinnacle of the Ability to Handle Large Emotions and Eliza tries to smile but her facial muscles look to be out of order as they do the work of pulling her lips back without an ounce of Happiness to help them and she says "Thank you so much Suzanne" as she takes the sandwich and the tea "Let me just—" she reaches behind the door and pulls the semi-dirty dishes out and she says "I did my best" by way of Apology

"No problem—You're not feeling well" Our Suzanne replies

CHAPTER EIGHTY-EIGHT

SChoy: Devonte, where are you?

SChoy: you haven't answered two days

SChoy: im fucking dying in here

SChoy: Eliza won't leave the elevator

SChoy: i need to talk to someone who doesn't, like, want me to be their mother

SChoy: or, like, someone who isn't RIGHT FUCKING NEXT TO ME

SChoy: it's brutal, never leaving. i didn't expect it to be this fucking crazy-making

SChoy: devonte?

SChoy: we have to move forward with some sort of plan

SChoy: you've had days to think about it

SChoy: i need help

SChoy: are you okay?

SChoy: devonte?

SChoy: I need her to be able to leave the room

SChoy: I need to be able to leave again

SChoy: devonte, you are the only one who knows how to do this, you have to

SChoy: devonte

SChoy: devonte i swear to fucking god

DAleb: i'm sorry suzanne

DAleb: i cant

SChoy: I CAN'T? what can't you do?

SChoy: you think you can't more than i can't?

SChoy: she's in my literal house

SChoy: eating my literal food and keeping me a literal prisoner

SChoy: and you can't?

SChoy: your life is fucking UNTOUCHED

SChoy: devonte?

SChoy: devonte, what the everliving fuckballs?

CHAPTER EIGHTY-NINE

We can't find her. We can't find her and it's frustrating. Or we can't find her and it means we are winning. Or we can't find her and we move on to the other women on whom we are tactically focusing for a time; we'll come around to her again when she surfaces. We cackle with glee; she is cracking. She is cracking and we love it. We have found the weak places and tapped them with our sharpest hammers. Doesn't she know that none of this is dangerous, that we will only hurt her if she doesn't disappear? Or we desperately want her back. We want her to show any sign that she knows we're still around. She is so much fun to consume. Her fear is a delicacy.

What surprises us is that we also wish desperately for Suzanne to send up a flare, any flare at all. Even though she's abrasive. Even though she's the social justice warrior. We love to slurp her shock, surprise and horror off her bones as well. It's not the same kind of love we've grown into with some of the others. Nothing like JP, for instance. Nothing close to that. But this sucks for her. It just fucking does. She could have nothing to do with this, and were it not for some overzealous volunteering, she would be relatively untouched—The Inspectre can't find her, after all. She is no JP, who got whirlwinded into this; she is no Preston, tempted with a siren song, fallen victim to females. She just raised her hand at the wrong time, thinking she could be a superhero. We love to see it—someone masterminding their own downfall, out in the open.

Eventually, we will come to know the outside of this freakshow building that they're in. Eventually, we will know the view from the window on the first floor, in particular. And we will hear what the degenerates inside think about this, those faggots, those people pretending to be made-up genders, who are infiltrating our normal fucking game space. They will converge upon Suzanne as though she could fix the crazy girl, as though Eliza is her responsibility. And we know that is the worst feeling; we hate being responsible for others. Even being responsible for ourselves is exhausting.

Or. Or. Suzanne is purely selfish. The Inspectre is targeting her too, after all. Perhaps she's staying in, scared of her own accord.

Or Suzanne was voluntold, she didn't volunteer at all. Eliza guilted her into offering housing and now Suzanne is being kept prisoner. She feels like someone volunteered her to be a janitor without her consent; constantly cleaning up the spilled milk, those human-shaped puddles.

But that is not now. For now, we can't find them. We don't know exactly what she does in meatspace after she is finished chatting with Devonte. What we do know is that moments after that chat is time-stamped, Chimera the Protector appears in Windy City, and she appears alone. We also know that she is not visible for more than twenty-eight seconds. Then even her digital self is gone, gone, gone. Fuck this shit.

CHAPTER NINETY

Preston is on the third floor of Fancy Dog Games. It should be rife with debugging, but when he feels unprovoked panic begin to rise in his chest, he tells everyone to take lunch. "The whole team? All five of us at once?" Devonte asks.

"Yep," replies Preston. "You deserve it." Preston squeezes his temples with his hands and Devonte knows that Preston needs some time, some privacy. So they all go to the taco place and we imagine Preston rekeys the elevator to let only his ID onto the third floor for an hour or so. He must need some privacy. Then he embarks on playing *Guilds*, for real, for the first time in—fuck, months? A year? We are not sure. He wants to forget about Eliza, about Dog and his sad stump where a tail used to be. He's in a cone, and Preston has hired a fancy dog walker, armed with treats and vetted near to death to make double, triple sure she is not The Inspectre. But he thinks The Inspectre is likely a man, that women don't generally do things like this.

Preston spent enough time as Human Man in virtual reality only to declare it working, up to par. Now he really takes a look at himself, looking down at his hands. His lair, a simple cube room set apart from the rest of the world, doesn't contain much. Certainly no reflective surfaces—mirrors didn't seem important before the headset. Using his almost unlimited in-game power, the perk of being the CEO, he replaces one wall with mirrors. He need not pay—his money counter always reads an eight, lying on its side. Infinite credits. We are so jealous. He gets the woman; he gets the money; he gets the fame. And the world of Windy City is his bitch.

He sets his eyes upon the default character he inhabits. Human Man. He moves his arms and Human Man's arms move. He paces back and forth and he sees this amalgam of parts pace as well, slightly stiff. When more sensors come out, as hardware advancements march forward with time, that will be fixed. He isn't worried. The cape flows out behind him and Preston smiles—the physics are spot-on. His team has made a world steeped in scientific laws for his heroes, his villains, to break with flight and teleportation and electricity shooting from their fingers. He is sad the second this thought materializes—likely he'll never get to see Circuit Breaker like this. Or he is angry that Eliza has so thoroughly ruined the launch. Or he's numb, still, from Dog's tail being amputated, and touching this is like poking a surgical scar—it zaps through him in the not-feeling. Though Human Man's head dips, looks to the floor, his face doesn't change. It is chiseled; stoic. And not only is it devoid of emotion, it looks nothing like him.

Preston doesn't feel the same things his players report feeling— we've heard him say he does, but he doesn't. He feels disconnected from this bag of options he chose almost at random. Yes, it was a lie, back when he called them his favorites. He doesn't have favorite options. He chose efficiently. Or he was so overwhelmed at the time, he created the narrative that made him sound smooth on television. We think that's a tragedy, like a wizard who can never revel in his own wondrous spells. Perhaps, he thinks, if it looked more like him, he'd feel at least a shadow of the magic he helped make. Unlike everyone else in the system, he and Brandon can both alter their features after selection. We watch as he creates his first self-portrait, as honest as he can make it. It's from memory too. A life-size sculpture. Preston stands before himself, creating himself. Examining himself. He keeps the cape—he finds it actually is his favorite, no lie this time. Not a random choice.

He's been selecting, shaping, sculpting for but ten minutes when his alert goes off. When he'd realized he hadn't coded any component of the game himself in the same amount of time he hadn't played it, he refamiliarized himself by adding in a few lines, just for him. So he knows, even though he is not friends with her, that Suzanne is online. He would know if Eliza signed on too, but he knows as well as we do that this won't happen. And he knows his code has worked because he knows every time Devonte plays, even when he is not Runner Quick. He wants to be close to them, to those shut in Suzanne's house (or apartment? He doesn't really know. He has looked up the address but has not yet used Google Street View, which he will do soon), without actually being there. He wants to poke at his bruise without injuring himself further.

We wonder why. He could move on. Out of sight, out of mind. And Eliza is definitely out of sight. Perhaps he feels a sense of responsibility. Eliza has convinced him he is partially to blame for events unfolding the way they are. Perhaps he is lonely—Eliza was his girlfriend, after all, or perhaps his whore, and he mistakenly thought her friends were actually his as well. Or perhaps he is operating within a moral code—people appear to be in trouble (even though we know they're perfectly safe as long as they behave how we want them to), and so he feels protective. Or perhaps he is like us—curious. Watching. Entertained.

Preston uses another one of his CEO powers. "Suzanne," he says, and she hears his voice in her ear. She is startled—she appears where she last was, outside the city surrounded by trees that have, since she and Eliza split them and scorched them, grown back. She knows instantly who it is. She looks around, but no—he's not there. She's never considered he could do things others couldn't, project his voice where his character isn't, but she supposes it makes sense. Owning the world; that is a superpower. Omniscient. Godlike.

"You're not supposed to use real names in-game," she whispers into the air with a voice still watered from crying.

Preston can hear the recent tears. "I know. I'm sorry. I'm—I don't know what I am." It is the truth. He pauses, and Suzanne can hear him breathe. "Do you want to talk?"

"Yes," she says, and she is surprised at how quickly she answers. Or she says, "I don't know. I don't know what I am either." Or she says, "Not like this. This is creepy." Or perhaps all three, one after the other. We are learning quickly that many things can be one thing. As we are inventing this world, this story, we are learning that there are few absolutes. Few single options.

"I'll teleport you," he replies. He is nervous. He isn't sure where it is coming from, but we know. He's about to show someone his new self for the first time. To unmask is vulnerable.

Preston is surprised when Chimera materializes in his all-but-empty lair—he expects Suzanne's avatar to look more like her. Instead, she is a sphinxlike creature with giant arms and wings. She is barely human, save for the elegant head.

Suzanne is just as surprised—like everyone else, she knows what Human Man looks like. But standing before her is an approximation of Preston—the same swooped hair and symmetrical smile. She gasps— she's never seen an avatar look so realistic. Partly, it is because this is her first time using Vive. But it's also because Preston is the only person she's ever met pretty enough to be replicated almost exactly by choices in a computer game.

At the same time Preston says, "You're not you," Suzanne says, "You look like you." They both smile and laugh behind their headsets, but Chimera and Human Man only stare at each other as though they are mesmerized.

When they breathe the sighs of stopping, Preston is excited to have something driving thoughts of Eliza, of this crisis, out of his head. "So do you feel anything?"

"What do you mean?" Suzanne asks, puzzled.

"Like, your character doesn't look like you. But people report Windy City as feeling like reality. Like their bodies are actually here."

Suzanne pauses to think, turns toward the mirror. "I don't know. This is my first time playing this way."

"Seriously?"

"Yeah. We've been busy."

"I guess that's understandable. You should take some—alone time." Preston doesn't mean it to sound strange, sexual, and he winces. Luckily for him, Suzanne can't see that. She sees only Human Man.

Suzanne is elated. She feels recognized, understood. She does need time to herself. "I think you're probably right." She turns back to the mirror. "I don't know, though. I don't know that she has to look like me for me to feel—connected, I guess is the word." She tosses her head side to side and sure enough, Chimera's hair bounces and flows. It is so realistic. "I've played as her for so long. She's part of me."

Preston bites his tongue—he almost says that she sounds crazy, like one of those stereotypical basement boys who are too hyped up on cyberspace. He stops himself because she is vulnerable right now. Or because he figures she might be right. Human Man, as he was originally designed, represented a part of him. Perhaps he hadn't felt connected because Human Man was only the worst part, the grasping desire for more, for better, for optimization.

Instead, he says, "So I ask this only based on my very recent experience and not because I think this is how, like, games should go, but if you haven't played as yourself, how do you know if, relatively speaking, you wouldn't feel more connected than you do now?"

Suzanne laughs. "I guess I don't."

"Wanna see?"

"You mean make a new character?"

"Sure. Why not. For the lulz."

They spend the rest of the hour whispering into each other's ears, sculpting Suzanne, selecting every arch of eyebrow, every curve of hip from the eerily detailed character-creation menu. She is both subject and object in this moment. He pays such close attention to every part of her. We are both jealous or we are not; it is Suzanne, after all. Harsh warrior; shrewish ruiner of fun; melting snowflake. But. It is art; it is intimate.

CHAPTER NINETY-ONE

@theinspectre: I notice @HumanMan isn't seeing you at all @BrightEliza. I'd know if he was.

@theinspectre: Is that because @BrightEliza and @yrface are holed up like a couple of dykes?

@theinspectre: Are you too busy fucking @yrface to notice everyone hates you, @BrightEliza?

@theinspectre: Some politician said some girls rape easy, @BrightEliza. I can't remember who it was.

@theinspectre: But I bet he was talking about you, @BrightEliza.

@theinspectre: I bet you fuck easy, @BrightEliza. I bet you rape easy

@theinspectre: you're a coward, @BrightEliza. You too, @yrface. Hiding from me, from this.

@theinspectre: You're just afraid to be wrong, @BrightEliza. You're afraid of a healthy debate.

@theinspectre: Come out and debate us, @BrightEliza. Come out and play.

@theinspectre: .@BrightEliza, have you listened to your phone lately?

@theinspectre: .@BrightEliza, they're coming to take you away, ha ha.

CHAPTER NINETY-TWO

Lewis dreams of severed tails. He dreams of a slow cutting, of watching the blood well around soft curling fur, of guiding the offending hand, of wielding the scalpel himself. He is remarkably clear-eyed about it. *I know I am dreaming of Dog's tail and it is my fault* he writes in his Day One journal every single day since the incident occurred. In his dreams, he always winds up transparent, as though he has given something of his essence, and covered in blood. He looks down at his own hands—they are spotted too. "Out damn spot," he says, and then he wakes, sweating, feeling like he is drowning. He does not cry out. But he does fall out of bed. His sheets are soaked and he thrashes against them. They cling. They pull. He slowly untangles himself.

"Lewis? Lewis, are you okay?" Mrs. Fleishman walks into the room without knocking. "I heard a thump."

We have not zoomed in on Mrs. Fleishman in a while—on either Fleishman, if we're honest—but she's been gone the longest, a tertiary character as mothers often are. She is lying awake when she hears the thump and she comes running down the hall. She's been listening for him. She's barely slept herself. She is so confused, and she is very worried. It makes her bite her cuticles. She's made herself bleed so many times in the week since Lewis's friend was fired. We pity her for what is to come. We blame her for what has happened. We know that

Mrs. Fleishman can't win. Mothers never can. Not in Disney movies, not in D&D games, not on the therapist's couch.

"God, Ma. It was just a dream," he says. He climbs back into his bed and pretends to sleep. He hears his mother pad down the hall. He does not sleep after that—neither of them do. His phone counts up from 1:37 to 2:03 to 2:25. He stares at the ceiling, wired and fearing water, severed tails and blood. He thinks about his endless Steam library—he wants to play something, but nothing appeals. He selects *Guilds* out of habit, but when he sits in front of his computer, something keeps his hand from reaching out to turn it on. He doesn't understand what.

Understanding his whys and hows has never been Lewis's strongest suit. In that way, we can't trust his thoughts, his self-awareness, his Diary, which we have under our control, as clear-eyed as it might sound. His reactions are animal. We have to speculate so much more with him, even though we ostensibly have the most concrete replication of his inner monologue, the most of anyone we're watching. He must be far more complex than what he writes; it doesn't make sense if he isn't. Funny, it's not what we would've predicted. Most of us look so much more like Lewis, act so much more like Lewis, have experiences that are closest to Lewis's. We would've predicted logic, order, in the way he sees the world and himself. Instead, the way he sees the world is clear, but the way he sees himself is muddy water. Is that us? Are we like that too?

Our brains grind on that stone, clinging tight to one difference: that he is in a rigid stasis; we have grown and changed in the telling and retelling of this story more than Lewis has. He paces his living room, watching a city that never goes dark.

Let's jump ahead a bit and look at how many nights Lewis dreams of the tail. December 17–24, 2016, his Day One obsesses over a single question: *Where is it? Where is the tail?* We don't know either. Where is it? Where is the tail?

He goes to work sleep-deprived and works with two new people on his development team, hired almost immediately one after the other, bang bang. Both male. We don't care about their names because it doesn't matter. Consider them NPCs; they are not players in this game. They are generic people who turn out generic code and listen to whatever Lewis tells them to do. And Lewis hates them for it. He bashes out most of the real work himself, assigning mundane tedium to these two bags of skin who never complain, never want more.

Lewis misses Jean-Pascale something fierce. He tries to email him, tries to email him eight times over, ten more after that; no response. He even starts to miss Eliza—it sneaks up on him when he is going through the NPC programmers' code. It surprises him—the thought that he would rather have Eliza back than either of these two men, both of whom have degrees and proper training and have paid their dues. Both of whom chug energy drinks and listen to classic rock through oversized headphones while working. There is something motivating about having a nemesis. Who is he, if not the opposite of her?

He begins to stay later and later at the office because he knows he can't sleep. Even if his body is tired and he needs to drink coffee or soda or Rockstar to do work, to keep his eyes open, he knows he won't be able to close them once in his bed. And even if he could manage to slip into sleep, he'll only be in that "virtual reality" state for two, maybe three hours before he dreams of slicing apart an animal, seeing the white of bone as he peels back skin with his fingernails. Before he wakes up drowning.

So he begins spending the night at the office. He ignores frantic texts from his mother (*where r u?*) and catches naps on couches, dreaming of tails, tails, blood and the missing tail, almost as soon as the white noise in his mind gives way to black. *It's the most reliable thing about me right now*, he writes. At least there are no sheets to get tangled in.

He misses Preston too. It's only been a couple of weeks since this all started, and Preston still comes into the office, but "miss" is, nevertheless, the right word. Preston, who's been acting weird, disappearing, closing the third floor off for long stretches of time. Lewis thinks he's coming up with something new down there. Or that he's pining. Either way, Preston is totally different, as is working on *Guilds*—the creative spark is gone, the game is just a game with Brandon in charge. It isn't a world; only pixels. It doesn't feel imperative to play. He can't name the emotion wedged into the interstitial space between his heart and his diaphragm. He can't figure it out, but we can: responsibility. He feels responsible for Preston's sorrow or mania, for Preston's absence. He whispers to himself in the back of his own head: your fault, your fault, your fault. And Lewis is so rigid that he can't flow around this information. Can't figure out how to adapt to it, erode it or excise it.

He begins to shake during the day. His heart beats fast and his legs threaten to dump him on his ass. Brandon questions why he is there so late, so early, overnight, and Lewis says, "I'm just working. There's a lot to do with new people around." Brandon nods, puts on a solemn face and lectures halfheartedly on work-life balance. Then he gets on a plane for a meeting in California because truthfully he doesn't give a flying saucer.

With a liter of orange soda in hand, Lewis forces himself to turn the game on at three in the morning because there is no more work to be done. The office isn't creepy in the same way his home is, but it's still empty. A void. He wants to fill it with something, and *Guilds* used to work so he figures he'll give it a try. He keys himself into the third floor. He'll play with Vive.

Tonight, his lair is familiar, but not comforting. The library-esque quality of his plush digital furniture, his rugs imported all the way from imaginary in-game desert artisans, the cold fire in his fake fireplace: it all feels flat. Meaningless. Like trash. He itches to break all the glass—there is so much glass here. All of Black Hole's possessions. He is so angry. What is Doctor Moriarty without his sidekick? But he stops himself, because that would be nuts. Because what if Jean-Pascale forgives him and comes back, plays again. Lewis prides himself on his stability.

He walks around the space. Doctor Moriarty (no tagline) doesn't feel calm or authoritative or any of the things Lewis normally feels while inhabiting this body. He feels manic. Jittery. He remembers that, should Jean-Pascale forgive him and play again, it won't be the same.

Black Hole is being transformed into an NPC villain, full-time, and JP's account has been discontinued. He did it himself. He'd killed Black Hole with just a few deleted lines.

Lewis pings the other two backend guys. "Doctor Moriarty (no tagline) would like to invite you to join his Guild. Only Lawful Evil and Neutral Evil characters may respond." He paces his lair for a couple minutes, waiting. He practices at his blackboard, increasing some skill points. He smokes a pipe made of pixels. No one responds; likely they are asleep. Lewis and Doctor Moriarty are bored.

So he decides to cause mischief. Real mischief, because, in the past, that has always brought him joy. He is in possession of one of the rarer items in the game—an antique printing press. He has plenty of paper (Paper X4562), enough to make some flyers.

Bounty, the flyer says. *Photos of Circuit Breaker in compromising positions. Will wire 10 credits to anyone who can provide. Never forget her lewd behavior, never forget how she fell from grace.*

He stops at two flyers when he realizes that his original plan—unlocking her account and letting the hackers go for it once more—will get him fired. And that these in-game flyers will be easily traceable to him. But he can't resist a tiny bit of mayhem. He sends each of the flyers to the NPC programmers. It is such small mayhem, nothing like his masterminded plans of yore, when the consequences didn't spill out into the physical world. And for a few moments, he wonders if getting fired would be such a bad thing, if he shouldn't cause larger chaos and screw the meatspace consequences. But he stops himself, because giving up his job would be nuts—would be perceived as insane. And Lewis, as we said and will say again and again, prides himself on his stability.

He removes his headset and sleeps, arms and legs splayed out like a da Vinci drawing, on the bare concrete floor. He sleeps light and fitful and dreams of blood and knives and finding the tail in the garbage can on the subway platform. He resists checking the game each time he wakes, resists the appearance of needing a reaction. Someone to ping back from the void, to validate, to agree.

Lewis falls asleep in earnest around five and wakes again around six thirty. He peels himself from the floor and checks the game: both his teammates have accepted the invitation, declaring their intention to move lairs, to perhaps repurpose the celestial observatory that Black Hole used to call home. "We could sell all that stuff," one says. "And really make something spectacular." The second one sends an in-game screenshot encased in a virtual Polaroid photo frame. It is of the day Eliza had been hacked, the day Circuit Breaker engaged in that afore-mentioned lewd behavior. In the photo, which Lewis can hold in his hands as Doctor Moriarty, NPC Programmer Two's character, in a masked getup similar to the Phantom of the Opera, is having a go with her. "I was there," it says in mock-handwritten scrawl on the bottom of the photo. "Never forget."

Lewis thinks he should feel better. But he doesn't. And he can't ar-ticulate why. He wires NPC Programmer Two ten credits, as promised. He makes a full pot of coffee for the early-comers in the physical world. He is not a monster, he thinks to himself. He makes the coffee. He considers his co-workers.

At ten in the morning, Lewis is in a meeting with our NPC programmers when his vision goes a bit purple, a bit spotted. He is beyond registering alarm—he's had visual artifacts for days. He figures lack of sleep will do that to a person, and it'll all go away as soon as he falls back into a regular pattern. Any day now. But when the colors clear, Dog is in the room. But he is huge, as if Lewis has put on the Vive and Dog had been scaled to the size of a cow. Even if he were the size of the real Dog, Lewis knows Preston hasn't yet brought him back to the office. Might never bring him back. He sits stock-still behind the two men, who are laughing and joking about the flyers. That's when the alarm happens, the panic. Lewis reaches up to touch his face, to make sure the headset isn't on. But it isn't. And yet. There he is. Dog, looking at Lewis with sad, accusatory eyes. Dog, not in a cone but minus one tail, bleeding a river onto the floor.

"Thanks for the ten credits," Programmer Two says. Lewis's eyes widen as Dog, that real, solid Dog, stands. Deliberately. He points like a hunter, which Dog has never been, with his nose. If we were to draw a line between it and Lewis, it would connect with Lewis's forehead, right between the eyes.

"What, man?" Programmer Two continues. "You don't remember wiring me the ten credits? It's just ten credits, man, no big—" He is interrupted by Lewis standing up and scrambling backward, knocking over his chair. The wall is directly behind him; the collaboration rooms are small. He presses himself against it.

"No," Lewis says, "no." He doesn't shout. His words are small. His actions, however, are large and jagged and attract attention through the glass windows. He means to control himself, but he can't. Fear. It's all fear, and he is sweating. Then he is enclosed in a tank of water. It is a deep blue, it's murky. It obscures everything, but the chains holding him down are visible. He sees his own face: the vignetted visage of this phantom is pressed, grotesque, against the glass. He bangs at it with a fist and Lewis can see the sound waves ripple through the water. Bubbles rise from his nose and mouth as Dog gets up and leaves the room, turning his bleeding behind on Lewis.

Lewis gasps for breath. He is drowning or being squeezed; he can't seem to make his chest expand enough. He is taking in sips of air between gulps of water. Everyone is locked in a tank; everyone is drowning. But we know better. We can see that nothing is happening in the room with him. There are no tanks, there is no grand escape trick or any bleeding Dog. There is only Lewis, breaking down against the wall.

"Dude, are you okay?" says NPC Programmer One. Lewis screams, tiny again, as he watches Programmer One's ear cleanly sever from the side of his head. "Bro"—he turns to NPC Programmer Two, whose fingers begin to unzip themselves one by one from his hand, leaving five exposed bones and cascades of blood in their wake—"let's go get help, okay? Because he is not okay." They leave the room; the tank stays. Lewis cowers until he passes out. He is taken to the hospital, sedated and released into the care of his mother.

These are all things that we know for sure. We post his whole Diary on r/Bright, this daily log. From there, it is tweeted. It is published in its entirety on Medium, placed side by side with news articles, tweets from Fancy Dog co-workers, all the reporting on what happened after. We read it voraciously. We devour every single word.

CHAPTER NINETY-THREE

SChoy: okay so

PDog: yes. okay.

SChoy: it got weird

SChoy: i think we can both agree it got weird

PDog: yes. we can agree on that.

PDog: it was unexpected. for sure.

PDog: but like bad weird?

PDog: suzanne?

SChoy: no, not bad weird i dont think

SChoy: but against company policy weird probably

PDog: well i mean

PDog: its not like we never tested the patch

PDog: like, people at the company have done this before

PDog: with each other

SChoy: pretty sure not like that

PDog: what are you talking about

PDog: mechanically, its the exact same thing

SChoy: tell me preston

SChoy: did you have to wash a pair of boxers after you tested the sex patch completely platonically?

PDog: now that question isn't work appropriate

SChoy: luckily we're not working

SChoy: i bet the employees testing the sex patch didn't moan into the microphone

SChoy: just a fcking hunch

PDog: okay yes.

PDog: i'm sorry

PDog: if you felt, like, pressure in any way

PDog: if things are going to be weird for you now

PDog: ill do whatever it takes to fix this

PDog: i'm really sorry

SChoy: don't be

PDog: ?

SChoy: don't be sorry

SChoy: i clicked yes

SChoy: or i guess not clicked

SChoy: what do we even call that now? there's no click with these remotes

PDog: we say "selected"

SChoy: well then

SChoy: i selected yes. i chose to do this

PDog: youre not mad?

SChoy: no

SChoy: in fact

SChoy: i have a little proposition for you

PDog: ?

SChoy: we can continue this

SChoy: it was nice

SChoy: like a vacation from my life rn

PDog: i cant pretend it wasn't nice for me too

SChoy: just dont get weird or fire me or anything, okay?

PDog: can i ask you something?

SChoy: ?

PDog: whyd you do it? select yes?

SChoy: idk

SChoy: id never done something like that before

SChoy: mostly curiosity

PDog: ouch

SChoy: ?

PDog: i mean, like

PDog: i dunno what i mean

PDog: i guess i hoped you liked me a little at least

SChoy: i don't dislike you

PDog: ouch again. you really don't pull punches, do you?

SChoy: not really. but like i don't know what you want me to say

SChoy: its not like were having real sex

SChoy: this is like fucking chat roulette or whatever from a million years ago

SChoy: its just getting yr rocks off. its not real

SChoy: i guess i want to continue because its fun and its free and im locked in my house and we have neat chemistry

SChoy: were both climbing the walls in here

SChoy: whyd you do it?

PDog: idk

PDog: I guess I just wanted to connect.

PDog: with you. with this.

SChoy: this?

PDog: the vr, Windy City

PDog: i made it and mostly now i feel nothing about it

PDog: i only feel like . . . pressure

SChoy: i hear that

SChoy: that's all this is. steam release

CHAPTER NINETY-FOUR

After a few days of what he thinks might be purgatory, Devonte pays to fix Aunt Ida's door. He sends them home with assurances it won't happen again. He is about 57 percent certain.

Now he sits, deflated, dimly conscious of the deep bruise on his left ass cheek. That is from his cousin David. No amount of space or time can make them grow the fuck up. Alone at last, he tries to play a record but he is too antsy to sit and enjoy it. He swigs some whiskey from the bottle and decides to play *Guilds of the Protectorate*. He slips on his Vive.

But when he gets to his character selection screen, he stands staring at the life-size Runner Quick, trying to make himself select. Proceed. Runner, we've mentioned before, looks so much like Devonte. He is dark with smart eyes and a mischievous smile. Devonte sighs. The point of games, sometimes, is to escape the real world. The real world is too hard right now; it is too difficult to be himself. There is too much weight on everything. There is too much at stake. It is all, simply, too much.

Now we pause, here, because not all of us are great fans of what Devonte does next. For some of us, it makes us uncomfortable and we cannot put our finger on why. Theoretically, there is absolutely nothing wrong with it; one of Devonte's favorite books is *Ready Player One*, so it's an action that is consistent. We wonder, though, how many Black people we accidentally interact with; who hears us at our most honest? Would we be able to tell if someone was infiltrating? Will they unmask us on Twitter, come for our jobs, get us fired for banter that is otherwise completely acceptable? We've said it before and we'll say it again: the world isn't safe for normal white men anymore.

Devonte selects build new character instead. And he builds the lightest-skinned white boy he can build. Red hair, Roman nose, freckles. The works. He, too, has laughed at the Eddie Murphy sketch, but the voice whispers in the back of his mind: will it be different? Does everyone throw a party when he leaves a room? Will he be able to tell if they do from a computer game? How close is it to real life? What would it be like to not worry about his dreadful cousins being SWATted? Besides, he thinks, he doesn't want to encounter Suzanne. Or worse, Eliza. He hasn't heard from her and he takes that as a supremely bad sign. But she has to understand. Has to. The world is a dangerous place for someone like him. Hasn't she considered that? If he slips and doesn't turn on true invisibility, if Eliza and Suzanne are pinged that he is online and they try to find him, they won't. He can slip into a crowd, a lowly level one, and wait until they leave. Would it be worse, he wonders, if his friends didn't come looking for him?

Finally, he sets himself loose in Windy City. This time, he can fly instead of run. He carries a bow and arrow—when he levels up enough, he'll attain a wolf companion. He can see very, very far away. He possesses True Strike—he can shoot even when someone has half cover; when he levels up enough, three-quarters. He wants as much distance between himself and the rest of the world as possible. He wears a cape. His name: Lone Hunter (no tagline—it sounds better without one).

The first thing Devonte notices about flying through the world as Lone is the silence. No pings, no prodding, no "look"s or "he works here!"s. The second thing he notices is: nothing. He supposes he expected more of a climax, and he laughs a little. There shouldn't be a climax to creating a new character. That's all it is; making a new skin.

Easy as a few selections. Easy to remake a body to fit tonight's whims. The flight is the most impressive thing about this, on the Vive. It no longer makes people nauseous to stand still and soar at the same time, but he half expects it to. It only feels a little strange, like standing in the aisle of a moving local subway train while looking through neighboring windows of an express train, passing quickly. His body adjusts and before long it's as if humans have always been able to fly and he feels like he should be able to do this in the physical world as well, is mad that he can't. He has a dream like this at least once a month. Where he takes off into the sky with no wings to assist him.

He flies into the city proper and touches down, looking to pick a fight. With a brand-new character like this, he needs easy XP fast. So he goes to where The Hooligans hang out—a particular overpass where sullen preteen boys make throwaway characters to heckle and harass passersby. As Runner, he's taken great joy in walking into the shadows there and, when someone shoots a gun or a laser at him, wiping out the lot of them before they can react. He smiles thinking about it— about how time almost slows for him, about walloping each smug little shit in the back of the head. It'll take more, with Lone. He is brand-new, after all, the equivalent of a shaky newborn lamb. But these kids make throwaways, like we said, and they hoot and ah when they get eviscerated fantastically. It'll take more, but it won't take that much.

He smirks and advances. He can hear them, see their typed script. He knows they're there, and he waits. He waits for someone to start some shit.

He is so surprised when he comes out the other side and nothing happens, as anticlimactic as making a new character itself had been. Puzzled, he tries again. No one hurls a missile at him. No one even makes an outdated "your mom" joke.

Devonte's face throbs under the headset. He thinks he knows why, why they've fucked with Runner and not Lone. But what if it's just because he's level one? Or because when he walks through here as Runner, he has that stupid badge by his name indicating he's a Fancy

Dog employee? There are a million reasons why they're not targeting him right now, he thinks. But what if it *is* that particular reason? He signs off in disgust. He is too tired to play anyway. He spends a lot of time staring at his ceiling in bed. His body is exhausted, but his mind keeps talking to him. He feels insane.

CHAPTER NINETY-FIVE

We are obsessed with what goes on where we can't see it. A black box. In short, we still cannot find Eliza or Suzanne and it is making us froth at our collective ever-hungry mouth. We want to make sure we mark time passing. Time is passing. Slowly, excruciatingly. If we were in a cheap movie, we'd see days being ripped off a desk calendar in a wibbly soft focus. Days pass and Lewis goes to work, sedated and sleepless after his breakdown. He is getting no better. Days pass and Suzanne continues to sign on, meet Preston. She's borrowed some of the equipment from work (express mailed to her by Preston himself). Preston's taken to playing at home now. Something he hasn't done in ages. Turns out, an empty apartment is perfect when reality is virtual. Days pass and Devonte gets used to his new alter ego and has very mixed feelings about it. Days pass and we still haven't found them, have not yet come to be acquainted with the outside of the warehouse.

CHAPTER NINETY-SIX

Of course We know what's going on because We can see and hear them—Hear them especially—Our Suzanne has set up VR equipment in her cubicle and We are going to have to have a talk about her not Sharing Her Resources And Knowledge with the Collective and also We understand the need for Personal Space and Boundaries and wouldn't subscribe to the capitalist notion that every single thing she does must somehow pay us a return on our Time and Friendship—she especially loves to play when We are using the recording studio because it grants her the (false) sense of privacy that the noises never escape the cork walls—They Certainly Do—and We are used to the Sounds of Sex and it is No Big Deal and We know she is up to something and We want to know what's going on—who she's Seeing and what software she's using and We want her to *Get It Get It Get It Girl* because she hasn't brought someone home in a long time and We were worried she wasn't using her Queerness to its Fullest Advantage and also We don't place a person's total value on the Sex they have and also there's no hierarchy in identities (excuse Us) it just sometimes seems the Straight People Are Not Okay

Eliza largely remains in the elevator—she waits and she sleeps and she listens to Our sounds and hears the soft moaning We know is coming from Suzanne but Eliza doesn't know that because We are always fucking Someone and Each Other and unless one knows Us very well Our Noises are indistinguishable and anyway she is too busy cocooning—forming her chrysalis and Healing from the trauma—We worry though—We worry that she is crossing from a Healing-Space into one of self-harm and We are all trained in Police-Free Bystander Intervention in the event of self-harm—it's Community Care and We must help her Emerge

It is morning and Eliza wakes when the elevator doors shudder to life—she springs from bed as they close behind the curtain and the entire space lurches toward the ground floor and when the doors open again she is wide-eyed and feral with fear—she'd be snarling if she weren't human

We say *It's okay* from beyond the still-drawn curtain—*Open the curtain—We just want to talk—We are worried about you*

Eliza slowly peeks her face through the curtain to face Us—the Many-Headed Hydra of the Sixsterhood-minus-Our-Suzanne and she doesn't remember all our names in the swirl of her despair and panic and that's okay because We deeply appreciate a person's limits in a time of duress—We are an undulating sea of Purple Hair Dye and Septum Piercings and Mesh Shirts and Mullets and Leg Hair and Matte Lipstick—every body a Good Body and everyone a Babe—One of Our hands is on the big red lever that controls the elevator guest room

Before you say anything—We decree—*We want to acknowledge the ways We have disagreed on Our course of action this morning as there is a wide swath of Acceptable Best Practices in this kind of Situation and reasonable minds can differ on the best way forward*

Yeah like you are reacting perfectly reasonably to a Shitty Situation and We just want to be clear about that

but there are a couple of things We want to reassure you about? because We don't want you to be this scared?

We're not gonna let anyone in and this place is technically leased to a business so no one's going to find you here At All—it's not a logical fear and also All Feelings Are Valid and your fear is reasonable fear

Right—and even if someone does find you? We have a Community

Safety Plan in place and We're not gonna let anything happen to you and you can take a look at it if you want—We built it on post-it notes and they're on a poster board by the fridge in the kitchen and We think it's pretty good!

Second thing is it's totally fine to have a mental health meltdown right now but this is a Community that Supports folks in getting Help, so—you don't have to do it today and you don't have to do it tomorrow but We are going to make sure you get to a Therapist because No One should have to go through this without a Therapist

Third thing is you are relying too heavily on Our Suzanne—no single Community member should bear the weight of sole responsibility in a Crisis Scenario

Yeah Our Suzanne has been weird and not the good kind of weird—not the normal kind of weird—

So We need to think of ways for you both to Co-Exist here and maybe for you both to Get Out Of The Building for a little and We Intend to have a Community Strategizing Vegan Dinner about it after the holiday

Yeah It's Christmas Eve Eve so like We said—Not today and not tomorrow—We're having our Winter Holiday and Solstice Tree Trimming Ceremony tonight anyhow and We'd love it if you joined Us and tomorrow morning is a Nice Big Breakfast that We all make Together and it'll just be weird if you sit in this elevator through all of it—so you don't have to go out but like maybe explore the Sixsterhood today? you took a tour but you really haven't seen everything and you can use any of the equipment you want!

We've had a Community meeting and decided to put a whole bunch of fabric over the windows and We think probably that'll be a little bit easier

"And I'm painting on it gosh it's so much fun check it—"

Anyhow—a stern look—Wander today—you don't even have to change out of your pajamas if you don't want to but We want to remind you that there is laundry here and you smell like death

"Oh My God You Cannot Say That—"

"What? it's laundry—she should do some laundry instead of changing into the same three things—"

"Let her see the warehouse fuck don't give her chores!"

"I can't give her chores Bunny it's not a hierarchy and I don't have the power to give her—"

Eliza is a little stunned and We think it's because she wasn't aware that We cared—but of course We care! it's impossible to see someone go through something like this and not care and she says "I could—uh— I could get out of the elevator I think—do laundry—walk around the warehouse"

Good—now! Actual Breakfast! We can see your ribs through your shirt and you can't just have Our Suzanne bring you toast forever

Eliza looks around and asks "Where's the tree?"

It's getting delivered this afternoon

This perks Eliza's ears up because it is so strange to her that she forgets her fear for a second—"You can get Christmas trees delivered?"

Solstice Tree, We reply

CHAPTER NINETY-SEVEN

@BrightEliza: I'm done

@Fleishmaster: I know.

@BrightEliza: you're an asshole

@BrightEliza: I don't mean I'm done in the industry, I don't mean I'm done at life

@BrightEliza: which I'm sure is what you're hoping for

@BrightEliza: I'm done letting your actions have all this power over me

@BrightEliza: I can't leave a goddamn building because of you, but I'm not going to let you make me afraid like this anymore.

@BrightEliza: and maybe you haven't been fired (Lord fucking knows why not)

@BrightEliza: and maybe I don't have the power to make sure you don't get hired again if you are

@BrightEliza: but just so you fucking know

@BrightEliza: as of right now, at least, I have options

@BrightEliza: If I run off into the woods somewhere and become a hermit, it's because I CHOOSE to

@BrightEliza: I can keep working in the industry, I can come back to Fancy Dog or go to See No Monkey, whatever I want, I'm good.

@BrightEliza: despite your efforts, I'm even more sought after than before

@BrightEliza: and I have friends. People who are helping me out right now. A community of actual, IRL PEOPLE.

@BrightEliza: you. What do you have? You had one friend and that dude is GONE.

@BrightEliza: you had the game, but hey, with him gone, is that fun anymore? Or is that just another reality you have to maintain?

@BrightEliza: all you have is this one job and a whole HOST of people who aren't going to touch you with a ten foot pole. I bet even your mother is ashamed of you.

@BrightEliza: if you were wiped off the face of this planet this second, the only person who'd care is Brandon

@BrightEliza: because your code wouldn't be in on time and he'd have to hire someone else to do it

@BrightEliza: congratulations, Lewis Fleishman.

@BrightEliza: the only worth you have in this world is the work you do for others, in service of their ideas, not yours, you vulture

@BrightEliza: rot in hell

CHAPTER NINETY-EIGHT

See No Monkey: Hello Ms. Eliza Bright! My name is Courtney and I'm in charge of booking your travel for your contract work in Santa Cruz! I would love to get some information from you about your flight preferences/requirements, your known traveler number if you have one, dietary restrictions and some (rather arcane, my apologies!) information to help us get you some temporary housing.

Eliza: Hi Courtney! Last I heard, See No Monkey wasn't too sure about scheduling something with me because of all the recent responses to my firing (my apartment was broken into, my boss's dog was attacked). Am I to understand that's changed?

See No Monkey: I do see in my notes that you've had a bit of upheaval and I'm supposed to book you for after the holiday so you can make sure your travel documents are in order. But I don't see anything about the offer being rescinded.

Eliza: Oh! Awesome! Thank you! I'm really shocked and grateful.

Eliza: Quick question before we get started—am I allowed to tell people that I'm flying out there in January to do some work with you?

Eliza: Is it something that's public knowledge?

See No Monkey: it can be!

See No Monkey: We didn't make any announcements because we wanted to protect your privacy as much as possible.

Eliza: Thank you. That's very considerate. I'm sorry to be such a bother, it must be a little annoying having to deal with someone in my situation.

See No Monkey: It's not a bother!

Eliza: Thank you. Do you mind if I publicly say that I'm going out for a contract period?

See No Monkey: Sure! We can put a post on our blog too. It would be a nice little coordinated announcement. I'll loop in PR to double check/make a strategy.

Eliza: You don't mind doing it so close to Christmas?

See No Monkey: Nope, not at all. We're here.

CHAPTER NINETY-NINE

@BrightEliza: Really excited to say that I'm doing some work for @SeeNoMonkey in the New Year! #success #thankyou #raisetheshield

We wonder—is her computer good on location? Or will she inadvertently broadcast the data? It must be from her computer, her phone is long gone. We scour it. Should she have hashtagged it Gamergate? Is she out here to get a rise out of all of us? If so, hashtagging it Gamergate would be the most effective. But perhaps redundant; we're all watching her anyway.

@SeeNoMonkey [verified]: We're excited too! RT @BrightEliza: Really excited to say that I'm doing some work for @SeeNoMonkey in the New Year! #success #thankyou #raisetheshield

@SeeNoMonkey [verified]: Read more about our decision to offer @BrightEliza some contract work. Excite! bit.ly/739e-28

Notifications start pouring in. She scrolls through the rest of us: tepid, angry, a very few of us offering congratulations (why are those cucks still among us? Is their number growing?). She finds the one she was looking for.

> **@theinspectre:** @SeeNoMonkey @BrightEliza no. I will not let this happen.

> **@SeeNoMonkey [verified]:** good thing for all of us you don't work here, @theinspectre! #byefelicia

We imagine Eliza, a cold look on her face. Is that—is it fear? Suffice it to say we think the expression on her face in this moment is fear. She is a scared little girl.

CHAPTER ONE HUNDRED

Why hasn't he called?" Eliza asks and We are not sure why she wants The Inspectre to torture her—perhaps she is turning into a masochist? it is now hours later in the afternoon and We've been keeping an eye out to make sure nothing Explodes—waiting for The Inspectre to act and for Lewis to write back more than one line and We are ready with a Community Response Plan—the sun on the walls is orange and all that's happened is Eliza has done laundry so it has been like watching the sand in an hourglass drip like liquid—Delightfully Boring with no outbursts and We Rejoice because We've chosen the correct Intervention

An hour until decorating!

Where the fuck has Suzanne been all day?

We're worried about he—

Eliza peels herself off the deep couch before We finish Our sentence and exits into the stairwell and she closes the door behind her because she doesn't want to hear about how she's been killing Suzanne—she feels bad enough already and she's listened to Us all day and could use a little more time in places We are not and it's a cool space and she's not near done seeing all it has to offer

She begins to poke around the warehouse again—she is jittery and wants to run laps and she is not a person who is usually so-inclined but she still isn't keen on leaving and as large as the warehouse is its many nooks and piles and obstacles do not make it ideal for running laps indoors—Yoga sounds Too Calm—she wants to punch something Over and Over and Over again and she wonders if We have a punching bag? We do not because We are split on the implications and We have bandied about arguments like *Radical Self-Defense in our racist police-state* and *the glorification of violence for sport* and *Christ it's Just Exercise people not everything has to MEAN something* and *but We have our Powerful Anger Circles to process Our Inherited Rage and We don't need to enact capitalism as a Coping Mechanism*—but even as We approach Punching-Bag-As-Theoretical-Philosophical-Practical object there is always something We agree on much easier than a punching bag and so we spend our Pooled Community Resource budget on the tub with jets and the bidet and the aerial rig and the candy thermometer and the new amplifier and the *Guilds of the Protectorate* shared account—Self-Care and Creativity and Luxurious Food and No We Do Not Have A Punching Bag

She winds up in the near-empty space with the computers and the Vive—its spaciousness is beautiful and elegant and with the fabric over the windows the early-setting winter sun diffuses in the room like a faint perfume—one Vive sits on the table—it's not Eliza's—she left hers in her apartment and she'd asked Devonte (when he was still speaking to them) not to bring it with the rest of her things because she never wanted to look at it again but things feel different now than they did and she doesn't think anyone will mind if she futzes around with this one and in actual fact We are hoping she does because then maybe she will Contribute to the Feminist Unity Project after all—she puts the Vive on over her eyes and spends an hour drawing in 3D with a starry sky as her backdrop—something she hasn't tried before but eventually the novelty wears off and she wants to hit something again

She figures she'll try to "Go Out" with her newfound Courage and Community-Induced Positive Attitude—not real out because that's too dangerous but out on the internet in virtual reality where the consequences at least pretend to be imaginary—the problem is that there's only one MMO with that capability—well two if We count that archery one but it's not what Eliza would call a fully-fledged MMO—she takes five minutes to think it over while doodling with the light pen in a luminescent purple—if she plans to continue in the industry she can't stay out of it forever—at some point she'll have to go back and she figures The Time To Be Bold Is Now and as long as she doesn't play as Circuit Breaker she figures she'll enjoy it okay and there's been enough distance and she can Create even more distance with a new body that she is not so attached to—she hopes

The problem is solved almost as soon as she launches the program because We are set to automatically log in—We are not more careful because the data is everyone's property and We are not more careful because the character is not reflective of any single one of Our desires and We are not more careful because to be perfectly honest all our energy went to Our upcycled closed-circuit security system that doesn't give any data to the NYPD because it was a higher priority and even in Our extended state with Many Brains working on one thing there is still only so much bandwidth and this didn't seem as Important

Eliza makes a decision that We might describe as a Moral Grey Area but also it's not one because it's not as though We didn't tell her to make herself at home—she lets it log on despite feeling a little bit weird about accessing a communal account that isn't hers but reasons it is just left open for Anyone to use and Anyone must include guests not only the folks who live here and it's probably the only option because her account is likely still shut down anyway because she told Preston not to give it back to her and when she thinks his name she feels her stomach turn to marbles and they roll around her body as Disparate Feelings—is it Longing? Regret? Guilt? Anger? all of them of course—Every Feeling under the sun and she pushes them back together to cohere her narrative as best she can and continues forth as an amalgamation of the Sixsterhood—Our Communal Superhero—as Tinker Taylor

It takes Eliza a second to get used to Tinker Taylor's vantage point because They (We) are almost unnaturally short—she looks down at

Their (Our) hands and they are green and webbed with bulbous finger-tips and Eliza grins with half her mouth and sets out toward a reflective building—a Joyful Curiosity replaces less pleasant feelings and what a good distraction it is to delve into Our Minds and Bodies this way because she knows—We all know—that a character says so much more about a person than they even realize—so what does a group Creation say about the Collective?

She laughs when she gets to a place where she can properly see her whole reflection because it is evident We had good fun creating this character—Tinker Taylor looks like an X-Files-style alien—Their (Our) eyes are big and black all the way through and as Eliza waits and stares, the program takes over and processes little movements that happen when an avatar stands idle so Tinker Taylor blinks and green lids shutter over giant orbs and Their (Our) head tilts to the side like a puppy hearing a child's distant whistle—They're (We're) dressed in loose mechanic's overalls with wrenches and unnamable tools hanging from loops and pockets and bandoliers—Eliza thinks They're (We're) Adorable and so Safe—this body isn't her body even though she is a passenger and that is a much better way to "go out" for the first time in—how many days? she doesn't really remember because everything's run together

Eliza pulls up the stats overlay—Their (Our) alignment is Chaotic Good but that's a given and They (We) haven't played as long or as hard as Suzanne or Eliza so Their (Our) level is way lower—Tinker is a Darling but Occasional experiment and They (We) are multi-classed to reflect all our varied wants—it's a very different way to look at building a character than Eliza is used to—Circuit Breaker has leveled up only in power over electricity and Chimera relies on a lot of body-bonuses to provide her well-rounded powers but Tinker's primary class is "Inventor" and the big alien brain helps with it—the secondary class is "spy" and one more level in spy grants the first shape-shifting ability so Eliza decides she'll do enough menial tasks to accumulate enough points so We can take another spy level if We want

She's just about to collapse the stats overlay when she sees that Tinker Taylor's one and only friend—Our Suzanne—is logged in but not as Chimera—she is logged in as Suzanne and it is as We suspected but Eliza's feeling is more along the lines of What The Ever-Loving Fuck so she selects the map—it's as simple as pointing her hand down at it and pulling a trigger as though she is shooting herself in the foot and Suzanne is nowhere that Eliza recognizes and her brows furrow underneath the headset because it's almost like she's in a room entirely removed from the world of Windy City with nothing else around it

She checks Tinker's inventory and finds what she is looking for—a teleportation device—which are usually pricey but Inventors can make them—they only work for people in your friend list or already-visited teleportation hubs and so using the map she teleports to Suzanne's location

She blips from the City into a bare room with mirrored walls and reflected in every panel are two people having sex—it sends a jolt through Eliza's body because she isn't used to This Much Sex and without processing any more information she seeks a place to hide and to fumble with her teleportation device and bamf out before she's noticed but after the initial wave of embarrassment and the urge to leave, the content of the image finally hits her and she drops her hands to her sides—the people having sex are pumping away doggy style and with every movement he makes she lurches forward and sinks back and it is so realistic and her hair—her long wavy hair—bounces and her mouth opens and glistens with spit that isn't really there and her eyes look up to the ceiling and it looks like ecstasy—Eliza knows the animators did well but she couldn't have imagined the almost photo-realistic full-sized bodies of Preston and Suzanne having sex in front of her when they'd tested the patch with lifeless grey mannequin characters

She's never heard the sounds before either because no one had gone this far during Circuit Breaker's assault and that's what sells it— the juxtaposition of what are clearly sex sounds with what is almost sex—it makes it into Unmistakable Carnal Fucking and it makes it into something like—Intimacy? Love? Both Suzanne and Preston are moaning and Preston is cursing over and over and We wonder if it is familiar in a way that sends anger and panic and the feeling of being discarded through Eliza's veins in one sudden surge? We are not sure— it might be because plenty of bosses coerce their employees into having sex and perhaps she is also in love with Our Suzanne and perhaps it is Both And More And Otherwise but We are not sure so We shouldn't speculate—Eliza drops the teleportation device from her limp hand as she accidentally hits the release button and it falls end over end slowly and clatters to the ground—Our Suzanne hears the noise and her face turns toward the source of the sound but her facial expression does not change—her eyes still stare upward and her mouth remains slack because it is only a simulation after all—it is Very Creepy

"Oh God—folks come on get the fuck out—I—" but Eliza doesn't hear the rest because she logs off and leaves the teleportation device behind—a Cinderella's slipper for a newer age

CHAPTER ONE HUNDRED ONE

When Our Suzanne bangs down the stairs and bursts into Our Solstice Tree Decorating her mouth open and ready to explain herself and beg us not to tell her friend, Eliza is already sitting there with her lips pursed and Our Suzanne says "Oh! you're out!"

"Yup"

And even though not one single head turns toward the two Our Entire Attention is focused on the pair—We continue to string cyberpunk lights that We hacked together from spare parts and test strands and throw switches on a truly massive tree that We sized to remain undwarfed by our warehouse's high ceilings—it is a brilliant display of electrical engineering with a large crescent moon adorning the top and soon We will light it and Everyone will clap but We are stalling in order to watch the Drama play out and Hold Space for conflict and so the two can equalize before the Finale so that they might truly enjoy it with Us—We don't want a temporary fight to mar an otherwise Beautiful Community Tradition and if waiting an extra hour would prevent it why not? We make the motions of tree decorating without making progress

"I'm glad" Our Suzanne says in a way where We can tell she isn't really glad

Eliza stands and tries to figure out how to signal to Suzanne that she's been caught out—she wipes her hands on her borrowed Hand-Sewn Winter-Themed Pajama Pants which We lent her and were politely (perhaps too politely but nonetheless gracefully) accepted

"Suzanne I—" and she pauses because unsure of where to go next and she wonders if she should outright say it rather than drop hints? what's the emotionally mature way to react to your best friend having virtual reality sex with another consenting adult with whom you have a contentious and confusing and charged (and potentially sexual) relationship? how do you say that it hurts your feelings and it makes you feel discarded and distant? that you are hurt because you weren't told and weren't asked and were suffering while she had such fun? do you yell? do you cry? it's strange waters to navigate and We'd be equally lost even though We are so practiced at Peaceful Conflict Resolution—the difference is that We are usually clear on what We want and what We feel even if We aren't clear on what has happened but that is because We have a High Emotional Intelligence and Eliza isn't clear on those things At All and We can see the journey on her face and it is one of pain and meta-pain when she's not clear on what the pain is about and it is in this moment that Our Suzanne understands that something intensely personal is about to go down in public and that she will be Embarrassed in front of Us if it does because Suzanne is an intensely private person— even with Us, her people

"We're about to start putting decorations up!" she says too brightly "Here—have they shown you my favorites yet?" and she leans down and We think she picks a box at random but maybe they are in fact her favorites—they are soft golden stars made of felt and sewn with basic straight stitches around the edges and hung from deep blue ribbons and Our Suzanne holds one out and when Eliza doesn't take it she loops it around an errant finger (frozen in mid-gesture) such that Eliza looks decorated herself—"And have you tried the gingerbread yet?" Our Suzanne plows ahead "The Sixsterhood has—We have—a mean gingerbread recipe"—she reaches down and grabs one of the decorated Genderless Gingerbread People and moves it toward Eliza's face so fast that Eliza reacts without thinking and she opens her mouth and closes her teeth around the Gingerbread Person's head—it is a sight to behold—the ornament still swinging from Eliza's finger and ginger-bread feet sticking from her mouth while she looks at Our Suzanne with a Sourness Heretofore Reserved For Her Enemies

Eliza lays the ornament back on a box lid and bites the head off the Gingerbread Person and as she swallows it down it forms a sticky lump in her throat like she's trying to ingest wallpaper paste and she lays the headless snack down right next to the ornament and she says "I'm not feeling super well again—I think I might go to bed?" she turns her attention to Us "I'll see you all for breakfast—thank you—for including me I mean" and We murmur Comforting Noises that sound like *Yes Yes Enough For One Day* but contain no actual syllables and no words in any language—only Concerned-Satisfied-Nurturing sounds

Once Eliza is up the stairs (the elevator earlier returned to its original spot) Our Suzanne turns to Us and asks "Come on guys, who told her?"

We blink because while we Know now We don't Really Know because We didn't Experience it—We have pieced it together but We haven't Seen it with Our eyes like Eliza has

Told her what?

Suzanne blanches

CHAPTER ONE HUNDRED TWO

Eliza trudges down to breakfast after a largely sleepless night of wondering what it means that she is jealous and betrayed and angry? she knows what Our Suzanne did wasn't explicitly out of bounds and it wasn't explicitly sex and yet she feels this bubbling soup of feeling—We wonder if mad is entirely the correct descriptor in this moment?—and perhaps We should focus on what We can absolutely tell by looking—She Is Tired—We know that for sure

Our Suzanne also hasn't slept very well because she feels embarrassed for being caught and embarrassed for being embarrassed and stupid for sleeping with her boss because she should know better and she doesn't think it's sex either and she feels as though she has done something wrong even though she cannot quite pinpoint what the wrong action was but she knows she wouldn't have hidden it if it didn't feel wrong on some level

It is Christmas Eve Morning and We sit at the long table eating vegetarian sausage and vegan egg substitute and facon bacon—It is a feast! and Our Suzanne is already seated at the table as Eliza joins and their eyes lock and they cast them back down again at their breakfasts— Eliza butters toast

It becomes Unbearable—the jovial conversation begins to strain under the weight of strange behavior and Our smiles no longer extend past Our mouths to Our eyes

Finally—

Okay enough—you two go downstairs and work it out

Yeah We gave you time yesterday to process your conflict and regroup but you didn't take it

Better to handle it now than let it fester!

You're killing Our Breakfast Vibe

Do you need a Powerful Anger Circle or—?

And because the Collective voice is powerful Eliza and Suzanne oblige

For a while they simply stare at each other and then Eliza asks "Why'd you sleep with Preston?"

"Oh come on" Our Suzanne says sourly "I didn't sleep with Preston—it's a game—"

"Well the noises you were making"—and Eliza pauses as she realizes tears are beginning to leak from her squinted eyes—"suggest otherwise"

Suzanne doesn't have a response to that (not a real one) so she counters with "It's a goddamn game Eliza—our bodies weren't in the same room—I just needed to blow off some fucking steam and it's not like the world is rife with people I can fucking talk to right now"

"Suzanne—you are my best friend and we're locked in a warehouse together—this is—this is mean—there's a Kind Way to do this and an Unkind Way and this is Unkind—Unkind all the way to the middle"

"Well if you want to talk about a Kind Way and an Unkind Way you've been treating me Unkindly since you got here"

"Treating you—how even? how even do you fucking figure?" Eliza's vocal volume begins to escalate and it echoes on the high ceilings

"I open my home to you—I agree that yes I can't go to work because likely The Inspectre is watching me too—We know that's true! but instead of—I don't know—actually talking to me and hanging out with me in my own fucking House-Turned-Prison you leave me to field questions from the Sixsterhood who all have Opinions about the way this should be handled! I hate other people's opinions! other people's opinions are my day job!"

"Oh fuck off Suzanne do you think I did any of this On Purpose? do you think I would have chosen this for you or for me?"

"Well what you did choose to do is make me serve you food and made my roommates build literal accommodations for you—" Our Suzanne walks over to the giant swaths of fabric covering the warehouse windows and they are floor-to-ceiling pieces slowly becoming art installations "—all because of baseless irrational fears—No One can find you here! No One! and Not Once did you say thank you to them or to me—Do you know—" and she pauses to wipe her eyes with the back of her hand because she's crying now too "—Do you know what it takes for me to do this? Eliza I'm an intensely private person—I don't even like having my address on forms for work—There's a reason that neither you nor Devonte—" her voice cracks when she says his name "—have ever been here before"

"Well first off if you didn't want me here you shouldn't have offered"

"It's not like I don't fucking care about your safe—"

"Let me finish—Second these fears are completely rational or have you forgotten the Dog incident already? fucking long memory you've got there"

"No one is going to find you—"

"He's watching you too Suzanne! you already agreed! We know it—there's no question here! and you just said it—you said your address is on forms for work! well we know how secure Fancy Dog is so excuse me if I'm feeling less than comforted right now and finally—" Eliza walks over to the huge expanse of fabric—it is a white muslin next to three entire bolts of some flower-patterned thin brown fabric like something out of the 1970s that has resurfaced in the era of slow fashion and fad thrift stores and each little bloom is so tiny one might confuse it for polka dots—Eliza looks up to the ceiling where it's taped intensely but not so intensely that it couldn't be severed for Dramatic Effect "—finally this—I didn't ask for this! I didn't ask for the Sixsters to do anything!"

she gathers the fabric in her two fists and from all the way upstairs We hear Our Suzanne whimper behind her and We can almost feel her put her hand out in protest but That's Art Babe-y Nothing Is Permanent "And I don't need it! I don't need it anyway! I am fine!" she begins to sit her weight down and pull as hard as she can and instead of the tape giving way the weave on the flimsy fabric does and she tears through it like The Hulk—all the while screaming "I am fine! I am just fucking fine! I am fine!" It feels so good to lose it—to really truly lose it—and to move her whole body—to make big arcs through the air with her arms and to windmill ferociously and to pump her legs and to throw what We could only consider to be a temper tantrum and see THIS IS WHY WE HAVE THE POWERFUL ANGER CIRCLE

When she is left holding giant wads of satisfyingly-torn fabric and trailing them like she's wearing a pretentious and poorly constructed dress—that is when she sees The Profile that looks like it should be on a coin someday and here is Preston standing outside the window in the middle of turning around—he'd been facing away—he has Dog with him who appears to be fine save for the cone of shame—Party hat! Eliza corrects herself because that's what the vet called it but that is the last rational thought she has as Preston mounts the stairs to the entry while poking at the camera and the speaker

We can see Preston now as well—We were dimly aware of him or at least dimly aware of his public persona but this is the first time We have seen him in person—in Meatspace—We can Read him to Filth nearly instantly as his close-up face broadcasts onto our televisions because everything about him screams "I do not know what I am doing" and he is so young—younger than many of Us—and he has The Feral Look of the Creatively Constipated—the Look that arrives when combined with Perceived Hyper-Competence and Public Pressure—every time he has an idea he is convinced it will be his last—Preston's original Human Man is made entirely of default settings with an alignment of True Neutral and it is sad to really see him and understand why: if ideas are finite resources then why put any creativity into this at all? middle skin tone and middle brown hair and Middle Middle Average Average Average with the default red unitard and blue cape—it's constant fear and We can tell he hasn't figured it out yet—Making Art is like cutting plants or giving gifts—you have to Release and Trust or things won't grow and you have to move forward with Abundance and Open Hands and the Understanding that The Muse doesn't visit hoarders

"Fuck!" Eliza screams and that is all that rests between her ears right now—the only thought is screaming curse words "Fuck fuck fuck" she slams her ball of tattered material to the ground and stomps toward the stairwell and to where the door opens out into the world

"What the—" Our Suzanne walks up to the window where Eliza had only seconds before been standing "Oh" she says

Eliza rips the door open and says into the bright sunlight "you've got to be shitting me"

CHAPTER ONE HUNDRED THREE

Preston is easy to follow, so we follow him. Follow him to this very spot because there are so many angles, so many strands and we have to hold them all in our hands at once for the whole thing to make any kind of sense. In the morning on Christmas Eve, he wakes up and Dog, in his cone of shame, is standing by the bed. Staring. He is no longer facing the wall in the corner. He tentatively wags his butt-stump and Preston's heart soars into his mouth, into his fingertips. For the first time since this all started, he feels hopeful.

Dog points his nose toward the door and spins back around, looking soulfully into Preston's face, begging, pleading. Preston actually laughs at how silly he looks. It is so early. Five in the morning. He hasn't been doing much at work lately, and he figures even if he took the day off, no one would much notice. Until the day previous, he'd been spending hours on the third floor every afternoon, accomplishing nothing. Everyone is convinced he's inventing the future of gaming, but we know better. We know he's slumming it with that slut. One word echoes in his head, in ours too: charlatan. He is fooling them all.

Preston has made too many bad decisions to be our king anymore. He's succumbed too hard, and for too long. Let his elite status muddy his moral, ethical waters. And what were we expecting? Fucking Chad. Fucking Chad pretending at being a real, upstanding gentleman. We hate Preston Waters.

He pushes that thought—our thoughts—away, swats them with his hands as he swings his legs out of bed. He knows that today, today he will try to do work. Today, when he goes to the third floor on Christmas Eve, he will use the Vive to access a virtual whiteboard. He will do what he's been resisting for so long—he will make Fancy Dog Games into a true plural. It is over, he thinks. The worst of everything is behind him. Eliza is behind him. And now this—whatever it was—with Suzanne is behind him too, since they got caught. Life will go back to normal today, and tomorrow he will fly, early in the morning, to his parents' house for Christmas. We do not hate Preston Waters after all. Long live Preston Waters.

But he has to make amends, he thinks, and he hatches a plan that we all think is a terrible idea. He thinks he's out of the quicksand; he is completely unaware of its ever-present pull. Goldfish never notice the water that they're in. He decides that since it is almost a holiday, he can swing arriving late. Around ten. That gives him five hours. He grabs Dog's leash, his own coat. He feels buoyant; he is wrong to feel buoyant.

After he unlocks his four fancy new locks and ushers Dog down the hall and out the elevator, he spends two hours walking. In the false dawn, everything is misty. Dewy. He walks into Central Park when he gets to it, taking his time. In the half-light, statues look as though they are of another world, reaching out of the fog toward him and the sky. Dog pees on everything. He shies away from strange men, joggers in orange knit caps wearing socks pulled up to their knees, but he is better. Everything is better. The cold and the wet are transformative.

He turns east and leaves the park, only half admitting to himself where he is going next. He walks across town until he is staring at the bridge to Queens. He stops for a second, surprised at himself. He realizes his legs are cramping, wobbling like sticks made of Jell-O. He looks down at Dog, who is panting hard. He hails a cab to take him the rest of the way. He drops an intersection into the air, one that he has unwisely memorized.

When he gets to Suzanne's neighborhood, he is exhausted and

confused. Where could a person live, here? And yet, there's a Starbucks on the corner. It is still New York City, after all. He pops in to buy himself some time, some energy. All he had, he left in Manhattan.

The morning light is just cresting the warehouses, turning their brutal façades orange, when he finds himself on Suzanne's street again. He still isn't sure he wants to knock on her door. So he checks his coffee cup. "Peter," it reads. He snorts. Then, to waste a few more minutes, he gets Dog to sit and holds his coffee cup out, name facing his iPhone camera. He whistles and, as if Dog is also determined to make the best Instagram photo, he cocks his head to one side, the cone transforming instantly from sad to adorable. Preston Instagrams the photo, #nofilter because everything is golden in the sunrise. Perfect. It is also #LongLiveDog. We are glad to have the photo; we are elated. We love that he feels safe enough with us to have ignored all previous warnings. Because if he doesn't do this, in this exact moment, there is no end to the tale, not a swift one nor one that's satisfying. If he doesn't do this, we have to leave the narration up to the fags and the females, relinquish our story-making capabilities or our truth-telling capabilities. He watches the hearts tick up for thirty seconds before he takes a deep breath, puts his phone in his pocket and grabs Dog's leash off the ground.

He mounts what he thinks is Suzanne's stoop to—what is this? A warehouse? He stands on tiptoe to look at a security camera mounted in the entrance. Suzanne isn't particularly technical, he thinks, not compared to the rest of his office. Is this perhaps an addition since Eliza's gotten here? Eliza is this technical, and her life is such that she might want a camera at the entrance—

Oh God. He realizes the optics of what he is about to do. He is about to walk into a house with Eliza, who he has fired and has certainly slept with in meatspace, and Suzanne, who he has not fired but has slept with in cyberspace. What am I doing? he thinks. This is a bad idea, he thinks. And we scream and we throw our figurative popcorn. Yes, you dipshit, this is a terrible idea. None of us think it's a good thing to do, even though we understand. We understand the siren song of women and bad choices, but we as men are supposed to rise above all that. He is about to straighten up, about to turn around and walk away, not knowing he's already tipped the scales. But the door bursts open and, surprised, he jumps up, spilling coffee over his fingers. Dog leaps back down the stairs, butt-stump reaching between his legs. "Uh," he says. He can't think of anything else to say.

"You've got to be shitting me," says Eliza.

We see her.

We're coming to take you away, ha ha.

CHAPTER ONE HUNDRED FOUR

We will now look in on Lewis, because it's an important day for him as well. More important a day than for Eliza, even. More important for him than for us. The most important day he'll ever know.

It is the first time Lewis Fleishman sees raw sun in a week and a half. His experience of daylight has been filtered through windows and sunglasses, which hide the evidence of his experiences at night. The sunglasses remain until he reaches the Apollo Theater. He stands in front of the red letters, dead in the blue sky, and takes the sunglasses off. No one around here knows him, so no one points out that he looks like hell.

He has a vague and mistaken inkling that Eliza and Suzanne are somewhere around here, and so he's come up on the subway. He realizes Harlem is a big place, he likely wouldn't find them even if they were here. He makes choices at random, convinced he will eventually stumble upon Eliza because they are drawn to each other. Their fates are two sides of the same coin. They have more in common than they don't. He hasn't checked Twitter. If he were to, he might know everything that we know. He might know he's in the wrong place. And his phone sits right there, in his pocket. He could check it at any time; all the information is right there at his fingertips, and it's pinging away his location. But he never reaches for it. As it stands, he cracks his frowned mouth open and laughs at himself. Of course he isn't turning up in front of Suzanne's apartment, wherever it may be. He is being insane. Grinning, he reapplies his sunglasses. Or is it a grimace? To the outside observer, it looks like he is enjoying a nice morning; the city strings up large snowflakes made from Christmas lights on 125th Street each year, nestled neatly in the crosses of power lines. It wouldn't be out of the ordinary for someone to be happy.

Except we know Lewis Fleishman doesn't give a flying saucer about Christmas or things being pretty. He experiences everything as though he is wearing wool armor—the twin smells of fried Popeyes and the salty rot of the fish market are delivered to him as though through a mask, and the flowers look false against the December air; they have no business being that bright. A bell ringer's bell doesn't penetrate the cotton in his ears, placed there by sleeplessness. He sees the flash of a red Santa hat (or was it a red ball cap? Rare in Harlem, but we are everywhere) and thinks to himself, fuck it all.

What strikes him, of course, are the people. He knows, rationally, that their body parts aren't unzipping finger by finger, ear by ear. But all the people have been unzipping since Eliza talked to him for the last time, regardless of how hopped up on medication he is, regardless of how many times he leaves messages on his doctor's answering machine. Even his mother's face is marred by ever-shifting carnage. And if he isn't careful, if he doesn't keep his mind actively focused on the blood, the gore, he begins to lose his color once again, becoming the drowned magician of his childhood nightmares, unable to escape his chains. And then he is surrounded by water.

Something in the alleyway. There is always something in the alleyway, it is New York City. Everything is grime. It could be anything— discarded cardboard boxes melting in the cold-wet, dropped chicken bones, human feces. But this time he swears he sees a dog's tail, severed, long and white with cloudlike curls of fur wisping off it, wrapped in butchers' paper or newsprint or just there, on the ground. His doctor has told him none of this is real; he walks quickly past, trying to forget the image. An eerily concrete iteration.

"Excuse me." He stops a man with no nose.

"Yes?" this noseless man says.

"Which way to the George Washington Bridge?"

The noseless man's eyebrows raise.

"I'm meeting a friend," Lewis stumbles. "For—for some biking." People bike across that bridge, right? "He's returning my bicycle at the bridge and we'll go from there."

Lewis knows the lie is weak, but the man with no nose points anyway. "You're way too far south," he says.

But Lewis shades his eyes. He could get on the subway, get there in a minute. But maybe between here and there he will stumble upon Eliza. Then he can tell her she won. "It's a nice day," he replies. "And I've got all the time in the world."

CHAPTER ONE HUNDRED FIVE

We can see them now. Framed in the window, we're now capable of imagining exactly what this conversation is. "No, no. He doesn't get to come in." Suzanne runs to the door, hands outstretched. "No."

"What—what is this place?" Preston asks.

Suzanne raises an eyebrow. "A warehouse full of artists. Surprised you don't know that, considering you seem to have the rest of my paperwork memorized." Then there is silence. One breath. Two breaths.

"What possessed you?" Eliza asks.

"To what?" Preston responds, though he thinks he knows the answer already. Time, time, he is buying himself time to think of what, exactly, possessed him.

"I mean, for starters, to come here?"

"I recognize my choice is a little unorthodox—"

"Stupid," Suzanne interjects. "Your choice was stupid."

For a beat we think Preston will get defensive, or have a Conversation as though he is at the office. Instead, he lets a breath escape his lips, as though he is deflating. "Alright. Yes. It was stupid. I did a stupid thing."

"And you know what other stupid thing you did?" Eliza asks. She can feel the electricity buzzing in her face. Her hands feel like they are going to float away. We don't think she is talking about the very stupidest thing he's done; no one in this room is aware of it yet. But we are. We are so, so happy.

"I imagine it was, uh, what we did in the gam—"

But he can't finish his sentence. Eliza barrels right over him before he can even finish his *m* sound, let alone the rest of the thought. "I mean, that was weird. And yeah, pretty tremendously fucked up. More fucked up for you than Suzanne, honestly, since you're the CEO and therefore her boss, but no. What I was referring to, what I think is particularly stupid, is after you play knight in shining armor and stash me in a cab, sling me over your shoulder and carry me naked into a public street, hide me in your apartment. After you suffer some consequences for that and I drag your bleeding dog to the vet's office, you peace the fuck out. You. Don't. Contact. Me. Once. That's the fucked-up part I'm focused on." Of course that's what she's thinking about. Women are always thinking about their goddamn boyfriends.

"Well it's not like you contacted m—"

"Don't even start," says Suzanne. "I told you she wasn't leaving her room, I told you she was upset. I told you she was climbing the walls in here! You have her burner phone number. You could've called her."

"Thank you, Suzanne," Eliza says, surprised that she is coming to her defense after they'd been yelling at each other moments before.

Or:

"I mean, that was weird. And yeah, pretty tremendously fucked up. More fucked up for you than Suzanne, honestly, since you're the CEO and therefore her boss, but no. What I was referring to, what I think is particularly stupid, is the fucking radio silence on behalf of Fancy Dog. What, you're just like entirely unaware of anything but Dog's tail getting hacked off? We're only going to condemn that? We're not going to, I don't know, post any messages of support for one of your former employees that's being stalked? Do anything to try to clear my name with this absolute basket of deplorables you've cultivated as your most devoted fanbase? Hell, even just retweeting the See No Monkey announcement with a thumbs-up would've been less *absolutely fucked* than saying *nothing*." Of course that's what she's focused on. "You care so much about me and my career and my safety when we're face-to-face, but when it comes to engaging with the real consequences of having a moral fucking backbone, when it comes to putting your *own* money on the line for those trendy feminist beliefs you're paying lip service to, profiting off of, suddenly it gets *very* quiet in here."

Suzanne turns to Eliza. "And you know who else is doing this, by the way? I didn't tell you because I didn't want to, like, bother you. But this whole cold-footed hero bullshit? Devonte is doing it too."

"I knew he wasn't contacting me, but I thought he was, like, giving me space or, like, unsure what was going to get me tracked. But he isn't talking to you?"

"Yes. He apparently 'can't.' Whatever that means."

"Oh, he can't?" Eliza turns back to Preston and points an accusatory finger back at him. "And I suppose you can't either?"

Preston stutters. "Eliza, what you're suggesting is—it's not poss—"

"Well you know who can't?" Eliza shouts at both of them. "You know who definitely can't? I can't."

"And you know she can't opt out of any of this?" Suzanne sticks her thumb out in Eliza's direction. "You can. You and Devonte can, apparently. All these man children running away when something gets real tough."

Fuck you, Suzanne. This is not their problem. It's yours. We intend for it to be yours, because wouldn't it be better? Wouldn't it be better if the Elizas and Suzannes of the world simply didn't work in games? They wouldn't be harassed; neither would we.

"And you know who hasn't opted out of it even when she could've? Suzanne."

"Thank you, Eliza."

and We can hear them too because We have Converged and Crashed and Collided and We are watching Eliza Bright in this moment—all of Us are— and We need to pause for a word on Friendship because the others wouldn't know what this is if it Bit Them In The Literal Ass—most people say friends when they mean acquaintances and any people they don't hate but when We say Friends We mean what is true—Family—the people We have and hold forever, even when We look at them and see only rage—where We can go from screaming at Each Other to screaming with Each Other in that binary way like a switch flipping—No to Yes and False to True—even after everything happens that's about to happen and even after Eliza and Suzanne don't live in the same state they will go on being Friends and that's Our meaning of Friends—Heartfriends—Chosen Family and We Embrace Eliza by proxy because Our Suzanne is Ours and they are Each Other's for years and years to come and this is the sort of Kinship that We need to survive in this unfeeling world and it is Sad—Sad in the same way Preston is Sad—that the others don't get to know it and they don't understand it and they scramble for it in their mythmaking and their obsession and their constant pinging into the internet void as they pray in desperation that the others are listening—but they do not have the "and" in them—not really

"Well what do you propose I do?" Preston says. He tries to continue, to say that they don't know what it's like, running a company. They don't know what it's like realizing he's been taking hours upon hours doing nothing and no one at work has missed him an ounce. Everything's kept going. Without him. But he doesn't say that, because those aren't feelings he's been aware of until this moment. He stoppers his mouth, looks at the ground.

"I propose that you leave," says Eliza. "This is really uncomfortable."

"Well. Okay then. I will." He turns around and walks down the steps.

Eliza remembers something. "Preston?"

He turns around, something hopeful in his eyes, as though he were Dog. Begging, pleading. Eliza is extremely happy because she feels no more conflicted feelings at all. Only one. The very clear desire to haul off and punch him in the mouth. She is proud of herself for resisting. "I forgot to tell you," she says. "Jean-Pascale didn't doxx me. Lewis did. You can fix that. That's what you can do." She watches him walk away.

Then she turns to Suzanne. "I'm sorry I made this really hard for you."

Suzanne snorts. "Please. It just sucks, you didn't have any control over it. It just—sucks. But thank you. Apology accepted, though certainly not required. I'm not sorry I did—whatever it was—with Preston. I don't think it was sex. I don't think it was inherently wrong. It's just a fucking game. But I am sorry it hurt your feelings. And that I did it, like, now when I knew very well you were going through a rough time. And I'm sorry I kept it from you."

Eliza really wants to accept the apology because some part of her believes Our Suzanne's correct that it's just a game but she's not one hundred percent sure she believes it in her gut because one part of her isn't all parts of her and We all know it is not a Real Apology—sorry to have hurt your feelings never feels good and We know because We have all done it before and Our Suzanne knew Eliza would hate this cyberfucking—she knew and she rationalized and she did it anyway without telling her simply because she wanted to— there's a Kind Way and an Unkind Way—Eliza said it and We agree— Unkind all the way to the middle—but sometimes people are Unkind and sometimes it's even the ones We love the most and who love Us the most do a shitty behavior and they set a Boundary and they take care of their own Need and it's the antithesis of Our own and We can't control that nor would We want to—We can only revel in the Closeness of it—that's just the way the world is

The door is still open. We can still see them as well, stare upon this gateway to hell. During all the shouting, Eliza's eyes have gotten used to the sun. It's beautiful out. Winter, sure, but warm for the season. A few other people walk by on the street, walking dogs. She feels sad she didn't once reach down and pet Dog while he was right there; she thinks maybe she won't get another chance. Come out and play, Eliza.

"You know what?" she changes the subject. "I think I will go out. Like, out out. For real." She puts her foot across the doorjamb and feels no fear.

"Wait," Suzanne says. "Coat." She ducks into the closet and retrieves it, hands it over. Eliza slings her arms into it and climbs down the steps. "Wait," Suzanne says again. "Are you sure?"

"Yeah," Eliza replies. "I won't go far. I won't be long. You said so yourself. It's unlikely, at this point, that he can find us. Maybe"—and she brightens, here, at this thought—"maybe he's given up. Maybe he's gone back home. He scared me pretty good. He probably got what he came for." And she half convinces herself this is true. "I'll be back in, like, thirty. I just—need a walk. A walk, and then I'll make more pancakes to make up for the ones we ruined with our fight."

"Okay," Suzanne says. "But more than half an hour and I'll send a search party."

Suzanne trudges up the stairs, a little bit mad at herself. "Sorry to have hurt your feelings?" she is thinking. She knows it sucks and yet—Suzanne absolutely cannot apologize if she thinks she's done nothing wrong; she can't even bring her mouth to make the words. About half-way up to the kitchen, she looks down at her phone, looks at Twitter. She flies back down the stairs, breathless, gesturing toward the screen as she wrenches the door open and squints down the street. The time for breathing is short-lived, we think. It is breath-catching, heart-stopping, something out of a horror movie. Yes, yes, yes. A horror movie for us to consume. "Eliza!" she yells, and no one answers. People stare and Suzanne stares back, seeing if any of them look suspicious. But there's no Eliza on the street.

We, of course, can see it too. The tweet.

It is a retweet: Preston's Instagram, automatically pushed to Twitter with If This Then That. It is a photo of his "Peter" coffee cup and Dog. In the background, where the uninitiated wouldn't see her, where no one would notice her if they weren't expressly scouring social media, is Eliza yelling in the window, tearing fabric to pieces. Her face is distorted by her wide-open mouth, ugly, like fangs on a rodent, but it is unmistakably her. Her glasses. Her distinct overbite. The retweet is quoted; The Inspectre has something to add:

"I'm coming to take you away, ha ha."

CHAPTER ONE HUNDRED SIX

O kay," Suzanne says to the air. "New plan." She grabs her phone and starts texting Eliza. She's telling her to stay the hell away. To get on the subway and go to a stop she's never been to before.

Suzanne hits the send button a few times and her stomach drops as she hears the buzz. She looks to the floor near the windows, where sits a pile of balled-up fabric, and sees Eliza's burner phone, dropped and forgotten.

"Shit," Suzanne hisses. "Shit fuck piss."

While her eyes are still on the phone, it begins to ring. She walks over and picks it up. It says Buffalo, New York.

Luckily, she is prepared. She grabs the phone and takes the steps two at a time, running straight for the laptop, wherever it is in that abomination place that we can't entirely conceptualize. Finally, when she will lose him if she doesn't pick up, she answers. "Hello," she says, trying to mimic Eliza's higher voice. Suzanne concentrates very hard on how Eliza sounded on television, not how she sounds in real life. She steadies her breath as best she can, even though she is scaling stairs at a clip.

"Eliza?" he says, the name sandwiched between heavy breaths, his mouth too close to the receiver.

"This is she," Suzanne says and winces. Eliza would have never said that.

"I've found you, I think." Suzanne is surprised. The voice is mellifluous, childlike and tenor at the same time. She can picture him, younger, singing in a children's church choir. She isn't sure what she expected, but it isn't this: the voice of an angel.

"I ran here," he continues, "took an Uber, before you could move. Before you could go anywhere." Suzanne slides into the guest bedroom, looking frantically for the laptop, and she can hear the laughing and glass-clinking of the Sixsterhood's breakfast. It's best they not know, so she doesn't alert them. She finds Eliza's laptop, pops it open and launches a program. It's janky, lines of code and a window with a Google map ported into it. And taped right onto the computer, just under the keyboard in the space where a wrist might usually rest, is a piece of paper with some Verizon log-in credentials scrawled on it.

Wait.

What?

CHAPTER ONE HUNDRED SEVEN

We can't believe it.

We can't believe it.

All that time she'd been hiding away, she'd been hacking the phone company. Putting together all the pieces she needed to catch him. We look for our evidence, we scour her chats and our imaginations. While she'd been slowly losing her mind, her response hadn't been to simply lie there, like we thought. Her response had been to do something. To, in the absence of any sort of savior, save herself.

CHAPTER ONE HUNDRED EIGHT

Eliza: this is Eliza

JP: copy

JP: I'm glad you used my phone number, I didn't think you'd talk to me again

JP: Is everything okay.

Eliza: I need some help

Eliza: Switch to Signal? Will be texting from Suzanne's number.

CHAPTER ONE HUNDRED NINE

Suzanne: this is Eliza

JP: this is confusing

JP: how can I help?

Suzanne: I feel like I missed the very thing I need right now because I learned to do this shit as an adult

JP: this shit?

Suzanne: programming

Suzanne: some people like you and Devonte learned because you were out there lawbreaking and I learned from fucking YouTube

Suzanne: I've never hacked anything

Suzanne: there are too many consequences when you aren't a kid

JP: and you need to now?

Suzanne: yes

Suzanne: I've made the software

Suzanne: to track down the inspectre, next time he calls

Suzanne: I'm gonna pick up and make him keep talking

Suzanne: but I need a verizon employee's log in and pasword

Suzanne: *password

Suzanne: to make it work. To use their data

JP: that is very, very illegal

JP: phone companies are super litigious, too

Suzanne: I know

JP: you have to be one hundred percent certain you won't get caught

JP: and you know, it's never one hundred percent certain

Suzanne: I know

Suzanne: but I can't live in an elevator forever

JP: I have follow up questions regarding this turn of phrase

Suzanne: never mind

Suzanne: the point is, the police aren't helping me, the inspectre hasn't stopped and I've had enough

Suzanne: I have to do something

JP: and what are you going to do when you have that information?

Suzanne: well if it's nowhere near here, probably I'm safe, and so that's something

Suzanne: but if it is, I'm not sure yet

Suzanne: I have to figure out how to tell the police where he is without letting them know we broke the law

Suzanne: but as far as I'm concerned, that's a problem for another day

Suzanne: the point is, is getting a phone company employees username and pw something you have experienced in your checkered past as a cyberpunk youth?

JP: oh yeah, absolutely

Suzanne: great.

Suzanne: can you help me break into whatever to get it?

Suzanne: I don't even really know where the data and shit is stored

JP: oh that's not how you do it

JP: that's script kiddie shit

JP: computers are fast and stupid and bad at a lot of things

JP: but they're good at being secure, most of the time.

JP: people are terribly insecure, though

JP: people can be tricked faster and easier than backdoors can be found and exploited

Suzanne: I'm not a social engineer

JP: I'd offer to do it for you, but there's one problem

Suzanne: your accent, yes, that's why i wanted you to help me get it some other way

JP: yeah.

JP: when I was young and French in France, that of course was not a problem

JP: but now, I don't know how much of a red flag it'll be

JP: i also always have socially engineered at least one thing out of people in order to compromise data, so honestly i don't think i could do it any other way

Suzanne: welp

Suzanne: im fucked

JP: I don't think you are

JP: you're gonna do it

Suzanne: me?

JP: yeah

JP: you're going to make a phone call

JP: and you're going to get sensitive information from a Verizon employee

Suzanne: I am?

JP: yes

JP: you're going to pick someone in sales or in customer service, they're the easiest

JP: if you come up with a reason that there's money involved, that someone's going to buy something or stop buying something, sales-people lose all their common sense

JP: customer service are conditioned to help

JP: I'd call "from a store"

JP: if you look online, they probably put their store numbers in their "locate a store" urls

Suzanne: thats crazy

JP: thats common

Suzanne: but my caller ID

JP: here, here's a way to get around that

CHAPTER ONE HUNDRED TEN

We have seen the evidence with our eyes and we still can't believe it. Maybe she has never really been afraid to leave. Perhaps staying in the elevator night and day had been a product of finishing something as the sole maker of it. Of figuring out how to trick a hapless, corn-fed Verizon employee into giving her sensitive information. Of reading everything she could about Defcon hacks and Kevin Mitnick, catching up on the lessons a childhood of rule-following can't teach. Rule-breaking is usually about curiosity and a sense of immortality, two things people lose as they grow older; we suppose fearing for her life has been good motivation.

We are reeling. Angry. We mistrust ourselves, our leaps into logic, our guesses to fill in the blanks. Had she and Suzanne even fought? What if they'd spent days together, side by side in the elevator, plotting? What if Eliza was totally okay with Suzanne sleeping with Preston in-game? What if, instead, they fought over something else? The ethics of the plan? How best to break the law without being caught? Whether or not to involve JP? Or perhaps it went smoothly the entire time, something most of us can't picture. If we were locked in a room with even our best friend, we would drive each other insane. We know she pulled down the fabric. We have a photo.

Or what if Eliza never knew that Preston and Suzanne had fucked in the game? What if she never put on the Vive, never saw the uncanny, reality-adjacent behavior. What if? What if Suzanne and Preston never slept together? What if they spent hours in the game with each other talking about something else? What if both of them made impeccable, professional decisions? What if they put that stuff in the G-chat as a diversion? Or bait! What if they were plotting too? What if they used Preston's high visibility as a provocation, what if they asked him to post that picture to lure The Inspectre into calling Eliza, into showing himself in this neighborhood into which most people would otherwise never venture? Perhaps Preston was supposed to show up on this day, at this time, and take a photo in which Eliza was plainly visible. Perhaps our strange anti-protagonists had enough of waiting for The Inspectre to stop or make a move. Perhaps it wasn't an accident that Eliza's phone was still at the Sixsterhood, ready for Suzanne to use while Eliza made herself a plain, irresistible target.

We find this unlikely, given what happens next.

It's too dangerous. If they'd really planned it that carefully, they could've done all of this and waited for The Inspectre to show up, staying safely inside. They could've called the police on a physical human stalking his way around the warehouse and the police would've had to do something.

Or maybe it's some combination of all of this, where they're all flying by the seat of their pants because they are only people, imperfect people. Planning strange, imperfect plans and responding to failure the best ways they can see. We are more optimal players than that; that is probably why we've gotten stuff wrong, why we didn't know she'd written the program. We can see the whole thing, respond to all of it at once. They can only see from their limited perspective. We've been analyzing the moments we know for sure as though they have made the best, most logical decisions at every turn. The ones we would expect them to make. We've already realized an inconsistency; how did The Inspectre get the burner phone number? Did someone leak it, put it in their Google contacts? Suzanne? Preston? Devonte? Or did she forward her old number to it? Was it an accident, or did they trap our comrade?

What else have we gotten wrong?

CHAPTER ONE HUNDRED ELEVEN

Y ou have to understand," The Inspectre says. "You broke my
favorite game. You destroyed a world."

"The world is still there," Suzanne offers. This is harder
than it looks on television—selecting the right locker-combination of
words that would click into place and open up a new conversation.
She will say she sweat through the entire conversation, and that she
could smell herself by the time she was done. "I just knew he couldn't
hurt anyone while he was on the phone with me," she will say. "Or at
least that I would know about it. If he did." She will never admit that
she did anything except field this call; she will never admit that she
was party to hacking Verizon to find out where he was. She will only
say that she knew where Eliza was going, and so when the phone call
came in, she immediately followed. We won't be allowed in the court-
room, of course, but rumors will circulate that as she tells the story,
her eyes flick to the left. As if she is back in the elevator bedroom,
concentrated, collected, all action and fury—as if she's transported
back to now, where we are.

"It isn't the same," he doesn't yell, exactly. It is more a forceful talk,
a theatrical voice that rises from the belly. She nearly drops the phone
when she realizes The Inspectre is imitating Lewis; at least, imitating
the voice Lewis uses for Doctor Moriarty. "It's being taken over. It used
to be a safe world, a better world. But with every one of you who worms

her way into it, it becomes more and more like reality. Like—" he stops. Suzanne's breath catches in her throat.

A low *huh-huh-huh* emanates from the phone. Suzanne wants to throw it far away; he sounds so much like Lewis hamming it up, performing for his fanboy spectators. We wonder how long The Inspectre has been watching them—the employees, Preston. Everyone. Because this kind of imitation, it can't have started with Eliza, with 80085, with all that followed. It's too detailed. Too practiced. How long has he been obsessed and no one's noticed because this is normal? "You are not Eliza," he states. He sounds extremely sure.

"Yes, I am," Suzanne asserts, but her voice is shaky.

It doesn't matter, though, because a red dot blinks into existence on Eliza's screen, marking her digital map around the corner and down the road. Suzanne leaps up.

"Cunt!" The Inspectre or Keith Mackey hisses into the phone. His voice loses the angelic quality and becomes hard-edged, mean like razors. "I'm coming for you next." He hangs up.

Suzanne bursts into the dining room with the phone still in her hand. The Sixsterhood all turn their many heads and stare at her as she screams, "Taser! Taser!"

One of them stands immediately, no questions asked, and rummages through a drawer. Another does have a follow-up question. "Here?"

"No, no. Out there." And perhaps there are more questions to be answered, but at that moment someone passes her the weapon and, like a sprinter being passed the baton, she is once again out the door. The Sixsterhood sits in silence at the breakfast table for a breath. Two. Then they burst into frenzy.

CHAPTER ONE HUNDRED TWELVE

I t's hard to decide who to follow, with everyone converging like this. Everyone's slamming into each other, many pinballs in a machine, ricocheting. And it's hard to parse. What if even the parts they talk about later are falsehoods, built for public consumption out of half-truths and public relations strategy? But we'll start with Eliza, who puts her hands in her jean pockets. She realizes she isn't wearing a bra, but her coat hides it, so she doesn't much care. She tries to decide where to go, with her half hour and her fraying nerves, her buzzing fingers and face. She feels pins and needles on her lips. She is angry or she is upset or she is relieved that she can still set foot in the world. She walks in a giant circle. Walks in another giant circle.

She decides that she will get snacks. Snacks that she picks, with her own hands, and not skimming from the Sixsterhood's communal fridge like a mooch. She has a little cash in her wallet still from the women, the ones from *Last Week Tonight*. She has her heart set on a few bags of chips, each a different flavor, and perhaps some onion dip. The kinds of things the Sixsterhood would never have in favor of homemade sourdough and artisanal granola made in a ceremony on Saturdays. No, Eliza feels she (and Suzanne) deserve some honest-to-goodness junk food. So she strolls into the bodega on the corner. A police siren wails by and she jumps, turns around.

This is when The Inspectre arrives outside the warehouse. He phones Eliza, and we've already heard the conversation he has with Suzanne. But what's important to know is where he walks—he realizes he hasn't brought anything. No snacks, no bottle of wine, no nothing. It's rude to do that, to show up at someone's house, especially on Christmas Eve, without bringing something to share. At least flowers. Because then Eliza will know it's just a joke, just a puzzle, just for the lulz. He pictures sitting down with her, with Suzanne, and they will be so impressed that he found them. Perhaps they will introduce him to everyone, to Black Hole and Doctor Moriarty and Human Man, even. Perhaps he will get hired—everything he's done has been genius level. He's resisted giving her any way to figure out where he was—in a hostel not too far from here. They'll see he's not a monster; his only crime is being smarter than everyone, needing the challenge. And as long as she confesses her sins, says she won't try to ruin the world for his brothers again, he doesn't see why they couldn't be—

But wait. They are lying to him. They are trying to humiliate him again. His fantasy comes crashing down around him. Because as he is browsing for a bottle of wine and talking on the phone, he looks out over the aisles and sees Eliza, absorbed in rows of neon bags, trying to select chip flavors that complement each other. The kind of caloric waste served at a fifth-grade sleepover. She actually giggles, her spirits lifting at the thought. It will be a fine Christmas Eve after all. Perhaps they can watch *The Muppet Christmas Carol* all together in the living room. In pajamas. Things are looking up.

"Cunt!" he hisses into the phone. "I'm coming for you next." Keith Mackey hangs up and grabs a bottle of wine at random. They think they can fool him. But he knows what Eliza looks like—they think he is an idiot. Both of them have to pay for that. And Eliza has to pay especially for giggling. Giggling, he thinks, at having devoured Preston Waters perhaps. Does she maybe take delight in her evisceration of this great man, her invasion of the gaming territory?

Or no. Perhaps not that violent, not right away. Here is something we know about Keith: as he grabs the bottle of wine, he isn't sure how exactly he is going to make her pay. He thinks perhaps he'll confront her—give her the opportunity to compliment his prowess. He imagines she'll admit her own inferiority. She might say something like "You really had me going there." Or "Good game." And in return he will be magnanimous. He will say, "All this is okay, little lady, just don't go ruining any more games."

Before he rounds the corner, before he comes up behind her with that bottle of wine in his right hand, strangled by its neck, he thinks about what winning the game might look like: she quits. That is what he wants. If *Guilds of the Protectorate* is his favorite universe, then See No Monkey's *Ancient Magic* is a close second. He has subscriptions to both. Eliza's taken down one—he wants to make sure she doesn't take down the second. He wants her to leave Preston Waters alone so he might eventually recover and return, triumphant, as Human Man. Every man. If she had just quit instead of moving companies, he could've gone home. He could've stopped. If she'd sat down quietly, he wouldn't need to keep hunting her down, need to keep teaching her a lesson.

He imagines Eliza will then apologize for wrecking the game. That maybe other would-be sirens will stay out. He doesn't think girls don't belong in games, exactly—they just should make their own, play their own, and stay out of his. Or they shouldn't change the culture. It's thrived without the influx this long, after all. The niche has always been healthy. But what happens when it all becomes mainstream? What happens when the kids who beat the shit out of him when he was little grow into games? What happens when the girls who laugh at him, who tease him, who would never date him invade as well? His palms begin to sweat when he sees her body closer. It is small. Smaller than he imagined before. Smaller than we imagined before.

There are legitimate fears here. The fear of your unique culture being sublimated, being overrun. The fear of dilution. But they're all mixed in with what The Inspectre does next. And so we ask ourselves, does one lead to the other? Is that how we got here, with us running the world by accident? But we like to think we wouldn't do what he does next. Would we? We are afraid; we are so afraid. And if we have reason to be, doesn't that mean we should be allowed to defend ourselves? We are more marginalized every day; it's not a good era to be us.

He is behind her now. He clears his throat. "Eliza," he says. He is doing his best to imitate Black Hole. He succeeds to a point—even the faintest touch of Jean-Pascale's accent, the pronunciation of Eliza's name as Ee-liza. But his voice breaks because he is nervous.

Eliza is in the middle of reaching for barbecue chips when she jumps and turns, both startled and half expecting to see Jean-Pascale, though this voice is crackling and much higher than his. For two confused blinks, neither speaks. Eliza runs her eyes up and down The Inspectre. Here is where we finally meet Keith Mackey's physical body. The young man who the world nudges closer and closer to acting out with every #YesAllMen, with every desexualized game, with every subreddit that autobans KotakuInAction participants. He is our tragic hero too. Set in motion by circumstances beyond his control.

If we weren't, on the whole, so averse to describing men in terms of food, we might say that Keith resembles a clear glass of half-and-half. But it's not only the half-and-half that is important here, it is also the glass: a translucent quality. He lives, stereotypically, in a basement. He is very pale. He blinks widely whenever he forgets his sunglasses upon exit, like some sort of burrowing creature when faced with the hard, harsh light of noon. Eliza takes in his skinny body, his short stature, his blonde almost-see-through eyebrows. And his obvious youth. At his oldest, he could be nineteen. Maybe twenty.

"You're The Inspectre?" she asks. Let's zoom in here, because that question mark is important. If Eliza instead states a breathy "You're The Inspectre," things would go differently. If she's wearing a dress and stockings and an elegant pea coat with shining buttons; if she looks like an ingénue but with Lara Croft lips, maybe. If she sighs and swoons with fear or admiration, almost definitely. But Eliza stands before The Inspectre with sweatpants and a puffy down coat and barbecue chips and, above all, a question mark. Punctuation is important. Her mouth twists into a grin. "But you're a kid." Her glee reaches fever pitch. Her fear need not be so strong; her life has not gone to shit nearly as much as she thought.

The almost-translucent Keith Mackey turns the tomato red of a classic Nintendo 64 controller. "I—I," he says, his voice vaulting higher with each syllable. We know he is trying to say, "No. I'm nineteen. Not so much younger than yourself." But we also know why he can't get it out. The anger at the dismissal, the disdain. Eliza is turning the dial up with every breath, every word, every smirk, every movement of her eyebrow. Everything about Eliza makes Keith Mackey furious.

A laugh is on Eliza's lips when Keith turns away. A giggle is boiling up, evaporating into the air when the bell rings on the bodega door once more. "Eliza!" Suzanne shouts, turning her head in all directions. She looks like an owl meme.

Eliza begins to shout back, "I'm fine, he's just a kid. It's all just kid st—" But her mouth is stopped by a full bottle of wine, smashing her face and shattering. Eliza feels her face crack from ear to ear, the warmth of what was once inside coming out. This is how pumpkins must feel, she thinks, during Halloween.

CHAPTER ONE HUNDRED THIRTEEN

Preston walks Dog to the corner and takes a Lyft to work. He isn't sure exactly what he'd been expecting. But he's grateful to flee.

He dreads walking into the office. The new normal, since Dog, since Eliza, since all of it: everyone watches him, and not in the good way. Not in the popular way. He barely has to move eight feet, from the elevator to his glass room, and yet. And yet. He feels every single eye touch his skin. It is the strangest sensation, being watched that way by everyone on his floor. Everyone in the collaboration rooms. The wide-eyed pity; everyone hushed quiet as though they'd been talking about him seconds earlier. The weight on Preston is obvious and so we look. Whisper. Everyone afraid to break him.

Today, he exits the elevator to the same stunned silence. He keeps his gaze turned to the floor. He jumps when he hears the first clap. Other hands begin clapping. It's a sputter, then a cheer. He looks up—people are standing at their desks and clapping. Dog's stump isn't pointed between his legs either. He whips his cone around, trying to take in all his favorite people. Preston begins to smile. His employees are clapping his dog back into work. And Dog likes it.

Preston feels like his old self for a second. He puts his hands up. "One at a time, one at a time. He's still pretty shaken up." But he lets Dog off the leash and Dog accepts his audience gracefully, even when people break the rule and pet him two or three at a time. He licks. He jumps up onto people's thighs. Preston watches the transformation and thinks perhaps they've turned a corner here. Perhaps things aren't so bad at Fancy Dog anymore. Especially since he's got something he can do now, immediately. Something he can put right.

He gets to his desk and sits. He G-chats Brandon. They haven't spoken face-to-face since Dog. Brandon sent him an Edible Arrangement the day after. That was it. And they certainly haven't had a face-to-face meeting since Preston started virtually schtupping Suzanne (they must have done, we think). He would never tell Brandon. And that is the first moment in this whole exchange we'll dive into: Preston realizes that he and Brandon aren't friends anymore. It is obvious to us, but he realizes something less obvious: he and Brandon aren't even really co-workers. With the entire HR department in the middle of replacement, Brandon dealt with Lewis on his own, and he did it poorly—a work-from-home arrangement until Lewis's meds are fine-tuned, but Lewis is still expected to shoulder the backbreaking load of an unofficial team leader. If Preston had been more present, would things be different now? Midnight tonight might go very differently. But we can't really know, because it didn't happen. Preston abandoned his company, his child, and Brandon ran things as Brandon does, and not once did they talk about it. Let's instead look at the G-chat: "want a meeting. come ASAP."

"be there in ten," Brandon types back.

An eerie calm washes over Preston and he knows something is about to happen. He is close to something. He sips his coffee and looks out the window. He thinks his life might go better now, might go differently. And if he's feeling it internally, then external factors will go his way as well. When he gets home, he'll call Eliza. He'll call Suzanne. Or email, he's not sure just yet. But he'll wholeheartedly apologize. He'll invite her back. He'll hire a security guard or something. A security detail, even. Hell, he'll figure it out. It's that kind of morning. The worst is over. He is excited: this feeling of being right on top of something he doesn't know yet is the same feeling he had before he outlined *Guilds* to Brandon while getting high in their dorm room. He stands like this for a while, barely breathing, his skin buzzing with newness. With proximity to realization. He doesn't want to scare the feeling away.

"Preston."

Preston turns and finds Brandon at the door. He doesn't know where the ten minutes went, but half his coffee is gone. He figures the time must have passed. "Brandon," he replies.

"I wanted to tell you in person that I'm truly sorry about Dog."

Preston cocks his head to the side, so much like Dog in the photo. "He's here, you know." He gestures out to the clump of employees. Dog is getting the pet of his life.

"Oh. I didn't see, sorry. Well, congratulations. Everyone loves him. You've seen the hashtag, right? Long Live Dog?"

"Uh. I used it this morning."

"I think a woman who works here started it. Susan? Her handle is—"

"Yrface. Yes. Suzanne." There's an awkward silence and Preston rubs his temples. "Do you want me to have a talk with her about it? It probably breaks, I dunno, some policy, but I don't think it's conduct unbefitting of a—"

"No, no. Why would I want that?" Brandon interrupts, his slash of a mouth tilting sideways, a smirk. "Preston, Dog's story and that hashtag have done more for us, publicity-wise, than any press release we've put out. We're getting calls for you to do the talk show circuit about all this—which, I've given you some time, but you're doing, by the way—and we're at our normal steady holiday increase in account sales for the first time since all this started. If anything, you shouldn't give that girl a talking-to. You should give her a raise."

"Brandon, I am not going on talk shows to describe how a psycho stalker chopped my dog's tail off. He's doing much better now. I'd really prefer to let this die."

"We'll talk about it later."

Preston sets his coffee on the desk and frees his hands up so his body language can be direct, convincing. Leader-like. "It wasn't Jean-Pascale who doxxed Eliza. It was Lewis Fleishman. We have to take care of this."

Brandon pauses, tents his pointer fingers in a here-is-the-church-and-here-is-the-steeple style. He touches the steeple to his lips. "Why?" he asks.

Preston shakes his head. He must not have heard correctly. "What do you mean, why? Because Jean-Pascale didn't do it and Lewis did. We need to fire one and apologize and attempt to rehire the other, if he'll even come back."

"I have a better idea," Brandon says. "We do nothing."

"Excuse me?"

"We. Do. Nothing." Brandon holds up one hand and ticks his fingers off with the other. "Right now, we have one tried-and-true dev on team B. That's Lewis. The other two are trainees—brand-new to the company, even. If we fire Lewis, that leaves us with two brand-new people and a spot to fill."

Preston makes a move to interrupt, but Brandon keeps going. "Before you say we'll just rehire Jean-Pascale, you said it yourself: if he'll even come back. He might not, because if what you say is true—and I'm not convinced it is, we'll get to that in a moment—then we fired the guy for no reason and publicized that he doxxed a female employee. We essentially wrecked his career—do you think he'll agree to work for us again? I don't, personally, because I wouldn't. Then we have evidence to consider. Where did you get this statement from?"

Preston waits for a second to see if he is supposed to answer the question. "Eliza," he says, after a beat.

"Exactly. And where did Eliza get her information?"

"I'm not sure. But I imagine Jean-Pascale."

"Right. So." Brandon starts to pace the office. "On the one hand we have anecdotal evidence from two people whom we have fired. He could have paid her, they could be in cahoots or something, whatever. And on the other hand we have actual data that we collected from our own computers using an outside firm and people whom we have not fired, and that evidence says Jean-Pascale did it. Whom do you think we should believe?"

Preston grits his teeth. "Personally," he says, "I'm inclined to believe Eliza. Lewis seems to have gone—"

"And finally," Brandon interrupts, his eyes narrow and his voice loud, "even if what you say is true. Even if Jean-Pascale didn't do a damn thing and Lewis is the fucking spawn of Satan or something, why would we stir the pot? We are just starting to come out of this hole. It's Christmas. New accounts should've been cropping up like wheat in the Midwest and we're just, *just* seeing that bump. We are finally, finally getting some good PR here and we are finally seeing some of that Christmas spirit as a result. You"—he points at Preston, who leans back sharp as if he's been shot—"said it yourself. Just let it die. Just let it die."

"Are you hearing yourself right now?" Preston finds himself standing and yelling, something he has never done on the Fancy Dog premises. Is this the precipice? Is this what he feels he's on the edge of? "Fuck feedback right now, are you listening to your own words? Christ, we started Fancy Dog so we could have a fucking human place to work. So we could be in a place that cared about more than the bottom line—that cared about innovation and fun and the people. But you don't sound human anymore. This company isn't human anymore."

Brandon crosses his arms and shakes his head and chuckles, sneering. "You buy into that corporations-are-people-too bullshit, huh? That somehow, because we're running it, this place can operate like some kumbaya hippie's GI tract? Here's the thing, Preston. Corporations aren't people—they're organizations. They're made up of a goddamn bunch of people. Investors, employees. I have a responsibility." Brandon pounds one fist on his chest. "Me, I have a responsibility to the bottom line because I have a responsibility to 'the people.'" He extends his arm out to the glass wall, palm up and open, dramatic. "You, you're a fucking pansy. And if it were just you, Preston, and your weird corporate culture and your ideals and your bullshit—it's all bullshit, we're still a fucking company—you'd run this place into the ground. You can't make a goddamn decision to save your life. You've been on the third floor being cagey for a week, maybe more. You've barely been here. If it were just you, where would all your people be? And you, you have the audacity to stand there and call me inhuman? To call me a robot, is that it? Some corporate, capitalist robot. Well I'm the corporate capitalist robot who keeps Fancy Dog in the black and I say we do nothing."

Preston's mouth bobs open and shut, a fish on land, not quite dead but very much not breathing. Brandon's hand is still out toward the glass and, for lack of anything better to look at, Preston's gaze follows Brandon's gesture. He looks through his wall and everyone is staring, their open mouths mirroring their leader. Everyone, that is, except for Joe. Remember Joe? We've met him before. Joe with the hearing aids. Joe with the mad lipreading skills. Leaky Joe, who's one of us. Who tells us things. Who always knows things first. Joe is looking at his computer. When he finally looks up, he can barely contain his glee. There is something new happening. There is something special about the way he carries his body as he walks up toward Preston's office. His co-workers look at him with a mixture of awe and fear—what could possibly make him interrupt this fight? We know. We've known since it happened.

"Preston, Brandon," he says. "The Inspectre found Eliza. She's on her way to the hospital now."

"What?" Preston says. He feels like the floor has dropped out from underneath him. It's exactly like the Portal demo for the Vive—he was one of the first to try that one—except he's not standing in virtual reality. He doesn't have a headset on. This is real. It's very, very real.

"Turn on the news. It's even on cable."

Preston's office does have a TV and it does have cable news. Mostly he uses it to display things from his computer screen even larger, but now he searches for a remote he knows must be around somewhere. When he finds it, he turns on ABC. They barely know anything, these journalists; they haven't been watching this closely at all. They're promising contextual interviews with The Women from *Last Week Tonight* in the next half hour. They're promising updates. It is like a real news story. Like a real tragedy. Like a celebrity has been hurt. They have interviews with witnesses. They have Suzanne pushing her way through a crowd, refusing to talk, getting in the back of an ambulance with, Preston can only assume, Eliza. They've blurred her face in the footage. "Disturbing" is what the anchor calls it. Blurred because it "may be disturbing to some viewers." Sources say a stalker found her after her former boss posted a photo in which she was present. We say that. That is us. We are the sources. We have happily been in the news since November 9th, and we happily are again. And again. And again. Preston hears the reason, hears his fault. He lunges for his phone and looks at Twitter. Sources say. We say. Preston confirms.

When he rips his eyes from the phone, the first thing he sees is Joe's face. He is eating it up. He has one hand on his chest like he is shocked, and a smile on his face. And with a pang, Preston realizes what we already know: Joe loves being this close to a good shitshow. Joe loves a good story. Joe is our mascot, our stand-in. Joe is us. He barely knows Joe, but now he thinks Joe is an asshole. "For Chrissakes," Preston yells. "Really? Really? You're smiling?" His body spasms and he stomps the ground with two feet and throws his hands in the air—he looks like a Preston doll dropped by a child. "No," he shouts. "No, this is over. You can't even hide that you're happy." Joe steps back and his face doesn't change. "You're a dick, Joe. You've been leaking things from my office since you started here and I thought I couldn't say anything about it because you're deaf. I thought you didn't know what you were doing, that you thought it was information everyone was supposed to have. But no, you're just a dick."

Brandon tries to interrupt, tries to keep Preston from saying something Joe can sue them over. "Now I don't think—"

"And you." Preston rounds on Brandon. "You fire the wrong guy and keep him fired. And you don't fire the right guy. You say you don't trust Eliza, you don't want to rehire her, and you don't believe her. Well maybe not believing her is what got us here in the first place, did you ever think of that? We're so behind on the holiday bump it's going to affect us, maybe for years. And look. You said we're finally climbing out of the hole, but look at this—" Preston gestures to the television, the coverage repeating now because that is how the world works. When no one has anything meaningful to say, they repeat. They repeat. "This isn't climbing out of the hole. They won't even show her face. She might be dead. No one's said anything about that."

"And then there's the rest of you." He runs the two steps to the glass wall and presses his hands against it. At any other time, we might laugh: he looks like a mime whose creation had suddenly solidified. "You look at me. You all look at me. Like a fish in a bowl." We think it is interesting that he chooses fish—he could say shark in a tank. He could say bear in a zoo. But those would be too powerful, wouldn't they? Because Preston understands, finally, what he is on the precipice of. This is the second moment we'll zoom in on. The feeling of edgeness, of closeness, is replaced. It is sudden, the change. Binary. Yes, no. True, false. Precipice, falling.

No. Not falling. That's not the right word. Because Preston finally decides that he will not be a fish in a tank, not be on display for us to look at. Fishes in bowls have no agency, and he will take that agency. He will take it back. "Falling" is not a word that implies agency. No. Precipice, leaping. Precipice, flying.

Preston imagines how he sounds to those on the other side as he screams—the wavy, octagonal sounds that shouting makes underwater, when syllables crash together, words sound like they're being spoken into tin cans. Everyone's ears and eyes are satellites, listening for the syllables of his opening mouth, marveling at how stupid he has been. How he got Eliza caught. How Brandon thinks he'd run this company into the ground. But it isn't just the glass wall. It isn't just his physical space. It is everything. The whole office is watching; the whole internet is watching; we are watching.

"This was your choice," Brandon says. And it is unclear what he means—what the choice was. But probably he is referring to the trans- parent wall. Or starting a company. Or being famous enough to draw our attention.

"No, it's not. It's not my choice anymore." Here it is. The leap. "I quit." Preston shouts until his throat feels red.

"Preston, this is your— You can't just—"

"Yes," he says. "I can. I can just not show up to work until you fire me—until the board votes me off the island. I can resign. Publicly! Or I can—" and Preston begins to laugh. He laughs so hard he doubles over. He throws his arms out wide and hugs himself around the middle, stomps his feet again. Brandon joins Joe in backing away. But we don't. We stay right up in his face. We stay right up in his mind. It seems crazy to the outside observer, but we sense something else here. Triumph. Or the thrill of emotional cliff diving. Or finally getting free of Eliza's siren song. Or finally succumbing to it in its entirety.

"Preston, man, let me—" and we think perhaps for a moment Brandon is truly concerned for his friend, because this is not a way he has ever seen Preston. No one has, because this is not a thing Preston has ever done. Brandon does not get to finish his sentence, though, so we remain—will always remain—a little bit in the dark on this one.

Preston pops up with the enthusiasm of morning toast. He runs behind his desk, still laughing, and he grabs his desk chair with both hands. Laughing and laughing, tears streaming down his face from all the deep belly heaves it takes to maintain hysteria. Wheels first, he throws his chair into the glass wall. Everything shatters. Let it shatter, he thinks. Let the whole thing shatter.

Brandon is at Preston's desk in an instant. He leans over and grabs the phone. "Security," he says. His eyes are wide and he does not turn his back to Preston, his former captain and former friend.

"Don't bother," Preston says. He starts for where the door would have been, but stops. Instead he steps over the low metal fitting that once held his office wall. His shoes crunch the jagged fragments—everyone is silent. Everyone hears. It is very final. It sounds like a car accident or a man stalking away after an explosion. He calmly walks to Dog, re-leashes him, gets in the elevator, and leaves.

CHAPTER ONE HUNDRED FOURTEEN

I t is the sound Suzanne will never un-hear: the dull thud, almost like being hit with a baseball bat, combined with a sound like cutting meat. She doesn't have much time to think or to see—she only has the instant to hear and react. She has never fired a Taser before. She points the weapon at the kid with half a bottle, bloody, in his hand, white wine pooling with red at his feet to make a horrid zinfandel, and she pulls the trigger.

His body goes rigid and he drops the jagged glass remnant—the pop, the electric buzz and the second crash set people screaming again. Two run out—some duck and hide in aisles. She doesn't know how long she should keep tasing him, but we know. We have Google. Thirty seconds. She doesn't hold it for that long. She finds it very disturbing to tase someone.

She releases the current and, as he'd been turning around to face her, he topples into the metal aisle stand. He and all the snacks go down in a thunder, topped with a crinkle. He doesn't move immediately.

Suzanne's first priority is Eliza, but she sees someone is already there. A big block of a man in a white uniform and covered in deli meat, grease and ketchup kneels over Eliza and covers the mouthpiece on his phone— not a smartphone. He is the butcher. "The police and the ambulance are on their way," he says to the unconscious woman—the woman without a face, with gaping cuts and holes and broken teeth where just moments ago she'd had features. Eliza's eyes crack open. We aren't sure if she's truly conscious or if it's a bodily response, something her brain doesn't have to tell her to do. We wonder if she is on the way to being dead. "No," he says. "No, don't do that—keep 'em shut. Trust me." Her head moves almost imperceptibly up and down, the tiniest nod.

"Her neck—is she bleeding? Where's she bleeding from?" Suzanne asks him. She's looking right at her friend, but somehow she can't see any of it. It's as if her mind is censoring it. Her eyes are simply not telling the rest of her what's going on.

"No," the giant man says. He sounds like a cartoon of himself, a rumbling voice made quiet and bookish by a gentle nature. "There's actually not as much blood as you would think," he says. "Everything is just fine. Just fine."

The Inspectre begins to stir amid the bags of chips and cookies and boxes of crackers. Suzanne says, "Fuck," because she could've grabbed zip ties, but she hasn't. So she drags The Inspectre off the rack by his ankles, plants him facedown in the middle of the floor, and sits on him, cross-legged.

"Miss, miss," the cashier says. "Do you need some water or something?" He wipes his hands against his pants. Suzanne attempts to respond and finds herself shaking, dry in the mouth—probably that's what the cashier sees in her, why he asks. She clears her throat. "Yes," she says, trying her best to sound calm. She notices her own voice sounds far away in her ears. "Water would be great. Thank you." She tries to say this as if she isn't sitting on a person, a person who is now twitching and trying to buck her off.

"Don't even think about it," the butcher growls. The Inspectre goes limp.

With her water in hand and the sirens echoing, bouncing off buildings, she texts Devonte:

"im fine. eliza hurt. tazed inspectre. police coming."

Suzanne sips her water.

CHAPTER ONE HUNDRED FIFTEEN

I t is for this reason Our Frequently-Absent-But-Doing-His-Best Friend Devonte doesn't see Preston's Meltdown—

He is at work when he gets this text and he runs to the elevators and pushes the close-door button over and over again while blood rings like bells in his ears and he calls Our Suzanne when he gets outside and he completely forgets his inability to deal and that he's been distancing himself from the situation because when it comes to an Emergency he is Present and Ready

"What happened?" he says without saying hello

"We're headed to Flushing Hospital in Queens—Can you go back and get her clothes and her toothbrush—oh maybe not that—maybe take care of her laptop?"

"What does that mean, take care of—"

"No time they're here we've gotta go"

"Does that mean bring it or—" but Our Suzanne is already off the phone as Devonte is shouting the question into the receiver

"Shit" he says and he hails a cab because it's faster than calling a Lyft

We all know what's happened by the time he gets to Us and We open the door for him immediately upon his arrival

Have you seen this? We ask and We pull him to the giant television We so rarely use for cable and there it is—the same news coverage the others saw with Preston

"Oh Fuck" Devonte says "oh Fuck oh Fuck oh Fuck"—he finds himself grabbing the sides of his head like Preston does "How bad is this?" he asks the air or Us or maybe even God because he doesn't know and it is this inability to assess if his friend got punched or if his friend is about to die that is so scary and destabilizing and We do not answer him because We do not have any answers and after a few seconds he says "oh I need to get her stuff—I need to go—where—?"

But before he's finished asking the question We are already leading him to the elevator—Eliza's bag is in the corner and he grabs clothes and starts getting organized and that's when he sees the computer on the bed and this story might go very different if he simply shuts it and puts it in a bag but as he doesn't know if the drive is standard or solid state he sits down to power it off before turning it sideways and that's when he sees the janky program and the now-grey dot on the map and with an almost audible click he knows what "take care of her computer" means

"No—No no no Suzanne—no" he softly pounds his head into the mattress

What?

Devonte squints up at the elevator doors—the curtains are pulled back and We are all here, the Entirety of Us, and We look in as One— flashes of worry echo across Our collective faces like small electric signals as though together We make up one computer or one brain

"Suzanne tased The Inspectre—she said she tased him and that means she's probably going to be arrested because it's illegal to have a Taser in New York and it's even more illegal to use it"

Oh We know but We don't call the police around here—no one does

Devonte sighs and says "well they might be here anyhow to search for things if she gets arrested which means"—he gestures to Eliza's computer—"this is a real problem"

By the time he's finished with his sentence, about half of Us have disappeared because We can think of several other things that would definitely be problems and Devonte's brain begins to spin its wheels— what does he do with the computer? a small ugly voice whispers between his ears that he could just leave it and We can see this journey written on his face and on his body—the girls broke the law—the girls broke the law so so many times and he hasn't yet and he doesn't have to—he can feign not understanding and leave the computer here or bring it with him—but no he's already mentioned it to Us so Our Suzanne would surely find out and then his Friendship with both of them would truly be over—and he is correct that We would certainly tell but that isn't what stops him from doing it—the next voice in his head is less ugly and it says that's not the kind of person you are and it says you are Noble and Good and Fuck the law and Fuck the cops and be a Renegade and be a Friend

He picks up the computer and wonders how to dispose of it Thoroughly and Completely? he exits the elevator and walks in a circle twice with the open laptop balanced on his hand and he heads for the front door—into the river maybe?

Here We say and he looks up—one of Us stands in the doorway with several other faces peering out from behind and We hold out a baseball bat—*There's a good floor for it this way and when We're through We'll each take pieces in our pockets and dump them*

Devonte steps through the door into the large room with the aerial silks rigged to the ceiling with the recording studio at the back which one of Us ducks into and We press a few buttons and the song "Still" pumps through the speakers piped into the bigger rooms and piped into everywhere—"Really?" Devonte says with caustic judgment masking terror because he is about to destroy evidence and it is the first illegal thing he's done since college when he let himself know better—when he started to internalize that the rules the white boys followed weren't the same standards to which the world holds him and this one feels like a much bigger deal with both the action and the consequences in meatspace—nothing virtual about it

Devonte takes a deep breath and he delivers the initial blow to the offending computer and he is Scared and he is Elated—Glee rises in his throat because there aren't many times in one's life that one gets to wreck something and enjoy pure destruction—it is Cathartic in a way virtual destruction only dreams of being—Devonte and Us—Us and Devonte—We take turns slamming Down and Down and Down Again until the technology is Pulverized and We are all sweaty and Laughing and it no longer seems so all-encompassing when it's Reduced To Pieces—to Trash—Our Devonte is now one of Us like Our Suzanne and Our Eliza and We will hold him forever—We sweep pieces into sandwich bags and slip them into pockets and We all leave together and as Devonte sets out for the hospital he imagines the debris snaking through the city—deposited into garbage cans and dumped onto streets—impossible to reassemble

CHAPTER ONE HUNDRED SIXTEEN

And now, a partial list of things that happen so we can move time forward very quickly to the important bits. The end bits. The bits we remember and take with us, instead of the bits that are simply bits:

When Eliza gets to the hospital, her attentive parent is informed. Well, both are informed, but her attentive parent responds. Her mother gets into a cab immediately. We haven't met the mother yet. We forgot she had parents.

Suzanne is allowed to ride with Eliza to the hospital, but when the police show up, she is handcuffed and taken away.

Eliza is actually doing better than expected. She is pumped full of morphine while she waits and is finally wheeled into surgery, where they repair much of her face. They will do her teeth later—she will get dentures, then implants. Her jaw is broken; it is wired shut. She is stitched up. They do their best not to give her one hell of a facial scar, but that isn't really possible.

Devonte pays for Suzanne's bail. When Suzanne gets home, she PayPals him a large sum of money, but he decides the instant she sends it that he will never accept the payment.

Reporters call everyone. When they call Samantha Delphine Stewart, she agrees to go on television. That cunt, that shrewd cunt—she looks good on camera and she knows it. People will see it. She has already capitalized on her proximity, and she will again and again and again. The only thing worse than the Elizas and Suzannes of the world are the Delphines, the ones who seem like they are for us, with us, and then turn around and stab us from behind while we are fixated on their goodness, their kindness. Someone breaks up with someone. We want it to be JP who does the dumping; we are not sure it is.

Suzanne and Devonte go back to the Sixsterhood, where Suzanne asks what happened to the computer and, wisely, no one will tell her. Suzanne gets dressed for real and they head back to the hospital. They wait in a waiting room while Eliza's mother watches her daughter's eyes crack open. Mrs. Bright leans in close to her face and whispers two things: "I'm so glad you're alright," and "You're quitting."

That gets us to about eight at night.

CHAPTER ONE HUNDRED SEVENTEEN

L et's skip to midnight. Or rather, to a few minutes before. 11:58 or 11:59. We promised we would get here.

Lewis doesn't really drink, not outside the game. He doesn't care for it, the feeling of losing control. But he weaves as he walks along the George Washington Bridge. He is not drunk, not off of alcohol, but off of deep regret and severe insomnia. It has taken him all day to get here with us. He knows nothing about Eliza, nothing about the crack in her face. He knows only that she is right; he knows only the few stars he can see through the light pollution. There are more than he thinks there should be. He wonders how many of them he's hallucinating.

We don't want him to do this. It is a permanent solution to a temporary problem. There are many of our cast we would tell to go kill themselves—Eliza, Suzanne, Devonte once he's back openly defending the other two. But we don't want Lewis to kill himself. Because most of us? Most of us are most similar to Lewis. This loss stirs in us the same feelings as seeing our deep tendrils sunk into The Inspectre, or perhaps his deep tendrils sunk into us. We think of ourselves one way, but how much of ourselves do we not see? What does it say when one of us is so rigid he breaks? How close are we all to the same? How important is it, that unbendable sense of self? Of right? Where is the line between being walked on and being adaptable? How bad are we right now?

And if we are wrong about so many things here, what else? What else are we clinging to, desperately, that will, after our tortured demises, prove to be incorrect?

We feel complicit in this, this death. If we keep watching, if we keep reading, if we keep writing, then he dies. It is almost easier to stop telling the story before that—to let him sink into the river on his own time, without us pushing forward. Pushing him forward. But then, we think, if we do that, if we stop, this whole moment is nothing more than voyeurism. We want to elevate it to witness. So this is the truth; this is what happens. And because it happens, we will tell it.

Lewis steps to the edge and looks at the sky. He thinks of nothing. Or he thinks about how wrong he's been, about the damage he's caused, about Dog's tail and being plagued by an ever-present severing, getting Jean-Pascale fired, how worried his mother will be, about everyone but Eliza. Or he does think of her—he doesn't know about their histories in games like we do, but maybe he does get the sense of similarity. Maybe he does think about the thin line connecting them, the one he put there when he decided to create himself in opposition to her. To people like her. Or maybe he thinks only the phrase "you're right." Or "you win." But we don't want to believe that; we don't want to think of him as petty in his last moments.

He steps off the edge at 12:01 on Christmas Day. He realizes, weightless, in the air, that when he hits, when he breaks the surface, he will be surrounded by water. He will be in a tank of his own construction, one from which there will be no escape. Or he realizes he has been in there this whole time. He comforts himself by looking skyward, by counting and recounting, in this infinite moment, the stars.

Lewis Fleishman is dead. Long live Lewis Fleishman.

CHAPTER ONE HUNDRED EIGHTEEN

Eliza's face is broken. Her jaw, her nose, her teeth spidered and cracked like the wine bottle she'd been hit with—her once-convex mouth is now concave, pushed in as if it were nothing but soft wax. Her eyes are blackened, brilliant shades of purple that are almost pretty. Her face is lined with slices, paths, gashes; later Eliza will describe this feeling as her skin falling away in ribbons. We will all shudder and touch our faces; we will wonder what that feels like.

After surgery and stitching, her jaw is wired shut and she is stoned on painkillers. This is unfortunate, as her mother talks like a tempest. Her mother, just as petite but much prettier, hailing words against the silence. These words are all about packing Eliza's apartment up, about her moving back to Westchester, about finding a new industry where people don't get smashed in the face with wine bottles.

It doesn't take long, of course, for one of us to tweet that @BrightEliza was asking for it. Or perhaps @BrightEliza deserved it. All the websites cover the response—tech, business, feminist. The televised news outlets added social media tickers to their already-graphic security camera footage. Across the bottom of the screen, broadcast by an algorithm, run scathing tweets we type through hissed teeth. For twenty-four hours we all watch as the anchors warn us of the graphic nature of the footage to follow. We watch Keith Mackey, with his skinny arms and blonde transparent eyelashes, glance to the wine bottles and heft one up. We watch Suzanne Choy throw her arm out. We watch soundlessly as his arm rockets toward Eliza's face—it almost looks sped up. Some of us cover our eyes, some of us don't. But the channels cut away from the footage before too much blood runs onto the floor. The anchors never really discuss the tweets, which we like. Providing "context" for our written thoughts usually means liberal bullshit when it comes to mainstream media. Leaving them there for viewers to truly decide what they think about them; that's exactly what we want. Our numbers grow.

One of us rips the security camera footage and puts it on YouTube. Whenever we Google "Eliza Bright," it is in the top section of the results—playable, with a triangle smack in the middle. The views on it tick up and up and up. One of us sets it to music. It is taken down due to copyright infringement.

When the police come to speak to her, she is barely conscious and can't talk. From her perspective, their words sound mushy, amorphous, like vinyl played backward and watered down with pain and opiates. Moist. Everything is moist and slippery and she can't hold on to them, those words. Instead, she sleeps. Time passes. She is not sure how much.

Suzanne and Devonte come, after Devonte bails Suzanne out. Mrs. Bright begrudgingly lets them in when Eliza's eyes shoot open. They bring her pens and a journal and the tablet from her apartment. Suzanne, under the guise of comforting her, leans her head close: "We never hacked anything. I knew where you were going. Got it?" Eliza ticks her head slightly, up and down. Not enough to jar anything, but enough to feel the pull. She is green with the sensation.

It is Devonte who sees the tweet and reads it to the room: @SeeNoMonkey [verified]: We stand with Eliza Bright #raisetheshield #enough.

"I guess you still have the job," Devonte says. "I guess they'll wait for you." But Eliza is already asleep.

Mrs. Bright, however, purses her lips. She says nothing. In fact, she does not say one word to either of them, no matter how many times they visit. She nods and grunts when they address her. Mrs. Bright makes no distinction between us and Eliza's two comrades. To her, we are all the same thing: dangerous, the reason her daughter near about has no face. We should also zoom in on what's not said: by now, everyone knows about Lewis. Everyone except Eliza. The TV is kept off in favor of audiobooks, podcasts on subjects so far away from the internet or technology or games that neither she nor Lewis will ever be mentioned. That's her mother's doing.

Her father finally comes, which is no good at all. She drinks her meals through a straw and listens to their plans for her future. "You'll take it easy for a while, rest and heal," they say. "Then we'll find you a job—one of our firms will have something open. Of course you'll move back with us for a while, until you're up again. Oh, won't that be fun?" they ask to the air and they mean it, from the place where clueless people believe things. Eliza tries to grimace, then grimaces because her attempted grimace makes her grimace in pain; her face constantly hurts and she hasn't looked at herself in the mirror yet—she can't see her mouth underneath the bandages anyhow, and even so. She doesn't want to. Not yet.

Her parents begin to leave for more and more of the day, but they always end on the same note: "Why didn't you tell us this was happening?" Eliza can only shrug. She won't reach for the tablet or the journal, won't clarify her position—she wonders why they didn't know, without her running to them like a child. They are trendy people—they should have heard about it. "We had no idea. It's just games, after all. We didn't think it would be a war zone." Eliza has to admit they have a point there.

During one of these sessions where her parents talk and Eliza listens, Devonte and Suzanne sit in the corner eating fries out of a paper bag. Eliza keeps staring at them darkly, eyeing each wonderful potato as they so easily pop each crispy strip into their mouths. This makes Suzanne hide a giggle behind her hand. Devonte stares straight into Eliza's eyes and chews, deliberate. If Eliza could, she'd smile. But she can't. So she settles for flashing them her middle finger.

The whole crew stopped by unannounced. She wants Devonte and Suzanne to stay, but she wants her parents to leave. There is nothing to be done about it. Devonte and Suzanne keep their heads close together as they listen to the monologue, the hand-wringing, and finally their goodbyes. Still, Eliza types nothing. But she is having a lot of thoughts. We can tell; so can her friends.

"Is that really what you want?" Devonte asks as he uses a straw to break the lid perforation on some sort of smoothie. He tries to mix it a little better before handing it over—the protein powder is still visible in nasty clumps. "To quit and go back into advertising or PR or whatever the fuck that was?"

Eliza can't move much of her face, but she risks the pulling sensation to raise a single eyebrow. She gestures for the tablet and he hands it over instead of the smoothie.

> **Eliza:** im not quitting
> **Eliza:** i wish i could say those words with my mouth. i think they'd feel more...something.
> **Eliza:** monumental.
> **Eliza:** something.
> **Eliza:** i wasn't sure before, but now im sure

Devonte's and Suzanne's heads are pressed together, better to see the screen in real time. Suzanne lets out a hissed "yes" at the appropriate moment.

Devonte waits until the end. "You better tell See No Monkey," he says.

> **Eliza:** i already did
> **Eliza:** smoothie please

She takes a sip.

> **Eliza:** this is abysmal

Eliza: wtf are you guys doing eating fries in here

She stares darkly at the brown bag and looks straight into Suzanne's eyes as she sips her meal through a straw. "Don't hate me because my jaw is ambulatory," Suzanne says. She flips her beautiful hair and shoves a handful of fried potato in her mouth. She smiles, the food sticking out in all directions. Devonte mock gags.

They are back, this group. We won't say to normal, but they are back. They still haven't told her about Lewis. When will it be time for that? We are full of resentment. They get joy; Lewis doesn't.

CHAPTER ONE HUNDRED
NINETEEN

This is where Preston disappears—after Our Devonte and Our Suzanne tell Our Eliza about what they'd heard from work about his glass-smashing crack-up and she tries to text him but all the texts go unanswered

The Reddit Men do not know where he is but We at the Sixsterhood do—he and Dog don't even have to sell much to pack a car full of every possession Preston holds dear and they drive across the country to rural Oregon where Preston lives alone with his dog in a farmer's cottage which is entirely free of Wi-Fi in exchange for his help with the bee-keeping and he is actually very good at it—among other new hobbies he also learns to brew beer and on his first night there he throws his phone into a pond and he doesn't miss it at all but one day he will and he will return sometime in the nebulous and distant future—he will return when he has filled three journals with Ideas and the first thing he will do is hand the journals to his new creative team whoever they may be and it will be a Gift—an Offering—an Invitation to use them all—All The Ideas—with abandon because the bees and the buds and the beer will teach him the thing We already know—there will always be More if he just keeps Making

CHAPTER ONE HUNDRED TWENTY

See No Monkey: I must admit, it's weird to do hiring via G-Chat.

See No Monkey: it's absolutely no bother, of course, but all the same.

Eliza: Yeah, I know what you mean. But no worries, I can move my mouth enough to talk a little now! It just hurts after a while. This isn't permanent, though, I'm told. Plus I don't sound great—it'd be really hard to hear me over the phone.

("Ugh, Eliza, delete most of that, no one wants to know, don't hit send." "Okay, Devonte.")

Eliza: I agree. No worries, I'll be back to talking in no time.

("Yeah, that sounds good. Like it ain't no thang. Don't roll your eyes at me.")

See No Monkey: Well this brings us to the last part—constructing your team. We happen to have a lot of openings—our growth has been almost exponential as of late, and we're on-boarding like crazy. Is there anyone you'd like to recommend for hiring at See No Monkey to work on Project Roam?

("Well?" "Fancy Dog blows, I'm in." "Suzanne?" "Actually—yeah. Maybe. No more CS though—maybe PR? I can't picture leaving the Sixsterhood. But also I can. For a bit at least." "We could live together, like all three of us." "Do you think Preston?" "Nope. That's insane. He's probably long gone. Plus you owe that turd nothing." "He's not a turd." "He's a turd.")

Eliza: I'd like to recommend Devonte Aleba, a developer at Fancy Dog. Suzanne Choy as well, she's a customer service representative now, but would like to move to PR and communications. If we're developing a game, we'd like her to be the voice of it. And I'd like to recommend—

("Eliza are you okay?" "Yes, dipshit, I'm fine. Just thinking." "Sometimes I think I liked it better when you weren't talking." "I am literally only pausing for a hot second, stop fucking babying me, I'm fucking fine.")

Eliza: And I'd like to recommend Jean-Pascale Desfrappes, he is currently available and specializes in gameplay development.

("No shit." "Really? Really, Eliza?" "Yep.")

CHAPTER ONE HUNDRED TWENTY-ONE

Eliza calls Jean-Pascale. She's worried she's done it in the wrong order. But when she gets him on the phone, it feels like a weird conversation to have. Like, heads-up, you're probably getting a job offer today and maybe I'll wind up being your boss, hope that's cool? Eliza flushes red and speaks softly and carefully into the phone. She asks him to please come over.

"To the hospital?" he asks. We can hear the nervous in his voice.

"No, no," she clarifies. "I'm going outpatient as we speak. Getting all my shit together, just waiting on someone to sign something. My apartment."

"You're—" Jean-Pascale clears his throat. "You're going back to your apartment?"

"Yup."

"That—does not make you nervous?"

"JP. It's already happened. The worst already happened. The doorman knows. Suzanne and Devonte shipped a bunch of stuff to my apartment, including a video doorbell thing like they have at the Sixsterhood. It's like a fort. I'll be fine."

"Someone's staying with you? Your parents?"

"I have banished my parents. Don't worry about that, you won't have to deal with them."

"I didn't mean—"

"Devonte is spending the night. On the couch, don't get the wrong—"

"Oh, no, I didn't think that—"

"Listen, just come over in, like, an hour? Hour and a half? It's important."

"Uh. Okay." He hangs up.

When he does arrive, the doorman knows to send him right up. When he walks in the door, we have to pause. Because they each see the other in ways that are valuable to us. Eliza's face is literally shaped differently. There was so much surgery. The bandages aren't so complete as to obscure her head anymore, and Jean-Pascale takes in the scars peeking out, the drain taped to her neck, how swollen she still is. It is everything he can do not to sit her down on the couch and start making tea, making soup—but those are hot, she can't drink them anyhow. The bruises are fading, but they're still green. When they're that deep, they don't go away so quickly. He is relieved to see her mouth still protrudes, but he can't see what her teeth look like. We know she has no front teeth for now. A cosmetic dentist will eventually fix that and she will receive a handmade pop-up card from Suzanne that says "Happy Dental Implants Day, Remember To Duck Next Time."

Eliza hasn't yet looked at herself in the mirror. She can feel her face is different, but she's not ready yet. Jean-Pascale, however, looks like hell. He clearly hasn't slept well; his eyes are surrounded by dark circles, which is—was—normal for Lewis, but not for him. There's an abrasion on his arm (we know it is from moving Delphine out of the apartment, scraping his skin on the doorframe while lugging boxes, but Eliza doesn't). And his eyes, on top of the dark circles, are red and sad. "JP. What the fuck happened to you?"

"It's been rough since Lewis."

"Since Lewis what?"

They are almost immediate, the tears he tries to corral behind his eyelids. They spring to life when Jean-Pascale realizes the news he's responsible for. He glances toward Devonte's face, and it is hardened.

He will not do this job, this reveal; he continues to stock the fridge with almond milk, the cabinets with protein powder. He looks away.

"Jean-Pascale," Eliza repeats. "What did Lewis do?" JP tries to answer, but as Eliza stares him full in the face, takes it in, she answers her own question. "He's dead, isn't he?" And how she knows to jump there, we'll never know. She'll never know either. Just a feeling she has, which we suppose makes sense. When two people's lives are that inextricably linked, when each feeds the other's flash point until it is blinding, how can there not be a witchy tingle, a sixth sense?

Instead of them finding a way to awkwardly congratulate each other over jobs well found, the evening becomes one of mourning. "He was a bastard," Eliza says. "But I didn't want that for him, not really. Didn't ever want that."

CHAPTER ONE HUNDRED
TWENTY-TWO

No one ever searches the Sixsterhood. Suzanne, however, is in so, so much trouble. A lawyer, hired by a mysterious moneybags in rural Oregon, finds her way to Suzanne. A very, very good lawyer. Rather than spending four years in jail or paying five thousand dollars, she is downgraded substantially. A one-thousand-dollar fine later, and Suzanne is free to move to California to start her new job with See No Monkey. Elitism. Money makes everything go away for the powerful.

Keith Mackey's parents, however, refuse to pay for a fancy lawyer when they find out what their son has done. It takes months but he finally pleads guilty. He gets a prison sentence; it will be appealed, be reversed later. He fades into obscurity, but we remember him. He's an example of our finest and of our fears—among us, he alone had the courage to take a stand, to fight a real battle in the war for the latest frontier, for men's ability to be men in the newest world of our creation. But he doesn't return to us. We are not sure why—what a waste of all that potential. Perhaps he is simply spent, like a burnt match ignited fast and bright, and we aren't. We are, in shadow, ruling the most powerful nation in the world. It is an argument for subtlety. We are learning.

CHAPTER ONE HUNDRED TWENTY-THREE

Lastly, there is this moment, much later, also relevant:

See No Monkey releases details on Project Roam, now commercially called *Zombie Zombie!* It is an augmented reality game built for smart watches and phones that requires the participants to take over buildings in their city using location services, to tag other players in the real world by placing their device where another device has recently been.

"Given your history with location," Trevor Noah asks on *The Daily Show*, "isn't that dangerous?"

Eliza Bright shakes her head. Her scars have a weird effect—the deepest cuts had formed an arch on either side of her mouth; she looks as though she's carved a smile into her skin. Disconcerting. Like the Joker. Even when she is being serious, she is grinning, dimpled. "No, it isn't dangerous—players can play in general population, or they can opt to completely separate and play the game only with their friends. And"—she does smile here, in a real way—"when you're within ten blocks of your apartment or any other location you select as frequent and important, 'mystery mode' is automatically activated—and you can increase that radius as well. It's also part of the world of the game— I won't tell you why, that'll be spoilers—to delay in-game reactions by twenty-four hours. It makes sense in the plot, but it also serves so players can play without giving away who they are and where they are right away. I made this game with people like me in mind—once it happens to you, you can't really turn that mindset off."

"So why do this, then? Make a game that's playable in the real world, instead of another VR game?"

"I'm going to push back on calling it the real world, Trevor, because the virtual world is just as 'real.' The consequences of it are still very real, though its virtuality attempts to convince us otherwise. It's a dangerous thing, to fragment our society even further by actively turning that part of our brain off, the part that connects with other people in the flesh, and to convince ourselves that the things that happen in games and online aren't important. The lack of community in meatspace—"

"Meatspace, is that what you call it? That's absolutely disgusting, I do not like that."

The audience laughs and Eliza continues. "Yes, meatspace, physical space, whichever you like. The lack of community in physical space is what gives rise to stalkers like Keith Mackey, and what gives rise to the weaponized nerd populations today. The lack of human interaction is how young white men can be radicalized on the internet and turned into real, violent white nationalists." We boo, we hiss at the television. "So that's why, I suppose, I couldn't resist making something you play in person, that encourages you to interact with the physical world around you, where you live. It might seem like flirting with a personally dangerous concept, and perhaps some of that is true. Perhaps I just like danger. But really, when it comes down to it, I want to use gaming and technology to bring people together. Not to isolate them further."

The audience applauds and Trevor Noah continues. "So when will this game be available?"

"Actually, we're releasing the beta versions now, as I'm on the air. If you go to See No Monkey's website, you can register to be a beta tester in San Francisco, Los Angeles and New York City."

"So I could play this game right now?"

"Yes, if you wanted. In fact—" Eliza touches her smart watch. "I'm taking over your building right now, in New York City, and I don't even live here." The studio audience laughs and applauds.

We vow to never play it. Or we download it to our phones right then and there. Trevor Noah continues: "That might not have been the greatest sales pitch, because, and I say this with complete respect, no one is going to fuck with you."

Tonight, some of us are running around New York City, finding each other in bars and theaters and parties, anonymous like spies and giddy in telling no one who we are, seeing slow wars over buildings and points, hits and takeovers rack up. In the spaces where everyone knows each other, perhaps some of us ask, "Are you playing right now?" But part of the fun is in not knowing who is who, who might "bite" and make us into Zombies.

Eliza Bright looks straight into the camera. "Come get me, Zombies!" Fearless.

ACKNOWLEDGMENTS

A writer never writes alone, or at least I certainly haven't. Total myth that it's a solitary gig. I have an embarrassment of riches in terms of community and a scroll long enough to stretch to the moon of folks to thank.

A huge thank-you to all the professors and workshop leaders, both at The New School and not, who have impacted this book and the way I approach writing—Helen Schulman, Luis Jaramillo, Laura Cronk, John Reed, Sharon Mesmer, Honor Moore, Susan Bell and Namwali Serpell. A special thanks to Shelley Jackson, your two-page literature seminar assignment turned into my graduate thesis when I simply never stopped writing it, and to Tiphanie Yanique, thank you for advising me on that thesis, which eventually became this book.

Massive gratitude to my thesis group for helping me solidify so much of this text through your generous praise and critique—Julie Goldberg, Catherine Bloomer, Brady Huggett and Erin Swan. An extra-huge thanks to Randy Winston for doing all of that and also, somehow, being physically next to me in space during every major milestone from finishing the book to selling it. I can't wait to buy you lunch while you hyperventilate because your book just sold; I can't wait to write in Hungarian Pastry Shop with you again.

And thank you to my writers outside that thesis group—to Cory Saul, thank you for reading this book through just to tell me that I had not made the Reddit voice too mean; to Calvin Kasulke, I will never forget the way you helped crystallize the Sixsterhood voice by saying, "these are the kind of people who have soft-core porn Instagrams by accident because they never wear clothes"; and especially to Nat Mesnard, thank you for reading multiple drafts over weekly beers and pointing out every time I got something grievously wrong about the making or playing of video games (any errors that remain are mine and mine alone).

A massive thank-you to Christopher Hermelin—a better agent for me and for this book does not exist on this planet or in the multiverse, if I'm honest. Your astute feedback, belief in the project and perennial ability and willingness to correct people who misgender me is unparalleled and highly appreciated. (And a massive thank-you to Lexi Wangler and Alexandra Franklin for both reading the book in its early stages and helping me seek representation without sounding as zany and anxiety-ridden as I likely am.)

Thank you to Millicent Bennett and Seema Mahanian—y'all's incisive edits and deep understanding of what the hell it is I'm trying to do here have impacted me and my work deeply. Seema, you have helped make this book great in ways I never could have done without you and I will be grateful forever.

Thank you to D. J. Capelis and The Octagon, for inspiring the Sixsterhood and letting me sleep in your elevator shaft that one time. And to Bren Christolear, for being the first friend who read the first tiny bit of this book. And to every single nerd who has ever played Dungeons & Dragons with me.

Thank you to Richard, Berit and Dave Osworth for making me into a person who can take insane creative risks while only flinching a little; it's y'all's fault that this book is so hard for me to describe to other writers in bars.

A thank-you so large I couldn't wrap my arms around it to the friends who came to my rescue at the tail end of making this book real: Nate Zeiler, Quinn McIntire, Megan Skwirz and Sam Komenaka.

ACKNOWLEDGMENTS

Thank you for letting me do the last round of edits in your house during a pandemic. And additionally, thank you to the countless friends who stayed up late and talked me through every last-minute meltdown, made sure I could both eat and cry when I needed: Adrian White, Abby Ryan, Carolyn Yates, Eli Stevens, Jeanna Kadlec, Carmen Rios, Carrie Wade, Keely Weiss, Isaac Fellman, Angus Andrews, Archie Bongiovanni, Sarah Hansen Shields, Liz Rubin, Chrissie O'Neill, Gavin Greco, Orion Guerra, Lou Bank, Vanessa Friedman, Bridget Sullivan, Brian Doyle and Renée Stairs. And thank you to everyone else who has listened to me endlessly process this book for six entire earth years; I am sorry if I missed your name here.

And finally, thank you to Laura Chrismon, my heart-friend. You have been my strongest, most steadfast support for twenty-three years. May we play *Gloomhaven* and watch *The Labyrinth* and shout at each other for another twenty-three to come.

A. E. Osworth is Part-Time Faculty at The New School, where they teach digital storytelling to undergraduates. They've spent eight years writing all over the internet, including a stint as Geekery Editor for *Autostraddle*. Their work has also been published in *Quartz*, *Catapult*, *Electric Literature*, *Guernica* and *Paper Darts*, among others.